HAWAIIAN WILDFLOWER

BETTY JOHANSEN

Copyright © 2010 Betty Johansen
All rights reserved.

ISBN: 1450542913
ISBN-13: 9781450542913
Library of Congress Control Number: 2010900972

Hawaiian Wildflower is a work of fiction. Names, characters, incidents, places, and organizations are the product of the author's imagination or are used fictitiously. Any resemblance to actual persons or events is purely coincidental.

This book is dedicated with adoration and praise to

Jesus Christ, the Lord of glory,

who loves me and gave Himself for me.

My Thanks

I owe an eternal debt of gratitude to my family and friends who help me and brighten my life in ways too numerous to mention and often in ways that exceed my understanding. With regard to this book, I would like to extend special thanks:

1. To you, the reader. Words fail me to express the depth of my gratitude to all of you who spend your valuable time and/or money to read the words I have written. In doing so, you are supporting me in one of my most treasured dreams, and it is my prayer that the Lord will bless you by bringing your most treasured dreams to fulfillment.

2. To Joyce Bryson and Terri Johansen who believe in me far more than I believe in myself.

3. To Adele Chong who read the manuscript with great care and attention and kept me from making a number of blunders in my narrative concerning Hawaii.

4. To Terri Johansen, Joyce Bryson, Adele Chong, and Kathy Highley for reading the manuscript and offering their opinions and guidance.

5. To Polly (Susie) Allison for making it possible for me to have the time I needed to complete this novel.

Characters

This list of characters is provided for reference while reading the novel. (In some cases, situations change; therefore, the descriptions given apply to the characters at the time they are introduced to the story.)

1. Nettie (Jeanette) Jamison West–owns Spring Up West

2. Qiana Jamison–Nettie's half-sister, owns Spring Up South

3. Dillon West–accountant, Nettie's husband

4. Jeremy West–Dillon and Nettie's 13 year-old son

5. Dr. Phillip Jamison–cardiac surgeon, Nettie and Qiana's late father

6. Bethany Jamison–Nettie's mother

7. Shelley Jamison–Qiana's mother

8. Maylea Kanaka–the Hawaiian wildflower

9. Scot Sanford–a fitness trainer and university student, majoring in computers

10. Trolley (Tra-la-la)–Maylea's housekeeper

11. Dolly Tatum–works for Nettie, manages Spring Up West

12. Matt Tatum–Dolly's father, retired engineer from NASA

13. Cecili Wells–works for Qiana, manages Spring Up South

14. Judge Franklin Meyer–Shelley's employer

15. Anita Patton–divorce lawyer

16. Dan Ebersole–Dillon's lawyer (wife, Connie Ebersole)

17. Jeremy's buddies: Kurt Mayfield
 Ronny Stamps

18. Lance Bellamy, M.D.–obstetrician

19. Velma Jackson–client of Nettie's at Qiana's fitness center (husband, Harold Jackson)

20. Glen Bristol–Dillon's computer technician (wife, Hayley Bristol)

21. Lubbock police officers:
 Jed Daly–chief investigator on the case
 Farley Gunther
 Allen Latimer–rookie

22. Dr. Irving van Vleet–Lubbock medical examiner

23. Ethan Holmes–criminal lawyer

24. Dillon's family:
 parents–Dick and Regina (Reggy) West
 sister and brother-in-law–Rilee and Shane Norris
 nieces–Ruth (8) and Lydia (5)

25. Dr. Gregory Rand–owner of vacation home on Oahu

26. Alana–caretaker for Dr. Rand's Oahu home

27. Dr. Greg Rand, Jr.–son of Dr. Gregory Rand, married to Alana's daughter Kalea

28. Kimo (Jimmy) and Paulo (Paul)–Alana's youngest and oldest grandchildren

29. Windsong Towers waitresses: the nervous waitress (Puna)
                                   Kiana–head waitress
                                   Julie

30. Oahu police officers: Nate Zang–detective
                            Officer Parker
                            Luke Kalama–body guard

31. Kevin Vickery–accountant on Oahu

32. Kidnappers: Thor–gravelly voice
                        gruff voice
                        boss–soft, deep voice

33. Kun Yee–owner of Windsong Towers

34. Caleb Hancock–Maylea's high school sweetheart

35. Annette Hancock–Caleb's mother

36. Sarah–Trolley's sister

PART I

A Day in April

Chapter 1

Huge yellow eyes gazed into Nettie's soul. Nettie gazed back. And trembled. Beads of sweat formed on her upper lip.

Why wouldn't the owl fly away? Why was it staring at her? Why her? And what would it do if she looked away? Or closed her eyes?

More minutes passed. Nettie and the great white bird waited with gazes locked. Then the bird's eyelids began to close over the yellow orbs. Slowly the haunting eyes grew narrower until they were gone.

Nettie gasped in relief. She shut her own eyes tight and put her hands over them for a moment. When she looked again, the owl was gone.

Her scream caught in her throat and she couldn't get it out. Again and again she opened her mouth to let out the piercing shriek, but no sound escaped.

Quaking, she searched the sky for the ghostly figure. How could it have disappeared so quickly? She couldn't have closed her eyes for more than a few seconds. And now it was lurking out there, waiting. Waiting to swoop down on her when she least expected it!

Nettie opened her mouth to scream again and this time the ringing telephone wakened her and the scream escaped. She sat straight up in bed and so did Dillon. "Nettie, it's only the phone," he said urgently. "Why are you screaming? It's only the phone."

He picked up the handset, mumbled at it, then handed it to Nettie. "Your Mom."

It took all her concentration to control her voice as she whispered, "Mom, what's wrong?"

"Nettie, put on black clothes and come to my house. Hurry." The hoarse voice was almost unrecognizable. "Nettie, hurry!"

"Do what?" Nettie asked.

"Black clothes from head to toe. How long will it take? Fifteen minutes?"

"Mom, what's wrong?"

"Nettie, are you coming?" The strangled voice was on the verge of tears.

"Mom, tell me what you're talking about ... Mom? Mom!"

Nettie punched the "off" button and looked at her sleeping husband. Dillon was already breathing deeply again. She could be pursued by horrifying owls and her Mom could turn into a mad woman, but it wouldn't disturb *his* rest.

Ten minutes later Nettie, dressed like a cat burglar, parked in front of her mother's house. She raced up the sidewalk and tried the front door. It was locked. "Mom!" she called. "Mom, I'm here. Open up!"

"Nettie, quit yelling!" Bethany Jamison yanked open the massive door and pulled her daughter into the front hall. She, too, was dressed like a shadow. Even her salt and pepper curls, which were always meticulously groomed, had been smashed flat under a black scarf. And Bethany's face, as she peered anxiously into the darkness beyond Nettie, was ghostly pale.

"Mom, what's wrong?" Nettie cried. "You're scaring me to death!"

"It's Otto," Bethany said. "Otto died."

Nettie's brow furrowed. "I'm sorry, but what's the big deal? He was more like Dad's dog than yours, wasn't he?"

Bethany pulled Nettie into her plush living room and glanced around, as if checking for spies. "Don't you see," she whispered hoarsely, "Otto never ate another bite after Phillip died. He loved your Dad more than I did, and now everyone will know. Oh, Nettie, I'm so ashamed!"

Nettie's refined mother, normally as calm as a summer day, was weeping hysterically.

Nettie drew her mother into her arms and held her until the crying stopped. "It's okay, Mom," she soothed, gently stroking Bethany's hair. "It's okay."

When Bethany lifted her head and dried her eyes, Nettie waited. In all her life, she had never seen her cultured mother fall apart so completely. Even at Phillip Jamison's funeral last week, Bethany's tears had been sparse and genteel. Nettie was afraid to speak for fear she would say the wrong thing and send her mother into another fit of weeping.

"Come on," Bethany said when she had regained her composure. She led Nettie to the den at the back of the house. The oversized maroon recliner where Dr. Phillip Jamison had spent many of his last hours was spread almost flat. The big German shepherd's front paws were on the footrest with his chin lodged on his paws. His haunches were gathered under his body, as if he were prepared to catapult himself forward upon his master's return.

Nettie's hand went to her mouth. "Oh, Mom, the poor thing!" she cried. "Why didn't you call the vet?"

"Call the vet!" Bethany cried. "Call him? I made him come over here!"

"What did he say?"

"He offered to take Otto to the clinic and feed him intravenously," Bethany answered. "But that would have just prolonged the suffering. Otto didn't want to be alive ..." her voice quavered, "... without Phillip." She shuddered and took a deep breath. "I need you to help me," she continued. "The city just planted a whole patch of petunias in the park down the street. I dug a grave for him in the flower bed, but he's so heavy–I was afraid to take him by myself."

"You dug a grave in the park?" Nettie gasped. "What for? Bury him in the back yard."

"No! Oh, Nettie, don't you see. I can't have him here in my own yard, accusing me ... accusing me ... every day accusing me."

"Mom, he's dead!"

"I don't care! Are you going to help me or not?"

"Can't we put him in the dumpster in the alley?"

The look Bethany gave her daughter was reproachful. "Oh, Nettie! What would your father say?"

"Nothing. He's dead, too!"

Giving Nettie one more indignant glare, Bethany marched through the kitchen and into the garage. When she returned, she was pushing her gardening wheelbarrow.

"What's that for?" Nettie asked.

"We're going to put Otto in the wheelbarrow and take him to the park."

"Mom, have you lost it?" Nettie asked, standing her ground. "We could go to jail for digging up a flower bed–defacing public property or something like that."

Bethany had positioned the wheelbarrow directly in front of the recliner. Now she straightened and faced her daughter. "Will you help me or not?"

Nettie looked at the big dog, then her mother. She sighed and said, "You know I will."

Bethany squeezed her daughter's shoulder. "Thank you, dear. If we get caught, I'll take the heat. We can say I'm crazy with grief and I made you help me. Anyway, we wouldn't go to jail; we'd only have to pay a fine."

"Whatever," Nettie said, bending over the dog. "You're the one who taught me to obey the law so if you want to teach me to *break* the law now, I guess it's your prerogative."

Together the women hoisted Otto into the wheelbarrow. "Now what?" asked Nettie.

"Did you bring your cell phone?"

"Never thought of it," said Nettie.

Bethany reached into her pants pocket and pulled out a tiny phone. "Take mine," she said, "and walk to the park. If you don't see any traffic on the way, call me, and I'll bring Otto."

Nettie bit back several sarcastic remarks and, instead, asked gently, "Are you sure you want to do this?"

Bethany nodded. "I *have* to do this."

"Okay." Nettie helped her mother get the wheelbarrow out the front door and down three steps onto the sidewalk. Then she strolled to the park at the end of the block. Tapping in her mother's land line number, she reported that not a person, a vehicle, or an animal was stirring.

In less than 10 minutes, Bethany joined Nettie at a newly planted flower bed in the small neighborhood park. "Do you think the hole's big enough?" she whispered anxiously.

"It's big enough for 10 Ottos," Nettie whispered back.

"Is it deep enough?"

"Mom, it looks like you were digging to China," Nettie said. "Come on. Let's do it."

The two women bent over the wheelbarrow, then Bethany stopped and straightened. "Wait! I've never done this before. Should we wrap him in something–you know, as a sign of respect?"

"Respect! Mom, we're burying him in a bed of petunias, instead of dumping him in a garbage can. What more could he want?"

"To be buried with Phillip," Bethany said softly.

"Tough nougies!" said Nettie. She picked up Otto's back end and waited for Bethany to lift the front.

Tears fell on Otto's black ruff as Bethany bent over him and heaved his head and front legs out of the wheelbarrow. The two women gently lowered him into the ground. To Nettie's surprise, he nearly filled the hole. She seized the shovel her mother had left beside a pile of sweet-smelling earth and scraped the soil onto Otto.

"There's too much dirt," she said when the hole was filled to overflowing.

"That's okay," her mother said, beginning to sound like her usual serene self. "Here, let me finish."

Nettie stepped out of the way and watched her mother spread the extra soil across the entire surface of the flower bed. "Okay, now hand me that box," Bethany said, pointing toward a sturdy file box that was barely visible under a row of shrubs.

Nettie hauled it out and saw that it contained all the new petunia plants her mother had removed when she dug Otto's grave. She carried the box to the flower bed and knelt down to help her mother replant them, but Bethany stopped her. "Let me do it. I know where every flower goes. You just hand them to me in order when I tell you. And watch for cops!"

"Watch for cops! Watch for cops!" Nettie muttered to herself. Who *was* this woman?

The job went fast with Nettie handing the plants to her mother and Bethany whisking them into the soft earth and patting the soil into place around them. They were on the last plant when Nettie cried, "Oh no, Mom, the root ball's broken on this one." She scooped it up, preserving as much dirt as possible on its roots.

Bethany dug out a small hole before she accepted the damaged plant. With infinite tenderness, she tucked the petunia into its fresh hole and patted the earth into place around it. "That's all we can do," she said. "Maybe it will survive."

"What about water?" asked Nettie. "Don't we need to water the plants in?"

Bethany nodded. "We need to, but there's no way unless we haul it from home in buckets." She paused and studied Nettie. "Do you want to do that?"

"No way," said Nettie. "Well, not unless we have to. Do you think they'll die if we don't?"

Bethany shook her head. "The soil is damp and they'll water again tomorrow if they have any sense. With the plants so fresh and the days so hot, they don't deserve to have a pretty flower bed if they don't water tomorrow."

Nettie grinned at her mom. "Right. And besides you'll come down here tomorrow to make sure they do!"

Bethany hid a little smile, as she began gathering up the shovel, box, and wheelbarrow. But she went still when Nettie suddenly called, "Mom, freeze!" She strained her ears to hear the sound of an approaching vehicle, but the night was still. So she looked around and found the reason for Nettie's warning. A skunk was scrambling toward them on the opposite side of the flower bed. Its tail floated over its back and its nose was low to the ground.

"What do we do?" Nettie asked, so softly that Bethany barely heard her.

"Just what you said," Bethany replied. "Freeze."

"Mom, I don't want to go home smelling like a skunk," Nettie wailed.

"Then, don't move. It doesn't care about us. It's looking for a meal."

The two women watched the skunk prowl along the opposite side of the flower bed until it disappeared into the hedge where Bethany had hidden the box of petunias. Nettie took a deep breath. "Let's get out of here!"

But Bethany put her hand on her daughter's arm. "Listen," she whispered. Breaking the silence of the night was an engine, moving slowly in their direction. "Quick! Let's hide this stuff in the hedge," Bethany said. "Get the shovel." She had already tossed the box into the wheelbarrow and now she thrust the wheelbarrow into the hedge.

"Mom, the skunk's in there!" Nettie objected, picking up the shovel.

"It's gone by now!" Bethany whispered. "Come on." She pulled Nettie toward the end of the hedge and out of sight behind it just before a police cruiser turned a corner and drove slowly past their hiding place.

When it was gone, Nettie leaned heavily into her mother. "We've got to get out of here before I have a nervous breakdown."

Bethany smiled in the moonlight. "Calm down. Now that he's driven past here, he won't be back any time soon. He may not come back all night."

"How do you know?" Nettie asked. "Are you familiar with police schedules?"

"Of course not!" Bethany shook her head. "But it stands to reason. Lubbock is a big place. Why should he keep checking on a tiny park in a peaceful residential neighborhood?"

"Because somebody might be burying a dog in a petunia patch," Nettie snapped. She pulled the wheelbarrow out of the hedge, deposited the shovel in the box, and began pushing the wheelbarrow toward the street. Bethany followed at a leisurely pace. The April night was cool, but her sweater was warm. If a person had to be out at 2:00 A.M., this was the perfect night for the excursion.

Nettie paused when she reached the street. "Mom, what's taking you so long?" she complained.

"I'm sorry," said Bethany, quickening her pace. "I forgot you have to go to work in the morning."

A shadow passed over her face and Nettie gasped. She scanned the sky, just as she had in her dream. Was it an owl? It couldn't be a *snowy* owl–not in Texas. But when she squinted up at the soaring figure, white moonlight reflected off the big bird. Nettie couldn't tell if it was an owl or not, but her heart said it was.

"What are you looking at?" Bethany asked, gazing at the starry sky. She had joined Nettie at the street and stopped.

"An owl."

"Oh. Come on, let's go home and have some hot chocolate," Bethany said, leading the way.

Nettie stayed, glued to the spot, watching the owl, until a cloud passed over the moon. In the darkness, the big bird disappeared and she began pushing the wheelbarrow after her mother.

In Bethany's kitchen, Nettie sat while her Mother bustled around, heating milk and pulling out cocoa mix and cookies. The scene had a familiar feel. How many times had Nettie sat here as a teenager, visiting with her Mother? Too many to count. In recent years, she was usually rushing around herself, helping with a meal. But tonight, she felt drained and her Mother was obviously hyped up. Nettie was content to sit and watch.

And talk. "When did Otto die?" she asked.

Her Mother paused and looked at her. "He was dead when I got up this morning," she answered, almost in a whisper. Tears were forming in her eyes again.

"Mom, he was just a dog! Nobody loved Dad more than you did. Don't you know that?"

"Oh, Nettie, you don't know. I wanted to. I wanted to love him the way I should, but I didn't. I couldn't. And he knew. He knew and he loved Otto more than he loved me." Tears rolled down her cheeks again.

Nettie rose, led her Mother to a chair, and took over the kitchen duties. By the time she had poured two cups of hot chocolate and set a saucer of cookies on the table, her Mother was in control of her emotions.

They sat companionably, sipping the hot liquid and nibbling at the cookies for a few minutes. Then Nettie said, "Please, tell me about it."

Bethany nodded and took a deep breath. "You know how they were. They did everything together. Otto even watched football with Phillip. And they took walks together. Your Dad fed Otto from his own plate. He talked to Otto. He never talked to me. Sometimes I don't think they even knew I was around."

"Yeah, I remember feeling the same way," said Nettie. "I hated it, but I never realized how hard it was for you to have to live with it day after day."

"Then when your Dad died, Otto found him first. I came in from the store that day and Dad was slumped over in his chair. Otto's chin was on his lap and Dad's hand was on Otto's neck. Otto sat there and whined at me until they came to take Dad away. And he never ate again. He loved your Dad more than I did."

"Mom, I don't believe that!" Nettie said. She studied her Mother. "Weren't you and Dad happy?"

"We were strangers," said Bethany. "I guess we were probably as happy as two strangers could be, living together all that time."

"How could you be strangers after 40 years?"

"We never talked about anything real. Just surface issues. Things like what he wanted for supper and where we should go for vacations. I don't know what his dreams were, so I don't know if he achieved them. I don't know what scared him or what puzzled him. I was jealous of Otto. He seemed to understand your Dad in a way I never could."

"Why *didn't* you talk? Why didn't you ask him about all those things?"

"When I tried, he was uneasy. So I quit trying. I was afraid my prying would cause him to avoid me or even leave me. And then, I began to resent him for not wanting to know *me*..."

Bethany's voice broke and Nettie waited for her to regain control. "I loved him so much, Nettie, honey. I adored him. And I hated him at the same time. I don't know how we ended up like that. I never meant to end up like that. And then your Dad retired and got Otto and ..." Bethany shrugged. "After he got Otto, they were the inner circle and I was outside. I didn't even hope any more after that. Hope died a long time ago."

"Do you miss Dad?" Nettie was almost afraid to ask. What if she had completely misunderstood her parents? What if they hadn't really loved each other, after all? Her hand trembled slightly and she set her mug of cocoa down without taking a sip.

But her Mother's answer, soft and heartfelt, returned Nettie's world to its normal orbit. "I miss him as if my own heart had died."

Nettie chose her next words carefully, not wanting to sound like a therapist. "Why do you think you feel so guilty? It seems like you're overreacting."

If she had expected to surprise her Mother with the question, she was the one who was surprised. Her Mother's response was instantaneous and intense. "Why? Because of Shelley and Qiana. Why else?"

"Shelley and Qiana?" Nettie asked. "What do Shelley and Qiana have to do with it?"

"I took Phillip away from them. It was selfish and evil enough to steal a woman's husband, but then not to be the perfect wife for him—well, that makes it even worse." Bethany's face was haggard and her voice broken.

Nettie was almost too appalled to respond. "Why are you dredging up ancient history?" she finally asked. "Dad divorced Shelley almost 40 years ago!"

"It doesn't feel ancient to me," Bethany confessed. "It feels as fresh as if it happened yesterday."

"Why? Mom, you're not making sense."

"It was adultery. It was a horrible, hurtful sin, and I ruined their lives."

"Whose? Whose lives did you ruin?"

Bethany stared at her daughter in amazement. "Shelley and Qiana, of course."

"No, you didn't. That's the stupidest thing I ever heard you say," Nettie told her Mother in her best no-nonsense tone. "Shelley and Qiana are both thrilled with their lives. Shelley works for one of the most powerful judges in the county, and Qiana told me last week that her Mother loves the job *and* the judge. As for Qiana–well, you know all about Qiana."

Bethany studied Nettie's face. "Do you believe Shelley's truly happy?"

"Yes. Totally!"

"And Qiana?"

Again, Nettie chose her words carefully. "Mom, Dad didn't abandon Shelley or Qiana. He worked his heart out his whole life to make sure both of his families had everything we needed. He was there for Qiana. You know that–she was at our house all the time."

Bethany shook her head. "It's not the same as having a whole family. And Qiana would have had a whole family if it hadn't been for me."

"You don't know that," Nettie countered. "How do you know Dad wouldn't have left Shelley for somebody else? Maybe they weren't a match."

Bethany's response was a question that knocked the breath out of Nettie. "Did your Dad cheat on *me*?"

"Mom! Of course not! Why would you ask that?"

"He cheated on Shelley. How do I know he didn't cheat on me, too? We were strangers–maybe it was because he had another woman somewhere. Maybe he shared his hopes and dreams, his fears and feelings with her. Maybe that's why he didn't need to talk to me."

Bethany was crying again. Nettie pulled her chair close to her mother and held her until she straightened up, dried her tears and said, "Go home, Nettie. I'm sorry to keep you out all this time."

"I can't leave you like this," Nettie protested. "You're jousting with a lifetime of ghosts. I can't leave you here to do it alone."

Bethany smiled wearily. "I'm too tired to joust any more. I'm going to bed. You do the same."

"Are you sure?"

"Yes, my love, go snuggle up with your good husband and be happy. If you'll do that, I can cope with my ghosties."

Bethany took the cups and saucers to the sink. She turned on the water and began rinsing them. At her side, Nettie put her arms around her mother's shoulders and kissed her cheek. "I love you, Mom."

Bethany smiled. "I love you too, baby."

Nettie's drive home was more sedate than her mad rush to reach her Mother had been. She was thinking–not so much about her parents' marriage, as her own. Dillon had seemed like a stranger for ... what? ... two months now? She caught her breath. Two months–his business trip to Hawaii had been two months ago. Was that when it started? Was he still angry that she had been unable to go with him on his surprise Valentine trip to paradise?

Okay, she *could* have gone. But she had refused. She should have gone in spite of everything. In spite of her heavy schedule. In spite of the unrelenting nausea that had plagued her. She smiled then and put her hand gently on her abdomen.

She knew now for sure–ever since this afternoon–why she had been suffering with morning sickness two months ago. At the time, she'd never given a thought to pregnancy, not when she'd had only 13-year old Jeremy, followed by three miscarriages. Not when the very thought of pregnancy filled her soul with black horror. Three babies she had lost and mourned. Three! She couldn't lose another. She couldn't. The grief would kill her, and Jeremy needed his mother.

She frowned suddenly. She hadn't told Dillon she was pregnant yet. Why not? Why hadn't she rushed to his office with the news the second she knew? Why was she holding back this precious secret that belonged as much to him as it did to her?

She didn't have an answer. She just had a vague sense of loss. Of abandonment. "So when are you going to tell him?" she asked herself, as she turned into her own driveway. She looked up at the dark, second-story window of the bedroom she shared with Dillon and answered herself, "I don't know."

Chapter 2

Dillon was sleeping soundly and never moved when Nettie crept back into their bed. She listened to his soft snores for a few minutes, thinking of the enormous yellow eyes waiting for her in her sleep. She never wanted to see those eyes again.

Suddenly she bounced off the bed, walked to the wall switch, and flooded the room with light. "Dillon, wake up. We're going to talk," she said.

Wincing, Dillon burrowed under the covers. "What time is it?" he asked.

"Time to talk!" Nettie plopped down on the bed, crossing her arms and legs. "I want to know what's going on. Where did you go? You're never here any more, not even when you're here."

Dillon's dark curly hair resembled a lop-sided bush as he sat up reluctantly and squinted at his wife. "What are you talking about, Nettie? I didn't go anywhere. If I'm here, then I must be here, right?"

"But you're not. Ever since you went to Hawaii, you've been different. Are you still mad at me for not going with you?"

Dillon gazed at her now, his eyes adjusted to the light. "No, I'm not mad," he muttered. "But you should have gone."

"I know, and I'm so sorry I didn't," Nettie said sadly, reaching out to rub his arm. "What can I do to make it up to you?"

Dillon's gaze fell and something like agony crossed his face. With a deep sigh, he said, "That's just it–you can't do anything."

Nettie studied him, trying to read him. "Why not?" she asked.

Dillon wouldn't meet her eyes. "Because I ... I need a divorce." When Nettie didn't answer, Dillon forced himself to look at her.

The expression of shock and horror on her face made him tremble. "Nettie ... I'm sorry," he quavered.

Nettie stared at him, waiting for him to explain the joke. After an eternity of silence, she managed to whisper, "That's ... not ... funny."

"No, it's not," Dillon replied, running his fingers through his thick, dark curls. "But it's ... a fact."

"You *need* a divorce?"

"Yes, I've gotten another woman pregnant. I have to marry her. I ... I *want* to marry her." Dillon's voice was low and anxious.

"Pregnant?" Nettie repeated. Her hands went gently to her own belly, which was beginning to bulge.

Dillon, watching, thought she was about to vomit. "Here, do you need me to help you to the bathroom?" he asked, reaching for her arm.

Nettie gave him a puzzled look. "The bathroom?"

"Yes. Aren't you feeling sick? A little bit sick?" he asked.

"I'm feeling a lot sick," Nettie said, "but going to the bathroom won't help." She crawled off the bed and walked shakily across the room to a rocking chair next to the window.

Dillon followed her, still pulling his fingers through his hair. "Do you want me to leave now?" he asked.

Nettie nodded, but her voice said, "No. I want you to stay here and get Jeremy off to school in the morning. I ... can't. *Then* I want you to leave."

Dillon nodded. "Okay. What else?"

"Who?" Nettie asked the dreaded question. "Who's pregnant?"

Dillon took the stool from the dresser, put it in front of Nettie, and sat down on it. "Her name is Maylea Kanaka. I met her in Hawaii."

Nettie's eyes widened. "And you brought her back here?"

"Of course not," Dillon said. "When I left Hawaii, I never expected to see her again. But when she realized she was pregnant, she came to Lubbock. I had no idea she was coming until she showed up at my office."

"When was that?" Nettie asked around the lump in her throat.

"Last week. The same day your Dad died." Dillon's voice was a low, sad rumble. "It was the most horrible day of my life. Maylea needed me, and you needed me."

Nettie looked at him quizzically, "But she gets you? We're married, but *she* gets you?"

"She *is* pregnant," Dillon pointed out. "Besides, I didn't think you'd want me when you found out about Maylea."

"And Jeremy? Did you think he wouldn't want his Dad any more?"

"I'll still be his Dad. I'll still be there for him," Dillon said defensively. "Just like your Dad was there for Qiana."

"And how do you know it's *your* baby?" Nettie demanded.

"Because Maylea is a sweet, naive little thing. I'm the only man she's been with since her husband died a year ago."

Nettie glared at him with a harshness he'd never seen in her face before. "Dillon West, you're too old to be so stupid," she hissed. Then she gathered up her cat burglar clothes and went into the bathroom to put them on again.

This time Nettie remembered to take her cell phone, but she didn't use it until she was parked in her Mother's driveway. Then she scrolled to her Mother's number, sent it, and waited until she heard Bethany Jamison's sleepy voice. "Mom, I'm outside," she blubbered. "Mommy, I need you."

Bethany got her daughter into the house and settled on her big, fluffy divan, then the story and the tears poured out. Bethany listened stonily, guarding against the flood burning her own eyes. The thing she had dreaded for nearly 40 years had happened, but it had happened to her daughter, not to her. "Dear God, it's not fair!" her heart screamed silently. "It's not fair for Nettie to suffer for my sins."

The story ended and the sobs softened as Nettie cried herself to sleep in her Mother's arms. Then Bethany lowered her daughter's head onto a pillow, tossed a light quilt over her, and trudged heavily into her own bedroom. "Why? Why? Why?" The question was a drumbeat that replaced her heartbeat and tried to shatter her chest.

...he hall, she paused in front of the wedding portrait Phillip ...en her on their 25th anniversary and studied her husband's handsome young face. She had been his office nurse 40 years ago and in awe of the cardiac surgeon who was a legend all over West Texas. When he had taken her to dinner for the first time, she had been too excited to eat. And soon, in spite of Shelley, his beautiful, young wife, he began spending evenings and nights with Bethany. She was hopelessly in love with him but desperately ashamed of herself for having an affair with a married man.

It took nearly two years for her to become pregnant and when she told him, he proposed immediately. He had divorced Shelley and married Bethany before he knew Shelley was pregnant too. Qiana and Nettie were born four days apart the next January, and Phillip always referred to them as his twins.

Bethany lay down on her bed and curled up in a ball. She had been waiting all these years for the axe to fall–waiting for the horrible fate that would avenge her youthful lust. But now the axe had fallen on Nettie instead of Bethany. Dillon, the son-in-law she loved like her own child, had broken Nettie's heart, just as Phillip had broken Shelley's heart. And now Nettie faced a lifetime of loneliness and heartbreak. "Oh, it serves me right," Bethany wailed. "It serves me right for taking Phillip away from Shelley. But if I'd known it would be Nettie who would suffer instead of me ... if I'd only known ..."

For history was repeating itself. Even the double pregnancy. It was too horrible to bear. "I *have* to tell Dillon that Nettie's pregnant, too," Bethany mumbled to herself, just before her eyes closed in exhausted sleep. But she wouldn't. Nettie had sworn her to secrecy and she wouldn't add her own betrayal to Nettie's burden.

The ringing of the telephone at her bedside wakened Bethany at 9:30. "Hello," she answered sleepily.

"Bethany, I'm so sorry to wake you. It's Dolly. Nettie's not here. There's a message on the answering machine saying she's not coming in today. I called her house, and Dillon said she might be with you. He didn't know. What's wrong? Is Nettie sick? What can I do? Why doesn't Dillon know where Nettie is?"

"Nettie's here," Bethany said, breaking into Dolly's frantic flow of words. "Let me see if she's up."

Going to find Nettie, Bethany smiled at the thought of Dolly Tatum. The lively young woman with short, dark, flyaway hair and huge blue eyes managed Nettie's fitness center, Spring Up West. She was intense and loyal and the talkingest person Bethany had ever met.

Nettie was in the kitchen, staring glumly at a cup of steaming coffee.

"Dolly's on the phone," Bethany told her. "Do you want to talk to her?"

Nettie shook her head mutely without taking her eyes off her coffee cup.

Bethany put the handset to her ear. "Dolly, Nettie's not feeling well today. Can you cancel her appointments and run interference for her?"

A momentary silence was her only answer. Then Dolly asked, "What's going on? Does Nettie need me there?"

Bethany studied her daughter a moment, then said thoughtfully. "Not yet. I'll let you know when."

"Okay," said Dolly, sounding businesslike. "Tell her I'll take care of everything."

"Thanks, Dolly. You're a gem."

Bethany pressed a button on the handset and turned her attention to her daughter. "Dolly says she'll take care of everything."

A fleeting smile of acknowledgment touched Nettie's lips, then she heaved a sigh and lifted a tissue to her eyes, which were beginning to well up.

"Did you get any sleep?" Bethany asked, pouring herself a cup of coffee.

"I think so," Nettie mumbled. "It didn't feel like I was asleep, but I guess I was."

"What would you like for breakfast?" Bethany asked, trying to sound cheerful.

"Nothing." Nettie hugged her stomach and grimaced. "I'm not hungry."

"You have to eat, sweetie. You're eating for two, remember?"

Nettie nodded. "I can't forget. Oh, Mom," she wailed suddenly, "why am I such an idiot? If I'd only gone to Hawaii with Dillon, none of this would have happened. It's my own stupid fault."

"If *you'd* gone to Hawaii without Dillon, would you have brought back a hottie?" asked Bethany, taking the seat next to Nettie.

"Of course not!" gasped Nettie, glaring at her mother.

"What if you were mad at Dillon for refusing to go with you?"

Nettie's glare faltered. "I wouldn't have replaced him over it," she muttered darkly.

"Right," said Bethany crisply. "So watch yourself. Not going to Hawaii was a mistake on your part, but it doesn't make you responsible for Dillon's infidelity."

Nettie shrugged. "Maybe. But it wouldn't have happened if I'd been with him. If I'd been where I should have been," she said sadly.

"Nettie, darling, you can't undo the past, so let's talk about the present. What's your plan?"

Nettie looked wearily at her mother. "I'm going to try to go on breathing every single minute of every single day for the rest of my life. Just try to go on breathing ..." Her voice faded.

"Please do," said Bethany drily, not betraying the fact that her heart felt as raw as if a bomb had exploded in it. "What else?"

"I don't have a plan, Mom," Nettie said, turning stricken eyes on Bethany. "But Jeremy has to be told." Her voice gained both strength and conviction then. "I won't tell him I want a divorce. Or that I quit loving Dillon. Or that we can't get along. None of those things are true, and I'm not going to lie to him."

Bethany nodded thoughtfully. "When do you want to talk to him?"

"He has to be told after school today," Nettie said. "Dillon will be gone–Jeremy has to know why."

"Okay, so you need to call Dillon and tell him to meet you at home at about 4:00 o'clock. Right?"

Nettie shrank into her chair. "I don't want to talk to him. Not yet. Maybe I can leave a message with his secretary."

"No, I'm going over there." Bethany's voice was determined. "I want to see his weasly little face when I tell him what I think of him.

I'll tell him to be at your house at 4:00 this afternoon. Anything else?"

Nettie looked up, but her gaze had lost its focus. "I don't know," she whined wearily. "I don't much care."

"Are you sure you don't want me to tell him about the baby?" Bethany asked.

Nettie shook her head. "I don't ... want him ... if he doesn't ... want me." She stumbled and sobbed over the words for they bruised her throat as they tumbled through it.

Bethany gently detached Nettie's fingers from her coffee cup and led her to the guest room, which had once been Nettie's bedroom. She pulled back the covers and guided Nettie into the cool space between the sheets. "You rest, my love, as long as you want to. When you wake up, we'll make some plans." She kissed Nettie's cheek, leaving behind a lovely Mother-scent that carried Nettie back to the deep, sweet comfort of childhood.

When Dillon West opened the front door of his home to find his mother-in-law on the porch, his face fell. "Bethy! Have you come to tar and feather me?" he asked.

Bethany winced at the pet name that only Dillon used. She had hated it when he first used it, but as she grew to love Dillon, she also came to love the intimacy of his nickname for her. "Please don't call me that," she said, sliding past him into the entryway.

After he had shut the door and turned to face her, she added, "I've come to tell you that Nettie wants you to be here at 4:00 to tell Jeremy you're leaving."

"Today?" Dillon sounded panicky. "I'm not ready to tell him yet. Can't we wait a few days?"

"Don't you think he might notice if you don't come home for dinner?" Bethany asked icily.

"Sure, but it's tax season. I always work late in April. Or Nettie could say I suddenly had to go out of town on business."

"Dillon West, it's bad enough that you're destroying my daughter's life. And now you have the temerity to ask her to lie to Jeremy about it? No! She's not going to lie for you." Bethany whirled, marched into the den, and settled herself in an easy chair.

Dillon followed uncertainly and perched on the edge of the sofa. For long moments, Bethany glared and Dillon fidgeted. Finally Dillon asked mournfully, "Am I making a huge mistake, Bethany?"

"You're making the biggest mistake of your life," Bethany said. Seeing the sober expression on Dillon's face, she added, "But it's not too late. Nettie loves you–she'll take you back."

"Oh, Bethy ... Bethany, I can't go back to Nettie. I've ... I've gotten another woman pregnant." There was a sob in Dillon's voice.

Bethany bit back the words she wanted to fire at him: *No, you've gotten two women pregnant.* Instead, making her voice as calm and reasonable as she could manage, she said, "Even so, you don't have to destroy your family. You'll have to support the child, of course, but I know Nettie will take you back–maybe not right away, but eventually."

"No!" Dillon stood, and his voice was hoarse and determined. "I can't abandon Maylea. I love her, and I want to be with her. Now if you'll excuse me, I'm trying to pack."

With a sinking heart, Bethany watched Dillon walk away. There had to be words that would bring him to his senses. She had to find those words. She rose and followed him into the hallway. But before she could think of a strategy, a beautiful woman appeared on the stairs above them. She was petite–almost childlike–with long black hair pulled into a pony tail and exquisite facial features. She was wearing a bright green silk top with flutter sleeves and spotless white Capris. Her high-heeled white sandals might have cost $250 if she'd gotten them on sale. A good sale.

"Sweetheart, what's taking ..." she began in a soft, lilting tone, but stopped when she caught sight of Bethany.

"Oh!" she cried, looking from Dillon to Bethany. "Are you Nettie?"

"Maylea," Dillon said in a stern voice, "this is Bethany Jamison, Nettie's *mother.*"

"Oops," Maylea said, with a little giggle. "I'm sorry, Mrs. Jamison." She walked down the stairs and put a hand on Dillon's arm with a possessive gesture.

"Bethany, I'd like you to meet Maylea Kanaka."

Bethany nodded coolly at the young woman who had to be *at least* 10 years younger than Dillon. Then she turned to her son-in-law. "What is she doing here?"

"Helping me pack," Dillon admitted. "I'm sorry you had to meet her like this."

"What exactly are you packing?" Bethany asked, starting up the stairs.

"Only my clothes and personal things," Dillon said, hurrying after her. "We're not looting the place, Bethany. I promise."

"But Dillon." Maylea's voice had lost its soft, lilting quality. "Half of everything in this house is yours. Half of the *house* is yours. You have a right to take ..."

Dillon turned on her. "I said we're not looting the place, and we're not." His voice was angry, and his face was hard. "Do you understand?"

Maylea pouted. "But darling, I only want you to have what belongs to you."

"And I'm here to *get* everything that belongs to me," he said, spacing his words as if he were speaking to a child.

Pausing, Bethany leaned against the bannister, and listened to the exchange. She obviously didn't know Dillon as well as she had believed she did, but she was pretty certain he wasn't putting on an act. He truly had no intention of ripping off his wife and son–well, besides shredding their hearts–but Maylea was another story.

"Dillon, I don't want that ... *woman* ... here in Nettie's house," she said decisively. "Either you take her back where she belongs or I will. Then *I'll* help you pack."

Maylea stomped a tiny foot and her dark eyes sizzled with anger. "I'm not going anywhere with *her*," she announced. "And I have a perfect right to be here. This house is half yours, Dillon. Stand up to her like a man!"

Without a word, Dillon seized Maylea's arm and led her through the kitchen into the garage. When Bethany heard his car engine start, she went into the kitchen and poured a cup of coffee. Remembering she'd missed breakfast, she turned on the toaster and began searching for a loaf of bread. She had no intention of leaving until Dillon was packed and had given her all of his house keys.

Chapter 3

Nettie woke with a start to find a face a few inches from her face. Inquisitive hazel eyes were studying Nettie in the same way an artist studies a subject. Nettie sat up with a gasp. "Qiana!" she cried, realizing it was her half-sister's presence that had wakened her. "Are you trying to scare me to death?"

"No, just trying to figure out what's wrong with you," Qiana said with an impish grin. She made herself comfortable on the bed, leaning against the headboard. "You know, some of your clients will gain 10 pounds in a week if they miss an appointment with you, so I was sure you must be deathly ill or you wouldn't hang them out to dry."

Nettie pushed at her shoulder-length, honey-colored hair, trying to restore some semblance of order. "I'm not deathly ill," she said, "just ... deathly sad." Tears sprang into her dark brown eyes.

Qiana dropped her light attitude at once. "What's wrong?" she asked with a worried frown.

Nettie sighed. She might as well tell Qiana and get it over with. Before long, she would have to tell everyone she knew–who better to practice on than her sister? "Dillon is divorcing me so he can marry a woman he met in Hawaii last February," she blurted.

It was Qiana's turn to gasp. "No!" she cried. "I don't believe that!"

Nettie shrugged and dabbed her eyes with the sheet. "I wouldn't either if Dillon hadn't told me himself," she said. And then tears overwhelmed her.

Qiana watched her weeping sister with dismay. She patted Nettie's shoulder awkwardly and went for tissues. In an agony of empathy she waited for the tears to stop and tried to think of a way to help.

Finally, Nettie took a deep, ragged breath and bit her lower lip. Her eyes were almost dry, and she faced Qiana with a shaky smile. "I'm sorry I'm such a baby," she said. "I can't seem to stop crying."

"That's okay," Qiana said. She gazed at Nettie uncertainly. "Do you want to tell me about it?"

"There's not much more to tell," Nettie said. "Mom's at the house, telling Dillon he's going to have to break it to Jeremy after school today. Oh! There *is* more–the woman is pregnant. I guess that's why he's determined to marry her."

"Pregnant! How long has he known her?"

"Only while he was in Hawaii, he says. She showed up at his office the day Dad died to tell him she's pregnant and he's the father," Nettie explained.

"Gimme' a break!" exclaimed Qiana. "You can't tell me he believes that rot!"

"He must–he's divorcing me," said Nettie.

"What an idiot!" Qiana rose and began pacing around the room. At 37, she was still an extraordinarily beautiful woman with short, dark brown hair that framed her face in natural waves. She was slender with a graceful bearing, the result of her years as a dance and aerobics instructor. As Nettie watched her, she stopped suddenly and asked accusingly, "Did you tell him he's an idiot?"

"Well, not that exact word. I think I said, 'You're too old to be so stupid.' Something like that."

"Oh good, that's better!" Qiana said, resuming her pacing. She roamed about the room, as restless as the tide. Finally, she stopped and returned to the bed. "Okay, I've got an idea," she said, her eyes alight with excitement. "Do you remember that movie, 'First Wives Club'?"

Nettie frowned. "No, I don't think so. What's it about?"

"Well, there are these three women–married to jerks–and the husbands divorce them because they want trophy wives. Well, it was something like that. Anyway, the three ex-wives get together and figure out how to get revenge on their ex-husbands. It's great!

They really make the men crawl. I know we can make Dillon sorry he ever met his Hawaiian flower."

Nettie was eying her sister in disbelief.

"What?" demanded Qiana. "It's the best idea I ever had!"

"I don't want revenge on Dillon," Nettie said. "Don't you understand? I love him."

"Love, hate–they're two sides of a coin. Yesterday you loved him; today you realize he doesn't deserve your love," Qiana said with finality. "Now come on. Nobody knows him like you do, and you'll never know him better than you do now. What's the best way to destroy him?"

Nettie was staring at her sister as if she'd never seen her before. "Qiana, love and hate aren't two sides of a coin. Maybe *self*-love and hate. But if I actually loved Dillon yesterday, then I love him today, too."

"Oh no!" Qiana cried. "Do you mean to tell me you want him back–you want that lowlife snake back? Please tell me you're not that lame!"

Nettie sighed. "I don't know if I want him back or not, but I don't want him hurt. I love him. And Jeremy loves him."

Qiana halted in mid-pace. Jeremy!

"Yikes!" she said. "I forgot about Jeremy." She smiled at the thought of her 13-year-old nephew who was one of her best buddies. "Well, so what? Jeremy's going to find out this afternoon that Dillon is garbage. So what if we embellish his understanding a wee bit?"

"QiQi!" Nettie exclaimed. "Is that what you thought of Dad–that he was garbage? He left your Mom to marry my Mom."

Qiana flopped back down on the bed and heaved a sigh. "That was different. I didn't know him then. If I had, I probably would have thought he was garbage–and told him so."

Nettie smiled. "Probably. But what *did* you think about him? Did you ever hate him for leaving you and your Mom?"

Qiana hesitated, as her memory roamed back over the years. "Sometimes I hated him because he was my Dad. But I don't think I hated him for leaving us. He had already moved out when I was born, so it seemed normal for him to live somewhere else."

Nettie nodded, thinking back also. "Mom still feels guilty for stealing him from you and Shelley."

Qiana was surprised. "Why? She was like a second mother to me. I never knew she had doubts."

"Neither did I until last night," Nettie said. She described the middle-of-the-night excursion to the petunia cemetery.

"Well," Qiana said after Nettie finished, "maybe Mom and I should pay Bethany a little visit and set her right about a few things."

"What things?"

Qiana pursed her lips for a moment. "Mainly that we're very happy. That we always had everything we wanted–Dad made sure we did. I'm not talking about having everything we *needed*. We had everything we *wanted*."

Nettie smiled. "He was a good man, wasn't he?"

Qiana nodded emphatically. "He was the best man I ever knew. Nobody worked harder." She paused and looked at her sister through moist eyes. "Do you think we could go to his grave together sometimes? You know, just to tell him we miss him and we love him?"

"I'd like that," Nettie said. "And I think he'd like to know we still feel like sisters even though he's gone."

"His twins," Qiana said, smiling and dabbing her eyes.

Nettie passed Qiana a tissue. "Dillon's a good man, too," she said. "I'd never do anything to hurt him, QiQi. Please, try to understand that I love him with all my heart."

"And you want him back?"

Nettie shrugged. "I don't know about that. He would have to do something to convince me I could trust him again."

"Something like what?" Qiana asked.

Nettie shook her head sadly. "I don't know of anything."

Qiana nodded approvingly. "Good. You had me worried for a minute there. I guess I'd better get back to the job. Shall we cancel your appointments for tomorrow, too?"

Nettie tried to measure her inner buoyancy and found herself in short supply. She felt like a party balloon that had been filled with sand instead of helium. "I don't know. I guess you'd better. Just in case."

Qiana nodded agreeably. "Okay, today and tomorrow, but that's it. If you don't show up the next day, I'll personally come bathe you, dress you, and haul you to work. That's a promise!"

Nettie smiled. "I'll keep it in mind."

Qiana walked to the door of the bedroom, then stopped and looked back. "What would Dad tell you if he were here?"

Nettie didn't have to think about her answer for more than a nanosecond. "He would say, 'You can't get strong in the good times'."

"That's right, 'You can't get strong in the good times'," Qiana repeated. "I usually wanted to smack him when he said that."

"Me too," Nettie laughed.

"So, are you going to stay here for awhile or go home?" Qiana asked.

"I'm going home as soon as Mom gets back and tells me Dillon is out," Nettie said.

"Good!" Qiana said. "And I've got an idea for a little surprise for Mr. Dillon. But I need some help, and I know exactly where to get it. I'll tell you about it when all my ducks are in a row."

"Qiana, no!" Nettie cried. But the door was shut and her sister was gone. "I don't want revenge!" Nettie told the closed door. "Please don't hurt Dillon."

She sighed and snuggled back into the soft sheets, trying to remember which of her clients were scheduled for the next two days. She and Qiana each owned a fitness center, given to them by their father on their 35th birthdays. "Two years ago," Nettie murmured to herself. "Has it been only two years?"

Of course, the sisters had already been managing the fitness centers under their father's direction for many years, at the time. Nettie, a nutritionist, had clients at both Spring Up South and Spring Up West. And Qiana, a fitness junkie, taught aerobic exercise and dance classes to customers and trainers at both sites. Two years ago Phillip Jamison had insisted on taking both of his daughters and their mothers to dinner on January 12th, halfway between their birthdays. Qiana, born on January 10th, was four days older than Nettie.

Their birthday gifts had been the deeds to the two businesses. Nettie received Spring Up West because it was closer to her home and, besides, now that her last name was West, it seemed fitting for her to have the business with the same name. Qiana became owner of Spring Up South, which was located a block from her apartment. The sisters' reactions had been typically dissimilar. Nettie had been hesitant, afraid of failure. Qiana had been jubilant, thrilled at a new challenge.

"What if I cause it to go bankrupt?" Nettie had wailed. "You're a wonderful manager, Dad, but I'm not. I don't have any experience as a business owner."

Qiana, instead of their father, had answered. "Don't be daft, JJ!" she cried, using a pet name from childhood when Nettie had been Jeanette Jamison. She threw her arms around Nettie. "You've been running that place for years. You'll still help me and I'll still help you. Dillon already keeps the books. We'll make both the gyms bigger successes than Dad ever dreamed of."

Qiana's excitement had rubbed off on Nettie, and they had poured gratitude upon their father the rest of the evening. Phillip Jamison had basked in their enthusiasm. Nettie smiled at the memory of her father's quiet pleasure, as he listened to his daughters make plans and dream dreams. As a cardiac surgeon, he had labored all his adult life to help the citizens of West Texas have the healthiest hearts possible. But what his daughters could do, using good nutrition and vigorous exercise to keep hearts healthy, was more useful than anything a doctor could do after a heart had been compromised by poor health or indulgent living.

Nettie let her thoughts linger on her father, so recently buried in the dry West Texas soil he loved, and shed a few more tears for him. There had been a time in her life when she had expected to become a doctor herself. To follow in his footsteps.

But when he heard her plan, Phillip Jamison had sat her down and asked her why she wanted to be a doctor. She told him she wanted to help people be strong and healthy, and he bluntly told her to study nutrition. "If you become a doctor, you'll become a doctor of *medicine*," he explained. "Medicine isn't about health; it's about sickness. You'll learn what to do to help people get well after they're sick, but that's not the same thing as helping them be healthy in the first place."

He had smiled wisely and sent her on her way to "think about it." And, because she trusted him, she had followed his advice. Over the years, as she rejoiced with clients who flourished under her care, she frequently blessed her father who had known her well enough to set her on the right track. And to save her from a career that would have made her miserable.

Nettie's eyes had closed and she was dozing off again when a timid tapping at the door wakened her. "Mom?" she asked with a yawn.

"It's me," came the distinctive drawl of Dolly Tatum.

"Dolly, what are you doing here?" Nettie asked, as the manager of Spring Up West peered around the door. "Who's minding the store?"

"Qiana. She wanted to talk to Dad. And when I heard how bad you felt, I just had to come check on you."

"She wanted to talk to your Dad?" Nettie repeated. "Why?"

"She didn't say, but I think it had something to do with computers," Dolly replied. She pulled the rocking chair close to the bed and perched on it. Her short, dark hair, as always, was held in place by a do-rag–a yellow one today–and she was wearing a long, loose yellow shirt over her leotards. Her huge blue eyes were riveted on Nettie's face. "You know, he goes around in overalls and a baseball cap, looking like a retired farmer, but he knew everything there was to know about computers when he worked as an engineer at the Space Center."

Nettie nodded, frowning. Matt Tatum was a regular at Spring Up West, not because he liked to exercise, but because he liked to keep an eye on his daughter–and on Nettie. Nettie knew he would do anything for her. What if Qiana talked him into hacking into Dillon's computers, and … and what? What might they do to hurt

Dillon if they accessed his files? And his clients' files? The thought boggled her mind!

"Well?" Dolly said.

Nettie looked up. "Well what?"

"What are you going to do? Are you going to let Dillon and his little chippie ruin your life?"

"No!" Nettie said, because she knew it was the right answer, not because she believed it.

"Good for you! You've been crying for what? A few hours now? That's about long enough, don't you think? I regretted every second I wasted crying over that half-wit husband of mine. Norman took off and left me with two little boys, and I nearly let him ruin me. But he wasn't worth a single tear I cried. I'm not going to let you waste any more tears or time on a man who's pathetic enough to walk out on a wonderful family like you and Jeremy!"

Nettie had heard Dolly's story countless times. When her children Mack and Tommy were five and two, Norman had left them for another woman. Just before the State removed the boys from their wounded mother, she had pulled herself together and found the job at Spring Up West. She never shed another tear over Norman. And she never let her boys get dirty or hungry again.

"So, what's the plan?" Dolly asked.

"I don't have a plan," Nettie confessed in a feeble voice.

"Then get one," Dolly ordered. "Sit up now and pull your guts together. I'm telling you–you're wasting your time moping around over Dillon West. He doesn't deserve it. What do you think–that he's going to come back to you because you're so pitiful? Because he feels so sorry for you?"

Nettie glared at her friend. "I don't want him back because he feels sorry for me," she said indignantly.

"Darn tootin'!" agreed Dolly. "Then don't lie around whining and feeling sorry for yourself. How would you like it if he walked through that door right now and saw you like this?"

Nettie glanced at the door anxiously and pushed her hair away from her face. "I wouldn't," she said.

"Okay. That's my girl! You need to do your crying at night when he's off with his new snuggle bunny. But during the day, when you might see him or his friends, you've got to look good. You've got to look *hot*! You get my meaning?"

Nettie nodded obediently. "Yeah. I never thought about it like that." She lifted her chin. "He's not going to see me looking pitiful." She gazed into Dolly's eyes defiantly. "I promise you that!"

"That's all I wanted to hear," Dolly said, bouncing up. "Now I'm back to the salt mines." She pushed the rocking chair back to its place at the window. When she turned, Nettie had wilted. "What's wrong?" she cried in alarm, rushing back to the bed.

"I don't know how. I don't even know what to do first."

"That's easy," Dolly said cheerfully. "Get a lawyer. Get a good lawyer and get an appointment for *today*."

Nettie nodded. "Okay. How do I find a good lawyer?"

"Call your Dad's lawyer. He'll know the best divorce lawyer in town."

Nettie smiled. Of course he would. She threw the bed covers aside and stood. "I guess I should call Qiana first and tell her not to cancel my appointments for tomorrow," she mused.

"Don't bother," said Dolly. "It was when she asked for your appointment book that I decided to come calling on you. I'd already cancelled today's appointments, and I told her to hold off on tomorrow's until I'd had a chance to give you a pep talk."

Nettie grinned. "You're pretty sure of yourself," she said.

"For good reason!" Dolly chirped. And then she was gone.

Chapter 4

Thirty minutes later, when Bethany stepped from her garage into her kitchen, she found Nettie at the stove, stirring soup for their lunch. Nettie's hair was wet, and she was wrapped in one of Bethany's robes.

"Well, you've perked up a lot," Bethany observed.

"Dolly came over," Nettie explained, "and read me the riot act. I have a 2:30 appointment with Anita Patton, so I showered and started lunch. May I borrow some of your sweats to wear home?"

"Of course. Anything you want," said Bethany. "Who's Anita Patton?"

"My lawyer." Nettie didn't look at her mother, but tasted the soup and stirred it industriously. She couldn't think about the meeting with the divorce lawyer without tears welling again. And she was determined to control the tears, instead of allowing them to control her. Bethany, sensing her daughter's precarious grip on her emotions, busied herself setting the table and rounding out their meal with fruit and crackers.

When lunch was ready, Bethany held her daughter's hand, and they bowed their heads. "Thank You, Father, for Your bounty," Bethany prayed. "We pray for wisdom and guidance today, and ask that You sanctify this food to nourish our bodies. In Jesus' name, Amen."

The two women ate in silence for a few minutes, and then Nettie asked, "Did Dillon say he would be there this afternoon?"

Bethany nodded. "He didn't like it, but he said he would come."

"He didn't like it?" Nettie asked.

"He wanted to wait awhile to tell Jeremy," Bethany explained.

"Oh." Nettie wasn't surprised. It was typical for Dillon to put off a difficult moment as long as possible. "In the long run, he'll be glad we got it over with early," she said.

"And I met Maylea," Bethany added.

Nettie stopped eating. "Where?"

"At your house."

Nettie's spoon dropped into her soup with a splat. "He had *her* at *my* house?"

"Not for long," Bethany said. She recounted the events of her morning for Nettie.

"And did he look weasly when you told him what you thought of him?" Nettie asked.

Bethany sighed. "I never actually got around to it," she said. "When he got back from taking Maylea away, he was so pitiful and so sorry that I didn't have the heart to grind him any deeper into the dirt."

"What was he sorry about?" Nettie asked, barely daring to breathe as she waited for her mother's answer.

"Sorry for hurting you. Sorry for hurting Jeremy. Sorry for hurting me …"

"But not sorry enough to drop kick his Island honey back where she came from?" Nettie asked.

"No, not that sorry."

"Do you think there's any possibility he's going to change his mind and come back to me?" Nettie asked. She had to know her mother's opinion before she kept the appointment with the lawyer that afternoon.

"It doesn't look that way," Bethany said. "Maylea is exceptionally beautiful–I suppose that's what this is all about. And she's not going to quit being beautiful any time soon."

Nettie nodded, took a deep breath, and forced herself to keep eating. "Qiana came over. She reminded me what Dad would say if he were here …"

" 'You can't get strong in the good times'," Bethany quoted before Nettie had a chance to say the words.

"Right," Nettie said. "I'm going to keep reminding myself to get strong–for Dad. It would make him proud, wouldn't it?" She looked up at her mother with tears in her eyes.

"Very proud," Bethany said. And her eyes were bright with tears, too.

Nettie arrived at her lawyer's office wearing a smart navy blue suit with her shoulder length hair pulled back in a chignon. Her eyes were dry and her movements crisp. She observed with approval that the office furniture was comfortable without being extravagant.

Anita Patton's secretary settled her in the waiting room with a questionnaire about marital assets. It took all of Nettie's will power not to dissolve into tears again, as she studied the questions and realized that the home and family she and Dillon had built together were about to be uprooted and dissected.

She had barely finished answering all the questions she could when the secretary came to usher her into the lawyer's office. Ms. Patton, a middle-aged woman, was both friendly and businesslike. "Any time you need to stop and cry, you go right ahead," she said gently. "I know how hard this must be for you."

Nettie smiled bleakly. "I'm trying to get past the crying stage, but thank you for being so understanding."

Ms. Patton looked surprised. "Didn't all this happen just last night? Or actually, early this morning?"

Nettie nodded.

"Well, don't expect too much of yourself. Twelve hours is a little early to be past the crying stage, don't you think?"

"I don't know," Nettie admitted. "I've been advised to do my crying at night when there's no chance Dillon or his friends will see me."

Ms Patton smiled. "You'll get a lot of advice in the days ahead, some of it good and some of it bad. You need to work your way through all the stages of this divorce in your own way. And be patient with yourself."

Nettie nodded again. "You're very kind. I'll try to do that."

Ms. Patton studied the questionnaire Nettie had handed her. "It looks like the main issues will be the child, the house, and the bank accounts. What do you think?"

"I think you're right," Nettie said.

"What about the businesses–your husband's accounting firm and your fitness center? And your separate retirement accounts? Is it your desire for the businesses and the retirement accounts to remain separate property after the divorce?"

"Yes, of course," Nettie murmured. "What else … ?"

"Everything could be split in half–or sold and the profits split–if your husband's income is higher than yours?"

Nettie shook her head. "That sounds like a big mess. Anyway, I usually make more than Dillon except during March and April. I'm not interested in his business, and I don't believe he'll be interested in mine."

The lawyer looked dubious. "Well, if you make more … we'll just have to see. In fact, why don't you give me the name of your husband's lawyer? I'll talk to him and see how much work we're going to have to do in order to reach an agreement."

"He uses Dan Ebersole when he needs an attorney," Nettie said, "but I don't know if Dan does … divorces."

"He does for his regular clients. If you'll give me Mr. West's office phone number, I'll check with him."

As Ms. Patton punched in Dillon's number and waited for her call to be answered, she said to Nettie, "You'll be wanting to stay in your home with your son, right?"

"Yes."

"What about house payments? Home owner's insurance? Will you need financial assistance from your husband to meet those obligations?"

Nettie shook her head. "I don't think so."

Ms. Patton looked impressed. "That's excellent." And then into the mouthpiece, "Yes, hello. I'm trying to reach Dillon West. This is his wife's lawyer Anita Patton calling."

It took Ms. Patton less than a minute to learn that Dillon hadn't called Dan Ebersole yet, but planned to contact him soon. "All right, then," Ms Patton said, "if you'll reconnect me to your secretary or receptionist, I'll give her my name and phone numbers. Please have Mr. Ebersole call me at his earliest convenience." A moment later she was rattling off her name and phone numbers.

Returning her phone to its cradle she said to Nettie. "Okay, here's what I foresee. We'll get the house in your name alone. You'll have joint custody of ..." She paused to glance down at her legal pad, then said, "... Jeremy. And you and your husband will divide the bank accounts equally. Does that sound reasonable to you?"

"You mean I'll have to pay my husband for half the equity in our home?" Nettie asked.

"No. I mean the house will become your separate property as soon as the divorce is final. You'll be responsible for the mortgage and upkeep, but I'll insist that you not be saddled with equity payments to Mr. West," said Ms. Patton.

"Well, then, maybe he should get more than half of our bank accounts," Nettie said timidly. "It doesn't seem fair for him to lose his share of our home. You know, to lose it completely."

"Fair!" snorted Ms. Patton. "Do you call what he's doing to you and Jeremy fair?"

"No, of course not," said Nettie. "But that's another issue. Dillon has always worked hard. He shouldn't be stripped bare after working so hard all these years."

Ms. Patton tossed down her pencil. "Mrs. West, if your husband is half as decent as you are, we need to abandon divorce proceedings and get the two of you into marriage counseling."

But Nettie was shaking her head. "It wouldn't do any good. His girl friend is pregnant. That's why he's leaving me."

Ms. Patton picked up her pencil again and began writing furiously. "I see. Then the first thing we'll demand is proof of pregnancy. And, trust me, I'll get you all the equity in the house and half the bank accounts, too. What else?" She was studying the questionnaire Nettie had filled out. "Your son is how old?"

"Thirteen."

Ms. Patton nodded. "So there's no chance that you're pregnant, as well?"

When Nettie didn't answer, the lawyer looked up to find her client in tears. "Uh-oh," she said. Picking up a box of tissues, she came around her desk and seated herself beside Nettie. She gave her weeping client a handful of tissues and rubbed Nettie's back soothingly.

"I'm sorry," Nettie blubbered, struggling to regain control. "I only found out yesterday, and I don't want him to know yet."

"That's a mistake," said Ms. Patton. "If he knew, he might come back to you."

Nettie shook her head violently. "No! I don't want him that way."

Ms. Patton sighed. "He'll have to know before the divorce is final," she warned.

"I know," said Nettie, beginning to regain her poise. "But I don't want it to look like I'm using my pregnancy to get him back. I only want him back if ... he wants me. And he doesn't."

"I understand," said Ms. Patton. "I still believe it's a mistake, but I do understand. And now I apologize for being abrupt, but you do realize, don't you, that I squeezed your appointment into a tiny crack in my schedule before I have to be in court?"

"Yes, of course," said Nettie.

"Very good. Make another appointment for next week, and we'll carry on." The lawyer seized her briefcase and started for the door. With her hand on the door knob, she stopped and addressed Nettie again. "I hope you realize what an exceptional woman you are. It's an honor to handle your case."

Then Nettie was alone in the office, mopping up tears and groping for her purse.

Nettie made a quick stop at the supermarket and hadn't been home five minutes when the doorbell rang. She glanced at her watch–3:35–typical Dillon timing. Now she wouldn't have time to change clothes. With a sigh, she went to the front door to admit her newly estranged husband.

He followed her to the kitchen where she poured two cups of coffee, adding a bit of milk and a teaspoon of sugar to his. After he had tasted it and thanked her, they sat in uneasy silence until Dillon cleared his throat and said, "Nettie, I hate myself for what I'm doing to you and Jeremy."

She glared at him. "Then don't do it," she said.

"I don't have a choice," he replied. "Maylea is young and helpless. I can't use her, then throw her away like an old newspaper."

Nettie shook her head in bafflement. "She's practically a stranger; yet you're saying her claim on you is stronger than mine and Jeremy's?"

Dillon met her gaze with defiance for a moment. Than his eyes fell and his shoulders sagged. "No," he said brokenly. "I'm trying to convince myself, but it's not true. No one has a stronger claim on me than you and Jeremy."

"Then why ... ?" Nettie couldn't finish the question, and it hung in the air between them.

Dillon shook his head mutely.

"Mom says Maylea is beautiful," Nettie said finally, breaking the silence between them with a voice that was weak and squeaky. "Do you think I'm ... ugly? Was it so terrible being married to me? Were you dreadfully unhappy? What did I do wrong, Dillon?"

Dillon's head snapped up. "No! You've got it all wrong! It's not you–it's me. You're wonderful! And beautiful! And I'm selfish and stupid. You're too good for me!" His voice broke when he added, "Way too good!"

Nettie watched silently as her husband struggled with his emotions. He was a stranger to her–a weak, vacillating man. Dillon had always been strong and confident, sure of himself and his decisions. Now he was this stranger–this beloved stranger.

She stood. "Do you want to talk to Jeremy alone or do you want me to be with you?"

"Which do you think would be better?" he asked, looking up tearfully as she laid her soft hand on his shoulder.

"I don't know," she answered truthfully. "I think it's going to be horrible either way."

Dillon shuddered. "If you think it's going to be horrible, please be there."

"Okay." Nettie walked to the sink where she had left a head of lettuce. She stripped and washed the leaves while Dillon studied his coffee in dejected silence. When he had emptied the cup, he brought it to the sink and stood watching her work.

"How did you find a lawyer so fast?" he asked. "And what's the rush?"

Nettie didn't look at him. "Dad's lawyer recommended her. And the rush is your girlfriend's pregnancy."

"Oh."

"Besides," Nettie added hesitantly, "are you ... living with her?"

Dillon reddened. "Well, it would be so expensive to live ... you know ... apart ..."

Nettie shrugged. "Not exactly the example I want my son to see."

"Neither do I," said Dillon frankly. "I won't bring him over until we're married. In the meantime, we'll take him to dinner or I'll come over here. Well, if that's okay with you."

"Don't bring *her*." Nettie's voice was harsh.

"She's going to be Jeremy's stepmother. You'll have to see her sometimes," Dillon said.

"Of course, but not here," Nettie said in a low, angry tone.

"Okay," said Dillon. "Not here." He watched Nettie work in silence a few more minutes, then said. "I forgot some things in my desk and upstairs. I'd better gather them now or I may forget."

Nettie nodded. She set a tomato on the cutting board and hacked it into chunks, never taking her eyes from her task as she listened to Dillon walk away.

Jeremy's re-entry into his home was typically noisy that afternoon. "Hey, Dad!" he cried as soon as he opened the door. His voice was bright with excitement. "Dad!" he yelled again before the door slammed behind him. "Come on," Nettie heard him add, "they're probably in the kitchen."

It was a rare day when Dillon arrived home before dinnertime. For his car to be in the driveway at 4:00 in the afternoon, and in the second week of April, no less, was nothing short of a miracle. Jeremy, a lanky youngster with his Dad's dark curly hair and bright blue eyes, appeared in the doorway, flanked by his two best friends, Ronny and Kurt. Nettie looked up with a smile. "Hi, boys! How was your day?"

"Fine now!" Ronny said.

"Yeah fine, now that school's out!" Kurt added.

"Where's Dad?" Jeremy asked impatiently, bypassing the small talk. "Did you know his car is in the driveway? Do you think he'll have time to shoot some baskets with us?"

Before Nettie could answer, Dillon appeared in the doorway behind the boys. "I'm pretty short on time today," he told Jeremy. "I'm here because I need to talk to you. Actually, your Mother and I need to talk to you."

Jeremy shot the briefest glance at his parents' somber faces, then turned to his friends. "Can Kurt go home with you, Ronny? I guess I won't be playing today."

"Sure," Ronny said. "Sure, but what's wrong?"

Jeremy shrugged, "I'll let you know."

As Jeremy escorted his friends to the door, Dillon and Nettie seated themselves at the dining room table–Dillon at the head and Nettie nearest the kitchen–where they always sat to eat. When Jeremy reappeared, his eyes were dark with dread. "Who died?" he asked. "Just say it and get it over with."

Before Dillon could speak, Nettie said gently, "Otto died yesterday, honey. Grandma called last night to tell me."

"Is Grandma all right?" Jeremy asked earnestly. He slid into his usual chair at the table and studied his parent's faces.

"She's taking it pretty hard," Nettie said, "but she'll be okay."

"Can we get her another dog?" Jeremy asked. "A puppy?"

"Maybe later," Nettie said. "I don't think she's ready yet."

"Is that why you weren't here this morning?" he asked.

Nettie's voice trembled when she answered. "I ... I slept at her house last night."

Jeremy nodded, still studying their faces. "What else?" he asked and it seemed to Nettie that he began to shrink into himself, as he prepared himself for the blow.

"Jeremy, son ..." Dillon began. He paused and cleared his throat. "Look, this is the hardest thing I've ever had to say ..." He stopped again and seemed unable to go on.

"Just say it," Jeremy demanded fiercely. "What's wrong?"

Dillon swallowed painfully. "I'm ... I've ... your Mother and I are ... getting a divorce."

Jeremy gazed unblinkingly into his father's eyes. "Why?"

"Because I've fallen in love with another woman, and I want to marry her," Dillon said, forcing his voice to flow as smoothly as possible. "It doesn't change how much I love you, and I'll always be here for you. Do you understand?"

Jeremy turned his gaze on Nettie and asked in an agonized tone, "Mom?"

Nettie drew a quavering breath. "We'll be all right Jeremy. Your father loves you, and you'll see him all the time. Truly. I'll make sure of it."

Jeremy returned his gaze to his father. "You told me a real man takes care of his family and lives up to his responsibilities," he said accusingly.

"That's right," Dillon said. "I still believe that."

"Then how can you divorce us?"

Dillon looked from Nettie to Jeremy, then hung his head. He seemed to shrivel up right before their eyes. "Son, I've just recently learned something about myself that I never knew before." The words were hauntingly soft and sad. "I'm not much of a man."

He rose and left his wife and son, sitting at the kitchen table alone.

Long, tear-stained moments passed before Jeremy lifted his head and spoke defiantly to his mother. "He's my Dad, and I still love him."

Nettie nodded. "I know. So do I."

A frown creased Jeremy's brow. "You *love* him? When Kurt's Dad left his Mother, she burned all his clothes and said she hated him. Isn't that how you're *supposed* to act?"

Nettie shrugged. "How can I love him yesterday and hate him today?" She gave Jeremy a grim smile. "I wish I did hate him. It would make everything so much easier!"

PART II

A Week in June

Chapter 5

Maylea sat on her obstetrician's examining table, swinging her legs and smiling. She was wearing a cheerful red and white pinstriped jumpsuit. Her long, dark hair floated past her shoulders to her waist. She looked like an expectant child, waiting for a lollipop. Dillon, seated off to the side and out of the way, felt his heart swell with longing, as he watched her. He wanted to give her everything she ever wanted. Make all her dreams come true. Be her knight in shining armor. Protect her from every ...

"I'll see you in a month," Dr. Bellamy said to Maylea. "Make an appointment on your way out."

Dillon's mouth fell open. That was it? Two minutes and the doctor was through with them? "Doctor!" he exclaimed. "Is she okay? Is the baby okay?"

The elderly doctor turned a quelling glare on Dillon. "Do you think I would let you walk out of my office if mother and baby weren't okay?"

"But look at her," Dillon objected. "She's not even showing yet, and she's ..." He paused to count on his fingers, "February to March, April, May, June–four months along."

Dr. Bellamy shot a curious glance at his patient before he said authoritatively. "No she's not. She's six weeks–eight at the most. And doing very well, I might add." Then he opened the door and disappeared into the hall beyond.

Dillon's heart sank. He stared at Maylea. "But you got pregnant in February," he said with a scowl. "That's four months ago. How can you be only two months pregnant now?"

"Sweetheart," she said in her most beguiling tone. "Don't you see? I must have lost that baby and gotten pregnant again right away."

"You lost the baby and didn't tell me?" He felt the foundations of his world shudder.

"I didn't know, you goosey-woosey," Maylea said, picking up her tiny purse and starting toward the door. "It's no big deal."

Dillon caught her arm. "But how could you lose the baby and not know? How could you become ... unpregnant ... without knowing it?"

Maylea's sunny mood clouded. "I had some spotting. It didn't seem like much, and I thought it was just ... normal. So I didn't mention it."

"Spotting? When was this?" Dillon's adoring tone had been replaced with a cold, harsh voice he'd never used with Maylea before. He squeezed her arm.

"Ow! You're hurting me." She jerked her arm out of his grip. "I don't remember when it was. I didn't think it was important."

"Was it before you left Hawaii or after you got here?" Dillon asked hoarsely.

"After I got here, of course."

Dillon glared at her, trying to untangle the meaning behind her words. "But your pregnancy test was positive during my divorce proceedings, so you were definitely pregnant then. Right?"

Maylea shrugged. "Maybe. I don't know. What difference does it make?"

"What difference does it make?" Dillon stared at her in astonishment. "The difference between I'm a happily married man or I'm the world's biggest sap. That's what difference it makes. So which am I?"

"You're a happily married man, of course," Maylea said, putting her arm through his and snuggling up to him with a confident little bounce. "Can't you tell?"

"I thought I could," Dillon said. "Suddenly, I'm not so sure." He studied his beautiful young wife for a moment. "But the positive pregnancy test we gave to the lawyers was yours, right? You were really pregnant then. Right?"

Maylea pouted prettily. "I shouldn't even talk to you–asking me a thing like that! Why do you want to hurt me? I thought you loved me."

Dillon repented. "You know I love you, but it's a shock, finding out you're two months along, instead of four. If I'd known ..."

Maylea paused at the door. "If you'd known, what? What would you have done if you'd known?"

Dillon shook his head.

"If you'd known, you wouldn't have married me? You would have stayed with that old crone in your safe, little world? You would be going with *her* to *her* obstetrician now, and I could be out in the gutter for all you cared?"

She shot through the door, slamming it behind her. When Dillon reached the hall, she had disappeared. He stopped at the front desk to pay the bill and make Maylea's next appointment for July 23.

When he stepped out into glaring sunshine, Maylea and her red sports car were gone. He sighed deeply, and moved toward his own sedate gray sedan. It was 4:30 and he was expected back at the office, but he suddenly didn't have the heart to return to an office full of papers and numbers and calculators. He excused himself with one, short phone call, then turned his car toward home.

When Dillon pulled up in front of the rental house he had found for himself and Maylea on 38th Street, the driveway was empty. Maylea had gone somewhere else. Dillon scowled at the empty driveway, and slumped down behind his steering wheel. Where was she? And what was going on–was she making a monkey of him? Had she really been pregnant when she arrived in his office last April? Or was it all a lie? What did a beautiful, young woman want with a stodgy, middle-aged accountant, anyway?

He suddenly felt like crying, but he got out of the car and went into the house instead. To his surprise, Jeremy was sitting in the front room, playing a video game with an old woman dressed in a purple Minnesota Vikings football jersey and black stretch pants.

She was tiny with bright black eyes and masses of gray curls. "Jeremy, what are you doing here?" he asked, his eyes glued to the elderly woman, who took over the game when Jeremy leaped up to greet his Dad.

"It's Friday. I'm here for the weekend." Jeremy, who had grown too old for hugging around the age of 11, wrapped his arms around Dillon. The hugging habit had reappeared after his Dad moved out.

Dillon returned the hug, but his eyes stayed on the old woman. "Who's that?" he whispered.

Jeremy glanced at her. "Don't you know?" he asked.

Dillon shook his head. "No! Where'd she come from? Who is she?" he whispered.

"She's Trolley. She let me in when Mom dropped me off. She can play circles around me," he added admiringly. "Well, at least, in the Cobra's Pit, she can."

"Trolley?" Dillon asked.

Jeremy shrugged. "That's what she said."

The screen door opened behind them, and Maylea came in, holding a hand to her head, still squinting from the harsh sunlight. She took in the living room at a glance and said imperiously, "Don't you think you should be getting dinner ready, Trolley?"

The old woman looked up with a bright smile. "Whatever you say," she replied. She rose and strolled into the kitchen, singing off-key in a crackling voice, "I've been working on the railroad, all the livelong day. I've been working on the railroad, just to pass the time away ..."

Maylea winced at the racket and dropped into a chair. Dillon stared at his wife. He was familiar with her childlike voice and her sex kitten voice, but this mistress of the manor persona was new to him. "Who is that woman?" he asked, motioning with his head toward the kitchen.

"She's going to be our housekeeper and cook for awhile," Maylea said, holding her head in both hands. "Just until I'm feeling better. You can call her Trolley."

"You hired a housekeeper without talking to me?" Dillon asked. "A housekeeper named ... Trolley?"

Maylea stood with an anguished look on her face. "I'm going to bed," she said. "And Trolley won't cost anything. She's going to be working for her room and board until she finds a place of her own."

"She's living here?" Dillon was aghast. "Where is she planning to sleep?"

"In the guest room, of course," Maylea said, making her exit.

"And where is Jeremy supposed to sleep?" Dillon called after her. The slamming of the bedroom door was his only answer.

Dillon looked helplessly at his son. "She's nuts," he muttered darkly.

"Don't worry, Dad," Jeremy said. "I'll bunk on the couch when I'm here."

"I guess we don't have any choice tonight," Dillon said. "When Maylea has one of her headaches, there's no use trying to reason with her. But we'll figure out something better before next weekend."

He looked around the small, crowded living room, feeling like a stranger in his own home. In the kitchen, Trolley was singing, "I wanna' hold your hand. Yeah, yeah, yeah …" Only Jeremy seemed real and familiar. "Get the b-ball," Dillon said. "I'll change clothes and meet you outside in two minutes."

Father and son played basketball hard and fast until Trolley called them to dinner. They came to the dinner table, laughing and sweating, to find only two place settings. "Where's Maylea?" Dillon asked.

"She ate a few pineapple chunks and said it was all she wanted," Trolley explained. "She has a violent headache, poor dear."

Dillon nodded, "Well, what about you? Aren't you going to eat?"

"I'll eat in my room if you don't mind," Trolley said. "I've been on my feet too much today, and they're starting to swell." She held up a booted foot for his inspection. "If I eat in the bedroom, I can put my feet up on a stool. The swelling will go down then, and I can get my shoes off."

"Of course," Dillon said, "if that's what you want."

"Mrs. West said she'd like to see Jeremy after dinner," Trolley said, taking off her apron. "Now, don't you boys worry about these dishes. You leave them where they lie, and I'll take care of them in the morning."

"Trolley," Dillon asked before she could complete her exit, "where did you get the name Trolley? Not from your Mother, surely?"

The wrinkled old face beamed. "No, from my grandchildren," she said. "They used to call me Tra La La because I sing when I work, but the little ones had trouble saying Tra La La, so they changed it to Trolley."

Dillon smiled. "How many grandchildren do you have?" he asked.

"Let's see here," Trolley said, "I believe it was seven at last count. Good night, now. I'll see you in the morning."

Dillon watched her leave with a worried frown on his face. "What's wrong?" Jeremy asked.

"I don't like having a stranger in the house," Dillon said. "What's wrong with Maylea, anyway, hiring her out of the blue like that?"

But Maylea couldn't be convinced that she had done anything wrong. "I checked her references, and they're fine. Her former employers speak very highly of her."

"Then why does she need a job with us? Why didn't she stay where she was?" asked Dillon.

"She lived in Minnesota, and the winters were too hard on her. She decided to come South, and she's trying to convince her sister to join her. Then they'll get an apartment together, and she won't need to live here any more. Of course, then we'll have to pay her."

Maylea was stretched out on the bed with an arm across her eyes, protecting them from the dim light of a lamp on the bedside table. Her expression said plainly that she was in excruciating pain and tolerating his inquisition at the cost of severe suffering to herself. Dillon watched her with frustration. How could she bring a stranger into the house and have no concept that it was a reckless, dangerous thing to do?

"I like her, Dad," Jeremy said. "We had fun this afternoon. And she's a *grandmother*! She's not going to hurt anybody."

Dillon nodded slowly. Trolley was the first thing Jeremy had liked about Dillon's new life. And Maylea *had* checked Trolley's references. So who was he to argue? He shrugged, and looked at Maylea's still form. "Trolley said you wanted to see Jeremy," he said softly, half expecting her to be asleep.

"Oh!" Maylea sat up. "I almost forgot. That's what a dreadful headache will do to you."

She smiled at Jeremy and pointed at the bottom drawer of the bureau. "Jeremy, sweetie, I need you to fill some capsules for me with my magic powder. It's in that drawer. Would you be a dear, and take care of it for me?"

Dillon shook his head and left. He had no faith in Maylea's "magic powder" from the island of Oahu, but he saw no reason to interfere with any placebo benefit she received from it.

Following Maylea's instructions, Jeremy carefully positioned 16 capsule sections into notches in a board. Then he poured her herbal powder from a huge jar onto the board and scraped it into the capsules. After he had capped each pill, he gave her two to swallow immediately, and put two in each compartment of a weekly pill container. The compartments already contained several tablets, which Maylea said were the vitamins and supplements she took every day. "Those wonderful pills are the reason I'm so strong and healthy," she told Jeremy with a confidential air.

He nodded obediently without pointing out that she had taken to bed long before nightfall. And, although she did no work except keep house, she needed a live-in housekeeper to help her.

"Mom works all day, then comes home and cooks and cleans. And she doesn't need a housekeeper," Jeremy told his Dad later. "What makes Maylea think she's so healthy?"

Dillon shrugged. "I don't know. And your Mom is six months pregnant besides. Look Jeremy," he added, "do you help your Mom around the house? She shouldn't have to do everything, and I can't very well come back and pitch in."

"Sure, I help some," Jeremy said. "But she doesn't usually tell me what to do, and I forget to notice."

Dillon nodded. "Me too. I didn't know how good I had it until I didn't have it any more."

Jeremy looked up in surprise. "You mean you wish you were back home with us?"

Dillon took a deep breath. "I don't know," he said. "I try not to think about it."

"You can come back if you want to," Jeremy said earnestly. "I can talk Mom into it. I know I can. She loves you."

Dillon gave Jeremy a surprised look. "She loves me?" he asked. "Why do you say that?"

"When you moved out, I told her I loved you anyway. And she said she did, too," Jeremy explained.

Dillon's shoulders sagged. "I should be horse whipped," he told his son, "for what I've done to you and your Mother, But I can't come back. I can never come back. I know you don't understand, but the truth is–your Mom is too smart to take me back, even if we both beg her."

Jeremy didn't answer, but in his heart he believed it was his father who didn't understand. He *could* come back. He could if he would.

Chapter 6

"A man shouldn't leave his wife, just because she puts on a few pounds, should he?" Velma Jackson demanded of Nettie. "I mean, what kind of love is it if a couple of pounds can kill it?"

Nettie shrugged helplessly. What could she say? Who could understand men? Who knew why they did *anything*? "It does seem pretty shallow to me," she told Velma. Then she frowned. "But you don't think he's going to come back to you just because you lose more weight, do you?"

"Who knows? Who cares?" Velma peered at her chart, trying to read it upside down on the crowded little desk Nettie used when she worked at Spring Up South. "How much did you say I've lost? Total, since I started seeing you?"

Nettie glanced down at the figures she had written over a period of six months. "Nearly 25 pounds," she said. "It's–let's see–23, to be exact."

"Right!" exclaimed Velma indignantly. "And Harold has the nerve to say, 'I told you if you didn't lose some weight I'd be out of here.' Then he picks up his suitcase and heads for the door.

" 'I lost the weight!' I screamed at him. 'Don't you have any eyeballs in your fat head? I lost 35 pounds, and you have the nerve to say I didn't lose any weight!' " She gave Nettie a conspiratorial wink. "I cheated a little bit on the amount. But I didn't know *exactly* how much I'd lost, so I made it sound better than it was."

"What did he say?" Nettie asked.

"He said nuthin'. He just marched himself out the door and drove away. And good riddance. That's what I say... ." Velma's words were cocky, but she was near tears.

"I'm so sorry, Velma," Nettie told her, passing a couple of tissues to her. She had never felt so much empathy for a woman who had lost her husband, because she'd never had to walk in her shoes before. Now she understood the pain and ached to the core of her soul for the chubby, little woman who sat across the desk in designer clothes, mopping her eyes with a handful of tissues. "Do you know what you're going to do?"

"Sure. I'm going to lose 30 more pounds. Maybe, then, he'll want me back," Velma said between gasping sobs. She looked at Nettie hopefully. "Do you think he will?"

Nettie shook her head. "I wish I could tell you. I wish I knew some way to help ..."

Ten minutes after Velma had gone, Nettie still sat immobile. She hadn't written a word in Velma's chart. All she could do was think of Velma's pathetic face when she said, "Maybe then, he'll want me back."

"Am I that pitiful?" Nettie asked herself. Harold Jackson wasn't coming back to Velma–any idiot knew it. He was obviously using Velma's weight as an excuse to leave her, but she was going to lose 30 more pounds, hoping to get him back.

Finally, Nettie let her head sink to the desk, burying her face in her arms. No woman ever wanted a man back as much as she wanted Dillon. Was she the biggest fool who ever lived? Ever? Since the beginning of time? And why did she keep longing, aching, praying for something she knew would never happen?

She let a few tears fall before she straightened and composed herself. She scribbled a quick progress note on Velma's chart, filed it, and picked up her purse. Thank goodness she could go home now. Home to Jeremy.

Her house had been a tomb all weekend while Jeremy was staying with Dillon and Maylea. But today, he would be there. He would be there to eat dinner with her. He would be there while she did the evening chores and relaxed with her feet up. She glanced at her ankles, which had begun swelling at the end of a long work day. Maybe she would go home and put her feet up to start with. They could order pizza in. What a great idea!

Nettie went to find Qiana so she could say her good-byes. But only Cecili Wells, the manager of Spring Up South, was seated at the big front desk. "I'm leaving," Nettie told her. "Have you seen Qiana?"

"Sure. She has Mr. Tatum in her office, helping her with something on the computer," Cecili said.

"Thanks," Nettie said, hiding her surprise. Since when did Matt Tatum hang out around here? He was usually at Spring Up West, visiting with his daughter Dolly or asking Nettie what repairs she needed him to do.

Nettie tapped lightly on Qiana's closed door, then opened it and stepped in. Qiana and Matt were both hunched over the computer screen, oblivious to Nettie's entrance.

"You did it!" Qiana squealed, thumping Matt on the back, and catching sight of her sister in the process. "Nettie, where did you come from?" she asked, moving to block the screen with her body.

Nettie caught only a glimpse of the columns of figures on the computer screen before Matt minimized it and turned to greet her. "Hi, Nettie, I didn't realize you were here," he said.

"What are you two doing?" Nettie asked suspiciously.

"Oh, Matt's just helping me with a program," Qiana said. "You know what a whiz he is! He *is* a *whiz*," she chanted, emphasizing the rhyme.

Nettie studied Matt for a moment, trying to decide if he had a guilty look on his face or not. Finally, deciding it didn't matter, she said, "Matt, you know how much I love Dillon, don't you?"

Matt's eyebrows rose. "Dillon? The cheating ex-husband who dumped you for a beautiful younger woman? You love him?"

Nettie shrugged. "I don't want to. But I've loved him for nearly 20 years now. I don't know how to stop. Besides, he's the father of my children." She touched her bulging abdomen gently. "Anyway, I wouldn't want anything bad to happen to him. You can understand that, can't you?"

Matt glanced at Qiana, as if for guidance, but she didn't notice. She was in attack mode.

"Of course–the father of your children!" Qiana snapped. "And how much child support is the father of your children paying?"

Nettie's eyes clouded. "None, right now. But he's had to start over. He'll pay child support when he can."

"Do you believe that?" Qiana waved an arm in dramatic appeal to Matt. "On top of everything else, he's not even helping to pay for his own children. And, mind you, there's a court order requiring him to pay child support, but does he care about the law? No!"

She snorted derisively. "But Nettie loves him and doesn't want anything bad to happen to him. Is that lame or what?"

Matt's eyes were compassionate. "Qiana, it's her life," he said quietly.

Nettie's eyes moved from her sister to her friend. Then she whirled and fled. They felt sorry for her. They pitied her. Well, why wouldn't they? She was pitiful.

Outside, the sky was dark with storm clouds and the air was heavy with humidity. Nettie drove home and pulled into her own garage before she felt composed enough to take out her cell phone and call Dillon. After the first ring, Maylea's fresh, young voice said, "Hello?"

"Maylea, it's Nettie West. May I speak to Dillon?"

"Nettie! I'm glad you called," Maylea said, then her voice turned cold. "I've been wanting to explain something to you. Dillon is *mine* now. We're married."

Nettie's own voice sprouted icicles. "You think I don't know that? What do you think I am–brain dead?" She punched the button to end the conversation, trembling with rage. Prissy little princess!

She took a few deep, calming breaths, then scrolled to Dillon's cell number. She had to remember never to call his land line again. When he answered, she managed to speak in her normal tone.

"Dillon, I may be borrowing trouble," she said, not bothering with preliminaries, "but I'm afraid Qiana may try to cause trouble for you."

Dillon had just dashed to his car in pelting rain when his cell phone rang. Now he sat in his parked car, studying the sky and frowning in puzzlement. "What kind of trouble?" he asked. "And why would Qiana want to cause me trouble?"

Nettie's voice trembled. "She thinks I should get revenge on you for divorcing me and since I won't she figures it's her responsibility to do it. Something like that. Anyway, I just found her and Matt Tatum looking at a screenful of numbers and columns–the same sort of thing I always used to see on your computer. They didn't want me to see what they were doing. And I'm afraid they may be trying to hack into your system so they can ... I don't know what ... ruin something. I just wanted to warn you ..."

Her voice tapered off, but he remained silent. She had no way of knowing that his mind was racing with possibilities and reeling with fear at the damage a vengeful hacker might do to his business. "Dillon, I'm so sorry," Nettie finally added when he didn't answer.

"No, Nettie. It's not your fault. I'm grateful you warned me. I'd better install a state-of-the-art firewall tonight. I just hope it's not too late. But, first, I'll go back inside and unplug everything."

"Okay, then. Bye Dillon."

"Bye, Nettiebug."

Nettie's mouth fell open. Nettiebug? When was the last time he had used his pet name for her? She couldn't remember.

"It just slipped out," she told herself sternly, as she climbed out of her car. "Don't get all excited about nothing!"

When she opened the door into her kitchen, the fragrance of baking bread greeted her. Jeremy was standing over the stove, stirring something in a pan. Outside, the sky had unloaded a torrent of raindrops mixed with marble-sized hail, but the kitchen was sunny and warm.

"Jeremy, what in creation are you doing?" she asked.

He looked up with a grin. "I made dinner. Dad showed me how to make spaghetti on Saturday. I have bread sticks in the oven. And there's plenty of salad in the frig."

"Jeremy! You didn't!" she cried, hurrying to the stove to see for herself.

"Meat sauce," he said proudly, stirring his concoction and watching the expression on her face.

"I can't believe it," she almost whispered. "I can't believe it."

And then she caught him in a bear hug and cried all over his shoulder. "You're the most wonderful son any mother ever had," she told him when she could speak. "I've had the most horrible day, but you've turned it into the most wonderful day! Thank you so much."

Jeremy, who had suffered through the mushy stuff with patience, beamed at his mother. "You shouldn't have to do all the work around here. Dad made me think about that this weekend. So I'm going to help more, but you may have to tell me what to do if I don't notice. And when the baby comes, I'll change its diapers sometimes."

Nettie kissed the top of Jeremy's head. "I'm going to change clothes, then I'll be back to help you finish up," she said, her energy suddenly renewed.

Jeremy nodded, smiling. When she got back, dinner would be on the table. And she wouldn't have to wash the dishes afterwards either! He plucked the bread sticks out of the oven and dumped the spaghetti and meat sauce into bowls. He put tongs in the salad and set it on the table. Iced tea in glasses. Dinner was served!

Meanwhile, Dillon had phoned Glen Bristol, his computer technician, at home. "Glen, I need you!" he exclaimed urgently. "Can you come to my office *now*? Or, if not, tell me what to do."

Glen glanced at his wife Hayley. She was in the middle of dinner preparations, and she was furious with Dillon for divorcing Nettie. Not that Hayley and Nettie were great friends, but they'd known each other in high school and Hayley seemed to see Dillon's abandonment of his marriage as an affront to all womankind. "Look, Dillon, it's not a great time. Can we do this tomorrow?"

Dillon's heartrending sigh was a tear jerker. "You tell me," he said. "Nettie just called and said her sister has found someone to hack into my system and damage my files–or damage something. She doesn't know what they have in mind, but Qiana wants to get revenge on me for divorcing Nettie. I'm going to unplug my computers, but I don't dare use them again until I have a state-of-the-art firewall installed."

Glen pulled a small notebook out of his pocket and, with one glance, saw that his morning schedule was packed. "Look," he said. "I can't come until after dinner–probably in an hour or so. In the meantime, you can go buy the software. You might want to call around before you go, because this program isn't in all the stores yet."

"Okay, let me get something to write with," Dillon said. He jotted down the name of the program Glen recommended. "Shall I call you when I get back here?" he asked.

"No, don't bother. You'll be back before I get there," Glen said. He lowered his voice to add, "You know I'm going to pay for this don't you?"

"What do you mean?"

"I mean Hayley is going to be livid when she finds out I'm leaving *her* to help *you*."

"She doesn't like me?" Dillon asked.

"Not since you dumped Nettie."

On his end of the call, Dillon was nodding. "Well, she has a lot of company. *Most* people don't like me anymore."

"Oh, don't be too sure of that," Glen said. "I know of a few bachelors who are thrilled with you!"

Dillon scowled. "What are you talking about? Are a lot of men hitting on Nettie?"

"Not yet. At least, not that I know of. But they're biding their time, waiting for her to get over you and be ready to move on."

"Like who?" Dillon asked belligerently.

"What's it to you?" Glen asked. "You've got your new, little floozy. Nettie is–how shall I put it?–up for grabs."

Dillon slammed his phone shut. He glared at the angry sky, which glared back at him. Did that huge storm cloud look like a vulture, poised to swoop down on him? He gazed at it. The cloud vulture was hunched forward with its imaginary wings half spread and imaginary beady black eyes fixed on him. "I'm not dead yet, so back off!" he yelled at it.

Then he tore his eyes from the sky and made a dash for his office. With ferocious jerks he snapped cords out of the wall. When he splashed back to his car, the sky was darker. His sedan plunged through wet streets in gale-force winds with chunks of hail hammering its pristine surface. His beautiful, sedate sedan would never be the same again. More than an hour later, soaked to the skin, he stumbled back into his office five minutes before Glen tapped on his door.

Entering, Glen said cheerfully, "I should charge you an arm and a leg for ruining my dinner. I'd rather starve than try to eat with a ticked-off chick!" He shed his raincoat and wiped his wet face with his wet hand.

"She was ticked off because of me?" Dillon asked, handing Glen a handful of paper towels.

"Oh yeah! She said to ask you what's wrong with you? Why would you leave a wonderful woman like Nettie for a plastic Barbie doll?" Glen mopped his face dry and seated himself in front of the computer. He gave Dillon a curious glance. "I've been wondering the same thing myself."

"Have you *seen* Maylea?" Dillon asked, settling himself at the edge of his desk to watch.

Glen shrugged. "Nope. You telling me that's all? You married her because of what she looks like?"

Dillon shifted uncomfortably. "Not exactly. She's also pregnant."

Glen began opening the package containing the new software. "So's Nettie. And, by the way, Nettie's not 20 anymore, but she's not exactly a dog herself. You better hope your plastic prize looks half as good in 15 years." He glanced at Dillon and added, "Not that *I'm* ogling your ex."

When Dillon didn't answer, Glen said, "I guess you're still in a honeymoon haze–I'm not here to dump on you. I'm just here to install this program."

Dillon smiled bleakly. "You're not saying anything I don't say to myself a thousand times a day. Every day."

Glen's hands went still, as he turned to study Dillon. "You saying you're sorry you married the new babe?"

"I haven't said that ... yet."

"But you think it?"

Dillon closed his eyes and gritted his teeth. "I'm trying real hard *not* to think it," he said.

It was after 8:00 and as dark as midnight when Dillon thanked Glen and locked the door of his office. At least the rain had stopped. As he walked to his car for the third time since 6:00 o'clock, he realized he hadn't called Maylea to tell her he would be late for dinner. He'd never kept her waiting before, but he had an idea she was going to make him sorry–*real sorry*–for his oversight.

Sure enough, Maylea met him at the door in a rage. She threw herself at him, pounding his chest with her fists. "Where were you? You were with *her* weren't you? First she calls here, and when you're not here, she finds you anyway. What were you doing? I know what you were doing, you lousy cheater. I should have known you'd cheat on me if you'd cheat on her!"

Suddenly she turned and fled toward the bedroom, weeping loudly. Dillon caught her and tried to pull her into his arms. "I had a problem at the office," he said, yelling over her sobs. "Maylea, listen to me. I've been at the office all evening."

"Then why didn't you call?"

"I forgot. It was a major problem, and I was worried. Why didn't you call me?"

Maylea's sobs had grown softer and sounded more genuine. "Because I knew you were with *her*, and I didn't want to talk to you."

As Maylea collapsed into his arms, weeping like a heartbroken child, Dillon's doubts flew out the window. She was so young, so tiny, so far from home. He had to take care of her. She had no one else. "Maylea, I won't cheat on you," he insisted. "Nettie called to tell me that her sister was trying to hack into my office computer. I had to get a firewall installed or Qiana could have ruined my business."

He held her, stroking her hair, until she pulled away from him, turning up a tear-stained face and gazing into his eyes. "Dillon, would you do something for me," she asked in her most beguiling voice, her eyes suddenly dry, "so I'll feel like I have a little security?"

"What kind of something?" he asked.

"You love me, don't you?" Maylea cooed.

"You know I do,"

"Then say you'll do it."

Dillon ran his fingers through his drenched hair. "I will if I can."

"You can!" she cried excitedly. "I'll show you." Taking his hand, she led him into the kitchen where she opened a drawer and took out a stack of papers. "Look, you sign here," she instructed. "It's a life insurance policy on you that names me as your beneficiary. See I've already got one for myself that makes you my beneficiary."

She beamed up at him, as she handed him the paper. Dillon's stomach began to churn. All his doubts flooded back in a rush, as he studied the document. "A million?" he asked. "A million dollars! Where do you imagine I'm going to get the money to pay the premiums?"

"There's money in the savings account," Maylea said. "We can use that."

Dillon tossed the paper back onto the table. "Maylea, even if I were willing to pay for a mil of life insurance, I would make Jeremy the beneficiary, not you."

"You mean, Nettie! You would be making Nettie the beneficiary because she's his mother–*she* would be getting the money!" Maylea's gentle weeping was over, and the harsh, angry voice was back. "You say you love me, but you don't! You don't care about *our* baby! You only love *her* and Jeremy!"

Maylea whirled and fled toward the bedroom again. This time Dillon let her go. He sat down at the kitchen table and began reading the insurance policies. She had actually done it–bought a life insurance policy for $1,000,000 and made him her beneficiary! Where had she gotten the money to pay for such an exorbitant policy?

And why? Why? Why? What if this money was what it was all about? What if she had married him so she could have him murdered, then walk away with a million dollars? It was ridiculous. Real people didn't do things like that, just people in the movies and in books. But it *would* explain why a beautiful, young woman would leave paradise to marry a dull, middle-aged accountant from Lubbock, Texas.

Besides, a woman with real character wouldn't have followed him to the mainland and destroyed his marriage. Even if she was cheap enough to sleep around, she should have enough class to raise the baby herself–with his financial support, of course–or put it up for adoption, instead of ruining his whole life. In other words, he had married a slug! He had divorced a lovely, gracious woman to marry a world-class bottom-feeder! How could he have been so blind? And stupid?

Dillon pushed the papers away in disgust. Then he went to his car and pulled out his cell phone. Driving to a nearby motel, he called his lawyer's office.

When the answering machine picked up, Dillon left a message. "Dan, I want something added to my will–I have one life insurance policy. One! Jeremy is the beneficiary. I don't have another one, and I'm not getting another one. I want that in my will. I'll call your office tomorrow for an appointment."

After he had registered at the Double T Motel, Dillon called Nettie. "I know it's late," he said pleadingly when she answered, "but I really need to talk to you tonight. Is that possible? And Jeremy can't hear this. I know I'm asking a lot ..."

"Dillon," Nettie interrupted him, "it's not a problem. Jeremy is spending the night with Ronny. Come on over."

"Thank you, Nettie. I can't thank you enough."

Chapter 7

Nettie felt nervous as she waited to hear the familiar sound of Dillon's car engine. Qiana and Matt had probably destroyed his business files, and he was coming to tell her he was suing them or charging them criminally. He would need Nettie to testify against them—what other proof could he get that they had done the damage? And how could she testify against her own sister and a dear friend like Matt? Matt had been a second father to her. And since Phillip Jamison's death two months ago, he had been especially solicitous of her feelings and her needs.

With a sigh, she went to raise the garage door. Dillon could park next to her car, and she would lower the garage door behind him. Hopefully the neighbors would never know he had come calling at 9:00 o'clock in the evening. It could only cause him trouble with Maylea.

The whole world seemed black, with roiling storm clouds low in the sky. The torrential downpour had mellowed into a mist and even the wind had slackened. But buckets of rain and sheets of hail could return at any minute. She trembled slightly with dread as she watched Dillon's car slide into place, then she tapped the button that closed the garage door.

"Look, I'm gonna' go straight to the bottom line," Dillon said when they were seated in the den with tall glasses of ice water. "Then I'll go back and explain and you can tell me if I'm completely paranoid or not."

He had automatically walked to the big recliner that was his favorite piece of furniture in the world and settled into it with a grateful smile. Nettie sat on the end of the sofa nearest to him and both placed their glasses on the end table between them. As Dillon located and repositioned a coaster, Nettie noticed that his hand was shaking slightly.

She frowned nervously. "Look, before you start, I have to say something. I don't want to testify against Qiana and Matt. Isn't there another way to work it out?"

"Qiana and Matt?" Dillon nearly laughed. "Qiana and Matt have nothing to do with this."

Nettie's eyebrows rose in surprise. "They don't? Then what's wrong? Why are you here?"

"I'm afraid," Dillon said, "that Maylea married me so she could take out a big life insurance policy on me, have me murdered, then cash in on my death."

Nettie was shaking her head in disbelief. "Oh, Dillon. What are you talking about? That child? I never heard anything so ..."

He interrupted with, "Just listen." He explained about the visit to the doctor's office. "She wasn't even pregnant when she arrived in Lubbock–I'd bet on it," he said angrily. "But that's nothing! Tonight she asks me to sign a life insurance policy that pays her a million dollars if I die. Or I should say, *when* I die."

He paused and sighed. "I feel like a paranoid fool, but I can't get it out of my head that she's going to murder me or have me murdered. Please tell me I'm wrong."

"It's the craziest thing I ever heard!" Nettie cried. "But if there's even the slightest chance you're right, then you have to do something to keep yourself safe. Oh Dillon, I couldn't bear it if anything happened to you. Jeremy needs you, and so do the babies."

She paused and cocked her head. "Do you know for sure she's pregnant now?"

"The doctor says she is. He says she's six weeks pregnant–eight at the outside."

"But she had a positive pregnancy test dated more than two months ago," Nettie said. "My lawyer saw it."

Dillon nodded. "What if she found some pregnant woman on the street, and paid her for a urine sample? Or just took her to the doctor's office, and sent her into the bathroom with the plastic cup? Why couldn't she do that?"

"Dillon, you *are* paranoid," Nettie said. "That's too weird!"

"No, it's too *devious*," he replied. "What if she's capable of being that devious?"

"Do you think she is?"

"I didn't ... until tonight. Now, I expect every minute that I'll see her coming through a door with a gun in her hand aimed at my heart." Dillon laughed nervously, but there was no humor in the laughter. "She's playing me, Nettie. She's been playing me since day one. I have a room at the Double T Motel for tonight–I don't ever want to spend another night in the same house with her."

Wrinkles creased Nettie's forehead. "Are you saying you're going to divorce her?"

"I haven't thought that far ahead," Dillon said. "Right now, I'm just trying to figure out how to stay alive."

"Well, you certainly don't need to throw money down the drain at some motel," Nettie said. "I have a guest room and so does Mom. Why don't you stay with one of us?"

Dillon shook his head wearily. "I don't want to get either of you involved. Maylea certainly won't blow *me* away until she gets my name on the dotted line, but she'd like nothing better than to get rid of you. And maybe Jeremy, too."

"Oh, Dillon, you're making her sound like a monster," Nettie protested. "Surely, you don't believe she's capable of murder."

Dillon thought long and spoke carefully. "I think I do." He pointed to the middle of his abdomen. "I have a feeling–right here–that she wants me dead. Come on, Nettie, look at me. Look at her. What does she want with me, anyway?"

Nettie smiled. "I can think of a lot of reasons I've always wanted you, but I'm not sure she's bright enough to care about intelligence and gentleness and a sense of humor and ..."

Dillon interrupted her. "I'm pretty sure she doesn't care about *anything* except money. She complains constantly about the cheap house we're living in and our second-hand furniture. She wants a million-dollar mansion with a swimming pool and tennis court, more spending money, designer clothes. But she has no intention of getting a job to help earn all that money."

"Oh Dillon," Nettie said softly. "How did you get yourself into this mess? It's my fault for not going to Hawaii with you, isn't it? I wanted to–the very idea of going to that beautiful place with the most wonderful man in the world was a dream come true. But I felt *so* sick in February–I couldn't bear the thought of being away from home when I was throwing up every morning."

Dillon rose as she spoke, sat down next to her, and wrapped her in his arms. "Nettie, stop! Don't you get it? It's not your fault! Maylea flattered me, and I fell for it. But my stupidity is no reflection on you. You're beautiful and kind and generous and loving. You're everything a man could want in a wife, and Maylea is a selfish child. It would serve me right if she actually did shoot me through the heart!"

When Dillon's arms enfolded Nettie, she felt as if she had come home. She leaned into him and let herself luxuriate in the comfort of his strength for a moment. But she didn't dare linger too long. She had grieved over him every second of every day for weeks. She didn't want to go through it again. So she sat up, pulling away from his arms, to answer him. "Dillon, that's ridiculous! You don't deserve to be murdered! And Jeremy doesn't deserve to lose his father!"

But Dillon had lost his train of thought. Having Nettie in his arms had momentarily banished Maylea from his memory. "Jeremy told me you still love me," he said in a low voice, searching her face hungrily for some sign of affection.

Returning his gaze, Nettie spoke frankly. "What good is love without trust?"

"Is there any way I can get you to trust me again?" he asked earnestly.

Nettie shook her head in amazement. "Not while you're married to someone else."

"Okay, then, after the divorce, will you go to counseling with me and see if we can find a way back to ... to trust?"

"Dillon, please! That question is all wrong. You're married to Maylea now–shouldn't you be trying to mend your relationship with her?"

Dillon's chin sank onto his chest. "Should I?" he asked wearily.

When Nettie didn't answer, he raised his head to study her face. "Yes, I guess that would serve me right," he said. "Do you think I should go back to her tonight?"

"No, of course not! I don't think you should get anywhere near her until you're sure she's not dangerous!" Nettie cried urgently. "Whatever else you do, Dillon, please don't give her a chance to hurt you!"

He nodded. "But how do I find out whether or not she's dangerous?"

Before Nettie could answer, the front door opened with a creak, then shut. She looked anxiously at Dillon. It couldn't be Maylea, could it? All this murder-talk was making her irrational! Both of them waited, listening to silence, straining to hear anything that would let them know who had entered the house.

"Hey, Mom!" Jeremy called, suddenly poking his head into the den before going to look for her in the kitchen. "Dad!" he exclaimed, catching sight of Dillon. "What are you doing here?"

He came into the room, followed by Qiana. They stared at Dillon and Nettie, seated cozily on the sofa. Dillon stood, as they entered, then helped Nettie to her feet.

"I'm talking to your Mother," Dillon said.

"Duh!" Jeremy replied.

Dillon looked at Nettie, saw no help from her, and added, "Maylea and I had a ... an argument, and I needed a woman's perspective on it."

Jeremy's face brightened. "You did? Does that mean you're coming home?"

Before either of his parents could respond, Qiana leapt into the conversation. "Coming home? What's wrong with you, Nettie? The man destroys your family over some trashy, little tropical tramp, and you can't wait to forgive him? I never heard of anything so stupid! Of course, he's not coming back, is he, Nettie?" She spoke the last three words slowly and emphatically, then repeated them, even slower. "Is ... he ... Nettie?"

Ignoring his aunt's impassioned plea, Jeremy looked hopefully at his Mother. "Can he, Mom? Can he come home?"

Dillon answered for her. "No, son, I'm not coming home. But I'm not going back to Maylea either."

Jeremy and Qiana looked at him with wide-eyed amazement. "You're not?" Jeremy asked. "Why not?"

But Nettie broke in. "Jeremy, I think the most important question before us is, Why are *you* here? And what happened to your shirt?" Jeremy was wet from head to toe and his left sleeve was dangling from a tear at the shoulder seam.

"Oh, yeah," Jeremy mumbled. "I forgot. Ronny and I were sort of fighting. We were in his front yard, and Qiana drove by and saw us. She made us stop fighting, then said she'd take us to rent a movie. We're going to spend the night with her and roast hot dogs and marshmallows in her fireplace. Is it okay? Can we? I didn't call because I had to come change clothes anyway."

"You were fighting with Ronny?" Nettie asked. "Why?"

Jeremy glanced at his father. "He said something I didn't like, and I hit him."

"They looked like they were about to fight to the death," Qiana added. "I thought maybe I should provide a diversion."

"What did Ronny say that you didn't like?" Nettie asked.

Jeremy gave her his please-don't-ask-that-question look, but she just waited, eying him sternly. Jeremy looked at Dillon again, then muttered, "Ronny said Dad is a bigger bimbo than Bill Clinton."

Nettie shook her head. "Jeremy, don't you know fighting doesn't solve anything?" she asked.

He hung his head and mumbled. "I know."

Nettie sighed and turned her attention to her sister. "Are you sure you want to put up with a pair of rabble rousers tonight?"

Qiana grinned in Jeremy's direction. "Sure, I can stand them for one night." What she really wanted was to park in Nettie's den until she was certain Dillon was gone. What if Nettie let him stay over? What if Nettie was so lame that she actually forgave him and took him back? It took all the self-control Qiana could muster not to launch into another tirade against Dillon.

"Okay," Nettie told her son. "Go change. And when you get back home tomorrow," she added in her firmest tone, "I want to hear about your apology to Ronny!"

"What about his apology to me?" Jeremy asked with a defiant glare.

"Certainly, if he chooses to apologize, I'll be happy to hear about that, too," Nettie said mildly. "Now scoot."

When Jeremy was gone, Nettie said to Qiana, "I assume you were on your way here when you intervened in Jeremy's fight–thanks for that, by the way."

"No sweat," Qiana said. "And I *was* headed here, but there's nothing I care to say in front of *him*." She scowled at Dillon.

"Just spit it out, Qiana," Nettie ordered. "I already told him you're trying to hack into his computer and destroy his business. So you might as well say what you came to say."

"Okay, I will. After your little speech, Matt packed up and went home. He said he wouldn't have any part of hurting Dillon since you still love him." She had been speaking to Nettie, but now she turned to Dillon. "But don't you think it's over, you sleazebag. I'll just have to find another way."

"Qiana!" Nettie cried. "Sleazebag? What's wrong with you? Why won't you leave him alone?"

Qiana, who never cried, was weeping openly, as she answered. "Because you're my sister, and I love you. And he stomped all over your heart, and he doesn't even care. He got you pregnant, then went off to play house with that ... that ..."

Unable to finish her sentence for the sobs, Qiana let Nettie pull her into her arms. "Qiana, I love you too, but you're not helping me by hurting the father of my children. Can't you see that?" she asked earnestly.

Regaining her composure quickly, Qiana pulled away and wiped her tears on her T-shirt. "I'm sorry I went off in front of Jeremy," she said contritely. "I won't let that happen again." She looked at Dillon. "I know you're his father and he needs you, so I won't talk about you in front of him."

Then she spun away from Nettie and strode across the room. Within seconds the front door opened and shut. Then Jeremy dashed in to kiss his Mom and hug his Dad before he hurried after Qiana. "Jeremy!" Dillon's stern voice halted him in the doorway of the den.

He turned.

"No more fighting, okay? It doesn't matter what anybody says about me."

Jeremy shrugged. "Sure, Dad."

Dillon relaxed then, and added, "But son, it means a lot to me that you were willing to fight for me."

Jeremy beamed. "You'd do the same for me," he said. Then he was gone.

"Qiana's wrong," Dillon told Nettie when they were alone.

"About what?" Nettie asked, returning to her place on the sofa and taking a drink of her water.

To her surprise, Dillon knelt down in front of her. "I do care about the pain I caused you and Jeremy. I'd rip off my own arm if it would take away your pain." He was so intense, Nettie was afraid he was about to cry.

"I know," she said, "but it's over and done, now. Let's forget it and move on the best way we can." She touched his face with a gentle caress.

Dillon nodded and stood. "Okay, Nettie, but I want you to know I'm going to spend the rest of my life trying to make it up to you."

Chapter 8

In a bed at the Double T Motel that night, Dillon tossed and turned. The storm raging outside couldn't compare to the storm raging in his mind. He couldn't sleep. He could only worry. About Maylea's intentions. About Maylea's baby–was it really his baby too? About finances. About Qiana's intentions. About the pain he had caused Nettie and Jeremy. About the child Nettie was carrying–what if she miscarried for a fourth time? How could she bear it? How could he bear it? He didn't deserve to live if she lost this baby because he wasn't there to help her, to support her, to take care of her.

And he replayed Nettie's words a thousand times when she called him "… the most wonderful man in the world …" It thrilled him that she had said it, but it also tortured him to realize he had thrown away a treasure in order to gain a trinket. "Oh, Nettie, my love," he moaned into his pillow, "how did I get to be such a fool?"

He had planned to go home the next morning to shower and pack his clothes. Surely, in the light of day, his deranged fears would evaporate. But they didn't. Instead, they took on new life. Maylea was young and beautiful. She would find an insurance agent who would fall under her spell just as completely as Dillon had, and the agent would accept her paperwork with Dillon's forged signature. Maybe she'd already found this mythical insurance agent. Maybe she was waiting for Dillon to come home right now–the spider waiting for the fly. Or maybe she would hire someone to do her dirty work for her. With a million dollars in the offing, she would have no trouble finding some big, bumbling boob who would pull a trigger in exchange for a few bucks.

Shivering with nervous tension, he rose and showered. The sky was still dark with clouds and the air heavy with moisture. Wearing the same clothes he had worn the previous day, he arrived at his office, weary and rumpled, 30 minutes earlier than usual. And the moment his watch read 8:00 A.M., he phoned Dan Ebersole's office for an appointment.

"He's tied up all day today in court," the lawyer's receptionist said. "I'm putting you down for 9:00 o'clock tomorrow morning. Is that time good for you?"

"Yes, I'll be there," Dillon said, feeling a letdown. Another day in limbo. Of course, Dan Ebersole couldn't solve any of his problems, but Dillon wouldn't rest easy until his will was amended in a way that would prevent Maylea from cashing in on his death.

With a supreme effort, Dillon put his personal problems out of his mind and turned his attention to the day's work. He was poring over an income tax form when someone knocked on his door.

"Come in," he called.

The door swung open, revealing a tall, muscular man with flaming red hair and an auburn mustache. Dan Ebersole. The lawyer dominated every room he entered, imbuing his clients with confidence and his opponents with apprehension.

Dillon sprang from his chair, nearly knocking it over in his excitement. He came around the desk with his hand extended. "I thought you were tied up in court all day."

Dan shook Dillon's hand with energy, as he explained. "We had an unexpected recess–something about the judge's new puppy being attacked by a pit bull. She barely lingered long enough to say we would reconvene at 1:00 this afternoon."

Dillon's eyes softened. "That's too bad! I hope the puppy makes it."

"I do too," Dan said. "Judge Harper is every lawyer's favorite judge–fair and soft-spoken, but always businesslike." He settled into a chair while Dillon walked back around his desk. "Anyway, as soon as I heard I had a couple of free hours, I headed for your office. That cryptic message you left me last night sent chills up my spine. What gives?"

Dillon prefaced his explanation with a disclaimer: "I'm probably paranoid, but ..." Then he told Dan about Maylea's million dollar insurance policy. "Even if I'm wrong, I'm not going back to her," he said in conclusion. "I can't bear the sight of her."

Dan, who appeared blustery and outdoorsy, still had the keen insight that made him an exceptional attorney. "You've come to your senses, haven't you?" he asked.

Dillon's expression was quizzical. "About what?"

"About Nettie."

"Oh." Dillon let his head fall onto the back of his chair. In a moment, he straightened and said, "Oh yeah. In spades. If I can't win Nettie back someday, then I hope Maylea blows me away today!"

Dan chuckled, then opened his mouth to speak. But Dillon intercepted his statement. "I know—you told me so. You nearly talked yourself blue, trying to convince me to stay with Nettie, but I had to be the hero. Maylea was tiny and helpless, and I had to be her knight, riding to her rescue on my big white charger!"

Dan was nodding. "Nettie was never helpless, was she?" he asked.

Dillon shook his head. "Never."

"Was that part of Maylea's charm?"

Dillon gave the lawyer a rueful look. "Yes, at first. But now her adorable, little-girl helplessness has mutated into a monstrous pool of quicksand that's sucking me into financial ruin."

"That's pretty strong language," Dan observed. "What haven't you told me?"

Dillon sighed and reddened. "It's embarrassing to admit, but you're my lawyer—you might as well know. I'm having to work like a mule to keep us out of bankruptcy. Maylea is trying to spend every penny we have or ever will have. The moment we were married, she bought herself a fancy, new sports car—dealer financed. I go home every night and search closets and drawers for the day's purchases, so I can return them the next day. I actually had to take out a loan to cover our bills, so I opened a checking account she couldn't access and put the money in it. Then she ran up two credit cards to the limit!"

"Well, Dillon, you may have forgotten how expensive it is to have a baby. Jeremy is what–a teenager now?" Dan said placatingly.

Dillon shook his head. "You don't get it. She's not buying things for the baby. She's buying things for herself–designer clothes, jewelry. Nettie never bought a designer dress in her life. Maylea has a closet full of them!"

Dan studied his client speculatively. "So what's your take on it? Do you think she's too stupid to handle money well?"

Dillon shuddered. "If I tell you what I think, you'll call the men in white jackets to take me away."

Dan held up both hands, palms forward. "No nut house attendants–I promise."

"Okay," Dillon said heavily. "Here it is. I think she's going to get rid of me–don't ask me how–then get rid of the baby."

Dan frowned. "You mean murder? And abortion?"

Dillon nodded. "Exactly. When she has a million dollar check from the insurance company, she'll have no problem paying the bills. And she'll be free to look for the next fool who can't wait to marry her."

Dan was nodding, his face set in stern lines. "I'd like to believe you're exaggerating," he said, "but one thing I've learned over the years is to trust my clients. Even if you're wrong, we can't afford to give Maylea the benefit of the doubt. So what do you want to do first?"

"Cut her completely out of my will, and make sure she can't finagle a life insurance policy that names her as my beneficiary," Dillon replied instantly.

Dan took a pad out of his pocket and made a note. "Okay. But, Dillon, you should keep in mind that you have a few years to live. A reputable company isn't going to pay out a million dollars if you die the day after you purchase the policy. Or the week. Or the month."

Dillon shifted uncomfortably in his seat. "Remember, I'm paranoid. And I know how persuasive Maylea can be. If there's any underhanded way to make it happen, she will. Even if she has to sleep with the head of the company and share the wealth, that's what she'll do."

Dan nodded. "I'll take care of your will. You take care of letting Maylea know she has no motive to murder you. Next, what about divorce proceedings?"

Dillon hesitated. "Nettie thinks Maylea and I should see a counselor and try to resolve our problems."

"That's what Nettie thinks?" Dan asked. "Interesting–what do you think?"

Dillon was slow to answer. Finally he said, "I'm not ready to make that decision yet. I'm not calling up a marriage counselor today, but maybe I'll be able to stomach the thought in a few days. Or weeks."

"And you certainly don't want Nettie to think that you bailed on another marriage. You have to convince her that you did everything in your power to make it work," Dan said.

Dillon nodded. "Something like that."

Dan shrugged. "It's your life. Okay, then, let's talk about your moving out. I advise you not to go to your home alone while Maylea is there. I have a friend on the police force–Farley Gunther–and I believe I can persuade him to meet you at your house. You can gather up the things you need right away–like clothes and toiletries–then we'll see about moving larger items at a later date."

Dillon gave Dan an admiring look. "That's a great plan! I've been trying to think how to get my things out of there without having to deal with Maylea again."

"All right, I'll give Farley a call," Dan said. He pulled a cell phone out of his pocket, scrolled through his contacts, and connected. After he had explained the situation to Officer Gunther, Dan said to Dillon, "How's 3:00 this afternoon? Can you be there then?"

Dillon nodded. "No problem."

"Here," Dan said, handing the phone to Dillon. "Give him your address."

In a matter of minutes the meeting had been arranged, Dan and Dillon had shaken hands again, and Dan departed as abruptly as he had arrived. Dillon resumed his seat, feeling a thousand pounds lighter. No wonder lawyers made so much money–they were as good as magicians, removing the weight of the world from their clients' shoulders. Dillon leaned back in his desk chair and enjoyed the sense of release Dan had left in his wake. He wasn't out of the woods yet, but maybe–just maybe–he would be able to bear up under the load of another day.

Dillon pulled up to the curb in front of his house at 2:45. It wasn't that he expected the police officer to arrive early, just that he couldn't sit still. He couldn't concentrate on his work. Ever since Dan Ebersole had left, all Dillon could think about was the unavoidable scene with Maylea. What would he say? What would she say? What would she do? What would he do?

And the biggest question of all, at this moment, where would he go? He couldn't afford to rent an apartment for himself since he was responsible for paying the rent on Maylea's house. And he would certainly have to support Maylea–well, Maylea and her car– actually, Maylea and her car and her baby–at least until a divorce judge decreed Dillon's level of obligation.

In his heart, Dillon wanted to go home. He wanted to chuck it all and drive to Dallas, crawl into his old bed in his parents' home, and let the world try to get along without him for awhile.

Although the afternoon was dark with low-hovering clouds, the muggy air was hot. Dillon got out of his car to wait for Officer Gunther. The police cruiser pulled up behind his sedan at 2:55.

"Farley Gunther," the young police officer said as he approached Dillon with his hand extended. "Please call me Farley."

"Pleased to meet you," Dillon said, shaking the officer's hand. "I'm Dillon."

"It looks like your wife is home," Gunther said, nodding at the shiny red car in the drive way.

Dillon nodded. "I'm afraid so. I was hoping she would be gone, and you wouldn't even need to stay."

Gunther shrugged. "It's no problem. I do this all the time."

"What? Go to the homes of feuding spouses to make sure they don't kill each other?" Dillon asked. "That's got to be the most dangerous job in the world."

Gunther nodded. "It has its moments."

The front door was locked, so Dillon used his key to enter. The house was cool and quiet. "Maylea?" he called. When there was no answer, he tried, "Trolley?"

He looked at Gunther and shrugged. "Maylea may be napping. She's pregnant, you know. I'll check."

Gunther waited in the living room while Dillon trod silently down the hall to the bedroom he shared with Maylea. Tapping lightly, he poked his head in. "Maylea," he whispered.

Maylea was there, lying across the neatly made bed. She normally didn't sleep like that—on top of the covers. He stared at her intently. She didn't seem to be breathing. "Farley!" he called. "Farley, come here!"

The police officer reached his side in seconds.

"Is she breathing?" Dillon asked. "Look at her. I don't think she's breathing. Do you know CPR?"

Gunther didn't answer. He just stepped over to the bed and put two fingers on Maylea's neck. Then he looked up, shaking his head. "It's too late. She's cool."

"You mean ... you mean she's ... dead?" Dillon gasped. "Do you know CPR? Can't you do *something*? What about the baby?"

Gunther took Dillon's arm and led him back to the living room. "Mr. West, listen to me. After the body begins to cool, it's too late to do CPR. And it's too late for the baby. Do you hear me?"

Dillon heard nothing, except a huge buzzing in his head. "She can't be dead," he told Gunther. "She can't be. She's healthy. And young. There's not one thing wrong with her—well, except for headaches every now and then. Please, call 911 and get an ambulance."

"Sit down," Gunther said, guiding Dillon to the sofa. "You wait here, and I'll take care of everything." He went back outside to call in reinforcements. If the woman had been healthy, the place had to be handled as a crime scene.

After he reached his supervisor and reported, Gunther rejoined Dillon in the living room. Seeing that Dillon was looking spacey, he spoke urgently. "Dillon, do you hear me?"

Dillon looked up at the sound of his name, but his face showed no sign that he recognized the young police officer. He frowned, as if trying to marshal his consciousness.

Although he wasn't at all certain Dillon was tracking, Gunther asked, "Who is ... Trolley? I think that's what you said. Remember, when we first arrived and your wife didn't answer, you called out 'Trolley,' or something like that?"

Dillon nodded, "Trolley is the housekeeper."

"Ah, and what's the rest of her name? Trolley what?"

Dillon was stumped. Gunther thought Dillon's confusion was a result of the shock he had just received, but Dillon didn't know Trolley's last name, or her real first name. He shook his head, feeling infinitely angry with himself for being so negligent. "Trolley is short for 'Tra la la,' because she sings when she works. But I don't know her last name. I don't know anything about her."

Gunther sighed. It was useless trying to pry information out of Dillon right now. Let him sit and recover awhile. Maybe he would be able to answer questions when the lieutenant arrived and took over.

Lt. Jed Daly, who would be chief investigator on the case, arrived around 4:00. He was middle-aged, paunchy, and short-tempered. When he found Dillon mainly unresponsive, he turned to young Officer Gunther and squeezed out of Gunther every minute detail he had learned since he met Dillon.

Then, avoiding the crime scene unit, Daly strode into the bedroom to take a look at the victim. Maylea was wearing a filmy pink negligee and matching robe. Her long black hair was fanned out on the bed around her. Lt. Daly took one look at her and gasped, "Who is she—Sleeping Beauty?"

"Her name is Maylea West," Gunther said.

Daily turned on Gunther and spoke with a growl in his voice. "Whoever hurt that child ought to be boiled in acid! Did you say she had a fight with the husband?"

"I didn't say they fought. I just said he was moving out," Gunther explained.

"He did it!" Daily snarled. "The yellow-bellied snake took a ..." He paused, and stared at Maylea. "What did he take? I don't see any blood. What's going on here, Gunther? How did he do it?"

Gunther spoke carefully, knowing how much influence the veteran cop had at the department. "Good question, Lieutenant, but I'm not sure the husband did it. He's been in shock ever since we found her."

"He's a good actor. Give him that!" Daly said. "But he did it. Look at her–why would anybody else want her dead?"

"I couldn't say," Gunther replied in his most respectful voice.

"All right. Let's go talk to the husband," Daly said. "Either he answers questions or we lock him up until he's ready to talk."

The two walked back toward the front of the house, pausing to talk to Dr. Irving van Vleet, the medical examiner, in the hall. "Doc, I want to hear from you the minute you know something," Daly commanded. "Anything! The minute you know *anything*."

"Yes, yes, I'll call you," van Vleet said. He was accustomed to, and not impressed by, Daly's dictatorial manner.

In the living room, the sofa where Dillon had sat for most of an hour was empty. He was nowhere to be found. His car was gone.

Daly turned on Gunther. "Didn't you tell him to stay put?"

"It didn't seem necessary," Gunther said anxiously. "He barely seemed to know where he was."

"That nails it!" Daly yelled. "He fled. He's guilty. Let's get him back!"

Without another word, Daly marched out of the house, strode across the yard, crammed himself into his unmarked car, and drove away. Gunther followed him out, then looked back at the house. Nobody needed him in there, so he got into his own car, called Dan Ebersole's office, and left a message with the secretary.

When Dan returned to his office at 5:30, he found a message from Farley Gunther that read, "Maylea West is dead. Lt. Daly believes Mr. West killed her. Mr. West has disappeared."

Dan muttered a few foul words under his breath and began making phone calls. Dillon didn't answer his cell phone or his office phone. Nettie wasn't home yet, and Dan wasn't inclined to talk to Jeremy about Dillon's latest predicament. Nettie wasn't at Spring Up West either—she had already left for home.

After a few moments of thought, Dan grabbed his suit jacket, locked his office, and headed for Nettie's house. She might not know where Dillon was, but he couldn't think of anyone in town more likely to know. And he had a gut feeling he'd better get to Dillon before Lt. Daly did.

Chapter 9

After Dillon's visit the previous night, Nettie had slept poorly. Upon arriving home from work, she collapsed in Dillon's favorite recliner. With the lights in the den off, her feet elevated on the foot rest and an arm across her eyes, she was nearly asleep when she heard Jeremy's voice saying, "Mom?" He sounded hesitant and far away.

Without opening her eyes, she asked, "What is it Jeremy?"

"There's a lawyer at the door. He's looking for Dad," Jeremy said. His voice sounded small and frightened. "Dad's not here, is he?"

Trying not to betray her irritation to Jeremy, Nettie lifted her head. "What's the lawyer's name?" she asked.

"Um, Ever ... something," Jeremy said.

"Ebersole?" Nettie asked, rising and hurrying to the door before Jeremy could answer.

Dan Ebersole, looking hot and tired, was waiting at the front door. Nettie welcomed him warmly and led him into the den. "Please sit down, and I'll get us something to drink," she told him.

Jeremy stopped her. "It's okay, Mom. I'll get it."

Nettie knew she wasn't doing a good job of disguising the panic that Dan's appearance had produced in her, so she tried to offset it by giving Jeremy a big hug and thanking him profusely. Then she joined Dan in the den. "What's wrong?" she asked urgently. "Please don't tell me Maylea has murdered Dillon. Jeremy said you're looking for him. Is he missing?"

Dan had seated himself on the sofa, and Nettie stood over him, kneading her hands. "Nettie, get hold of yourself," he said sternly. "I'm sure Dillon is fine, but I don't know where he is, and I need to talk to him." He pulled Nettie down onto the sofa beside him.

Nettie nodded and took three deep breaths. "I'm sorry," she said, speaking rapidly. "But he came over last night, and he was afraid Maylea wanted to kill him, so when I saw you, I was afraid she had."

She was on the verge of tears, so Dan held her frozen hands in his big warm ones until she began to relax. Then he said softly, "Now Nettie, I want you to stay calm for your baby's sake. Okay?"

Nettie's eyes widened in fear again, as she searched his face desperately. "Why? What happened?"

Dan stroked her back and repeated, "You have to stay calm. Can you do that?"

She nodded and took more deep breaths. Then she said, "Jeremy was going to fix us drinks. I'll go get them and make sure he has something to do." She paused. "Or do you want him to hear this?"

Dan shook his head vigorously. "No! Not yet."

Nettie rose, still feeling shaky. In less than a minute she returned, smiling, with two glasses of lemonade. "Jeremy is making our dinner," she announced proudly. "Apparently Dillon said something to him last weekend about helping me more around the house, and he has taken over most of the kitchen duties. It's such a luxury to come home in the evening and eat a meal someone else has cooked!"

"Hey, that's some kind of special kid!" Dan exclaimed. "Connie has to threaten to confiscate all kinds of electronic equipment to get any help out of our teenagers."

Nettie nodded. "Well, if I weren't pregnant and recently divorced, I'm not so sure Jeremy would bother. But he sees himself as the man of the house, now, which I guess he is. I hope I'm not taking advantage of him, making him take on too much responsibility for his age."

"He's about 13, isn't he?" Dan asked. "And he's probably free to do anything he wants all day while you're at work. Right?"

"He has a few chores—carrying out the trash, cleaning his room, mowing the lawn," Nettie said. She took a sip of the ice-cold lemonade. It was exactly what she needed to revive and refresh her.

"I think making dinner is the least he should have to do," Dan said. "You might pour on the praise and maybe even increase his allowance, but *don't feel guilty!*"

"I agree with you, but it's nice to hear it from someone else. Now, please tell me why you're here before I fall apart."

Dan took Nettie's glass out of her hand and set it beside his on the nearby coffee table. Then he took both of her hands in his. "Nettie, Maylea is dead, and the police think Dillon killed her."

Nettie blanched. "No! He couldn't have! Dan, you don't believe that, do you?" Her eyes were wild with fear.

"No, of course not," Dan tried to reassure her, but she was trembling all over. "Nettie, you have to calm down," he said urgently. "Listen to me—what do you think you're doing to your baby, right now?"

Nettie nodded. She leaned into the sofa, closed her eyes, and laid her hands gently on her abdomen. Slowly her breathing returned to normal, and the trembling stopped. Then she opened her eyes and said, "Okay, tell me about it."

Dan sighed. "I wish I could, but I've pretty much shot my wad already." He explained that all he knew was contained in a three-sentence note left by his secretary. "Dillon doesn't answer at work, so I was hoping he was here. I want to see him before he talks to the police."

"He stayed at the Double T Motel last night," Nettie said. "Maybe he's there." She found the phone number and punched it into the phone. After a short conversation, she told Dan, "He's not there. He checked out this morning."

"What about Jeremy? Do you think he might have heard from his Dad?"

"I'll find out," Nettie said, heading for the kitchen. It took only a moment to learn that Jeremy hadn't talked to Dillon all day.

"There's only one other place he could be," Nettie said, resuming her place on the couch. "At his parents' home. In Dallas."

"He couldn't be there yet, but he might be on the way," Dan said.

"Why couldn't he be there yet?" Nettie asked.

"I talked to Dillon this morning and arranged for him to meet a police officer I know at his house. The officer–Farley Gunther–was going to go in with him as a kind of buffer, in case Maylea tried to make trouble. Dillon was supposed to meet Farley at 3:00 this afternoon and gather up a few clothes and toiletries, things like that."

Nettie nodded. "And when they got there, they found Maylea dead?" she asked.

Dan blew out a long breath. "I don't know that for a fact, but it's a good guess."

"Do you know how she died? Or when?" Nettie asked.

Dan shook his head. "I've told you everything I know." He studied Nettie. Her color had returned and she seemed in control now, so he said what was on his mind. "If the police don't find Dillon soon, they're going to be knocking on your door. You realize that, don't you?"

Nettie's expression told him she didn't know that. "*My* door? Why?"

"Where else are they going to look for him?" Dan asked. "He's not at his office. He doesn't answer his cell phone. His home is a crime scene. He checked out of the Double T."

"Will they think ... I did it?" she asked breathlessly, almost too frightened of the words to express them.

"Not at first, but they may look at you if they clear Dillon," he said.

Nettie nodded thoughtfully. "Are you saying Dillon is guilty until he's proven innocent?" she asked.

"Not in the eyes of the law," Dan said, "but Jed Daly is another matter. He tends to fix on a suspect, then look for the evidence to support his conclusion."

Despair was written as plainly as words on Nettie's face. "Oh Dan, what are we going to do?" she wailed.

"My best advice is to get Dillon a good defense attorney," Dan said.

"Another lawyer?" Nettie asked. "Can't you defend him?"

Dan winked. "Not if he's smart. I don't practice criminal law."

"Right. I knew that," she said. "Who can we get instead?"

Dan looked dubious. "Based on the conversation I had with him this morning, I'd guess he's going to request a public defender."

Nettie gave him a worried frown, but persisted. "If you were in Dillon's position, who would you get to defend you?"

"Well, I believe I'd call up a neophyte by the name of Ethan Holmes. He's a little bit short on experience, but long on determination and loyalty. He's not as expensive as the old-timers with a track record, and I think Dillon may see that as a major asset right now."

"Dan, price is no object," Nettie said indignantly. "I want Dillon to have the best possible defense, and we'll find a way to pay for it."

Dan was shaking his head. "You know Dillon better than that. He's not going to accept charity, even from you. Or *especially* from you."

Nettie looked as if she were about to argue the point, then she shrugged. "We can cross that bridge when we get to it. Anyway, maybe it–the murder–happened when he was here last night. Then he'll have an alibi."

"We can always hope," Dan said.

"Look, tell me about this lawyer–Holmes, wasn't it? Then I'll let you go."

Dan grinned at the thought of Ethan Holmes. "He was in law school with my nephew in Austin, and they graduated five years ago. Ethan's buddies liked to call him Sherlock when he was on a case because he'd hang on to it like a bulldog until he found the solution."

Nettie was listening intently and processing Dan's words. "I guess he's the best we can do right now," she said. "Should I call him tonight?"

"No!" Dan exclaimed. "I'll give him a heads up tomorrow so he can start nosing around if he has time. But Dillon doesn't need to contact Ethan until the police contact *him*."

"In other words, I should mind my own business?" Nettie asked.

Dan smiled. "For now. Look, why don't you bring Jeremy in here so we can tell him about Maylea?"

Agreeably, Nettie went to get Jeremy. When they returned, Nettie said gently, "Jeremy, I don't know any details yet, but Dan has just told me that Maylea is dead."

"What happened to her?" Jeremy gasped, looking from Nettie to Dan.

"We don't know, but we think the police may suspect that your Dad murdered her," Nettie said.

"Aw, come on, the police aren't that stupid!" Jeremy protested.

Dan smiled. "They're not stupid, but they don't know Dillon so they'll have to find out for themselves that he didn't do it."

"Where *is* Dad?" Jeremy asked, giving his Mother a worried frown.

"We don't know that either," Nettie said. "Our best guess is that he's headed for Dallas to see Grandma and Grandpa West."

"There's a good chance the police will come here looking for your Dad," Dan added. "I don't want you to talk to them, Jeremy, unless your Mother is with you."

"Okay," Jeremy said, and his frown deepened. "Why?"

"Well." Dan considered his answer for a moment. "Sometimes police get so anxious to solve a crime that they'll twist your words to mean something you never meant to say. I'm not saying the police are bad guys. They're not–they're great! But murders sometimes make people behave differently than they normally would."

Jeremy looked at his Mother to see if she agreed with Dan. She nodded. "Son, don't worry about it. Just don't talk to them unless I'm with you."

"I won't," Jeremy said, "but what if they come here tomorrow while you're at work?"

"Maybe you should come to work with me tomorrow," Nettie said. "Couldn't you bring Ronny and Kurt? I'll drop you boys off at a movie in the afternoon. You can amuse yourselves in the gym in the morning, can't you?"

Jeremy nodded. "No problem. I'll go call them right now."

"Hey, pal," Dan called after him, "don't tell them about Maylea yet. We don't even know for sure how she died. It could have been an accident or something."

As Nettie walked Dan to the door, he said, "Now Nettie, there's one thing you have to keep in mind at all times. If the police–or the courts–clear Dillon, you and Jeremy are next on the list. So watch what you say."

Nettie had halted in mid-step. "Jeremy?" she cried. "They wouldn't!"

Dan stopped, too. "Sure they would. Did Jeremy like Maylea?"

"I don't know," said Nettie, feeling more flustered than she had since Dan arrived. "I don't think he exactly liked her. But he didn't hate her."

Dan opened the front door. "As far as you know," he said, "but he may blame her for tearing apart his family."

"Of course he does that! Who wouldn't?" asked Nettie. "But that doesn't mean he would hurt her."

"I know that. And you know that," Dan said soothingly. "We just want to make sure nobody else gets the wrong idea. That's all I'm saying."

After she had closed the door behind Dan Ebersole, Nettie leaned against it for a few moments, gathering her thoughts. Her first thought was that she would like to yell at Dillon–shriek at him! He had gotten them into this mess–all of them. Why? What had she done to deserve this grief? Her chin sank momentarily onto her chest. She would have to give that question some consideration when she had time. But now she had phone calls to make.

First Nettie called Dillon's parents to tell them Dillon might be on his way to Dallas. Then she called her Mother who was almost out the door before the words were out of Nettie's mouth.

"No, Mom, don't come over here now. We haven't heard from Dillon. We haven't heard from the police. We'll need you later, but right now I think we need to act like nothing has happened. At least, until we *hear* something."

Bethany finally agreed not to call out the cavalry after Nettie promised three times that she would call if she needed *anything*.

Then, with trembling fingers, Nettie began calling Qiana. First, she called Qiana's home and got no answer. Nor did Qiana answer her cell phone. When Nettie dialed Spring Up South, a young voice answered the phone.

"Is Qiana there?" Nettie asked.

"Yes, she's leading her exercise class," the voice explained.

"Please get her for me. Tell her it's her sister, and I *have* to talk to her now," Nettie said.

Qiana's voice was breathless when she came on the line. "Nettie! What's wrong?"

"I need to see you tonight. Not right now, because Jeremy and I are getting ready to eat, but afterward. Can you come over after your class?"

"Of course, but what's wrong?"

"I'll tell you when you get here," Nettie said. She had to see Qiana's face when she broke the news that Maylea was dead. Maybe, just maybe, Qiana's expression would give Nettie the information she needed.

After Nettie and Jeremy had finished eating ham and cheese sandwiches, Nettie asked carefully, "Jeremy, what time did you and Ronny get up this morning?"

Jeremy thought about his answer a moment, then said, "It was about 8:00, I think. Qiana said she had to be at work by 9:00."

Nettie nodded. "And what time did Qiana get up?"

Jeremy frowned. "How would I know?"

"I don't know," Nettie said. "What time did the three of you go to bed last night?"

Jeremy's frown deepened. "Why?"

Nettie shook her head. "Nothing. I'm just worried ... worried about everybody and everything. Forget it."

"Well, it was after midnight, if you must know," Jeremy said, "but I don't know what time it was."

"Okay, thank you, sweetie," Nettie said. "You go on. I'll do the dishes tonight. I *need* to do the dishes tonight."

Jeremy didn't have to be told twice. He headed for his bedroom and his favorite video game. As soon as the dinner dishes were washed, Nettie took a lawn chair to the front porch. She alternately sat and paced up and down the porch until Qiana's little blue car drew up to the curb.

Normally, Nettie had as much class as anybody, but tonight wasn't normal. The terror saturating her soul was scrambling her thoughts. So, as soon as she saw Qiana's car, Nettie bounded off the porch and across the yard to the car, cradling her stomach as she ran. Yanking open the door on the passenger side, she slid into the seat and, without preamble, asked, "Did you murder Maylea?"

Qiana's eyes widened. "Did I what?"

"Murder Maylea." Nettie seemed suddenly to recognize how outrageous her question was, for she added, "I'm sorry, Qiana, but I'm going crazy with worry. Maylea's dead and the police think Dillon did it. I'm so afraid you did it I can hardly breathe!"

Qiana gave her sister a pitying look. "That would be stupid, wouldn't it? To kill Maylea and throw Dillon right back into your arms. Why would I do that?"

"Well, if you framed Dillon and he went to jail ... you've been wanting to get revenge on him–what could be better than making him spend the rest of his life in jail?"

"What indeed?" asked Qiana. "But you can't really believe I would murder someone, can you?"

"Oh Qiana," Nettie said, her voice quavering, "I can't believe Maylea's dead. But since she is, I don't know what to believe. *Everything* is crazy. Everything is falling apart."

Qiana–recognizing the terror in Nettie's voice, in her face, in her demeanor–spoke quietly. "Okay, sis, here's what we're going to do. I'm going to put you to bed, then I'll hang around until Jeremy goes to bed." As Nettie opened her mouth to object, Qiana held up a hand. "Don't even start. You've got that wee babe growing in you. That means you need to be sleeping for two. Right? And how much sleep did you get last night?"

"Not much," Nettie admitted, "but how can I sleep when the police could ring the doorbell any minute, looking for Dillon? And I don't know where Dillon is! Qiana, what if the person who killed Maylea killed Dillon too?"

Nettie's voice rose hysterically, and Qiana took over. She led Nettie to her bedroom, sent her into the bathroom to put on a nightgown, then sat on the side of her bed, stroking her hair until Nettie fell asleep. "Sweet dreams," Qiana whispered. Then she kissed her finger and touched Nettie's tummy. "You too, baby."

Before she tiptoed out of the room, she picked up the handset of the house phone and removed Nettie's cell phone, which was on the dresser charging. She put both phones in the guest room, plugging in the cell phone so it could continue to charge. Next Qiana went into Jeremy's room and played three rounds of video games with him. He trounced her every time and never guessed that she was letting him win.

"That's it for me," Qiana said. "I'm going to sleep in your guest room tonight, so I can make sure nobody disturbs your Mom. She's beat, and it's partly my fault."

"Why is it your fault?" Jeremy asked.

"You heard me last night," Qiana said, "yelling at your Dad. Your Mom needs a sister right now, not a shrieking shrew!"

Jeremy grinned. "My aunt, the shrieking shrew," he said.

Qiana whacked him with his pillow, then went to bed. Soon the house was silent, and the peace continued through the night. But as Qiana told the Nettie the next day, "I couldn't have slept if I'd gone home, for worrying that you were being disturbed."

Meanwhile, Dillon arrived at his parents' home in north Dallas, stumbling with exhaustion. His mother fed him beef stew and sent him to bed. His father, upon hearing about Dillon's abortive attempt to retrieve his property, went shopping. At a nearby mall he bought his son underwear, socks, five changes of clothes, toiletries, and a suitcase to carry it all.

The next morning, after Dillon reported in to Nettie, Dick and Reggy West packed their son off to his sister's house in nearby Arlington. "You get some rest and get your bearings," his father instructed him. "The police won't find you at Rilee's–at least not quickly–since her name isn't West any more."

"The police?" Dillon asked. "Are the police looking for me?"

"They're bound to be–your wife is dead."

"But I don't want to hide from the police," Dillon said. "I should get back to Lubbock. Besides, my secretary is on vacation this week. I need to be in the office."

"I'll call Nettie and get her to hire a temp for your office," Mrs. West said. "You don't have to stay at Rilee's long but, son, you do have to get rested and think about ... everything."

"Think about what?" Dillon asked with a frown.

"About who killed Maylea, of course," his father exclaimed. "Otherwise, they're going to pin her murder on you!"

Chapter 10

Lt. Jed Daly leaned over his desk Wednesday afternoon, arranging the information on the Maylea West murder. When he had it spread out the way he wanted it, he sat back and rubbed his hands together with glee. He loved his job! What could be more fun than removing human filth from the streets of the city?

And this case? Well, this case was about to solve itself. The husband–Dillon West–was a ruthless monster. He had murdered one of the most beautiful women Daly had ever seen. And the motive was obvious. Shaking his head in disbelief, Daly picked up the million-dollar life insurance policy he had found on the kitchen table. West was so stupid he had left the evidence out in plain sight. Daly couldn't wait to put West behind bars. And he would, just as soon as he found him.

Daly brought his hand down hard on his desk. Where had the murdering scum gone? The ex-wife knew. And the kid. Daly was certain of it. But they weren't talking. Scowling, he made a low growling sound in the back of his throat. He would have to try again to wring the information out of them. Too bad he couldn't get the kid off alone. He was sure he could get Jeremy to talk if he could bring him in and question him without the mother hovering over him.

"Lieutenant?"

Lt. Daly looked up to see Allen Latimer, a rookie–a trainee. Daly loved trainees–they made superb gofers. "Latimer! Come in," Daly said heartily. "What's new?"

"I just talked to the medical examiner," Latimer said. "He wants you to let Mr. West know that the DNA test has been sent off."

Lt. Daly searched his memory and found no answer. "What DNA test?"

"Mr. West asked him to find out if the baby Mrs. West was carrying was his or not."

"What!" Daly roared. "When was this?"

Latimer stepped back at this unexpected outburst. "When was what?"

"Never mind." Daly was already punching in the number for Dr. Irving van Vleet. "Irving!" he said when the doctor answered. "What's this about a DNA test requested by Dillon West?"

"His wife was pregnant. He wanted to know if he was the father of the baby she was carrying. I sent him to the lab to give a sample."

"When was this?" Daly asked.

"Yesterday at his house, right before I talked to you. When I got there and told him who I was, he asked me if I could find out about the baby's paternity."

"And you said you could?" Daly asked.

"Sure."

"What did he do then?"

"He got up and left–said he was going straight to the lab for the test," van Vleet said.

"So that's where he got off to," Lt. Daly said, more to himself than to the doctor.

"Is there a problem?" van Vleet asked.

"Nope. No problem. Just a motive. *Another* motive. What about the poison? Have you identified it yet?"

"Not yet," van Vleet said.

"Okay, thanks Irving," Daly said and disconnected. He turned to Latimer with a Cheshire grin. "There's the second motive," he said cheerfully. "She was cheating on him. Add infidelity to a million dollars in life insurance, and we have a slam dunk. Now all we have to do is find him and lock him up until he's old and gray."

Latimer nodded, but he looked puzzled. He asked a lot of questions and didn't feel bad for doing it because he was, after all, a rookie. "Doesn't it seem strange to you that she had a life insurance policy, and he didn't? I mean, even an idiot would know that makes him look guilty."

"It was probably a mix-up at the insurance company," Daly said with a shrug. "Doesn't matter, we know it's always the husband. And I'll bet you a week's pay the lover boy's name will turn out to be Scot!"

"Right, the name on the housekeeper's note," Latimer said, referring to a message Trolley had left on the door of the refrigerator. "Where is that note? I'd like to look at it again."

"It's being checked for fingerprints," Daly said, "but I can quote it word for word. 'Dear Mrs. West, It's early so I won't wake you, but I have to leave. My sister broke her hip and I have to go to her. I'm so sorry to leave you in the lurch like this. Please call me if you need me—you know my cell number. Trolley. P.S. Remember to call Scot today.' "

Latimer studied the Lieutenant's face. "She knows something, doesn't she?" he asked.

Daly nodded. "No doubt about it. She probably saw the husband doing something suspicious—or maybe he was just at the house yesterday morning when he was claiming to be at a motel—and now the housekeeper is afraid she's next. So she cleared out."

"You can't blame her for that," Latimer said. "But it's strange how nobody seems to know her name. Have they finished searching the house?"

"Sure. It's a small place. Maybe West destroyed her employment papers or references—whatever there was to identify her."

"What about the victim's cell phone? Wouldn't the housekeeper's cell number be on it?"

"No cell phone found," Daly growled. "He took that too."

"Then maybe the witness is the reason the husband left," Latimer suggested. "Since he had the housekeeper's papers and his wife's cell phone, he must have known how to locate ... Trolley, was it? And he knew he had to kill her, too, to make sure she didn't talk."

"Very good, Latimer," Lt. Daly exclaimed with real admiration in his voice. "I think you've got something there."

"For all the good it does," Latimer said, "since we don't know where she is."

Daly drooped momentarily, but he was a man of action, so he scooted his chair back and said, "Let's go see the wife again. I'll get something out of her if it's the last thing I do!"

"The wife?" Latimer asked in surprise. "At the morgue?"

"Oh, the ex-wife. You know what I mean," Lt. Daly said irritably. "Come on."

He had barely cleared his desk when the phone rang. Latimer waited patiently while Daly took the call, expressing some excitement, then making a note on a piece of scrap paper. "We're going to make a stop on the way to Mrs. West's gym," he said after he replaced the phone in its cradle. "There's a Glen Bristol who was with Dillon West the night before the murder. Let's go see what he has to say."

※

The last thing Glen Bristol needed that afternoon was another interruption. But when he told his secretary to tell Daly and Latimer to take a flying leap, she replied urgently, "But Mr. Bristol, they're *police officers*."

"*Mr. Bristol?*" he thought. Then he said it, "*Mr. Bristol?*"

"Yes sir. That is your name, isn't it?" she inquired in her most formal tone.

"Okay, okay. Send them in," he said. "Let's get it over with."

When Lt. Jed Daly and Officer Allen Latimer entered Glen's office, he muttered to himself, "Mutt and Jeff. Laurel and Hardy." Of course, the tall, young one in his crisp uniform didn't look like a clown, but he was a distinct contrast to the older, burly man in his baggy civvies.

When the officers were seated, Glen asked briskly, "Now, how can I help you?"

"I just learned that your secretary phoned Dillon West's office to ask about a firewall you installed for him two nights ago," said Lt. Daly.

Glen nodded. "That's right."

"Did you see Mr. West that night?" Daly asked.

"Yes."

"Tell us about it."

Glen frowned. "Could you give me a hint? Are you asking me how to install a firewall?"

Daly rolled his eyes. "No, we're asking about Mr. West's frame of mind. What did he talk about? Do you know where he is today? Things like that ..."

Glen's eyes narrowed. "Why do you ask?"

"You haven't heard about his wife?" Daly asked.

"I heard she died," Glen said, "but I haven't heard any details. Since you're here, I presume she was murdered."

"We don't have the report from the medical examiner yet, but we have to assume foul play until we know otherwise," Daly said.

"And you believe Dillon ... murdered her?" Glen asked.

"Well, his behavior is decidedly guilty," Daly said.

"Like what?"

"Like disappearing," Daly said, looking smug. "So why don't you quit stalling and answer our questions? Did Mr. West say anything about his wife that night?"

Glen hesitated. He didn't like snitching on a client, but he wasn't inclined to protect Dillon if he *had* killed Maylea. Besides, he didn't have time to play games with a couple of cops, so he said, "Sure, he talked about her. He seemed to be having second thoughts about marrying her."

"Ahhhh," Daly said, drawing out the syllable. "What did he say?"

Glen did his best to recall and repeat the conversation in Dillon's office the evening before Maylea's death. When he finished, he recalled their earlier phone conversation, so he added, "I probably said something I shouldn't when Dillon called to ask for my help. This was before I saw him."

"What did you say?" Daly asked.

"He said most people don't like him since he divorced Nettie. So I told him all the bachelors in town are fond of him because now Nettie's free to see other men."

Daly gave Latimer a significant glance. "How did he take that?"

Glen shrugged. "It's hard to say. We were on the phone at the time, but he didn't sound happy about it. And he hung up on me."

Daly was struggling to hide his delight as he asked, "Is there anything else we should know?"

Glen frowned, trying to remember. "Well, there was something about ... Qiana, the ex-wife's sister. Apparently she's carrying a grudge against Dillon for divorcing Nettie. She might be able to give you some information."

"Mr. Bristol," Daly said, no longer trying to hide his glee, "you are a fine citizen and a credit to your parents. Thank you for your help. Would you happen to know how we can locate this Key-whatever, the ex-wife's sister?"

"She owns Spring Up South, the fitness center on the south side of town," Glen said. "Her name is Qiana—that's Q-i-a-n-a—Jamison."

"I know the place," said Latimer, who had been diligently taking notes throughout the conversation.

"Very good," Daly said. "Mr. Bristol, Officer Latimer will write up your statement and bring it by for your signature. Thank you again for your help." He fished around in his pocket and pulled out a dog-eared business card, which he handed to Glen. "Please give me a call if you think of anything else we should know."

Glen accepted the card and shook hands with both officers. When they were gone, he considered taking out a few minutes to feel guilty for spilling his guts about Dillon. But who had time for guilt? Not a computer tech–that was for sure! Two minutes later he was on the phone with a client and Dillon was forgotten.

Qiana received the representatives from the police department with a large measure of ambivalence. As much as she detested Dillon, her cheating, former brother-in-law, she was determined to protect Nettie, her only sibling. The fact that Nettie was actually a half-sister was a mere matter of semantics. And so she answered their questions with grunts, gestures, and monosyllables, not bothering to disguise her hostility.

"Ms. Jamison, we were given to believe that you're not fond of Mr. West," said Lt. Daly after he had asked several questions and failed to obtain any useful information from Qiana. "So it's hard to understand why you're being so evasive. Surely you know more about his life and affairs than you're letting on."

Qiana glared at him. "I'm *not* fond of Dillon, but I'm very fond of my sister. And my sister believes in his innocence. So, you tell me which I should trust–a policeman with an obvious agenda or a sister I've known and loved all my life."

Daly and Latimer exchanged glances. It wasn't an issue they cared to tackle, so Daly by-passed it. "Okay, let me ask you this. Is it your position that Mr. West did *not* murder his wife?"

Qiana looked uncomfortable. Then she shrugged. "Actually, I don't think he has the gumption to murder anyone." Her contempt was obvious in her voice.

"Aw come on, lady," Daly said. "It doesn't take any gumption to poison someone."

Qiana's eyes widened. "Poison? Maylea was poisoned?"

Daly nodded, never taking his eyes from her face. "That's right."

"How?" Qiana asked.

"We don't know yet. We're working on it," Daly said. "So tell me–does that change your opinion? Do you think Mr. West might have poisoned her?"

Qiana seemed to be considering the possibility, but when she spoke, it was to turn the tables on him. "Look, Mr. Detective, let me ask you a question for a change. Are you judge, jury and executioner? You seem to have decided that Dillon West committed this crime–are you considering any other suspects?"

"Like who?" Daly asked, not bothering to conceal his scorn at the suggestion.

"Like Scot Sanford," Qiana said.

Daly straightened in his chair. "Scot who?"

Officer Latimer came to attention also and began writing in his notepad.

Qiana looked from one to the other with interest. "You're looking at Scot as a possible suspect, too?"

"We might if you'll tell us who he is," Daly said. "His first name has come up in the investigation, but we didn't have his last name. Who is he?"

"He's a personal trainer. He brings clients here almost every day," Qiana said.

"And why would he be a suspect in the murder of Maylea West?"

Qiana looked unhappy as she answered. "I've never mentioned it to my sister, but he and Maylea spent a lot of time together here. And they didn't act like casual acquaintances."

"For example?"

"They were all over each other, and they didn't seem to care who noticed." She shrugged. "Not that anyone else *did* notice, but I did."

"So you think he was her lover?" Daly asked.

"It's possible," Qiana said.

"Okay, now we have a better motive for the husband to kill her. Why would the lover want her dead?"

Qiana frowned. "I'm not the detective–how do I know? Maybe he wanted her to leave Dillon, and she refused. I'm just saying Dillon isn't the only suspect."

Daly nodded. "Okay, we'll check it out. Thanks for the information, Ms. Jamison. And FYI, if Dillon West is actually innocent, then anything you tell us can only help him."

"Right," Qiana said in a cynical tone, "unless you've already decided he's guilty. Then anything I tell you will help hang him."

Daly tossed one of his frayed business cards onto her desk. "Call me if you think of anything else I need to know. About West *or* Sanford."

"Ma'am, would you happen to have an address or phone number for Scot Sanford," Latimer asked.

"Sure." Qiana flipped through her Rolodex to the S's, pulled out a card, and handed it to Latimer. He copied the information into his notepad, then handed the card back with a quick smile.

Qiana winked at him, and he blushed. Daly was already halfway to the car, and Latimer hurried after him, trying not to think about Qiana's bright hazel eyes and her lithe figure. She was actually five years older than he was, but he would have guessed she was five years younger. It took him a few blocks to get his mind off Qiana and ask, "Where are we headed next?"

"Spring Up West to talk to Nettie West," Daly said. "Maybe if I threaten to lock her up, she'll tell us where her ex is hiding out."

Latimer shook his head. "I don't think so. From what I hear, she'd rot in prison before she'd rat out a family member."

Daly sighed heartily. "Well, we've got to try. We're not going to get anywhere on this case without him."

Daly and Latimer had already been to Spring Up West that morning. When Nettie looked up from her desk and saw them again, she shuddered. "Now what?" she asked.

"The same thing," Daly said, walking in and helping himself to a chair. "Where is Dillon West?"

Nettie gave an elaborate, if unconvincing shrug. "How would I know?"

"Phone call, email, text message ..." Daly replied.

"Lt. Daly," Nettie said evenly, "Dillon West divorced me. He doesn't tell me where he's going or what he's doing any more."

"When was the last time you saw him?" Daly asked.

"Monday night."

"Where was this?"

"At my house."

"Why was he there?"

Nettie glared at him. "We already covered this ground this morning. He wanted to talk about his marriage."

"Because?"

"He wasn't happy," Nettie said.

Daly glanced at Latimer. The young officer's pen was idle. "Mrs. West," he said angrily, "you do realize, don't you, that I'm going to hound your every step until I have Dillon West in custody?"

"No, I don't realize that," she said. "And why would you take him into custody? He didn't kill Maylea. He wouldn't kill anyone."

"Because he doesn't have the gumption?" Daly asked.

Nettie frowned at his choice of words. "Because he's not a violent person. He was considering divorce, but he was going to see a marriage counselor first."

Latimer still wasn't writing anything, because she still wasn't saying anything new. "Look," Daly growled, "let's make sure you *get it*! The longer he stays away, the guiltier he looks."

"That's your opinion," she said, beginning to sound angry herself, "but it doesn't matter if he stays away until judgment day–he didn't kill Maylea!"

Daly muttered an expletive, stood, and stomped out. Latimer rose and trailed after him, stuffing his notepad into his shirt pocket as he went. Nettie watched them leave with a heartsick expression on her face. Surely Dillon hadn't killed Maylea. No, of course not! But what if she had attacked him? Perhaps in self defense ... .

She picked up her phone and dialed Spring Up South. Qiana answered.

"QiQi, it's me. The police just left, and I'm about to climb the walls. They think I know where Dillon is."

"And you don't?"

"Listen, can we talk?"

There was a short pause, then Qiana said, "I'll be there in ten minutes."

As soon as Qiana arrived, Nettie shut the door to her office and locked it. They sat close together on a low couch and spoke in voices barely above a whisper. "Qiana, he couldn't have killed Maylea," Nettie said earnestly. "I know he couldn't–unless it was self-defense."

She was trembling all over and Qiana wanted to say something comforting, but the suggestion of self-defense as a motive took her by surprise. "Nettie! You can't poison someone, then claim self-defense," she cried. "No jury in the world would believe it. *You* can't believe it."

"Poison?" Nettie gasped weakly. "She was poisoned?"

Qiana studied her. "The police didn't tell you that?"

"No. All they've done is demand to know where Dillon is. Why am *I* supposed to know where he is?"

"Maybe they've figured out what everybody on the planet except you and Dillon have known all along."

Nettie frowned. "What's that?"

"That he still loves you as much as he ever did."

Nettie looked up and her eyes were bright with hope. "Do you believe that, Qiana?"

Qiana spoke grudgingly. "I'm afraid I do. Not," she added emphatically, "that he deserves you!"

Nettie opened her mouth to answer; then her eyes widened, as a memory sprang to the surface. "Oh no!" she moaned.

"What? What's wrong?" Qiana asked.

"I know how she was poisoned," Nettie said.

"How?"

"Jeremy told me she made her own capsules with some kind of herbal powder. She thought it was a super tonic. All somebody had to do was put poison in the capsules instead of her powder. She'd swallow them and never know what happened!"

Qiana was listening and nodding thoughtfully. "Yeah! I bet you're right. And who else would have access to her capsules besides her husband?"

"That's the problem," said Nettie. "Who could have done it besides Dillon or Jeremy?"

"It definitely narrows the field," Qiana said. "I guess I should tell you what I told the police this afternoon."

"What's that?"

"Maylea had a boyfriend. His name is Scot Sanford. The two of them came into Spring Up South together all the time."

Nettie's eyes widened in disbelief. "Qiana! Are you sure?"

Qiana shrugged. "Well, I never actually saw them in the sack together, but they were all over each other. They didn't leave much to the imagination."

"Why didn't you tell me before?" Nettie asked indignantly.

"Right. So you could tell Dillon. And Dillon could dump Maylea. Next thing you know, he'd be begging you to take him back and you're just lame enough to do it."

Nettie stared at her sister a long time before she asked weakly, "Would it be so lame to take him back?"

"After what he did to you? I guess!"

Nettie stared at her sister for a moment, then dropped her head. "Yeah," she mumbled. "Yeah, it would be pretty lame." Then tears flooded her cheeks and Qiana held her until the tears were gone.

Chapter 11

Dillon opened his eyes Thursday morning to find bright sunshine streaming through the window and his five-year-old niece Lydia gazing solemnly at his face. "Unca' Dillon, are you 'wake?" she asked when he began to stir.

He opened one eye. "Almost. Are you?"

"Sure. I was 'wake a long time ago. Unca' Dillon, where's Aunt Nettie?"

Dillon yawned and stretched. "She's at home."

"Where's Jermy?"

"He's at home, too."

"Unca' Dillon."

"Yes, Lydia?"

She smiled shyly. "Thank you for coming to see me."

He laughed and pulled her onto the bed for a hug. "Thank you for *letting* me come to see you."

Lydia gave his head a tight squeeze and wriggled down to the floor again. "Unca' Dillon, will you come to Vacation Bible School with me?"

Dillon sat up and tried to mash down his unruly curls. He'd let his hair grow out at Maylea's urging after 30 years of wearing it short enough to thwart its natural tendency to kink. Now he'd shave it off himself if he had the equipment. Well, he could tend to that this afternoon. "When is Vacation Bible School?" he asked his niece.

"Momma says in one half of a hour," Lydia said carefully, so she would get the time right.

"Half an hour?" Dillon repeated, swinging his legs out of the bed. "Then I'd better move, don't you think?"

Lydia laughed excitedly. "Okay. I go tell Momma."

Dillon's sister Rilee had married Shane Norris, a Baptist preacher. Dillon knew the whole family would be at the church that morning–Lydia and her eight-year-old sister Ruth as students and their parents as workers. Maybe they could use an extra pair of hands today.

Shane and Rilee both tried to talk Dillon into staying home and resting, instead of spending the morning in the pursuit of youngsters. "You're so tired," Rilee told him earnestly, pushing a curl out of his face. "Why don't you go back to bed and get some more sleep?"

His face was sober as he answered. "I haven't been going to church much lately, Sis. Maybe that's part of my problem. Besides I slept all day yesterday. I'm tired of sleep."

Rilee couldn't argue with his logic. So she poured him a cup of coffee and handed him a box of cereal.

By 8:30 everyone was crowded into the Norris' minivan headed for the church. Shane glanced at his brother-in-law who was seated in the front passenger seat. "Look, Dillon," he said, "I want to point out that we had no idea you would be here today. I don't want you to get the idea that today's lesson is aimed at you."

Dillon frowned at him. "Why? What's the lesson for the day?"

Shane grimaced. "Our theme this week is 'The Life of a King.' It's about King David, and today we're talking about the fact that ..." His voice trailed off for a few moments. Then he continued. "... well, the fact that our actions affect other people, and our sins can hurt the people we love the most."

"Ah." Dillon absorbed this information, then gave Shane a wry smile. "I guess I'm the poster boy for today's lesson."

Shane said, "Pretty much." But he gave Dillon a sympathetic smile.

At 9:00 o'clock the morning's activities began. The first order of business was a skit by the teenagers, who presented the scripture lesson by bringing the children into the action. On this day, they had placed tables end to end in the large fellowship hall and seated the children in chairs around it, as if they were attending a banquet.

Looking around for Lydia and not seeing her, Dillon decided the younger children were probably not participating in the skit. He was about to move out of the way when he felt a soft, little hand in his and looked down to see Ruth. "Uncle Dillon, will you sit with me?" she asked. Noting that most of the adults were finding places among the children, he nodded his assent and let her lead him to a chair.

"Okay, listen up!" said the teenage girl who was acting as narrator. "We're pretending we're at a royal feast today. One of David's sons has invited all his brothers to come to dinner. What do you think you would like to eat if you went to a fancy banquet?"

"Pizza!" was the first suggestion.

"Hamburger," was next.

"A hundred bowls of chocolate ice cream!"

"You can't have just ice cream for dinner," another child said in disdain. "You have to eat your dinner *first* if you want ice cream."

"Okay," the narrator said, taking over again, "let's go on. In a few minutes, the royal servants will be bringing you cookies and punch, but we want you to pretend you're eating a big, fancy dinner. Okay?"

"Okay!" the children responded, looking eagerly toward the door where the promised refreshments would appear.

"But first, let's talk about yesterday's lesson," the narrator said, reclaiming their attention. "Who remembers what happened."

"I do!" said Ruth, raising her hand. "A mean boy hurt his sister."

"That's right," said the narrator. "Does anybody remember the name of the mean boy or his sister?"

Several children took a stab at it, but the names had escaped them, so the narrator said, "Okay, the mean boy was named Amnon. His sister's name was Tamar, and there was another brother named Absalom. Absalom was mad because his father, King David ..."

She paused and pointed toward the far end of the room. Another teenager, wearing a robe and crown entered and sat down in an office chair, which had been draped with a gold bedspread to represent a throne. Then the narrator continued, "... didn't do anything to punish Amnon. Can you think of a reason why David might not have punished Amnon?"

"Yes, because King David stole Bath-sheba and had her husband killed," said one of the older children.

"Do you think he might have had a guilty conscience about that?" asked the narrator.

Many of the children nodded and murmured, "Yes."

"Okay, now we're going to bring in the guests of honor–King David's sons, the princes of Israel," the narrator continued. At this cue, several boys wearing tunics entered and took seats at the head of the table. "Prince Amnon, will you stand up and give us a wave?" the narrator asked.

One of the newcomers stood and waved briefly before taking his seat again.

"And our host, Prince Absalom," said the narrator. "Will you welcome your guests today?"

Another teenager wearing a tunic entered and took his place at the head of the table. "Welcome, everyone!" he said in a voice that exuded charm. "I'm so pleased that you could be here today–I hope all of you will enjoy the royal food. And as for my brothers, my *most* honored guests, I welcome you to my home this day." He bowed slightly and the other princes bowed their heads in response. Then Absalom clapped his hands and teenage girls wearing bathrobes entered carrying cookies and punch. "Please, dear guests, enjoy yourselves." With this parting command, Absalom left the room.

Soon, all the children were munching cookies and drinking punch. "These cookies are good," Dillon told Ruth. "I think they're homemade."

Ruth studied hers a moment. "Maybe. Or they're from the bakery."

"So, if this is a royal banquet, what are you pretending that you're eating?" Dillon asked.

"I think they ate lambs back in those days," said the child next to Ruth.

"I think you're right," said Dillon. "What about hamburgers? Do you think they ever had hamburgers?"

"Maybe steak," was the contribution from a child on the opposite side of the table.

"Yummy!" said Dillon. "That's what I'm pretending to eat." He took a big bite out of his cookie.

The children seemed to have forgotten about David, Amnon and Absalom. In fact, Dillon had almost forgotten them too. And then there was a shout from the doorway and Absalom appeared with several more tunic-clad teenagers. "Attack! Attack now!" the prince cried. His small army descended on Amnon, brandishing plastic swords.

The children (and the adults) watched spellbound as Amnon fell to the floor and his attackers fled. Then a teenager stood and raced to King David to tell him the terrible news. King David responded with wailing and tearing of clothes, as he exited the room.

With the help of the narrator, the story continued. Absalom was exiled for several years. When he was allowed back in Jerusalem, he tried to steal his father's throne. At this point, Absalom came back into the room and walked among the children, giving them small gifts and asking about their health. He made wild promises and dispensed hugs and kisses.

At last, Absalom called in his army and drove King David out of Jerusalem. Then Absalom's army chased after David's army and there was a fight to the death. The soldiers in their tunics acted out this battle with much clashing of swords, yelling and wrestling.

When at last Absalom was killed, his army fled, and a messenger went to King David with the news that another son had died. As Dillon watched the teenager who was playing the grieving king, his own heart melted. King David had modeled sin, and his sons had followed his example. "And the wages of sin is death," Dillon muttered to himself as he watched the king weeping over his fallen son. "Dear God, what have I done to my family? To Nettie? And Jeremy?"

King David was led away, tearing at his clothes and hair and wailing loudly, "Oh Absalom, Absalom, my son, my son. If only I could take your place. Oh, if only ... ."

The narrator announced that the skit was over, and the children scattered to their classrooms. The adults followed until only Dillon remained in the fellowship hall. He wanted to find Rilee and offer his help, but his knees were weak and his heartache excruciating. He would rather be dead than cause Jeremy to follow in his footsteps–his adulterous footsteps. And so he sat in his chair, near tears, until Shane approached and said, "Come on, Dillon, let's go to my office and talk."

The pastor's study was small but cozy with comfortable arm chairs. Dillon sank deep into one and let his head rest on the back of the chair. Shane said, "Do you want coffee or something?"

Dillon shook his head. "I couldn't begin to swallow anything. Do you know what's amazing, Shane?" He continued without giving his brother-in-law an opportunity to answer. "I've thought about King David a thousand times since I met Maylea. King David eventually married Bath-sheba and their son became the next king of Israel. I told myself, 'Okay, the first son died, but they got past it, and God forgave him. Sure, David had his problems, but he was king. What king wouldn't have problems? The bottom line is that he was allowed to have Bath-sheba *and* Solomon *and* his kingdom. So he was all right in the long run.' I never once made the connection between David's sins and the actions of his other sons until today."

Dillon suddenly sat up very straight. "I can't let Jeremy be an Amnon. Or an Absalom. What can I do, Shane? How can I help him be a better man than I am?"

Shane sighed. "Do you know how often I hear that question in one form or another? There are no guarantees. We can't control our children any more than God could–or would–control Adam and Eve."

Dillon nodded and slumped back in the chair again. "If only there were a way to take it all back," he moaned.

Shane nodded. "If only ..." He waited for Dillon to continue and when he didn't, Shane asked gently, "Would you tell me about Hawaii? How you met Maylea? How she persuaded you to be unfaithful? How you felt about it afterward?"

Dillon leaned forward and put his face in his hands for a long minute, as he traveled back to that time and place in his memory. Finally, he said, "Maylea was a dancer at the hotel–Windsong Towers. Of course, I was in meetings and workshops all day, but our evenings were free. And Maylea picked me out of the crowd and kind of 'glommed' onto me. I don't know why–there were dozens of men younger and more attractive. She must have taken one look at me and thought, 'There's a sucker! I'll take him.' Anyway, the other guys were so jealous they teased me incessantly. 'Hey! does she know you're a bean counter?' Stuff like that."

"And you were flattered," Shane said with a knowing look.

"Oh yeah. Beyond all reason. I tried to tell myself she was just leading me on, but she kept saying I was *so* special. And I wanted to believe it ..." His voice trailed off.

"Then what?" Shane asked.

"She came to my room one evening and invited herself in. She was wearing white shorts and a floweredy halter, and her hair was soft and loose to her waist. I couldn't breathe, so she took over. Led me to the bed. Undressed me. Undressed herself ..."

Dillon paused and Shane waited silently until he continued. "The next morning was Thursday. I still had two more days of the conference–well, a day and a half–but I packed and went to the airport. I waited at the airport until I could get a plane back to the mainland. Nettie thought I'd made this great sacrifice by coming home early, and I was so ashamed I didn't even want to look at her."

"Then one day Maylea turned up on your doorstep?" Shane asked.

"She flew to Lubbock and came to my office," Dillon said. "When I looked up and saw her, it was the most horrible, thrilling moment of my life."

"How long was she in Lubbock before you told Nettie?" Shane asked.

"Nearly a week."

"So after knowing her less than two weeks, you decided she was worth more than a 15-year marriage?" Shane tried to keep the accusing tone out of his voice, but the very idea astonished him.

Especially since he had always known Dillon to be steady ... stable ... almost stodgy.

Shane was trying desperately to think of a reasonable response to this unreasonable behavior when Dillon asked, "Do you know what Nettie said when I told her Maylea was pregnant with my child?"

Shane shook his head woodenly.

Dillon winced. "She said I was too old to be so stupid. And I still didn't get it."

The phone rang then, and Shane reached for it. After a lengthy conversation, in which he asked several times, "Do you want to talk to him?" but never handed Dillon the receiver, Shane returned the phone to its cradle and reported the conversation to his brother-in-law. "That was your Mother. Nettie's Mother called her and said the police are hounding Nettie beyond endurance for information about you, and Mrs. Jamison wants you back in Lubbock."

Dillon half rose, saying, "I'll start right now."

But Shane stopped him. "Not yet," he said. "The mothers have your life all planned out. Your parents are going to drive your car to Lubbock tomorrow afternoon because your Mom is afraid the highway patrol will stop you and haul you to jail in handcuffs. Meanwhile, you'll fly home in the morning. Your lawyer–Ethan Holmes–will meet you at the airport. After you've answered his questions, he'll deliver you to the police station so they can ask their questions."

"Ethan Holmes?" Dillon asked. "Where'd he come from?"

"Your regular lawyer–Dan somebody–recommended him. Nettie's mother has already paid his retainer. Your parents are going to pay your bail if that's necessary. They'll be staying with Nettie and Jeremy while they're in Lubbock, and you will be staying with Nettie's mother. But Mrs. Jamison says you're going to spend your evenings with Nettie and Jeremy and wait on Nettie hand and foot until the baby comes. And if Nettie miscarries again, her Mom is going to have your head on a platter! Any questions?"

Dillon was shaking his head sadly. "I don't deserve their help. If the police think I killed Maylea, they should lock me up and throw away the key."

Shane shrugged. "We all need help sometimes. Now let me tell you the rest of the story since you won't be here tomorrow."

"The rest of what story?"

"The Life of a King," Shane said. "King David."

Dillon settled back into his chair. "Okay, tell me."

"The students will take up where they left off today, right after Absalom's death. David will moan and wail and grieve. He'll carry on until everybody in the audience is ready to strangle him. Then General Joab will come and ask him why he loves his dead enemy–Abasalom–more than he loves all the living friends who have supported him and fought for him. David will get the message and clean himself up. Then he'll go out to the people and they'll give him a royal welcome. He'll return to his throne and everyone will come and bow before him."

Dillon stirred in his chair and spoke with emotion. "It must have been hard for him, receiving the acceptance of his people after he had failed so miserably."

Shane nodded. "Probably, but he was still king and had responsibilities to fulfill."

Dillon's shoulders drooped, but he nodded.

"Anyway," Shane continued the story, "the grand climax of the week will be the Christmas story. Mary and Joseph went to Bethlehem, the city of *David*, to be taxed, because they were of the house and lineage of *David*. Jesus, the Messiah, was descended from *King David*, and to be in the line of the Messiah was the greatest honor a Jew could have. It is, perhaps, one of the greatest honors of history. So this man named David was a man who sinned greatly, repented deeply, and is remembered today as a man after God's own heart."

When Dillon looked up, there were tears on his cheeks. "I'd like to think," he whispered brokenly, "that I'll be able to find as much courage as David did, enough courage to go on."

Shane's gaze was intense. "You will, Dillon. I believe you will."

The next morning Dillon flew to Lubbock. No one was at the air terminal to meet him except a scrawny kid with tousled brown hair and piercing dark eyes. "Are you Dillon West?" the kid asked, extending his right hand. To Dillon's surprise, it was a deep voice, a man's voice.

Dillon shook the hand with some reluctance. "That's right. Who are you?"

"Ethan Holmes, your defense attorney."

Dillon scrutinized his young attorney. Holmes was wearing a crisp white shirt, open at the neck, and dark dress pants. He did have a few lines around the eyes, and Dillon realized he had the self-assurance of a man. "Are you old enough to be a lawyer?" he asked. He couldn't stop himself.

Holmes' answer was a boyish grin that took up most of his face. "Some day, Mr. West," he predicted, "you will brag to your grandchildren that you were defended by the great Ethan Holmes when I was barely out of law school. In fact, you may be able to tell them it was your case that catapulted me to fame and fortune. And for that, I'd like to thank you in advance."

Holmes seized Dillon's suitcase and led the way to his car. The first stop was Holmes' office where Dillon told his story. Holmes then delivered his client to the police station where Dillon was interrogated, arrested and locked up. But Dillon's incarceration was short. In spite of Lt. Jed Daly's blustering threats, the district attorney could not keep Dillon in jail.

What Lt. Daly did not know was that Nettie had phoned Shelley Jamison, Qiana's mother, and Shelley had spoken to her employer, Judge Franklin Meyer, and Judge Meyer had spoken to the judge presiding over Dillon's case. As a result, a reasonable bail had been set–*un*reasonably low, in Daly's opinion. Dillon's parents had paid the bail, then flown back to Dallas. And Dillon had returned, not only to work, but home. Home with Nettie and Jeremy.

Of course, he slept in Bethany Jamison's guest room every night, but in the evenings he helped Jeremy cook dinner and wash dishes. He played basketball with Jeremy on their own driveway and video games in their own den. On the weekends, he did laundry and mowed lawns. And every evening he and Nettie talked.

His life had regained a peacefulness and fulfillment he thought he had lost forever. Maylea was buried quietly with only a grave side service. Gone was her whiny nagging. Gone was the crushing weight of her mounting debt. Gone the fear of her infidelity, of her murderous intentions. Her car had gone back to the dealer. Her house was sublet. And many of her purchases had been given to charity in exchange for a tax receipt.

But Dillon was ever haunted. Haunted by the image of Maylea's form–improbably tiny and beautiful–lying as still as an ice sculpture on the bed they had shared. Haunted by his betrayal of Nettie. Haunted by the fear of a looming trial. Haunted by the future he may have inflicted on his son. Haunted by the wedding ring Nettie no longer wore.

PART III

The Month of August

Chapter 12

Ethan Holmes shuffled through the stacks of papers on his desk. How was he going to clear his client if he had nothing to work with? In the first place, Dillon was not the father of Maylea's baby–that was a big problem. As far as Detective Jed Daly was concerned, it was the ultimate motive for murder. Then there was the strange life insurance situation, providing a million dollars for Dillon, nothing for Maylea. It seemed proof of guilt to Daly, proof of innocence to Holmes.

As for means and opportunity, Maylea had been killed by a massive dose of morphine placed in capsules stored in the Tuesday compartment of her daily pill planner. What could have been simpler than for her husband to prepare the murderous pills and place them in the compartment for the day of his choosing?

Police had found fingerprints matching Maylea's, Jeremy's and Scot Sanford's on the plastic pill planner. At first, Holmes had been certain Scott was the killer, but neither he nor the police had found any other evidence. Most especially, they could identify no motive–he wasn't even the father of Maylea's baby. No one had cried at Maylea's service, except Scot, and his grief had seemed genuine and deep. Either he was an amazing actor or he had truly cared for her.

And where were the other mourners? Her parents, her siblings? Grandparents? Aunts, uncles? How could Dillon have no address or phone number for even one member of Maylea's family? What had she been hiding from him? Or was he the one hiding something?

Of course, the biggest question of all was, *Who fathered Maylea's baby?*

Holmes sat back in his chair to study on the flood of questions confronting him, and Trolley leapt to the forefront of his mind. She was the key to the case–he had no doubt of it. She had seen something or knew something. He had to find her. No one else was going to look for her. Lt. Daly had long ago moved on to other cases, confident in his belief that Dillon had murdered Maylea.

But *where* would he look? Holmes stewed over this question. Trolley had told Maylea she was from Minnesota, but he wasn't so sure. The police should have found her resume or references in the house, and they'd found nothing. Lt. Daly assumed Dillon had destroyed the papers, but since Holmes was taking the position that Dillon was innocent, there had to be another reason for the missing papers. And the only explanation he could devise was that there had never been any papers. Maylea must have known Trolley and hired her without any employment documents. So maybe Trolley was actually from Hawaii. Maybe he needed to go to Hawaii to search for Trolley.

He sighed and gazed out the window, imagining palm trees, ocean waves, and hula dancers. Did he dare tell his client he needed to go to Hawaii? Dillon, he knew, couldn't pay for the trip, but his parents might. Or Nettie's Mother. He sighed again and picked up the phone. Only one way to find out. He'd pitch it to Dan Ebersole. If the veteran lawyer agreed with him, he'd try Dillon.

It took most of the day to connect with Ebersole, but when he did and had explained why he needed to go to Hawaii, there was no response. Holmes frowned and waited. Finally he said, "Dan, are you there?"

In his most serious trial voice, Ebersole replied, "Yes, I'm here, and I have just realized that you're much too inexperienced to try such a weighty case. I should have kept it myself. I'm sure I can give Mr. West a much better defense than you can, you little whipper-snapper!"

Holmes was too astounded to respond until he heard Ebersole's suppressed laughter. Then he grinned. "Too late. It's my case now. How would you suggest that I proceed?"

"Call your client and tell him you need a co-counsel named Ebersole and we both need to spend two weeks in Hawaii researching his case!" Ebersole was no longer trying to restrain his mirth and laughter rang in every syllable.

"I could do that," Holmes replied, "or I could tell him I need to go alone for *four* weeks!"

After the two lawyers had spent their fantasies, Ebersole said, "If I were you, I'd call a war counsel. Get your client and his family together and tell them what you've told me. Let them be the ones to come up with the bright idea of sending you to Hawaii."

"Then you agree with me?" asked the earnest young lawyer. "A fact-finding trip to Hawaii is the next best step?"

"Sounds to me like it's your only hope for clearing your client," said Ebersole. "The police are through. And who can blame them? Why would they spring for an expensive vacation for one of their employees? Based on their theory of the case, there are no clues, no suspects in Hawaii."

Ethan Holmes was nodding vigorously. "You're right. Thanks, Dan, I'll give Dillon a call right now."

"One more thing, Ethan," Ebersole interjected. "Maybe you'd better include me in this little confab of yours. No charge to your client, but I can nudge things in the right direction if no one else takes the bait."

Holmes agreed readily. "That's very generous of you, Dan, and it will take some pressure off me."

Ethan needn't have worried. The conference had barely begun when Qiana said bluntly, "Someone is going to have to go to Hawaii."

Everyone who had an interest in the case was gathered around a big table in the law firm's conference room–Dillon, Nettie, Jeremy, Nettie's mother, Scot Sanford, Qiana and, of course, Ethan Holmes and Dan Ebersole. All of them turned their eyes on Qiana. Dillon, who had been slouching in his chair, wearing a lost look, jerked to attention. "Go to Hawaii," he repeated. "I don't have that kind of money, Qiana. I don't even know how I'm going to pay my lawyer."

Qiana frowned at him. "I don't recall asking you for money," she said, trying to keep the contempt out of her voice since Jeremy was seated next to Dillon, listening intently to every word.

"Why do you think someone needs to go to Hawaii?" Nettie asked.

Qiana shrugged. "You say Dillon didn't kill Maylea. Nobody seems to think Scot did it. So we have to find someone else–someone with a motive. Where are we going to look except where she came from?"

Dillon frowned. "Do you agree with her, Dan?" he asked.

"I do," said Ebersole. "And I'll be even more specific about it–the somebody you need to locate is that Trolley character. Her disappearing the same day Maylea died is no coincidence. Either she committed the crime herself or she knows who did."

"But she's from Minnesota," Dillon objected. "I'm sure that's what Maylea said."

"If Trolley is from Minnesota, where are her employment papers?" Holmes broke into the conversation impatiently. "References. A resume. An address. Maylea must have gotten some kind of information from her. Where is it?"

Dillon looked confused. "You're saying because we can't find any papers, she's not from Minnesota?"

"Come on, Dillon," said Qiana, as impatient as Holmes, "use your pea brain. Maylea must have already known her. So they must be from the same place."

"Oh," Dillon said, sinking back into his chair. "I get it."

Seeing an embarrassed flush spreading into his face, Nettie said reprovingly, "Qiana!"

"Okay, okay," Qiana said brusquely, adding to no one in particular, "but I wish someone would convince me Dillon didn't do it."

Jeremy leapt to his father's defense before anyone else could speak. "He didn't do it because he wouldn't do such a thing, Aunt Qiana!" His tone was furious and his eyes ablaze.

"Right. I'm sorry, kid," Qiana said, sounding sincere. She turned to Dillon. "I apologize. You don't have a pea brain—I know that because my sister wouldn't have married you if you did."

Dillon shrugged. "I've made some pretty pea-brained moves lately."

Suddenly Qiana flashed a disarming smile at him. "To tell you the truth, I'm getting pretty tired of being mad at you. I'm going to try to get over it."

Dillon offered her a weak smile. "Thanks," he said quietly.

"Okay, we're all in agreement that someone should go to Hawaii, right?" asked Ebersole.

He waited a moment and when no one disagreed, he continued, "So who should that someone be?"

"I'll volunteer," said Qiana. "I could use a vacation in paradise."

Nettie frowned at her sister. "Why you? You've never had any interest in clearing Dillon."

"Well, for one thing, because I'll pay my own way," Qiana said. "And for another, I love you, Sis, no matter how I feel about Dillon. And you believe in him. So ..." She paused, searching for words. "So ... I'm stuck believing in him, too."

Nettie nodded. "I love you, too. Thank you." She brushed the back of her hand across her eyes.

"Look, Qiana, you've made a very generous offer," Bethany Jamison said, "but you're not an investigator. Don't you think we need a professional? Dillon's whole future depends on our finding out who actually killed Maylea."

Qiana nodded. "Sure, that's true, but Thomas Magnum's not in business any more, so who are you gonna' get?"

Ebersole cleared his throat. "I suggest you send Ethan here. He's done enough investigating of his own cases in the past to earn the nickname 'Sherlock.' And while he's not a professional detective, I expect he could do the job. What do you think, Ethan?"

Holmes grinned at Ebersole. "Sure, I'd like the opportunity to go to Hawaii and clear my client, but we have another option. We could contact a detective agency there and let them take on the case." He looked inquiringly at Dillon.

Dillon shrugged. "I can't afford to do either, so I guess I'd better take Qiana up on her offer."

"Yes!" Qiana exulted. Then she glanced at her nephew and added, "And I'll take Jeremy with me if he wants to go."

Jeremy beamed. "Can I, Mom? Please!"

Nettie shook her head. "I don't know, sweetie. We'll have to see."

Jeremy's face fell, but he nodded.

Bethany smiled at Qiana. "How about this, QiQi? I'll foot the bill for Mr. Holmes and Jeremy, too, if he goes. But I really must insist on Mr. Holmes going. I think the stakes are too high not to send a professional."

Qiana grinned. "We don't need him, but the more the merrier. Right, Jeremy?"

Jeremy laughed. "Okay, let him come. We might need some help from Sherlock Holmes before we're through."

Smiles and a lightening of the mood followed Jeremy's remark. Dan Ebersole stood, excused himself with a wink for Ethan Holmes, and left.

After the door had closed behind Ebersole, Holmes changed the subject. "While we're all here, why don't we do a little brainstorming? Dillon and Scott, the two of you are the most likely to have information that would help us. How about if you tell us everything you know about Maylea, and the rest of us will try to pick up some germ of a clue from your information."

Dillon shrugged and said, "Whatever."

Scot Sanford was a tall, muscular university student. He had sandy blond hair and intense blue eyes. He sent a dark look at Maylea's widower, then turned his scowl on Holmes. "Why should I help *him*? How do I know he didn't kill her? In fact, I think he did, and I'd like to rearrange his body parts for the way he treated her." The young man, who was much closer to Maylea's age than Dillon was, glared at the older man, daring him to start something.

Dillon's eyebrows rose. "Really? How did I treat her?"

"You ignored her, begrudged every cent she spent, treated her like a two-year-old."

Dillon's mild manner held, as he asked, "Do you really believe that?"

"Of course I do," Scot sputtered angrily. "I would give everything I own for the opportunity to get you alone for two minutes in a dark alley and teach you a lesson you'll never forget."

Dillon sat up straight for the first time since Scot's tirade had begun, and gazed straight into the younger man's eyes. "Scot, I walked on egg shells every second I spent with that woman, trying to figure out how to please her. I took on new clients and worked longer hours, hoping I would be able to buy her enough designer clothes and jewelry to satisfy her. And while I was at the office with my nose to the grindstone, she was in the sack with you, feeding you fables about me."

Gone was the mild bookkeeper's tone. In its place sounded the deep pain and anguish of four months spent with a woman who had duped him, used him, and drained his assets. "She didn't come to Texas because she loved me," Dillon continued. "She came here to get everything she could from me before she threw me away and moved on to the next sucker. I doubt that she knew how to love anyone except herself. So if you think she loved you, you're as big a fool as I am."

He slumped back in his chair, drained and near tears.

Some of the fire had left Scot's eyes, but it was still smouldering near the surface.

"Okay, guys, let's move on," Holmes said. "Scot, if you really believe ..."

Nettie's voice stopped him. "Mr. Holmes, please ... I'd like to say something to Scot." She turned earnest eyes on the angry young man. "Scot, if you really cared for Maylea–and we all believe you did–then you should want the right person punished for her death. *Also* if Dillon is acquitted, which is pretty likely since he's innocent, then the police may come after me. *Or you.* All of us will benefit if we can find out who actually killed Maylea. Please help us."

Scot's resolve flickered, and he tossed another angry glance at Dillon. "You're an idiot, West. I loved Maylea, but even I can see this one is worth 10 Mayleas."

Dillon didn't look up when he replied dully, "I know."

Scot returned his gaze to Nettie. "Okay, Mrs. West, for *you*, I'll help if I can."

Holmes let out a long, relieved sigh. "Good! Thanks, Scot. Now, what can you tell us about Maylea? Do you have the names or addresses of any family members? Do you know if she ever committed a crime? Do you know of anyone in her past life who hated her or had a grievance against her?"

Scot shifted uncomfortably in his chair. "There are a few things I could tell you, I guess, but I need some kind of guarantee that what I say won't be used against me."

Holmes looked surprised. "Are you saying you've done something illegal?"

"No!" Scot nearly shouted. "I'm not saying that." He paused, took a deep breath and continued in a calmer voice. "But you might think I have if I tell you what Maylea wanted to do."

He had the full attention of everyone at the table. It was Holmes who said quietly, "If you haven't done anything wrong, then you don't have anything to worry about."

Scot nodded. "Okay, she wanted me to help her ..." He paused, took another deep breath, and said, "... be an identity thief." He waited for the gasps and indignant exclamations to subside. "I'm majoring in computer programming at the University, and she said we could be like Robin Hood, taking from the rich and giving to our poor selves."

Holmes had grown very serious. "Do you have the technical skill to actually do that?"

Scot shook his head. "I don't know. I never tried, but I was beginning to think about it. She could be very persuasive." He gave Dillon a meaningful glance.

Nettie looked at Dillon too and saw the shock on his face. "What, Dillon?" she asked.

"One time ..." Dillon began, faltered, then tried again, "... one time she playfully asked me if I'd ever considered embezzling from my clients. She said it would be easy to convince them that it had been a case of identity theft, and they would never suspect me. I was so horrified at the idea that she never mentioned it again, and

I convinced myself she was kidding. That she couldn't possibly be so ..." He searched for the right word and settled on, "... evil."

Holmes turned to Scot in excitement. "Now we're getting somewhere. Scot, had she ever been involved in such a scheme before? Maybe in Hawaii? And maybe she needed to get out of town quick!"

Scot was shaking his head. "If she had, she didn't tell me. All her talk was about what could be done, what she'd read on the internet, how she knew I was smart enough to do *anything*." He glanced at Dillon again. "I kept wondering why I had to be the one taking all the risk. I loved her, but I guess I didn't really trust her."

"And that's why you never tried your hand at hacking?" Holmes asked.

Scot nodded. "Right. But I might have tried if she hadn't died. She was starting to talk about dumping me and finding a guy with some real guts. I was afraid I was going to lose her, and I didn't see how I could live without her."

Nettie was shaking her head in amazement. "You didn't care that she was a ... a criminal?"

"I didn't think of it that way," Scot admitted. "I guess I was too love-blind to have good sense."

"Scot, I'd like to ask you another question," said Holmes. "Did Maylea ever suggest the possibility of ... I mean, did she ever ask you to kill Dillon?"

"Are you kidding?" exclaimed Scot. "That was our favorite fantasy. We'd get rid of Dillon and cash in a big life insurance policy." He paused and took in the severe expressions around the table. "Why? Do you think she was serious?"

"Maybe," said Holmes.

Scot looked genuinely shocked. "Hey now, I would have never killed anyone! I thought it was just a harmless daydream."

Bethany glared at him. "I wonder if there was ever a murder plot in the history of the world that didn't start out as a harmless daydream?"

"Okay!" Scot cried, holding up his hands in surrender. "I think we've established that I'm the bad guy here. So if you're through dumping on me, I'll see myself out." He rose and stalked out, slamming the door behind him.

After a moment of stunned silence, Holmes turned his attention to his client. "Let's go over this one more time, Dillon. You say Maylea worked at the hotel, Windsong Towers. That she was a hula dancer and a waitress, and you don't know anything else about her life in Hawaii. Am I accurate?"

Dillon nodded slowly, trying to remember. "She wouldn't tell me anything about her family, and I didn't have an address for her. She always showed up at the hotel in the evenings. She used to talk about the birds–the beautiful, free birds. She wanted me to stay in Hawaii longer so she could take me bird watching." He shrugged. "That's about all I remember."

Holmes nodded. He could just imagine where Dillon's thoughts had been when the exquisite Hawaiian girl was wooing him. They weren't the kind of thoughts he was about to mention in the presence of his client's son. And ex-wife. "Right," he said. "Well, I've contacted the police and the hotel–they've never heard of Maylea Kanaka. The hotel denies that she ever worked there."

Dillon shook his head helplessly. "It doesn't make sense. She was there every evening, serving drinks and dancing with the other girls."

"We'll need a picture then," said Holmes. "Either she changed her name or she was a poser, trying to gain credibility by giving the impression that she worked at the hotel."

Dillon nodded. "There's a wedding portrait you can take. It's the only one I have, but I don't want it."

"Good!" Holmes exclaimed. "I believe we're on the right track, now." He looked around the group. "Any other comments? Suggestions? Questions?"

"How soon can you leave for Oahu?" Bethany asked. "I'll make the arrangements if you like."

"It may not be easy to find accommodations," Holmes said. "I assume August is a pretty busy tourist month."

Bethany nodded. "Probably, but one of my husband's former partners, Dr. Rand–Greg Rand–has a vacation home on Oahu. I might be able to rent it or borrow it at fairly short notice."

"Whoa, that would be icing on the cake!" said Holmes.

"Bethany, that would be *strategic*!" gasped Qiana, flying out of her chair to give Bethany a hug. "Oh, I hope it works out so we don't have to stay in some stuffy hotel." She turned to Nettie then. "Now, Sis, let's talk about Jeremy. He has been like a *saint* this summer, helping out around the house, mowing the lawn–all that stuff! Now, it's his turn for a little fun. How about it? Can he come to Hawaii with me? We'll call you every day and tell you everything we're doing. Promise."

Nettie looked at Dillon, who smiled gently. "I'd have to agree with Qiana," he said. "Jeremy has earned a vacation."

Chapter 13

Jeremy woke up his first morning on Oahu in a comfortable twin bed. A fragrant breeze wafted through the window, and a ceiling fan kept the balmy air moving. He stretched and sat up, putting his feet on bamboo flooring. Immediately his grandmother's words came to him. Dr Rand, who owned this vacation home, had a caretaker who lived here year round. She made sure the house and grounds were kept up, and she cooked for any family or guests who were in residence. But Mr. Holmes, Qiana, and Jeremy were to be sure they didn't overload her. She wasn't their slave. They were to make their own beds, pick up their clothes, and leave the bathrooms neat and shiny!

Jeremy grinned to himself, remembering the serious expression on Bethany's face as she spoke and the salutes she had received all around. "It's not a joke," Bethany had said sternly. "If I hear that you've behaved like slobs, you're going to pay!"

He rose, pulled the sheet and coverlet into place, then headed for the bathroom. When he arrived in the kitchen, dressed in shorts and a T-shirt, he found Holmes and Qiana enjoying tropical fruit and pineapple juice. "Yummy!" he cried, joining them and reaching for a piece of fruit. "This is the life!"

"Did you make your bed?" Qiana asked accusingly.

Jeremy saluted. "Bed made. Clothes in closet. Bathroom neat and shiny. Did you make your bed?"

Qiana laughed. "Ditto, so I guess we're ready to start." She turned to Holmes. "I presume we're going to start at the Windsong Towers, right chief?"

Holmes grimaced. "How about you both call me Ethan?"

Qiana nodded. "Ethan it is. So did you make your bed, Ethan?"

He grinned, happy to feel like part of the group. "Bed made. Clothes in closet. Bathroom neat and shiny."

"As soon as I finish breakfast, I'm going to email Grandma, and tell her we're being good," Jeremy said.

"And she'll email you back that it's easy the first day. But what about the third day? And the seventh day? And the tenth? And so on," Qiana predicted.

Jeremy laughed and said, "Probably."

At that moment a jolly-looking woman appeared, wearing a wide smile that displayed a couple of missing teeth. "Good morning, Mr. Jeremy," she said. "Did you sleep good?"

"Sure! Like a rock," Jeremy told her. "And I'm just Jeremy, not *Mr.* Jeremy."

The trio had met the plump little woman, who introduced herself as Alana, the previous evening when they arrived. She had shown Ethan to the master suite downstairs, Qiana to a large bedroom on the second floor, and Jeremy to the room next to Qiana's. When Ethan had protested that he didn't deserve the master suite and Qiana should take it, she said, "No way. You're in charge here, so you take the boss's room. Bethany made it clear that you're running the show."

Alana had smiled happily at the little group, waiting for them to settle the issue. Then she led them into the kitchen where she served them fresh fruit and sandwiches. Her bubbly good humor made Qiana think Alana was happiest when she had someone in the house to care for. And this morning, serving them breakfast, she was still full of smiles and good cheer.

Jeremy took a huge bite of papaya and yummed contentedly. He had eyed the strange fruit with suspicion the previous evening. Now it was his favorite food. "Is this the best food in the world or is it being in Hawaii that makes it taste so good?" he asked.

Alana beamed at him. "Ours is the best food in the world," she said. Then she got down to business. "Now, Jeremy, my grandchildren–they wait to hear if you want to go boogie boarding today. You tell me. I call them."

"Boogie boarding?" Qiana asked. "What's that?"

"It is like surfing, only different," Alana said. "It is riding the ocean!"

Qiana looked alarmed. "I don't know about that," she said. "Have you ever gone boogie boarding or surfing?" she asked Jeremy.

He gave her an exasperated look. "You know I haven't. Look where I live. But I can do it. I know I can, Aunt Qiana. Please, let me."

Qiana looked at Alana. "How dangerous is it, Alana? My sister will kill me if anything happens to Jeremy." Glancing at her nephew, she added, "And I'll die of a broken heart."

Alana was shaking her head. "No danger. No danger," she insisted. "My grandchildren–they ride the ocean like the great whales. And they teach Jeremy, too. Besides, ocean is calm in summer–best time to learn."

With trepidation, Qiana gave her consent and Alana went to the kitchen to phone her grandchildren. They would pick up Jeremy on their way to the beach.

"What about us?" Qiana asked Ethan. "Shall we head straight for Windsong Towers?"

Ethan shook his head. "We may waste our time if we go there so early in the day. Dillon said he only saw Maylea at the hotel in the evenings. I was planning to go to some police stations this morning and see if anyone recognizes Maylea's picture."

Qiana nodded. "Okay. Do you mind if I tag along?"

Ethan smiled. "I was hoping you would."

"And Windsong Towers this evening?" Qiana asked.

"I think so," Ethan replied. "Maybe we can get Alana to make a dinner reservation for us at about ... well, what time do you think?"

"We should get there early before the staff gets too busy," said Qiana. "But then we would be ready to eat pretty early."

Ethan shrugged. "What time?"

"Is 5:00 too early?" Qiana asked.

"Not for me," said Ethan. "I can eat any time." Alana returned from the kitchen then, and he asked her, "Can you get a dinner reservation for us at Windsong Towers for 5:00 tonight?"

Alana gave him a puzzled look. "You eat as early as 5:00, you not need reservation."

"Probably not," Ethan agreed, "but just to be safe, would you do it for us?"

"Of course," said Alana. "I write it down. Then I not forget."

"Okay, make it for four," Ethan instructed. "We want you to come with us. We might need your help."

Alana's hand went to her heart. "Me?! Windsong Towers very expensive. I ... I ..."

"It's okay," said Ethan. "I'm paying. And we want you to come with us."

Alana's face showed her uncertainty, so he added, "It's business. We're looking for the old woman we told you about last night, remember?"

Alana nodded vigorously. "I help. Today I ask all my friends about this Trolley," she said.

"Thank you," said Ethan brightening. "We'll be grateful for your help. And tonight, if you're with us at Windsong Towers, you may think of something we wouldn't. So we want you to come with us."

Alana looked questioningly at Qiana. "Is it okay?" she asked.

"Of course," said Qiana. "You and I–we'll wear something pretty and make all the men wish they knew us."

Alana laughed nervously, but she looked pleased. Qiana was certain she was already deciding what to wear.

Alana's grandchildren arrived in a double-cab pickup with much shouting and tooting of the horn. Looking disgusted, Alana marched outside. Jeremy had dashed upstairs to put on his swimsuit, but Ethan and Qiana could hear Alana yelling at her grandchildren to come inside and put on some manners! Then a laughing, rollicking bunch of youngsters tumbled into the dining room. There were seven of them, ranging in age from young teens to early 20s, all with dark hair and deep tans.

Alana lined them up and introduced them, trying in vain to hide her pride. After she had pronounced seven foreign-sounding names, she returned to the tallest, a handsome young man. "This one," she said, "is oldest. He is going to be sure your Jeremy have good time and nobody get hurt. Am I right, Paulo?"

The tall, lean young man kissed his grandmother resoundingly on her cheek. "Of course you're right," he said. Then he turned to Qiana. "I promise to bring Jeremy back to you all in one piece."

Gazing into his earnest, dark eyes, Qiana thought she might believe him if he said the Earth was flat. "Thank you, Paulo," she said. "I believe you will."

Suddenly Jeremy was part of the milling crowd of youngsters, meeting them and repeating their names. Then before Qiana could warn him about sharks and sun burn more than twice, they were gone. The whole bunch of them had piled into the pickup, some seated in the back, and waved farewell to the adults who had followed them as far as the porch. Then the truck had pulled away with Paulo at the wheel.

Qiana looked at Ethan in dismay. "I hope Jeremy doesn't come back burned to a crisp. It'll ruin his whole trip if he does."

"Does he have suntan lotion with him?" Ethan asked.

"He has it, but he hates to wear it," Qiana said, gazing at the empty street.

"Never you mind," Alana said, taking Qiana's arm and leading her back to the dining room. "Paulo is going to *make* him put it on. Paulo is going to rub Jeremy down with gel. The gel–it last better in ocean."

Qiana looked hopeful. "Are you sure?"

"Yes," said Alana dismissively. "Now, you two. When do you want to eat lunch? I have food ready any time you say."

"No, don't fix our lunch," said Ethan. "We won't have time to come back here, so we'll find a restaurant when we get hungry."

Alana looked upset. "Restaurants expensive," she said. "I make lunch for you to take."

Ethan started to refuse, but Qiana didn't give him the chance. "Oh Ethan, what a good idea! Then we can eat anywhere we want to–maybe a picnic on the beach. Alana, you are such a sweetheart!"

Alana beamed, Ethan shrugged, and it was decided.

It was a long, disappointing day for Qiana and Ethan. Driving the compact car they had rented at the airport when they arrived, they visited a police station in every district on Oahu. They showed copies of Maylea's photo over and over again. Each time the result was the same. "Without the right name, how can we help?"

"Yes, I understand," Ethan said at each station, "but look on the back–I've written 'Maylea Kanaka'. That's the name we knew her by. Please keep the picture where you can find it quick, and when I have the right name, I'll phone you. Would you do that for us?"

At this point, he was content to deal with secretaries and receptionists, who were unfailingly polite and concerned. "When will you know the right name?" they asked.

"Maybe I'll find out tonight," Ethan said. "I *hope* I'll find out tonight. Then I'll call you tomorrow. Will you help?"

They were all eager to help the young lawyer from the mainland and promised to get the photo to the proper detective as soon as he let them know the name of the beautiful girl in the picture. Then Qiana would pipe up–unable to restrain herself–and ask if they'd ever heard of an old woman called Trolley.

"Trolley who?"

Qiana would shake her head and shrug. Then the receptionist would shake her head and shrug.

The only bright spot in the day was eating Alana's picnic lunch in a tropical paradise. Qiana had spotted the little park just after noon and Ethan had darted in front of oncoming traffic to turn left into the main drive. They found a picnic table and spread out fried chicken, fruit and generous slices of homemade bread.

"Everything is so beautiful I can hardly believe it's real," Qiana said, gazing around at the lush grass and the profusion of brilliant flowers as they ate. Palm trees shaded their picnic table, and a gentle breeze cooled them without scattering their paper plates and napkins. "The state of Hawaii must spend a fortune keeping their public areas perfect. There aren't even any ants in sight!"

Ethan nodded, "Well, tourism is probably their most important industry. I'm sure it's no accident that we all think of Hawaii as a paradise."

Before Qiana could respond, her cell phone rang. It was Jeremy. "I'm still alive," he reported. "I thought you might like to know."

"Are you having fun?" Qiana asked.

"The most fun in the whole world," Jeremy said. "Where are you?"

"In some park, eating a picnic lunch Alana packed for us. Where are you?"

"At the beach eating a locomotive," Jeremy said.

"Eating a what?" Qiana asked.

"Not a locomotive," yelled a voice in the background. "Locomoco."

"Did you hear?" asked Jeremy. "That was Kimo–Jimmy. He's 13 too, and he wants me to go home with him and play some b-ball when we leave the beach. Is it okay?"

"Our reservation at Windsong Towers is at 5:00, but Ethan and I want to get there earlier so we can talk to the office staff. What time will you be back at the house?"

There was a pause and confused murmuring, as Jeremy consulted with someone on his end of the conversation. After a few minutes, he said, "How about if I meet you at the restaurant? Jimmy says he can lend me some clothes."

"Okay, and invite Jimmy to eat with us if you want to," Qiana said. "That way you won't be stuck with a bunch of old people."

"You're not old, Aunt Qiana," Jeremy said. "But it'd be great if he'll come. He's a lot of fun. You're gonna' like him too."

Qiana was smiling broadly as she disconnected. She usually smiled when she talked to Jeremy. "Jeremy says he's eating a locomotive," she told Ethan. "But Kimo–aka Jimmy–says he's eating locomoco, or something like that."

She touched a couple of buttons on her cell phone. "Hang on a minute," she said. "I need to get Alana to change our reservation at Windsong Towers to five, instead of four, in case Jimmy comes."

After she talked to Alana, praising the picnic lunch and explaining about Jimmy, she smiled at Ethan. "Done."

"You put Alana in your phone book?" he asked. "I never even thought of it."

"Sure. I didn't want to have to memorize the number or keep up with a scrap of paper," Qiana said.

"You're one smart cookie," he said with admiration.

"Why thank you, Mr. Lawyer. I hope you're pretty bright yourself since you're in charge of my brother-in-law's case."

"Your brother-in-law?" Ethan asked. "Is that how you think of him? Even after the divorce?"

Qiana sighed. "They were married a long time. And I really believed in him–believed he wasn't like other men, believed that he was capable of being faithful. So when he destroyed my sister's life, I felt betrayed. Maybe I felt as betrayed as she did."

She rubbed at the tear that was forming in her left eye and hurried on. "But even when I was so furious with him, he still felt like family."

Ethan studied her carefully. "So there's no chance–not even the slightest possibility–that you killed Maylea and framed Dillon for the murder?"

Qiana's eyes opened wide. "You jerk! Where did you get an idea like that?"

Ethan shrugged. "Nettie is terrified of learning the truth. She's afraid you killed Maylea."

"Did she tell you that?" gasped Qiana.

Ethan shook his head. "No, but I can feel it. She's convinced Dillon didn't do it. And she has a gut feeling Scot didn't do it because ... where's his motive? So that leaves you."

Qiana suddenly felt too weak to sit up. She braced herself on the picnic table. "She asked me if I did it. I thought she believed me when I said I didn't."

"I'm sure she wanted to believe you," said Ethan. "But Maylea's dead. Somebody killed her, somebody with a motive."

"And I'm the only one with a motive?" Qiana asked.

"No, Dillon had a motive ..." Ethan's voice trailed off.

"So she had to choose between Dillon and me?"

"She had to choose between you and the father of her children. It's not about you and Dillon so much. It's about Jeremy and the baby she's carrying–she can't bear the thought of their father spending the rest of his life in prison."

Qiana took a deep breath. "Well, when you put it that way, I guess I can see her point."

"You're really close to your sister, aren't you?" Ethan asked.

"Actually, Nettie is my half-sister," Qiana said, "but Dad always called us his twins because we were born four days apart."

"And do you feel like twins?" he asked.

Qiana considered the question a moment before she said, "I didn't when we were growing up because we didn't live in the same house. But now–yeah, I do feel that close to her. We're always together, and we help each other with our businesses. Plus, Jeremy is practically my best bud."

Ethan gave her a sad smile. "I'm jealous of you. I have a half-brother who hates me. Of course, he's four years older, but he could have been my hero if he hadn't been so busy hating me."

"Why does he hate you?"

"Because my father left his mother to marry my mother when he was five. Of course, I was already a year old at the time. And Dad left *us* when I was four, so he had a father longer than I did."

"And his mother hated you and your mother, right?" asked Qiana. "That's where the poison came from."

Ethan nodded. "Probably."

"So where's your Dad now?"

Ethan shrugged. He looked sad and worn as he spoke. "I barely remember him. If it weren't for photos, I doubt I would know what he looks like–or what he used to look like. He moved to Houston when he divorced my mother."

"And he's still there?"

"I don't know." Ethan's voice sounded stronger and Qiana could see by the determined set of his jaw that he was putting the past behind him. "He set up bank accounts to provide child support for my mother and his other ex-wife so he wouldn't have to stay in contact with us. He didn't want to have anything to do with us–didn't want our existence to interfere with his new life."

He looked at Qiana. "What about you? Did you have a *real* father?"

She nodded, feeling even more grateful than ususal for Phillip Jamison. "He was always part of my life. I always knew he loved me, and ..." She paused a moment to consider her words. "... after awhile my mother realized she was happier living on alimony than she had been when she was married to him. So she taught me to love and respect him."

"Your Dad had to pay alimony?" Ethan asked, in amazement. "In Texas? For how long?"

"He didn't *have* to," Qiana said. "He chose to."

In the silence that followed her statement, both looked wistful. Ethan's was an envious wistfulness. Qiana's was nostalgic. She missed Phillip Jamison almost more than she could bear.

It was about 4:00 o'clock when Ethan, Qiana, and Alana walked into the lobby of the Windsong Towers hotel. Ethan was wearing a light blue, short-sleeved dress shirt and navy-blue slacks. Qiana had donned a simple, royal blue shift that clung to her slender figure. And Alana was decked out in a multi-colored floral muumuu, complete with ruffles and bows.

The lines at the check-in desk were formidable. Ethan sighed. "I guess we'll have to wait our turn with everyone else," he said.

Qiana and Alana followed him to the shortest line, which soon proved to be the slowest-moving. As they waited, trying valiantly to hide their impatience, a middle-aged Hawaiian man walked behind the desk toward an inner office. Seeing him, Alana yelled, "Aloha!" loudly and waved. Turning, he tried to determine who had hailed him. Alana waved again, snatched the photo of Maylea from Dillon's hand, and darted behind the desk.

Ethan and Qiana could hear her speaking to him in a strange-sounding language that they later learned is called "pidgin." Looking earnest and talking rapidly, she led him into his own office. Five minutes later, she rejoined them. They were still in line behind the same two groups of tourists, listening wearily to an argument between the desk clerk and a well-dressed woman who was determined to have a room with an ocean view.

"Come on," Alana beckoned.

Grinning in delight, Qiana and Ethan followed her away from the crowd at the desk. "Her name Lin Choi," Alana explained. "She never work for hotel, but sometimes she help out girls when they need to go somewhere."

"Like a substitute?" Qiana asked.

"Yes!" Alana bobbed her head up and down. "Like a substitute."

"Did the hotel pay her when she substituted?" Ethan asked.

"No. Girl pay her–the one who need her. Hotel only know her name. No more." Alana turned the photo over so Ethan and Qiana could see that she had written "Lin Choi" on the back.

"Alana, you're a marvel!" cried Qiana. "And Ethan is a genius for asking you to come with us." She hugged Alana and beamed at Ethan.

"I guess our next stop should be the bar," said Ethan. "Maybe we can find a waitress who knew Maylea or Lin or whoever she was." He led the way into a darkened room off the dining room. As soon as they were seated and a pretty young waitress appeared to take their order, he held out the photo and asked, "Have you ever seen this girl?"

The waitress took the photo and held it toward the nearest light. Suddenly she started and dropped the picture as if it had burned her hand. "Lin Choi," she said, as Ethan leaned over to retrieve the photo. "Why do you have a picture of Lin?"

"We're trying to find someone who knew her," Qiana explained. "Were you a close friend of hers?"

"Oh no! I know her name–that's all! What would you like to drink?" She was noticeably nervous, glancing around as if someone might hear her talking about Lin Choi and be angry with her.

"You order for me," Ethan said to Alana. "Something fruity and exotic."

"Me too," Qiana agreed.

Alana nodded. "I know just the thing," she said. She gave the order and the waitress hurried off, obviously relieved to be escaping.

"What do you make of that?" Ethan asked, frowning. "She acted like Maylea was a member of the mafia."

Qiana shook her head. "It looks like Maylea wasn't any more popular here than she was in Lubbock!"

"Not with women, anyway," Ethan said.

When the waitress returned, she brought three cool glasses, full of Hawaiian fruit and flavor. As she set them in front of her customers, Ethan said, "Please, ma'am, would you tell us which waitress at this hotel was closest to Mayl ... I mean, Lin Choi? It really is very important."

The young woman straightened and fastened her eyes on Ethan. "Why is it very important?"

"Well, because Lin is dead and her husband has been accused of murdering her. I'm his lawyer, and I'm trying to find out who actually killed her."

The waitress gasped and covered her mouth at the word "dead." "Lin Choi is dead?" she asked. "Lin Choi had a husband?"

"That's right," said Ethan.

The waitress turned wide eyes on the two women, and they nodded solemnly. "It's true," Qiana said. "Her husband was my brother-in-law until Lin came along and stole him from my sister."

The waitress nodded. "She wouldn't care if he was married. She would steal *anything* from *anybody*!"

"Did she steal something from you?" Ethan asked.

But the timid young woman was backing away. "I can't say more. It's all I know." And she was gone. Five minutes later a different waitress appeared to see if they wanted their drinks refreshed.

"What happened to the other waitress?" Ethan asked. "I hope we didn't upset her."

"You upset her very much, and she came to get me," said their current waitress. She slid into an empty chair at the table and said, "My name is Kiana."

"No it's not!" gasped Qiana. "My name is Qiana."

Kiana with a "K," was older than the first waitress, probably 10 years older and near Qiana's age. She studied Qiana with a "Q," who had dark hair, but skin that was lighter than most of the natives. "Are you Hawaiian?" she asked.

"No, I'm Texan," said Qiana.

"But you have a Hawaiian name?"

"Not really. Qiana is a type of fabric–it's soft and shiny and yummy-feeling. My Mom's name is Chantilly Lace, so she named me Qiana Silk. Of course, she's called Shelley, but I'm called Qiana."

"I think," Alana interjected, "that the spelling of your names is not the same. The Hawaiian Kiana is spelled with a 'K.' And you," she turned to Qiana, "how do you spell your name?"

"Oh, I see," said Qiana. "My name is spelled with a 'Q,' so it's not exactly the same name, after all."

"But it is pronounced the same," said Alana.

Qiana and Kiana smiled at each other companionably. "You're the only person I've ever met who almost had the same name as mine," Qiana said.

"If you move to Hawaii," said Kiana, "you may meet many Kianas. It means, I think, Diana in English."

"Hawaii would be a beautiful place to live!" Qiana said, enthusiasm shining in her eyes. "But my family is in Texas, so I'll probably stay there."

Kiana nodded. "Then you must come back often on vacation." Her tone was warm and inviting, but it became businesslike, as she turned to Ethan and said, "Now, about Lin Choi. I perhaps knew her best. I'm older than most of the girls, so I try to give them good advice for their lives–sometimes they call me their number two mama. What is it you want to know about Lin? Is she really dead?"

"Yes, she died in June. Someone put poison in one of her capsules. Did you know about her capsules?"

"Of course." Kiana's eyes were wide. "We all knew about her capsules. She tried to sell them to everyone. She said they were like a miracle–that if we would take them every day, they would keep us young."

"And did she have many customers?" Ethan asked.

Kiana smiled. "Not so many. My girls are already young. And she wasn't allowed to sell them to our guests."

"Did you know that she made her own capsules?" Qiana asked.

Kiana nodded. "Everyone knew. Lin Choi talked a lot when she had something to sell."

Ethan and Qiana exchanged a meaningful glance. Many more people knew about Maylea's capsules here on Oahu than in Texas. One of them could have followed her to Lubbock, knowing exactly how to kill her. It wouldn't have been hard to find her supplies–Jeremy said she kept everything in a bureau drawer.

Kiana, observing this exchange, said, "Why are you here asking about Lin Choi?"

"I am the lawyer for Lin's husband. He has been accused of murdering her, so I'm trying to find out more about her. I'm trying to find out who *really* killed her," said Ethan.

"Mmm, her husband ..." Kiana repeated with a frown.

"You sound surprised that she had a husband," said Qiana. "She wasn't already married, was she?"

"Oh no!" said Kiana. "She wasn't married, but she said she would never marry unless ..."

"Unless what?" Ethan prodded gently.

Kiana's dark eyes came up to meet his. "Unless she needed to leave Waikiki in a hurry. Or unless she needed to change her name in a hurry. Or some kind of emergency like that."

Ethan studied her a moment. "I thought you were going to say she would never marry unless she met a man who was filthy rich."

"Filthy rich *and* very old," Kiana agreed.

"Very old?" Qiana repeated with a shiver. "So he would die soon?"

Kiana nodded. "Yes. Lin always wanted her way. And husbands sometimes don't let you have your way."

"Okay," Qiana said, "let me see if I've got this straight. Maylea–or Lin–showed up one day at my brother-in-law's office, claiming to be pregnant. Do you think she came to Lubbock like that because she was in some kind of trouble here?"

Kiana looked sad. "I think–probably yes. I tried to help her be a better person, but she was a maylea, a wildflower. And she didn't want to be a good person."

"Maylea means wildflower?" Ethan asked.

Kiana shrugged. "So I've heard. My niece is named Maylea, and her Mother, who is from the mainland, tells me the name means wildflower. I think she found it on the internet."

"I don't understand," said Qiana. "Is 'maylea' the Hawaiian word for wildflower?"

"As far as I know," said Kiana, "there is no Hawaiian word for wildflower."

"Then I wonder where the word 'maylea' came from," said Qiana.

Kiana shook her head. "I have no idea."

"Anyway she chose to use the name 'Maylea'," Qiana observed. "She must have been proud of her wildness, as well as her beauty."

"Yes, I believe she was," Kiana agreed.

"Dillon, my brother-in-law, is a gentle, sensible man," said Qiana. "I don't know how Maylea could have made him act like such a fool."

Kiana released an unhappy sigh. "Lin was so beautiful and so vivacious–I believe she fooled many men who were very smart. But they weren't smart when they were with her."

"Do you have any idea what kind of trouble she was in that caused her to leave here so suddenly?" Ethan asked.

"I could make a few guesses," said Kiana, "but I don't *know*. All I can say is that one day she was here, just like always. Then we never saw her again."

"When was the last time you saw her?"

Kiana shrugged. "I believe it was April. Early April."

Ethan looked at Qiana and she nodded. "She must have come straight to Texas from Oahu. *And* when Dillon was here in February, she told him her name was Maylea Kanaka, so she must have known even then that she was going to change her name and leave."

Ethan gazed at the waitress pleadingly. "I know you're very busy, Kiana, but could you possibly stay long enough to tell us everything you know about Lin Choi? Maybe you'll say something that will help us."

Kiana leaned back in her chair and smiled. "I can stay a few more minutes," she said, "but I don't know if I can say anything that will help you." She paused, eyes closed, remembering, then began. "Lin came to us last summer. At first, she was like a vapor, here for a few moments, then gone. She would dance on the beach with our hula girls–dance as if she were one of them. Then we wouldn't see her again for two or three days."

"How did she know the dances?" Qiana asked.

"I think she must have been watching and learning," said Kiana. "Perhaps she would dance the parts she knew, then drop away to watch and learn another part. Anyway, after about two months, she could dance as well as any of them. And when we were terribly busy, she would take orders and bring drinks to our guests.

"One evening, one of my girls had a family emergency and needed to leave early. She asked Lin to fill in for her, and Lin did. After that, she filled in many nights but she often came to dance and help, even when she wasn't being paid."

"Why didn't she apply for a job with the hotel?" Qiana asked.

Kiana shook her head. "I begged her to do that. I said it was foolish that she worked so many, many nights without pay. But she always refused. She said she had a day job, and it was fun to come here at night to dance and see all the handsome men. She said 'handsome,' but I think now she was looking for rich men."

"You know, I've been thinking about that," said Ethan. "This is a beautiful, luxurious hotel, but it's not as expensive as some of the others. Why wouldn't Lin Choi work her way into one of the really expensive places?"

Kiana gave him a sad smile. "Perhaps it is because very wealthy people are more careful. They know someone may try to take advantage of them, and so they guard themselves."

Ethan nodded. "I bet you're right. And Lin knew that."

Qiana spoke up. "Do you know what Lin's day job was?"

Kiana shook her head. "About that she wouldn't give even a hint." She glanced at her watch and rose. "I must go. I hope you find what you're looking for." Then with a soft, "Aloha," she was gone.

For several minutes, Ethan, Qiana, and Alana sat in silence, trying to digest what they had heard–trying to understand the enchanting, elusive "wildflower" who had complicated so many lives. Finally Ethan said, "Why don't we go into the restaurant? It's almost 5:00."

He paid the tab and escorted the two women into the dining room, which adjoined the bar. In a few minutes they were seated again, studying menus that listed foods both strange and familiar. Two more menus were waiting for Jeremy and Kimo.

"I'm glad they serve some dishes from the mainland here," Ethan observed. "I'm in the mood for a big, juicy steak." Looking up he saw Alana's deep concentration as she studied the menu. "Now, you ladies order anything you want," he instructed, "even if it's the most expensive item on the menu. I'm paying and it's a small price for such delightful company."

Qiana wrinkled her nose at him. "Well, you're certainly full of it tonight, aren't you?"

He laughed. "I'm serious. You are the two loveliest women in this room and I am, of all men, most fortunate."

Qiana shook her head and turned to Alana. "So, Alana, what do you recommend?"

"My favorite is mahi-mahi with fruit salsa," Alana said, pointing to her menu.

Qiana found the entry, nodded and said, "Sounds heavenly. I'll try it." She looked at Ethan. "You're not really going to eat steak, are you? You can eat steak in Texas any day."

Ethan opened his mouth to answer, but another beautiful young woman with flowing black hair was standing at his elbow. Like the other waitresses, she was wearing a lei, a halter top, and a full, flowing skirt. Her eyes were riveted to the picture of Dillon and Maylea.

"Do you remember Lin Choi?" Ethan asked when he saw the expression on her face.

The waitress nodded, taking her eyes off the photo and transferring them to Ethan. "I'm Julie," she said. "Kiana told me that you want to know about Lin."

"Yes, we do," said Ethan.

Julie gave the photo another angry glare. "Lin sold me some jewelry—a diamond and sapphire earring and necklace set. She said it was worth $5,000, but she would sell it to me for $2,500. The jeweler said it was worth *at least* $5,000, so I bought it. Then, after Lin disappeared, the police came. They said the jewelry was bought with a fake credit card, and I would have to pay $8,000 if I wanted to keep it."

Her lip quivered and her voice broke. "I had to give the earrings and necklace back, but nobody gave me my $2,500 back."

"How awful," Qiana cried sympathetically.

Julie gave her the merest glance before turning back to Ethan. "Now Kiana says Lin is dead. Is this true?"

Ethan nodded. "I'm afraid so."

Tears were trickling down Julie's cheeks. "If Lin is dead, I'll never get my money back. I was always hoping they would find her and make her pay me."

She turned to leave, but Ethan touched her arm. "Please wait, Julie. Did Lin ever sell you anything else?"

Julie brushed her tears away. "Not me, but sometimes she had electronic equipment she wanted to sell cheap, and some of the other girls bought things from her."

"Like what?"

"Oh, a DVD player or an MP3 player ... um ... a digital camera once. Things like that."

"Did she say where she got those things?" Ethan asked.

"She said she had her own business. She had a way to locate stores that were overstocked in something. So she would buy a thing cheap, then resell it for just a little profit. If she sold enough things, she said she could make a big profit. It was the same way she had my jewelry." Julie's eyes were downcast as she related this information.

"And do you believe that's really how she got the things she sold?" Ethan asked.

"I did then," Julie mumbled.

"What do you believe now?"

Julie's hands were trembling and she clasped them together tightly. "Maybe they were stolen," she whispered. Then she looked up, tried to smile, and said, "I have to go now."

Before Ethan, Qiana, or Alana could try to stop her, Jeremy and Kimo descended on them with youthful exuberance. "Oh man, Aunt Qiana, I had so much fun!" Jeremy cried. "I don't ever want to leave Oahu!"

Kimo went to give his grandmother a kiss. Then he stood in the crook of her arm with his arm around her neck, as he said, "Jeremy is going to practice basketball with me. Maybe I can make the team next year. He's really good, Tutu!"

"I'm good because my Dad plays with me," Jeremy explained to Alana.

Alana smiled at her grandson. "Kimo's Dad is very busy man." Then she said to Qiana, "Kimo is my doctor's grandson."

Qiana had learned that when Alana said "my doctor," she was referring to Dr. Gregory Rand, her employer. "You mean one of your children married one of Dr. Rand's children?" she asked in surprise.

"Yes, my daughter Kalea is married to Dr. Rand's son–Greg, Jr. They fall in love as children and never stop loving," Alana said.

"Isn't Greg Jr. a cardiac surgeon like his father?" Qiana asked.

Jeremy and Kimo had taken their seats and begun looking through their menus, but Kimo looked up to answer for his grandmother. "My Dad is a cardiac surgeon *and* a cardiologist. He is the best doctor in the world."

Qiana smiled at him. "Well, since my Dad died last April, I won't argue with you."

Kimo looked apologetic. "I am sorry about your father," he said.

"Me too," said Qiana. "But mostly I'm glad I got to have him as my father. He was a cardiac surgeon, too. He and your grandfather were partners."

Kimo gave her a lovely smile. "Well, then he must have been a great surgeon, just like my Dad."

Qiana nodded proudly. "Yes, he was."

"You're talking about my *grandfather*," Jeremy said, looking up from his menu. He studied Kimo with new interest. "That means our grandfathers were partners."

"No wonder you ride the waves like a fish!" Kimo exclaimed, turning to Qiana. "Jeremy is a natural. Paulo showed him what to do and took him out into the ocean and Jeremy rode the board like he was born on it!"

Qiana wasn't sure how their having grandfathers in partnership explained Jeremy's prowess on the waves, but she didn't ask. Jeremy, already excited and buoyed by Kimo's praise, began explaining how the boogie board floated and he was attached to it by a tether. "So I couldn't drown," he said. "You didn't need to worry about me, at all!"

"And I see you didn't burn to a crisp, so you must have used your suntan lotion," Qiana said.

Jeremy nodded. "Paulo made me use some kind of jelly stuff. And he smeared some white goop on my nose. But I didn't mind. Paulo's tight!"

"And did you see any sharks?" Qiana asked.

"Naw, not even one." Jeremy looked disappointed.

"What about jellyfish?" Qiana asked. "I started worrying about them after you left."

"They won't be here for more than a week," Kimo said.

Qiana looked surprised. "How do you know that?"

"They come a little more than a week after the full moon. And the moon won't be full until Thursday," he said.

Qiana looked at Alana, who nodded and shrugged.

"Well, that's good to know," said Qiana doubtfully.

"Oh, we watch out for them all the time," said Kimo. "And the lifeguards put up warning signs as soon as they're spotted." He gazed earnestly at Qiana. "We always check the internet before we go to the beach, to see where the ocean is the best."

Qiana was impressed. She said to Jeremy, "Well, I guess we're the lucky ones to have made such good friends." Then she turned to Kimo. "I already feel a lot safer knowing how smart you are."

Kimo looked both pleased and embarrassed. He ducked his head to study the menu.

"May I have a hamburger?" Jeremy asked. "Do you think they have hamburgers here? I'm starved."

"Hey, me too," Kimo said, closing his menu. "Is it all right, Tutu?" he asked, not knowing who was paying for the meal or how much he was allowed to spend.

Alana looked at Ethan who said, "You order anything you want, son."

"Oh wait!" cried Qiana. "I should pay for the boys. I invited them." She turned to Kimo. "You eat anything you want."

Ethan gave her an exasperated look. "Would you mind your own business? This is my night, and it's my treat. Got it?"

Qiana shrugged and said, "Whatever." But she gave Ethan a quick grin of thanks.

The food was delicious and Jeremy expressed again his opinion that everything tasted better in Hawaii. As they ate, they discussed the activities of the day and the possibilities for the next day. Jeremy wanted to go snorkeling, but Qiana wanted to go too, and she wasn't ready to abandon the search for Trolley. So Kimo suggested that he and Jeremy pack a lunch and go hiking. Qiana looked wistful at the thought, but she said nothing.

"You don't have to come with me, you know," Ethan told her. "I'm here to work, but you're on vacation. You should go hike with them if you want or go snorkeling before the jellyfish get any closer."

Qiana gazed at him thoughtfully and realized that, as much as she wanted to see every inch of Oahu, she also wanted to be with Ethan. "I think," she said slowly, "that I'll stick with you at least one more day. Then we'll see."

She looked at Kimo then. "Unless we're taking up too much of your time, Jimmy. What do you usually do in the summer?"

Kimo gave her an impish grin. "Play with Tutu's guests. My kupuna kane, my grandfather, sends people over here all the time to use his house. And if it's summer and if they have kids, my sister and my cousins and I play with them. We take them wherever they want to go to have a good time."

Ethan smiled. "In a few years you'll be making a fortune as a tour guide."

Kimo laughed. "As soon as we can afford a helicopter, my cousin Kaniela–Danny–and I are going to open our own business."

"Unless you become a doctor like your father," said Alana.

Kimo shook his head. "Doctors work too hard. I want to have fun."

Alana smiled. "Your Dad said the same thing when he was 13 years old."

"Well, if I become a doctor, I'm not going to be a surgeon," Kimo said. "I don't want to cut people up." He glanced at his grandmother. "Is that what Dad said, too?"

She shook her head. "No, he never said that."

Kimo breathed a sigh of relief, then glanced around the table. "Hey, are we going to stay and see the hula show tonight?"

"We wouldn't miss it!" said Ethan. "But I wonder when it's going to start."

"It is at sunset on the beach," Alana supplied. "I ask when I call for reservations."

"What time is sunset?" Qiana asked, consulting her watch.

"About 35 minutes past 6:00," said Alana.

After they ate, and while they waited for sunset, Kimo and Jimmy scavenged the beach, examining shells and other treasures that had washed ashore. But it wasn't long before Kimo dashed back to the hotel and returned with a big canvas garbage bag. He and Jeremy continued their treasure hunt, but when they found trash, they tossed it into the bag.

Qiana, Ethan and Alana were strolling the beach and keeping an eye on the boys. Now Qiana turned to Alana in amazement. "How old did you say Kimo is?" she asked.

Alana watched her grandson with proud eyes. "Kimo 13, like your Jeremy. But we Hawaiians love our Islands. They are a gift to us from God, and we must keep them beautiful. We teach the children to show respect for the land."

"Why are they using that dirty old canvas bag," Ethan asked, "instead of a plastic garbage bag?"

"Plastic bags do much damage," explained Alana, "especially if they get in the ocean. Many sea creatures die if they are tangled up in plastic bags or if they swallow them."

"That's right!" said Qiana. "I read about that somewhere."

"In fact," Alana continued, "there is one place in the ocean they call the Great Pacific Garbage Patch where many currents meet. In that one place are more than three million tons of plastic!"

Qiana gasped, "Three million tons! Are you sure?"

Alana was nodding. "*Over* three million tons they estimate."

"What are they doing about it?" asked Qiana. "Is someone cleaning it up?"

Alana gave her a sad look. "Clean up three million tons of plastic in the middle of an ocean? Who can do this?" She shrugged. "But I think they are trying."

"How did all that trash get there," asked Ethan, "from ships?"

"Yes, partly, but they say most from runoff. People throw out plastic things. Rains take the plastic things to the rivers. Rivers take them to the ocean. Ocean currents take them to the Garbage Patch," Alana said.

"Wow!" Qiana said. "I'm going to be more careful about using plastic. I had no idea it was such a problem."

"And even the teenagers here care about keeping the Islands clean," Ethan marveled. "It's no wonder Hawaii is such a paradise."

Alana smiled sadly. "Not all teenagers are like my Kimo. Some of them only care about themselves."

"Just like the teenagers back home," Qiana said.

Alana nodded. "Yes. We are all the same no matter how much we are different."

By the time the group had wearied of walking and returned to the hotel, the sun was low in the sky. The musicians were playing and many of the hotel's patrons had begun to gather on the beach. Then the dancers came and spread across the white sand.

The performance was engrossing. Qiana found herself leaning against Jeremy as they watched the graceful, rhythmic movements of the beautiful hula dancers. A glorious sunset was a kaleidoscope of color behind them. Sometimes she almost forgot to breathe. Noticing that Jeremy seemed as bewitched as she was, she whispered, "What do you think?"

A long moment passed before he spoke. Then he whispered, "For the first time I'm beginning to understand what happened to my Dad out here."

Qiana frowned. Her mind churned. And then, with sudden clarity, she whispered back, "Me too."

In the gathering darkness, after the dance ended, Ethan guided the little group back to the rental car. No one was talking; they were half mesmerized by the beauty and fragrance of the Island. None of them noticed a shadowy figure behind them, following at a discreet distance. And none of them saw the small, dark car that tailed them first to Kimo's home and then to the senior Dr. Rand's house. When Ethan turned into the driveway, it continued down the street. But a few minutes later, it drove by again, and the driver saw that the rental car was now empty and the lights in the house were on.

Chapter 14

The next morning, Alana sent Ethan and Qiana to the police station in Honolulu, which she said was the hub of the police organization on Oahu. When they approached the front desk, the receptionist greeted them with a smile. "You were here yesterday," she said.

"That's right," said Ethan. "Do you still have the photo we brought?"

The receptionist held it up. "It's right here. And have you learned who this beautiful woman is yet?"

"Her name is Lin Choi," Ethan said.

The smile vanished. The receptionist picked up her phone and punched in a number. She spoke rapidly and had barely hung up and said, "It will be one moment, please," before an officer appeared behind her.

"Are you the people who found Lin Choi?" he asked Ethan and Qiana.

"We didn't exactly find her," Ethan said. "We're here on Oahu, trying to find out *about* her."

"Why is that?" asked the officer.

"She died last June," Ethan said, "and we don't know who murdered her. I'm a lawyer and my client has been falsely accused of the crime."

The officer nodded. "Well, I'd say you've come to the right place if you're looking for suspects. However, I'm going to send you to District 6 in Waikiki. The detective who knows the most about Ms. Choi is located there. I'll call ahead to let him know you're on the way. When you get there, ask for Detective Nate Zang."

Detective Nate Zang was a short, but powerful-looking man in his mid-thirties. He greeted Ethan and Qiana with knuckle-crunching handshakes and cordially waited for them to take chairs in front of his desk before he seated himself behind it. His manner and his tone were brisk and businesslike. "I understand you have information about Lin Choi," he said.

Qiana and Ethan exchanged looks. "Actually, we came to Hawaii hoping to *get* information about her," Ethan said. "We didn't even know her by that name."

Zang picked up a piece of paper from his desk and turned it over. When he did, the wedding portrait of Dillon and Maylea was facing Ethan and Qiana. "You knew her by the name Maylea Kanaka, I believe?" he said, reading the name on the back of the photo.

"That's right," said Ethan. He quickly explained the circumstances of their quest—about Dillon's dilemma and their relationship to Dillon. "It was uncanny," he finished. "Once she was dead the people around her realized that they knew almost nothing about her."

"And you've come to Oahu because this is where Mr. West met her?" asked Zang.

"That's right," said Ethan. "We're trying to find out everything we can about Maylea—or Lin—but our real goal is to locate the housekeeper she called Trolley."

Zang nodded. "Well, your information closes my case. I can't bring her back and indict her if she's dead. But I'll give you as much help as I can with your case. There are still many holes in my knowledge of Lin Choi. As you say, it is hard to find out about her."

He shuffled through a stack of folders and pulled one out. Opening it, he continued, "Ms. Choi was working in conjunction with an accountant by the name of Kevin Vickery." He glanced surreptitiously at his audience when he said the word "accountant" to see their reaction. They didn't disappoint him. Qiana gave a little gasp and Ethan sat up straighter, but neither interrupted him.

"Using the detailed information available to Mr. Vickery as an accountant, they were able to open fraudulent bank accounts in the names of many of his business clients. Then Ms. Choi would wander through a small business or doctor's office shortly after the mail had been delivered. Often she found a pile of letters, including checks from clients and customers, lying unguarded on a desk. She might ask to borrow the phone or she might just whisk them into her tote bag and be on her way if no one was paying attention to her. Then she would deposit the checks in the fraudulent bank account. It seems that she was so 'dainty and lovely,' as one secretary put it, that no one would suspect her of being a criminal."

"And this Kevin Vickery ..." said Ethan. "He was her accomplice?"

"He denies it," said Zang, "but he has been convicted."

"Convicted? So he's in prison *now*?" asked Qiana.

Zang nodded.

"Where?" asked Ethan.

"Here in Oahu Prison."

Qiana and Ethan exchanged looks. "Would it be possible for us to talk to him?" Ethan asked.

"For you, perhaps," said Zang. "I could make the arrangements."

"Please arrange for me to see him as soon as possible," Ethan said.

Zang picked up a pen and made some notes, with Ethan supplying the information he requested, including his cell phone number and Lubbock police detective Jed Daly's name. When he finished, he said, "I'm going to guess that you should be able to see Mr. Vickery by next Monday. Will you still be on Oahu?"

Ethan nodded. "We're scheduled to be here two weeks."

Seeing that Zang had stopped writing, Qiana asked, "What else do you know about Lin Choi? Was she involved in any other illegal activities?"

Zang looked grim. "Yes, it looks like she had quite a thriving little business involving credit card fraud. As I said before, she helped herself to any stray mail she found lying around at the businesses she was scamming. If she opened a letter and found offers from credit card companies, she would open a new account. Of course, she would use a different address–either Vickery's or a post office box–so the company being charged for her purchases wouldn't know about the account. We believe she also obtained credit card information from guests at the Windsong Towers. They would give her their credit card to pay for food or drinks, and she apparently wrote down the information from the card or took a picture of it with a cell phone. Then she would use the information to order items from the internet."

He paused in his recital of Maylea's crimes to run his fingers through his short, dark hair. "It took the hotel guests a long time to connect the thefts to the hotel because she always waited at least a month to use the information she had obtained from them. By that time, they were wracking their brains, trying to think of more recent situations where security could have been breached. In fact, she tripped herself up by using a card right away. It was about to expire, so she had to use it immediately or forfeit the opportunity."

"And she was too greedy to forfeit," Qiana murmured when he paused.

"Exactly," said Zang.

"But when people learned purchases were being made in Hawaii, wouldn't that clue them in to check the places they used their card while they were here?" Ethan asked.

Zang was shaking his head. "It might, but she only used stolen credit card numbers from people who live on the Islands."

"There were people from the Islands staying at the hotel?"

"Sometimes. But they didn't have to be staying at the hotel. They might be there for the evening–to eat or for the show," said Zang.

"Maylea was pretty crafty," Qiana observed.

"And she obviously knew someone who's a pro at counterfeiting I.D.'s," said Ethan. "She was able to pass herself off as Maylea Kanaka when she and Dillon went for their marriage license."

Zang nodded thoughtfully. "We'll have to do some research into that aspect of the case. We haven't looked into it since we didn't know she had changed her name. I assume you've already used her birth certificate to gather information about her?"

Ethan gave a heartfelt sigh. "It was a dead end. Apparently every piece of information was fabricated."

Zang frowned. "Hmmm ..."

"What?" Qiana asked.

"Well, she couldn't have been planning to use that identity long–not if she was using a bogus social security number."

Qiana paled. "What do you think she intended to do?"

Zang shook his head. "I'm not a speculator. I'll leave that to your imaginations." Changing the subject, he asked, "What about your accountant–Mr. West? Did she drag him into any of her felonious schemes?"

"She tried," said Ethan, "but he wasn't having any of it. So she hooked up with a fitness trainer who's majoring in computers at Texas Tech University there in Lubbock."

"And what kind of damage have the two of them done so far?" Zang asked.

"None that we know of," said Ethan. "The fitness trainer–Scot Sanford–admits that she was pressing him to try his hand at hacking, but he denies doing it."

Zang nodded and looked around. It was obvious his attention was beginning to wane. "Is there anything else I can do for you today?"

"What about Trolley?" Qiana asked. "Have you ever heard that name?"

Zang shook his head. "Nope. What's the rest of her name? Do you have a photo? Fingerprints?"

"No," Qiana said ruefully. "She was a housekeeper. Who knew we'd need a photo? And apparently she was some kind of cleaning machine–the police found very few fingerprints in the house. Every surface was spotless."

"I would like a list of Mr. Vickery's clients who were compromised," Ethan said. "Just the names and addresses of the businesses, so I can make the rounds and see if anyone has ever heard of Trolley."

Instead of answering, Zang leaned back in his chair and seemed to be studying the wall behind Ethan and Qiana. After a few long moments, he leaned forward and asked, "Did your detective ..." he glanced at his notes, "... Lt. Daly–did he have a picture drawn of this Trolley from her description? You know, by a police artist or a computer?"

Ethan scowled. "Lt. Daly settled on my client as the guilty party and moved on to his next case. He agrees that Trolley must know something about Maylea's death, but he's convinced her knowledge would support his position."

"He must be pretty sure of a conviction if he's not looking for her," Zang observed.

Ethan and Qiana exchanged glances. Zang was right, but they hadn't considered this point. Qiana suddenly felt nauseous and Ethan's heart rate quickened painfully.

Zang continued. "I've got a pretty good artist here on Oahu. What if I bring him in tomorrow to do a rendition for you? Do you think you could give an adequate description for him to work with?"

"I've never seen Trolley," said Ethan.

"Neither have I," said Qiana. "But my nephew has. It's his Dad who's been accused of the murder. I bet he can describe her."

"Okay, here's what we'll do," Zang said, standing. "If you'll wait in the lobby, I'll have a secretary print out the list of those businesses for you. Then tomorrow morning you bring your nephew here at 9:00 o'clock to talk to my artist. If the artist isn't available, I'll give you a call this afternoon and we'll reschedule."

"One more question," Ethan said as he stood. "What happened to all that money–the money Lin had been accumulating?"

Zang shrugged. "Who knows. She emptied the fraudulent accounts before she left–at least, the accounts we've located."

"And her partner ... um, Kevin Vickery ... did he have any of the money?"

Zang shook his head. "Like I said, he denies knowledge of any crime. And he wouldn't back down, even after he was convicted."

Qiana and Ethan thanked him repeatedly and each suffered through another bone-crushing handshake. "He's a wonderful man, but I hope I never have to see him again," Qiana confided to Ethan in a whisper as they waited in the lobby, both massaging their hands. "At least, not if we have to shake hands."

Ethan agreed. "The man has no concept of his own strength," he whispered back.

Ethan and Qiana spent nearly an hour looking for a place to eat lunch. They had decided they wanted a view of the ocean this time, but at a location that wasn't crawling with tourists. When Ethan finally pulled up to a shaded picnic table with a spectacular view, both breathed a sigh of relief. While they feasted on teriyaki beef and an assortment of fresh vegetables, Ethan spread out his map of Oahu and tried to locate the addresses on the list Nate Zang had given them.

"It's impossible!" he finally exclaimed. He pushed the map away and popped a cherry tomato into his mouth.

Qiana, who had been lost in her enjoyment of the scenery, started. "What's impossible?" she asked.

"Finding all these businesses in less than two months. We need a guide."

Qiana nodded. "Of course." She took out her cell phone and started to call Alana. But before the call could go through, she tapped the "end" button and frowned at Ethan. "Wait! We don't want to visit any of those places until we have the drawing of Trolley."

Ethan sighed. "That's true. I'm so eager to make some progress that I'm getting ahead of myself. Okay, so what do we do with the rest of the day?"

"For one thing, we need to call the other police stations we visited yesterday. We told all of them we would call today with Maylea's real name," Qiana said.

"Right you are," said Ethan. "And who knows–we might pick up another lead before we're through."

He pulled out his own cell phone and began punching in numbers, but Qiana said, "Don't do that yet. Let's enjoy our lunch. Then we can tear the list in half and be through in no time."

Ethan put his phone away. "You're right again." He turned his attention to his food and soon he and Qiana were both gazing at the ever-changing ocean while they munched on Alana's delicious lunch.

"See that yacht way out there?" Qiana asked, pointing.

Ethan nodded. "It's a beauty, isn't it?"

"How much do you think it cost new?" she asked.

"Oh, not more than a few million," Ethan said lazily. "Why? Do you want a yacht?"

She grinned. "Not for more than a few months. But wouldn't it be fabulous to go sailing off to anywhere in the world you wanted to go? Just take your home with you and go exploring!"

Ethan let his gaze linger on the yacht before he said, "I'd probably be seasick." He gave her a lop-sided grin. "I'm afraid I'm a land-lubber."

Qiana laughed. "I am too, but I think it would be fun for awhile."

They finished their lunch in companionable silence, then began making phone calls. Both had similar results. All the police districts on Oahu knew the name Lin Choi, but they had no new information to add. Lin was Nate Zang's case and they had funneled their information to him weeks earlier.

"Now what?" Qiana asked after she had completed her last call.

"Why don't you report to Alana, so she'll know our plans for tomorrow?" suggested Ethan.

"Okay, but we'd better go back to the car so I can plug in. I'm getting low on juice," Qiana said.

While she talked to Alana, Ethan drove along H1 toward the windward side of Oahu. His mind was preoccupied with thoughts of Trolley and Maylea so he was paying no attention to Qiana's conversation with Alana until she nudged him, pointed to the right, and said, "Turn here."

He obeyed, then asked, "Where are we going?"

"To a marina," Qiana answered. "We're going to meet Paulo and he's going to take us sailing."

Ethan's mouth fell open. "Doesn't anybody in that family have anything to do except entertain us?" he asked.

"Just drive," Qiana said. "We'll find a way to make it up to him later."

Muttering a few feeble protests under his breath, Ethan drove where he was told. Days, weeks, months, and even years later he blessed Alana for insisting that they let Paulo take them out onto the Pacific Ocean in his sailboat that day, for it was the best part of the trip for him.

At first when he stepped into the boat and felt it sway beneath him, his heart sank. He wasn't at all sure he wanted to be in this crate out on the biggest ocean in the world. "Listen, what happens if we get out there and the wind completely dies down?" he asked Paulo. "Will we have to row back to shore?"

Paulo grinned. "We're equipped with an auxiliary motor. You have nothing to worry about."

Ethan nodded, but he already felt a little green around the gills. "Don't worry," Qiana whispered, taking his hand and leading him to the padded passenger bench Paulo had pointed out. "He knows what he's doing, and we're going to have more fun than you ever imagined."

At the touch of Qiana's hand, all of Ethan's doubts were banished in a flood of giddiness. He took a deep breath and looked at her. She was smiling up at him, her eyes bright with excitement, her short dark hair framing her flawless complexion. In that instant, he came to the startling realization that he was gazing at the most beautiful woman he'd ever met.

She released his hand with a wink, turned toward her side of the boat, and reached to touch the lapping waves. Still slightly intoxicated by Qiana's touch, Ethan helped Paulo push off from the dock. And then he watched in awe as Paulo steered expertly through the maze of sailing vessels that blocked their way to the open ocean.

They had just cleared the marina and felt the boat leap forward when Qiana cried, "Oh no!"

Both men looked at her with concern. "What's wrong?" Paulo asked.

"I forgot suntan lotion," she wailed. "If I come back fried, Jeremy will never let me live it down."

Paulo grinned. He rummaged in a box under his bench, then tossed a bottle to Qiana. "We can't let you get fried," he said.

"Thanks, Paulo, you're a life saver," she said. After she had smeared the fragrant lotion on her face, arms and legs, she passed the bottle to Ethan. He did the same and tossed it back to Paulo.

The boat was sliding past rocky cliffs toward the open ocean. It was a warm day, but the breeze off the water was cool. A few wispy clouds decorated the sky, and the deep blue of the ocean was serene. Ethan and Qiana leaned back, stretched their legs, and let gentle sensations flood their souls.

Until that exact moment, Ethan had not realized how tightly wound he was. Trolley seemed a mirage to him–an old woman without a name. Even Maylea hardly seemed real. And yet, he had to locate the mythical housekeeper in order to learn who had murdered the mysterious beauty. Who could accomplish such a task? Who could locate a ghost in order to avenge a phantom? He had gone to sleep the previous night, cursing himself for not hiring a professional detective. He had wakened this morning, with his muscles tense and sore. And he had spent the day twisting his mind into knots, as his thoughts careened from futile theory to futile theory.

But now, suddenly, skimming over the surface of the ocean, every knot came loose. Every fear danced away on sea spray. Every doubt soared up, up, up into the tropical sky. He could breathe again. He could relax. He had his perspective back. If he found Trolley, he found her. If not, he could still hire a professional. He could almost feel the worry wrinkles falling off of his face.

An eternity passed–or a second–Ethan wasn't sure which–and then he heard Paulo say, "After we pass Makapuu Point, you'll see Rabbit Island coming into view." He pointed toward the shore as he mentioned Makapuu Point. "Rabbit Island is a bird sanctuary now, but it used to be a rabbit farm."

"How many rabbits still live there?" Qiana asked.

"None," Paulo replied. "They were upsetting the ecosystem so they had to be removed."

"Can we land on Rabbit Island and see the birds?" Qiana asked.

"Not unless you want to get in trouble with State government," Paulo said. "And I don't."

Qiana smiled. "I guess if rabbits were bad for the ecosystem, people would be worse."

Paulo nodded. "You don't know the half of it. Some tourists seem to believe it's their constitutional right to trample and trash and generally vandalize all they survey. If I had my way, I'd lock them up and throw away the key."

Qiana, listening soberly, nodded her agreement. "I guess when you ran out of space in your prisons, you could dump them in the Great Pacific Garbage Patch."

Paulo laughed. "My Tutu–my grandmother–has been talking to you, hasn't she?"

"Yes," Qiana said, "and I'm glad she did. I had no idea plastic was such a threat to marine life."

"We hear about such things all through our schooling," Paulo observed. "Most of us learn to love our islands and want to keep them beautiful."

"Speaking of school," Ethan spoke up, "do you go to college? Or are you employed full time?"

"I'm studying engineering at the University of Hawaii at Manoa," Paulo said. "This summer my classes are in the morning. Most afternoons I work for one of my professors but, when I get an afternoon free, I sail."

Ethan whistled. "Engineering! You must be a genius!"

Paulo shook his head. "Not me. I'm just doing what I love." He pointed shoreward then and said, "There's Rabbit Island. Watch for monk seals in the water. A few of them may still live on the island and fish in this area."

"What about dolphins and whales?" Ethan asked. "Any chance of seeing either of those?"

"Dolphins possibly. But not whales–it's not the season. They migrate, you know."

Qiana nodded. "Like birds."

Paulo was staring toward the horizon, a distant, hazy line where ocean and sky blended into one. "Are you two in a hurry?" he asked, returning his attention to Ethan and Qiana. "We'll head back soon if you like. Or we can take the whole afternoon and sail along the east shore."

"Oh, please, Ethan, let's not be in a hurry," Qiana pleaded. "It's so beautiful and peaceful out here."

Ethan was nodding. "Okay, no hurry. But be warned," he said to Paulo, "if we stay out here too long, I may never want to go back."

Paulo nodded sympathetically. "Many of us feel the same way," he said. Then he rummaged through the box under his bench again and pulled out two caps. "Here. You should probably wear these if we're going to be on the water for several hours."

Ethan and Qiana obediently put on the green and white University of Hawaii caps and pulled them low to shade their faces from the blistering sun. Then they settled back on their bench, with legs and arms outstretched in a lazy sprawl. The sailboat sped cleanly through the rocking waves. Sea breezes and ocean spray mitigated the scorching heat of the sun. And soon the aloha magic of the Islands seeped into their souls with a tranquilizing peace they had never experienced on the mainland.

While Paulo, Qiana and Ethan sped northward along the windward coast of Oahu, Qiana's cell phone–left behind in the rental car–was ringing urgently. Four rings. Ten minutes of silence. Four more rings. Ten more minutes of silence. The pattern repeated over and over as the sun reached its peak then began a slow descent.

Kimo had led Jeremy into the Ko'olau Range, along a little-used trail. It was a trail he knew well but, as he deftly led the way, he pretended with Jeremy that they were explorers. Ignoring the occasional tourist they met on the trail, the boys imagined they were the first to stumble across secluded nooks, brilliant with flowers, and waterfalls cascading into crystal pools.

Once a vine swung into Jeremy's face and he yelped while his heart skittered into double time. "Jimmy!" he shouted at his guide.

Kimo stopped and rushed to Jeremy's side. "What's wrong!"

"Snakes!" gasped Jeremy. "Don't we need to be watching out for snakes?"

Kimo laughed. "We don't have snakes on the Islands. And if we see one, we'll call 911 and they'll come take it to jail!"

Jeremy studied his friend, trying to decide whether Kimo was serious or poking fun at him. "No really," he protested. "Do you have any poisonous snakes that live in trees around here? A vine slapped my face just now and I nearly fainted!"

"I'm serious," Kimo said. "If snakes were allowed on the Islands, they could destroy a lot of birds that don't live anywhere except Hawaii. So even non-poisonous snakes aren't allowed to stay here."

"Wow, a paradise without any snakes!" marveled Jeremy. "I love it here!"

To eat their lunch, the boys perched on a rock next to a waterfall. The mist from the falls cooled and refreshed them, so they were soon ready to forge ahead in their explorations. It took them another hour to reach the top of the trail. At that point, they hadn't seen another hiker since they stopped to eat.

Before they headed back down the trail, they paused to gaze into a deep canyon, lush with vegetation. As they stood with their backs to the trail, two hooded men crept up behind them. One moment Jeremy was leaning as far as he dared over the edge of the canyon, the next moment a powerful arm was around his neck, pulling him into a muscular chest. "Keep quiet if you don't want a knife in your back," a gravelly voice ordered.

Jeremy's first impulse had been to struggle, but a knife was thrust into his face. "Don't move," the voice snarled, "unless you want to end up at the bottom of that ravine."

Jeremy froze. Adrenaline was surging through his body, but he forced himself to stiffen into statue-like stillness.

"That's better," the voice said. "Where is Lin Choi? If you lie, you die."

Jeremy gulped and croaked in a voice he didn't recognize, "Lin Choi?"

"Yes," the arm pulled him tighter and the knife touched his throat. "Maylea Kanaka. Whatever you call her. Where is she?"

"She ... she died," Jeremy stammered.

There was a long hesitation. Then Jeremy's captor said to his partner. "Get that one's phone and leave him. This one goes with us."

Still frozen in place, Jeremy listened to the sounds of someone dumping the contents of Kimo's backpack on the ground. "Don't move," a gruff voice ordered Kimo. Then, "I've got it."

"Okay, listen and listen good, both of you." The man holding Jeremy in a vise was speaking. "If you see something you shouldn't, it's the last thing you'll ever see. That's a promise."

The next thing Jeremy knew he was being dragged into the forest. As soon as they were out of sight of the trail, his abductor stopped, pulled the hood off his head and slid it over Jeremy's head, but with the eye holes in back. Jeremy's idyllic day in paradise had morphed into a nightmare.

Meanwhile, Kimo barely dared to breathe. "Okay, listen up," said the voice of the man behind him. "I'm going to turn you toward the trail, then I'm going to disappear. You look back or you come after us—your buddy is going to die. You pick up your things and head back down the trail. You got it?"

"Yes sir," Kimo whimpered. "I won't look. I promise."

As silently as he had approached, the man was gone. Kimo didn't even think of glancing toward the forest. Instead, he gathered a water bottle, a snack, suntan lotion, and the other items the man had strewn on the ground. Cramming them into his backpack, he began running down the trail. The original plan had been for him to call Alana when he and Jeremy started down so she would know when to come get them. But with his cell phone gone, he had no choice but to head for civilization as fast as his legs would carry him.

Kimo was nearly halfway down the trail before he met a group of four hikers. "Please help me!" he gasped. "My friend has been kidnapped and the kidnappers took my cell phone. May I use yours?"

Four hands reached for pockets or backpacks. Kimo took the first phone that was extended to him. First he dialed 911 and reported Jeremy's abduction. Then he called Alana. When he handed the cell phone back to its owner—a pretty, blond woman in her 20s—she said, "Come on. Show us where it happened. Maybe we can help your friend."

Kimo shook his head and backed away. "No, I can't. They'll kill him. They said so. They promised."

Before the hikers could try to change his mind, a helicopter appeared above the trees, then soared away in the opposite direction.

"That was them!" Kimo cried, staring at the vanishing aircraft. "I know it was!"

And he was right. As soon as the gruff-voiced man reported to his partner that Kimo had raced away like a scared rabbit, Jeremy's abductor began dragging Jeremy through the forest. Jeremy could see nothing except his own Nike-shod feet, his kidnapper's booted feet, and the soil and vegetation he was walking on. It seemed as if they walked for hours before he was shoved into some kind of vehicle. And when the vehicle sprang into life with a deafening roar, Jeremy's heart sank. He was in a helicopter. These men could take him anywhere. How would Kimo or Alana or Qiana or anyone ever find him?

Qiana and Ethan returned to their rental car feeling as light and free as air. But their levity turned to lead when Qiana picked up her cell phone and saw that she had missed 25 calls. As she listened to her voice mail, all the color drained from her face.

"What's wrong?" Ethan asked. His hand was on the car key, which was in the ignition, but he paused as he studied her face anxiously.

Qiana's cell phone slipped from her hand and clattered to the floor. Her limp hand fell into her lap and tears sprang into her eyes. "Jeremy has been kidnapped," she whispered brokenly. "They took Jeremy, but not Kimo." She lifted her eyes, so flooded with tears she could barely see Ethan. "Oh Ethan, what am I going to do? I should have never let him out of my sight. It's all about a murder ... a murder! I should have known there was danger!"

Her voice and her hysteria were rising in billows of terror. Ethan reached awkwardly across the car's console and pulled her as close as he could. "You have to calm down," he whispered soothingly. "Take some deep breaths and don't panic. I'll call Detective Zang and he'll help us. Okay?"

Qiana straightened and took one long, deep breath. When she spoke, her voice was calmer. "Detective Zang has been trying to call you, but you don't answer."

Ethan pulled his cell phone from his pocket and saw that it was nearly out of charge. "Here," he said, unplugging Qiana's cell phone and attaching his own, "let me get some juice flowing." He started the car and retrieved his messages. Within moments he was talking to Zang. When he finished and disconnected, he gave Qiana a bleak look. "They don't have a clue," he said. "But they're crawling all over Windsong Towers."

Qiana frowned. She was beginning to get some spunk again, and when she spoke her voice was stronger. "Do they think Jeremy is at Windsong Towers?"

"No, but they think someone at the hotel knows the kidnappers. How else would anyone know we're here looking for Maylea?"

"And that's why he was taken, because we're looking for Maylea?" Qiana asked.

Ethan nodded. "Kimo heard them mention Lin Choi, then Maylea Kanaka."

Qiana nodded. "I see." She closed her eyes and was silent for a long time. Finally, she seemed to have reached a decision. "I'm going to call Dillon," she said. She was disconnecting Ethan's cell phone now and reconnecting her own.

"Are you sure you want to do that?" Ethan asked. "We could wait until tomorrow morning, and Jeremy may be back safe by then."

"I know," Qiana said. "And I don't want to worry Nettie while she's pregnant and so afraid of losing the baby. But Ethan, I'm scared. I've never been so scared in my life. And my sister has a God she prays to all the time. What if I don't tell them so they don't know to pray? What if those monsters kill Jeremy and his folks never even found out in time to pray for him? I can't do it myself–I never pray ..."

She turned stricken eyes on Ethan. "Do you pray? Do you believe in a God?"

Ethan shrugged. "Well, I guess I believe there may be some kind of God but, no, I don't pray much."

Qiana lifted her cell phone and began jabbing buttons.

Chapter 15

Dillon West's greatest enemy for the past two months had been lethargy–lethargy born of self-disgust. As a result, before his cell phone rang, he had been slumped in an easy chair, staring into space. When he pulled the phone from his pocket and saw Qiana's number, his pulse quickened. Why was she calling him? She always called Nettie.

"Hello," he said, trying not to expect the worst.

"Dillon, it's Qiana," came the nervous voice from halfway across the Pacific Ocean.

"Qiana! What's wrong?" He knew something had to be wrong. He had never heard Qiana sound nervous before. Or afraid. Or doubtful. Qiana was always full of ginger and self-confidence.

"Look, Dillon, maybe I shouldn't have called yet ..." He could tell she was trying to keep her voice from trembling.

"Qiana, what's wrong?"

"I'm calling now because I know you and Nettie will want to pray." She was beginning to lose it again, her voice growing faint and broken.

"Qiana!" he roared.

"Jeremy has been kidnapped. The police are looking for him–maybe they've already found him. I'm only calling so ... you ... can ..."

Ethan took the phone from her hand and put it to his ear in time to hear Dillon say, "I'll be on the next plane out of here."

"No you won't," he told his client. "You try to leave Lubbock and the police will toss you in jail before the plane leaves the tarmac."

"Not if you don't tell them," Dillon said angrily. "You can't think I'm just going to sit here and worry!"

"No, I think you're going to stay with your wi ... with Nettie, and take care of her. I think if you believe in prayer, this would be a good time to practice what you believe. But you're not coming to Hawaii. There's nothing you can do here except help us pace the floor, and you're not going to jeopardize your case by jumping bail, just so you can pace the floor over here instead of over there."

This little tirade was followed by a long silence. Finally Ethan said, "Dillon, if you get on an airplane and come to Oahu, you can get yourself another lawyer." He pushed the button that disconnected the call.

Glancing around, Dillon was relieved to see that Nettie had not returned to the den. She had gone to take a bath and was taking her time. He had been waiting for a load of laundry to finish so he could transfer it to the drier before he headed for Bethany's house for the night. Now he called, in quick succession, Bethany, their pastor, his parents, and his sister Rilee. By the time he finished, Nettie had appeared wearing her favorite green and gold robe.

Seeing her in the doorway he went to her and took her hand. "Nettie, come sit with me on the couch. I have something to tell you."

Dillon had barely dared to touch Nettie in the two months since Maylea's death, but now he put an arm around her and pulled her close. Before she could ask any questions, he began in his gentlest voice. "Qiana just called. Jeremy has been kidnapped. I don't know any details yet. Qiana was too upset to talk and Ethan just yelled at me not to get on the next flight to Oahu." He felt Nettie trembling and tightened his embrace, as he continued. "Qiana called right away because she knew we would want to pray."

Nettie looked up, a light dawning in her eyes. So far, she'd said nothing. Now she nodded. "Yes, I want to pray."

As if on cue, the doorbell rang and in the next fifteen minutes, Bethany, their pastor, and three couples from the church had joined Dillon and Nettie in an impromptu prayer meeting. They were not a congregation that normally knelt to pray, but tonight all were on their knees, praying as if Jeremy's life depended on them.

And perhaps it did.

※

After a short helicopter ride, Jeremy had been hustled to a car. He was frisked and his cell phone removed from his pocket. A long, bumpy ride followed. Then he was dragged into a building and left in a dark, stuffy room with his hands tied behind his back. "Don't forget," the voice of his captor had said before closing and locking the door, "you see anything or anybody, it's the last thing you're ever gonna' see. You get my meaning, kid?"

"Yes sir," Jeremy said, nodding vigorously.

He had been shoved into a fairly comfortable arm chair where he waited for days. Actually, it was hours, but it felt like days because no chair is comfortable when a boy's hands are tied behind his back.

Still, he had finally fallen asleep with the words, "Dear God, help me," on his lips. He had repeated the prayer over and over, like a mantra, until his eyes closed and his head fell sideways against the back of the chair. The next thing he knew, someone was in the room and the light was on. He sat up, trying to hide the nervousness that swept through him like a West Texas tornado.

"So, you're being good, are you?" asked a soft, deep voice. It wasn't a voice Jeremy had heard before. This voice was wearing black, shiny dress shoes, he noted.

"I don't have much choice, do I?" he asked belligerently.

"Ah good, the kid has a spine. So tell me about Ms. Choi. I hear she's dead."

All of Jeremy's senses went on alert. And he silently prayed one more thing. "Please Lord, help me say the right things." Then he shrugged and asked, "What's it to you?"

"A fair question," the voice observed. "She took some of my money." He sounded angry now. "Actually, she took a lot of my money, and I want it back."

"I don't blame you," Jeremy said, "but how can I help?"

"You can tell me everything you know about her," the voice said, sounding calm again. Calm and imploring.

"I don't know much," Jeremy said, understanding all the way to the core of his being that his fate would depend on his answers. And Dillon's fate, too.

"When and where did she die?" the voice asked.

"A place called Lubbock, Texas. I think it was in ... June," Jeremy said, sounding hesitant.

"So if you don't know anything about her, why are you in Hawaii asking about her?"

"I'm not asking about her," Jeremy said. "I came with my aunt. Her boyfriend is the lawyer for the guy who killed Ms. Choi. So we came along for the fun of it. But it hasn't been much fun since you goons came along."

"Who killed her?" the voice asked.

"I guess her husband did," Jeremy said.

"Her husband? She was married?"

Jeremy shrugged. "That's what they say."

"What's his name?"

Jeremy shook his head. "I don't know. He's just some guy."

"What else do you know about her?"

"Nothing."

"And what have you found out since you got here?" The voice was beginning to sound annoyed.

"Nothing," Jeremy answered, sounding annoyed himself. "I went boogie boarding yesterday and hiking today. I'm not a lawyer–I don't care about some stupid case."

There was a short silence, then the voice asked, "What's the name of the newspaper where you live?"

"My family gets the *Lubbock Avalanche Journal*. I don't know if there's another paper in town or not," said Jeremy. Then he heard footsteps moving away from him. The lights went off, and the door was shut and locked again. He relaxed into the chair, trembling, and thanked God that he was still alive.

A moment later, he heard that same deep voice yelling in the next room. "You lamebrains! What do I want with a kid? He doesn't know anything. Check it out, Thor–June, the *Lubbock Avalanche*

Journal. If he's right, get him out of here. If he's not, throw him in a hole, and I'll talk to him again tomorrow." A moment later a door slammed.

"Get him out of here," Jeremy repeated to himself. He dared to hope it meant he would be released, not killed and dumped in a ravine.

About an hour later, the man with the gravelly voice, dragged Jeremy out of the chair and took him to a car. His hands were still tied, but he didn't dare complain. He barely dared to breathe. And he was amazed to realize it was still light outside. He hadn't been in the stuffy, little room all night–he was almost positive of that. So maybe he hadn't been in the room more than a couple of hours.

As his captor dragged him down the sidewalk, Jeremy noticed that a thundercloud and a lightning bolt were painted on the inside of his hiking boot. He stared at it, memorizing it, until he was shoved onto the back seat of the car. Then both front doors opened and slammed. It was probably the same two men who had brought him here, Jeremy reasoned. But they weren't talking so he wasn't sure.

After another long, bumpy ride in the car, Jeremy was dragged across a rocky beach and into the surf where a power boat was moored. He felt a tug on his wrists, then his hands were free. "Climb on," his captor ordered. Clumsily, Jeremy heaved himself into the boat, aided by the sliver of vision through the bottom of the hood. He stumbled and nearly fell when the boat dipped, as his companion pulled himself on board.

The gravelly-voiced man grabbed Jeremy's arm to steady him. "Okay, here's how it's gonna' go," he said. "Do you know how to drive a boat?"

"No," Jeremy said. "I saw my friend's dad drive one once, but I never tried it."

"Well, today you get your first lesson. I'm going to start you on your way, then I'll bail. You're going to sit right here ..." He shoved Jeremy down onto a bench. "... until you count to 100 *slow.* If you take the hood off before you get to 100, my pal is going to blow your head off. He has his rifle aimed at you right now, and he don't miss. Any questions?"

"Are you going to show me how to work the boat?" Jeremy quavered.

"No, you teach yourself–on the job training, you might say," the man said with a snicker. Then he called, "Shove off!"

Jeremy sat straight and stiff as the boat moved away from shore. He could hear the man walking away from him and feel the boat swaying with each footstep. Then the motor roared to life. As the boat began to pick up speed, Jeremy felt it rock as the man dived off the side. He counted out loud, "One ... two ... three ... four ... five ... six ... seven ... eight ... nine ... ten ..." And then panic hit him. He cried, "... 20 ... 30 ... 40 ... 50 ... 60 ... 70 ... 80 ... 90 ... 100."

On 100, he threw himself onto the floor of the boat, jerked the hood off his head, and waited for the rifle blast that would end his life. When no bullets hit the boat, he dared to peek over the stern. What he saw nearly made his heart stop.

Land was receding rapidly. The sun had set, and he could barely see the beach. He stood and raced forward to the wheel. Bullets no longer frightened him. He was speeding into the Pacific Ocean at a rate that took his breath away.

His mind catalogued the disasters that might await him. He could get lost in the Pacific Ocean. He might crash into an island. He could run out of gas. He might collide with another boat. He could die of hunger or thirst. Sharks might leap into the boat and tear him to pieces!

Frantically, Jeremy reached for the wheel. But before he touched it, he forced himself to take two deep breaths. He had a feeling that if he grabbed it and started yanking on it he could capsize. So he gently put both hands on it, and slowly began to turn it. He had to get headed toward land again, but he didn't want to go back to the same beach where had just left Mr. Gravelly Voice and Mr. Gruff Voice.

He was trembling from head to foot as he began to swing the boat in a wide arc to the left. He longed to find a way to slow it down because its velocity frightened him. But he longed to find a way to speed it up because he was desperate to get back to land before the Pacific Ocean swallowed him whole.

He had decided his only hope was to run aground on a sandy beach. But how was he going to identify a sandy beach in the gathering dusk? He could just as easily ram into a wall of rocks. His sweaty hands slipped on the wheel and he tightened his grip.

Well, he knew for sure he'd rather die by colliding with a rock wall than by disappearing into the Pacific Ocean and becoming shark bait. So he gently turned the boat to the left even further. As he peered toward land, he could see a white beach stretching in both directions. This was it–he was going in. Carefully he began manipulating controls until he found a lever that regulated his speed. He knew he had to slow the boat before he hit the beach, but he was terrified of slowing too much too soon. What if he stalled and drifted away from land?

"Father," he prayed, "please show me how to get back to Oahu. And please don't let me hit anybody in the water or on the beach. In Jesus' name. Amen."

Then he began beeping the boat's horn. First, he pushed it in long, loud wails. Then he remembered the Morse code for SOS and began tooting three shorts, three longs, three shorts. Over and over, he signaled ... SOS ... SOS ... SOS.

Sooner than he thought possible, the white beach loomed. He grabbed the lever that would slow him down and yanked it. Suddenly he was skidding across the sand, hanging on to the steering wheel with all his might.

When the boat shuddered to a stop, Jeremy sat down in the captain's chair and put his face in his hands. He wasn't going to cry. Somehow he was going to keep himself from crying. But the trembling was uncontrollable.

In moments, he felt the boat dip. Then strong hands were reaching for him, lifting him to his feet, trying to see if he was hurt. "What happened? Are you all right?" asked a middle-aged man wearing a touristy Hawaiian shirt.

Jeremy looked up into the face of a man about his father's age with dark, curly hair and friendly eyes. In that instant, he lost control. Dissolving in tears, he collapsed into the man's arms. "I'm sorry," he blubbered. "I'm sorry, but I was so scared." In a matter of seconds, he regained control, rubbed his eyes and peered around. "Did I hurt anybody? I was praying I wouldn't." He gazed beseechingly into the eyes of the kind stranger. "Please tell me if anyone was hurt."

"No, not at all!" the man assured him. "When we heard you tooting that horn and saw the boat coming in fast, we got out of the way."

Jeremy let out a sigh of relief. "May I borrow your cell phone?" he asked. "The kidnappers took mine. I have to tell my aunt I'm alive."

The man automatically reached for his waist, but he was still wearing his swimsuit. "Come on, we'll find one," he told Jeremy.

Ten or 15 people had gathered, and they eagerly reached to help Jeremy step out of the boat. When his feet touched the ground, he nearly fell, for his knees were still wobbly.

"Whoops!" said a woman's voice. She grabbed his arm, and he steadied himself against her substantial bulk.

"Thank you, ma'am," he said. "Do you have a cell phone?"

She beamed at him and reached into the pocket of a voluminous muumuu. "Here you go," she said. "You call anybody you like. And take all the time you need."

"Thank you," Jeremy said again. "I'll just call my aunt and 911." He had started tapping in Qiana's number, but now he stopped. "Where am I?" he asked.

"Ohikilolo Beach," said the man who had helped him out of the boat.

Jeremy had to hear the name several times before he called Qiana's cell number. When she answered, he said, "Aunt Qiana, I'm okay. I'm on Ohikilolo Beach."

"Jeremy, you're okay! Are you sure you're okay?" Qiana was talking and crying at the same time. And before he could answer, he heard her yell, "It's Jeremy! Ethan, it's Jeremy. Alana, it's Jeremy. Kimo, he's okay." Then she was back on the phone saying again, "Are you sure you're okay?"

"Yes, I'm positive," said Jeremy.

"Where are you? Say it slow."

Jeremy repeated, "Ohikololo Beach."

"Wait," Qiana said. "Say it to Alana."

"Aunt Qiana, it doesn't matter where I am now," Jeremy said. "I'm going to call 911. I'm afraid ..." He glanced around. "Well, I want the police to catch those guys."

"Okay," Qiana agreed. "We'll call a detective we met today. His name is Nate Zang, and he's been working on the case all along. We'll meet you at the police station unless he tells us to go to the beach."

"Thank you," said Jeremy. "And Aunt Qiana, do my parents know I was gone?"

"I'll call them this very instant," Qiana promised.

"What time is it in Lubbock?" Jeremy asked.

"It's after midnight. But that's okay. They're waiting by the phone."

"Aunt Qiana," Jeremy said, and his voice trembled. "I love you."

Then he broke the connection and called 911.

The impromptu prayer meeting had ended after an hour. When Qiana's call came through, only Bethany and the pastor were still waiting with Dillon and Nettie. And Nettie had cried herself to sleep in Dillon's arms.

Dillon snatched up the handset on the first ring. "Yes," he said tersely.

"He's okay," Qiana said. "That's all I know now, but he called me from a beach and said he was okay. He was going to call 911, and we're going to meet him at the police station."

Nettie was reaching for the phone, and Dillon handed it to her without a word. She had easily heard Qiana's excited words. "Qiana," she said urgently, "I want to talk to him. Does he have his phone with him?"

"I doubt it," said Qiana. "He didn't use it to call me."

"Tell him to call me," Nettie said. "As soon as you talk to him again, tell him to call me."

"Okay, sis. I'm sorry I didn't tell him to call you first, but he was in a big hurry to call 911 and get the police on the case."

"I know," Nettie said, trying to restrain a flood of tears. "But I have to hear his voice for a minute. For a second. Just for a …" She couldn't go on. She passed the handset back to Dillon and reached for a tissue.

The little group of four was having a hallelujah service, thanking God for Jeremy's safe return the next time the phone rang. Nettie answered it before Jeremy even heard it ring. "Baby, is that you?" she asked. "Are you all right?"

"Mom, I'm fine. Detective Zang is letting me use his cell phone. And Mom," Jeremy glanced self-consciously at Zang, "I'm not a baby."

Zang grinned and Jeremy grimaced. Nettie said, "I know you're not, sweetie, but you'll always be my baby. Always."

Jeremy sighed. "Okay, well, I know you've been worried, so I'll let it pass this time."

"Listen, Jeremy, I know you're in a hurry to talk to the police, but I want to tell you something. I want you to be the first to know." She paused and took a long breath.

"Okay, what is it?"

Nettie didn't dare look at Dillon when she said, "Well, I've been in a panic about you all evening, but your Dad was right here with me. I couldn't have made it without him, and I don't want to be without him any more unless I have to. So I'm going to ask him to marry me."

Jeremy couldn't think what to say for several long beats. Then it came to him. "Is Dad there now?" he asked.

"Yes."

"Let me talk to him," Jeremy said.

Nettie handed the phone to Dillon. "He wants to talk to you," she said.

"Hello, son," Dillon said. "I'm so glad you're safe." But his heart was racing, and he couldn't take his eyes off Nettie.

"Yeah, yeah," Jeremy said impatiently. "So are you going to marry Mom or what?"

Nettie looked up and met Dillon's gaze as he answered his son. "Yes, Jeremy, the very first second she'll have me."

"You mean you're not going to wait for me to get back from Hawaii?"

Dillon grinned wider than he had ever grinned in his life. "I don't believe children should be present when their parents get married," he said. "It doesn't seem quite proper."

"Okay," Jeremy said. "You have the wedding and I'll have the honeymoon trip to Hawaii."

Dillon's grin faded. "We'll have to think about that," he said. "I'm not sure it's a good idea for you to stay there."

"Please, Dad. I'll be careful," Jeremy said. But Dillon didn't hear him. Bethany had taken the phone and it was all Jeremy could do to persuade his grandmother that he was neither dead nor permanently scarred. While Bethany talked to Jeremy and the pastor tried tactfully to fade into the background, Dillon pulled Nettie into his arms and whispered, "I'm not good enough for you. I'll never be good enough for you. And I'll never forgive myself for hurting you and Jeremy the way I did."

Nettie nodded. "Thank you for saying that, but I have to apologize too."

Dillon's eyes widened in disbelief. "For what?" he asked.

Nettie's eyes were downcast as she spoke brokenly with tears in her eyes. "I should have told you I was pregnant. It wasn't fair not to tell you. Maybe you would have stayed with us, and Jeremy wouldn't have had to go through all this trauma."

"No!" Dillon's voice was soft, but intense. "I won't have you blaming yourself ..."

Nettie put her hand over his mouth. "Let me finish," she said. "I've been practicing this speech for days."

Dillon nodded. "Okay. But ..."

Observing their serious faces, Bethany and the pastor tiptoed quietly out of the room. The pastor went home, and Bethany went into the kitchen to make a snack.

Dillon and Nettie barely noticed their departure. "No buts. Just listen," said Nettie. "When you told me you wanted a divorce, all I could feel was rejection. So I rejected back. But I was wrong. I was trying to protect myself with pride and selfishness. And it was an ugly thing for a mother to do to her son–putting my own needs ahead of his. I want you to know how sorry I am for not telling you I was pregnant. Even if you didn't want me, it wasn't fair to Jeremy to push you out the door without letting you have all the facts you needed to make your decision."

She lifted her eyes to his, and her face was awash with tears. "I don't want to be with you if you don't love me any more," she continued, "but if it's possible, I want our family to be whole. So I'm asking–will you marry me again?"

Dillon couldn't believe his ears. After all he had done to her and to Jeremy, Nettie was heaping blame upon herself. "You're wrong," he whispered through a throat so tightly clenched he could barely croak. "You're so wrong to blame yourself. It's all my fault. All you did was try to deal with the impossible position I put you in."

He reached for a tissue and gently dried her face. "I think you're too smart to want me back," he said. "But if you do, I'll marry you again. And it will be the happiest day of my life."

Nettie's smile was sunshine to his heart. "I do," she said. "I do want you back."

"I want you back, too," he said.

Jeremy handed the cell phone to Detective Zang. "My Mom and Dad are getting married again!" he announced exuberantly.

Zang grinned from ear to ear. "Well, now, that's what I call a happy ending."

Jeremy beamed at him. "Me too."

Before Zang could ask Jeremy the first question, his cell phone began to jingle. He glanced at the screen, then frowned at Jeremy before he answered, "Zang here."

"Detective Zang, my name is Bethany Jamison. I'm Jeremy West's grandmother," said the voice on the U.S. side of the Pacific Ocean.

"Yes, Mrs. Jamison," Zang said.

Jeremy grimaced and sighed. What did she want *now*?

"Detective, how long has it been since my grandson had anything to eat?" Bethany asked.

"Good question. I'll ask him," Zang said. Lowering the phone, he asked, "How long has it been since you had something to eat?"

"At noon," Jeremy replied.

Zang's eyebrows flew up. He covered the mouthpiece of his cell phone and bellowed, "Parker, get in here."

Almost immediately a uniformed officer appeared in the doorway. "Parker, this is Jeremy West. Take him to the break room and get him anything he wants to eat, just a snack to tide him over. And while he's eating his snack, have a pizza delivered here." He looked at Jeremy. "You like pizza?"

"Sure!" said Jeremy. "Especially pepperoni."

"Get a big one," said Zang. "His family is coming and they probably haven't eaten either. In fact, get two—two of the biggest they've got."

When Parker and Jeremy were gone, Zang lifted the phone to his ear again. "Okay, Mrs. Jamison, we're getting him fed. He hasn't eaten since noon. Is there anything else I can do for you?"

"Thank you, Detective," said Bethany. "Yes, I'd like you to hire a body guard for Jeremy for as long as he's there. I'm prepared to give you my credit card number if you like. Or I'll send the gentleman a check. You tell me the best way to handle it."

Zang smiled. He liked this lady's style. "Mrs. Jamison," he said, "I know the perfect man for the job. You give me your address, and I'll have him send you a bill."

By the time Qiana, Ethan, and the pizzas arrived, Zang had arranged for one of his police officers to take off a week or so and serve as Jeremy's body guard. That done, he joined the group in the break room and ate a couple of slices of pizza himself.

Jeremy, who had been too frightened to be hungry, suddenly felt ravenous. He polished off half a pizza by himself. Then Zang led Jeremy, Ethan and Qiana back to his desk. "Okay, Jeremy," he said, "start at the beginning and don't leave anything out."

Jeremy had mentally rehearsed and relived his adventure over and over. Now he had no trouble reporting every detail from the miniature painting on his captors' boots to the sounds of their voices. When he said the name "Thor," Zang straightened and studied his face. "Did you say 'Thor'?" he asked.

Jeremy nodded.

Zang shook his head. "They were so careful and yet they let you hear that name." He was frowning. "Not very bright of them," he mused to himself.

"Do you think it was a trick?" Qiana asked. "Was there some reason they *wanted* him to hear the name?"

"Like they were trying to put the blame on someone else?" Zang asked.

Qiana shrugged. "Yeah, something like that."

"It's possible," said Zang. He turned to Jeremy. "Let's go over it one more time–the man who said 'Thor' had shut and locked the door of the room you were in. Right?"

Jeremy nodded.

"Maybe he just got careless," said Zang. "If he did ... well, if he did, we've got a starting place."

"Not many Thors on the Island?" asked Ethan.

"Only one I know of," replied Zang. Then he turned to Jeremy. "And he had a lightning bolt painted on his boot?"

Jeremy nodded and described the boot decoration for the second time. "There was a black, fluffy-looking cloud with a yellow zig-zag of lightning coming down from it. Like this ..." He helped himself to a pencil and a pad of paper from the detective's desk and made a sketch.

Zang tore off the sheet and set the drawing aside. "Good work, son. This picture may come in handy. Go on–what happened next?"

Jeremy finished his story, trying to minimize the terror he felt when he faced a dark ocean in a runaway power boat. But he fooled no one. Qiana and both men congratulated him on his courage.

"You're not only brave; you're very bright," Zang observed. "If you'd let those guys know who you were, it might not have gone so well for you."

Jeremy nodded vigorously. "That's what I thought. And that's what I want to talk to you about. I'm afraid for my Dad. Now that the goons know Maylea's dead, they're going to think my Dad has their money. Won't they go after him?"

The adults exchanged looks. "That's a good question," Zang said. He turned to Ethan. "Any chance of getting police protection for Mr. West?"

Ethan snorted. "Not likely! They have Dillon pegged as Maylea's murderer."

Zang nodded. "Yes, I spoke to your Lt. Daly today." He winked at Jeremy. "Perhaps we should bring Mr. West to Oahu where we can give him some protection."

"If he leaves the jurisdiction, they'll hunt him down and lock him up," Ethan said. "And Jeremy tells me his folks are planning to remarry. That's not going to sit well with our local detective either."

Jeremy looked up, surprise registering on his face. "How come? What difference does it make to the police if my Mom and Dad get married?"

"A wife can't be forced to testify against her husband at his trial," Ethan explained. "So they may think the marriage is evidence that your Dad has something to hide–something your Mom knows about."

Worry frowns creased Jeremy's forehead. "I don't want them to get married if it's going to make my Dad go to prison," he said. His voice was breathy with anxiety.

"Don't you worry," Ethan said. "I'll talk to your Dad and help him with the decision. Anyway, if we can find out who murdered Maylea, then it won't matter if your folks get married."

"But can you?" asked Jeremy. "Find out, I mean?"

Ethan glanced at Detective Zang, then returned his gaze to Jeremy. "We have to," he said. "That's all there is to it–we have to."

Chapter 16

Morning came quickly after the late night, but Ethan, Qiana and Jeremy were at the Waikiki police station at 9:00 o'clock to meet the police artist who was going to draw Trolley. He was a rumpled man in his 50s with thinning gray hair and light brown eyes. He shook hands all around, then turned his attention to Jeremy. "You're the only one among us who knew this Trolley, I believe?"

Jeremy nodded. "That's right." Then he grinned at the man and added, "You can start by drawing Granny Clampett."

The artist grinned back. "You talking about Granny from 'The Beverly Hillbillies'?"

"Yes, but Trolley's hair is short with lots of curls. It reminds me of Dad's after he grew it out to please Maylea," Jeremy added to Qiana. "Except Trolley's is gray instead of black."

"What does she like to wear?" the artist asked.

"I only saw her one weekend," Jeremy said, "and she was wearing a football jersey and black sweat pants."

"The team?"

"Vikings." Jeremy hesitated before adding, "Number 10, I think."

"Tarkenton, I'll wager," the artist muttered to himself, as he began drawing.

The image that emerged delighted Jeremy. "It's her!" he kept exclaiming. After directing the artist to loosen the curls, shorten the nose, and deepen the wrinkles, he stood back in amazement, gazing at the likeness of Trolley. She gazed back with the familiar wry twinkle in her eyes and a half smile on her lips. A purple

Minnesota Vikings jersey and black sweat pants covered her spry little body.

"It's perfect!" he told Qiana. "I think she's going to start singing, 'I've Been Working on the Railroad' any minute."

Qiana grinned at him. " 'I've Been Working on the Railroad'?" she asked. "Was that a song she sang often?"

"I think it was her favorite," Jeremy said. "She sang it all the time."

Zang was summoned to see the finished product and, assured by Jeremy that it was the "spitting image" of Trolley, he disappeared with the drawing. Ten minutes later, he returned with a handful of copies for Ethan. "What's next?" he asked the little group of Texans.

"I've got the list of businesses that Maylea and her accountant defrauded," Ethan said. "Alana is going to take us around to all of them so we can show people the picture of Trolley."

Zang nodded. "And what about you, young man?" he asked Jeremy. "Have your parents ordered you back to Texas?"

Jeremy shook his head. "They wanted to, but since my Grandma hired a body guard for me, they decided to let me stay."

"I'm glad to hear it," said Zang. He turned to Qiana. "I've asked an officer named Luke Kalama to hang out with Jeremy and Kimo today, and we'd appreciate it if you'll let the boys go up in a police chopper with him and take a look around." He returned to Jeremy, saying, "It turns out that both the helicopter and the boat those goons used to abduct you yesterday were stolen. Of course, we have the boat back, but we'd like to locate the helicopter. It's always possible that we'll pick up a stray fingerprint or some other kind of clue. What do you think?"

Jeremy's face was alight. "Oboy! Can I, Qiana? Please. A helicopter ride–oh man!"

Qiana studied Zang's face. "Would you let your child fly in a helicopter with this guy?" she asked.

"I would, and I have."

Qiana smiled. "That's good enough for me."

After meeting Officer Kalama, Ethan and Qiana left to pick up Alana. Luke and Jeremy headed out to get Kimo in Luke's open-air jeep. Both boys were too excited to sit still. "I've never ridden in a helicopter," Jeremy confided to his body guard, who insisted on being called Luke.

"You're going to love it!" Luke promised. Then he glanced at the back seat where Kimo was fidgeting excitedly. "How about you, Kimo? Have you ever flown in a chopper before?"

"I have," said Kimo, "but never on a police case! Do you really think we might find the stolen helicopter?"

"I think it's possible," Luke said. "Which way did it head after they grabbed Jeremy?"

"Toward the leeward side," Kimo replied. "I watched until it was out of sight, and it never turned back."

"Good job," Luke said approvingly. "If you ever want to join the force, call me. I'll give you a recommendation."

Kimo beamed. He'd never thought of being a policeman, but now he considered it. It would sure beat being a surgeon like his Dad! But still, he had his plans with Kaniela to open their own charter helicopter business. ...

"Hey Kimo! You back there?" Jeremy yelled.

"Course I am! Whaddya' want?"

"Which trail were we on yesterday?"

Kimo gave Luke instructions, and soon the three of them were soaring above the emerald island of Oahu, peering intently into ravines and glades, searching for the stolen helicopter that had spirited Jeremy away the previous day. "Even if we can't find it," Jeremy said enthusiastically, "this is one of the greatest days of my life!"

"Maybe you'll move to Oahu and go into business with Danny and me," Kimo said.

Jeremy grinned at his new friend. "Maybe I will!"

The quest that drove Ethan, Qiana, and Alana was as fruitless as that of the three in the air, but much less fun. A few of the people they questioned thought Trolley looked familiar, but no one knew who she was.

Ethan sighed as they all climbed into Alana's car for the 10th time. "They yell and screech at us as if it's our fault Maylea stole their money. As if we're in cahoots with her. Like we're friends of hers."

"They're venting," said Qiana. "They need somebody to take it out on, and we're probably the closest link they've found to her."

Ethan made a wry face. "Well, they couldn't detest her any more than I do, and I'm tired of being linked with her. The only problem they have is theft–we're dealing with murder."

"But she wasn't the murderer," said Qiana. "She was the murderee, so you can't hold her responsible."

"Why not?" growled Ethan. "I don't know of anybody who was asking for it more. If she'd developed a little character, she might be alive today."

The 11th stop was at a small, informal flower shop. While a salesgirl was staring at Maylea's photo, trying to remember her, a customer leaned over Trolley's picture, which was lying on the counter. "Trolley?" she said uncertainly. She held up the picture. "Is this Trolley?"

"Trolley who?" Ethan asked, barely daring to breathe.

The woman thought for a long moment before she said, "I don't think I know her last name."

"Well, then, how do you know her?" he asked.

"I used to see her in the grocery store occasionally. You know, the one around the corner. I noticed her because she was singing 'The Yellow Rose of Texas,' to herself–soft, almost under her breath."

Ethan and Qiana exchanged glances. " 'The Yellow Rose of Texas'," he repeated. "Did she say she was from Texas?"

"I don't know if she actually said it, but I got the impression that she was." The woman frowned slightly. "Why do you have her picture? Has something happened to her?"

Ethan nodded. "You might say that. She witnessed a murder, then disappeared. We're hoping we can find her, but we don't even know her real name. Anything you can tell us will help."

The woman wrinkled her brow as she struggled with her memory. Seeing that she seemed to have drawn a blank, Qiana retrieved the picture of Maylea and held it out. "What about this woman?" she asked. "Have you ever seen her?"

"Yes, I do remember her," said the woman, "She was with Trolley at the grocery store one time. I thought they were discussing what to cook for supper, but I'm not sure. As soon as I greeted Trolley, that younger woman slipped away. At first, it seemed to me that she didn't want to be seen with Trolley, but I decided I was being silly. She probably went to get whatever they'd decided to buy."

"Did Trolley say anything about her?" asked Ethan.

The woman shook her head. "Trolley acted as if she didn't exist. We visited for a few minutes about the weather and such, then we parted. I didn't see the younger woman again."

When it was clear the woman had told them all she knew, Ethan handed her his card with his cell phone number on it. "Please call if you think of anything else," he pleaded. "*Anything!*"

Leaving the flower shop, Ethan, Qiana and Alana made a beeline for the grocery store around the corner. And, although it felt as if they showed Trolley's picture to a thousand shoppers and clerks, not even one of them remembered her. "Well, that's that," Ethan observed as they piled into the car again. "What's our next stop, Qiana?"

Glumly, the three continued making the rounds of the various shops and businesses Maylea had targeted, but they got no new leads. Just more yelling, threats and anger.

Meanwhile, Luke, Jeremy, and Kimo had flown the island from tip to tip and side to side, stopping briefly for lunch. By midafternoon, Luke sighed and said, "Unless you guys have somewhere you want to go, just for fun, I'm ready to call it a day."

"Maybe," Kimo said, "they left the chopper at some heliport, right in the middle of a bunch of other helicopters."

Luke looked thoughtful. "You know, maybe that's exactly what they did." He got on the radio and gave instructions to someone on the ground to call around to the helicopter services on Oahu. That done, he headed for home. "Tell your grandmother," he told

Jeremy, "there's no charge for today. This was police business, and I'll be paid by the department."

Luke and the boys had turned in the helicopter and headed for Luke's jeep when his cell phone vibrated. He opened it, spoke briefly, then put it away. "They found it," he said. "You had a good idea Kimo. It's being checked out right now."

The three high-fived each other all around and climbed into the jeep. Luke handed his cell phone to Jeremy, "Call your folks and see when and where they want to meet," he instructed.

Ethan, Qiana, and Alana, thoroughly exhausted after their tedious day, said they would pick up the boys at Waikiki police headquarters in fifteen minutes. They had visited every business establishment on the list, and found only the one woman who so much as knew Trolley's name. The two groups met in the parking lot and were exchanging the tidbits of information that had gathered that day when Detective Zang joined them.

After exchanging greetings and listening to reports from Luke and Ethan, he said to Ethan, "I've made arrangements for you to see Kevin Vickery tomorrow."

Ethan's face lighted up. "That's great news! I've been wishing for a way to expedite the process."

Zang nodded. "Vickery expedited it. He begged to see you as soon as possible. I suspect he's hoping you can help him get out of prison."

"Whew!" Ethan whistled. "I don't know how I could do that."

Zang shrugged. "I guess that's his problem." He told Ethan when and where to go for his meeting with Vickery, then bid the little group goodbye and went back inside.

"How about tomorrow we go snorkeling?" asked Luke. "I know a good reef that's less crowded than some."

"Yeah!" cried Jeremy. "That'd be super. Can Qiana come too?"

Luke looked at Jeremy's attractive aunt and grinned. "Of course!"

Chapter 17

At his first sight of Kevin Vickery, Ethan did a double-take. Vickery had an average-sized, athletic body and a mop of dark curly hair. Although his facial features were unlike Dillon's, his overall appearance resembled uncannily the man Maylea had married.

"Your name is Holmes?" Vickery asked. His voice was low and weary.

"That's right," said Ethan, offering his hand. Vickery's handshake was firmer than Ethan had expected, judging by his voice. "I appreciate your seeing me," he said.

Vickery shrugged. "What else have I got to do?"

Ethan seated himself across from Kevin Vickery. "Would you be surprised to know that your appearance resembles the appearance of my client, Lin's husband?"

Vickery didn't even look up. "I wouldn't be surprised or interested. The only thing that interests me is what you're going to do to get me out of this hell hole."

"Me!" exclaimed Ethan. "Getting you out of here is *your* lawyer's job."

"My lawyer, the public defender?" sneered Vickery. "He couldn't get me out of a one-room cabin with five open doors."

"You used a public defender? Why?"

"Why? Why?!" Vickery cried. "Do you think I had a penny left to my name after Lin Choi finished with me?"

"Oh," Ethan said, "I see what you mean."

"Well, get on with it. What are you doing here?"

Ethan opened his brief case and handed over the picture of Trolley. "Have you ever seen this woman?" he asked.

Vickery glanced at the picture. "Sure, that's Trolley, Lin's housekeeper."

"Trolley?" Ethan repeated. "What's her real first name? Her last name?"

"Beats me," said Vickery. "She's just an old woman. Who cares?"

"I do. My client does," said Ethan. "My client has been indicted for Lin's murder and Trolley is the only one who can help him."

"Your client was married to Lin?" Vickery asked.

"That's right."

Vickery actually put his head down on his folded arms and began to cry. "Why him? Why wouldn't she marry me?" he sobbed. "I want her back. Please get her back for me."

Stunned, Ethan protested, "But she's dead. And she's the reason you're in prison. Why would you want her back?"

When Vickery made no response, Ethan ordered, "Buck up, man. I need your help. Why would you want her back anyway? She's about as low as any lowlife I ever heard of."

Still no response except sobbing.

"Look, Kevin," Ethan tried again, "what was so great about her except her beauty? One thing. Tell me one scroungy reason you want her back besides the way she looked."

The sobbing seemed to lessen. After a few moments, Vickery straightened up and stared at Ethan. "You're right," he said. "There's not another reason." He seemed about to tear up again. "What's wrong with me? Why would I let a woman ruin me just because she's gorgeous?"

"I'm a lawyer, not a psychologist," Ethan said, "but I think it's safe to say you weren't alone. My client left one of the loveliest, finest women I've ever met in order to marry Maylea ... I mean Lin. He hadn't known Lin two weeks when he dumped a fabulous wife and a great 13-year-old kid."

Vickery looked interested. "And was he destroyed when she died?"

"Hardly," said Ethan. "Maybe that's why the police have him pegged as the murderer."

"How'd she get her hook in him?"

"He's an accountant like you," Ethan said, noticing the quickened interest in Vickery's bearing. "He came here last February for a seminar and Maylea attached herself to him. Then, in April, she showed up at his office in Lubbock, Texas, claiming she was pregnant with his child."

"I remember that seminar," said Vickery. "I was there. And Lin–what did you call her, Maylea?"

"Yes, she told Dillon her name was Maylea Kanaka."

Vickery nodded. "Very interesting. About that time–February–she was declaring her undying love for *me*." He gave a little snort. "Maybe it's my kid."

Ethan shook his head. "Nope, there was no kid. At least, not then. She did manage to get pregnant in time for the divorce, but she was only two months pregnant when she should have been four."

"Lowlife," Vickery muttered, almost to himself. "I'm beginning to see what you mean."

"Are you kidding?" asked Ethan. "Didn't you get it when she swindled your clients and left you holding the bag?"

Vickery shook his head. "I've spent every day I've been here making excuses for her. Making excuses and waiting for her to come back and rescue me. I was sure there had to be some kind of mistake. Some way she was an innocent victim ..."

"I'm sorry, man," Ethan said, and meant it, "but she wouldn't come back to you even if she were alive. She's already milked you dry."

Vickery nodded glumly. "So much for that fantasy."

Ethan took another stab at his objective. "Look, I desperately need you to tell me everything you know about Trolley. I can't even get a handle on her real name–first or last."

Vickery gave the lawyer a piercing look. "Okay. I'll help you if you help me."

"How can I help you?"

"Well, for starters, ask her husband to return the money she stole from my clients. Maybe then I'll have a prayer of getting out of this stinking place!"

"Her husband?" Ethan asked. "Her husband doesn't have any money. She was doing her best to drive him into bankruptcy."

Vickery scowled. "Then where is all that money?"

Ethan shrugged. "One of the things I was hoping to learn from you."

Vickery studied him a few more moments, then said, "Okay, I'll tell you what I know. It's not much so what's the point of holding out? I don't know the old woman's real name or her address. All I know is that one day she was in Lin's house, cooking and cleaning. When I asked about her, Lin said she was a pitiful old woman who needed a job."

"Did she live with Lin?"

"I'm not sure," Vickery said, "but I think she did."

"And you have no idea how I might find her?"

Vickery shook his head. "No clue. And I don't think Lin liked her. Sometimes I saw her glaring at Trolley or covering her ears when Trolley sang."

"Did Trolley like Lin?"

Vickery thought a moment before he said, "Trolley was like an owl, circling ... circling ... circling ... waiting for her prey to come out of its burrow. But she never betrayed an emotion. She just waited–waited with that cheerful, grinning exterior."

Ethan sat back to think. Finally he said, "You're describing a cat and mouse relationship. And I think you're saying Trolley is the cat and Lin the mouse. Right?"

"I don't know. Maybe." Vickery lapsed back into his lethargy. "Who cares?"

"Maybe *you* should care. If I can find Trolley, she might know where the loot is," Ethan said. "If that's the case, maybe I *will* be able to help you."

Vickery brightened a bit. "Well, in that case, I wish you all the luck in the world."

"Look, just for my own information, would you tell me how Lin got you into this mess?"

Vickery sighed deeply. "I had my office at my house and apparently Lin was coming over when I wasn't there and going through my files. I found her at the house once when she wasn't supposed to be there and she said she was waiting for me as a surprise. Of course, I believed her."

"And that's all there was to it?" Ethan asked. "At least, from your perspective? You never suspected she was up to anything?"

"Not even once," Vickery said. "I thought the police had gone off their *trolleys*–sorry, I couldn't resist–when they arrested me."

Ethan smiled grimly at Vickery's trolley joke. "What about Lin– did you ever meet her parents or any member of her family? Do you know if they live on Oahu?"

"No idea," said Vickery. "When I asked about her family, she changed the subject."

Ethan nodded forlornly. "Okay, one last question," he said, rising to go. "Where was Lin's house?"

Vickery laughed mockingly. "Don't get your hopes up. The police went through every inch of it, and so did I. There's nothing there. Nothing except rotting memories."

To Qiana's delighted eyes, the beauty below the tropical ocean rivaled the beauty of the Islands themselves. Brightly colored fish darted among brightly colored plants in a sun-dappled wonderland. A sea turtle cruised below her at one point, and she even caught sight of a shark in the shadowy depths.

The distant shark didn't frighten her. Nothing could frighten her. Her senses were mellowed in the warmth of the caressing ocean. She let her limbs float freely, barely bothering to propel herself through the water. Why bother? Let the tide carry her where it would. Her breathing was slow and relaxed through a bright yellow snorkel tube. The gentle peace that engulfed her was hypnotic–a sedative. She wanted to stay awake and enjoy the enchanted kingdom below her. At the same time, she wanted to drift into dreamland and stay forever in this lovely state of tranquility.

When Jeremy swam up beside her and tapped her shoulder, she almost swallowed the mouthpiece of her snorkel. Her startled expression sent Jeremy into spasms of silent laughter. When he was through laughing, he cocked his thumb toward land. Qiana nodded and reluctantly began swimming toward shore.

"I want to do that every day," Qiana said, nodding toward the ocean, as she and Luke spread out the picnic lunch Alana had sent.

"What–snorkel?" Luke asked.

"Yes. In that great, big, luscious ocean."

Luke grinned. "I've heard that a few times."

"And does anyone ever mean it?" Qiana asked.

"They all mean it, I think, but almost none of them stay," Luke said. "In the end, the call of home is too strong."

Qiana nodded. "For me too, but I'll never forget this morning. Thank you for bringing us here, Luke."

"My pleasure," Luke said, as Jeremy and Kimo galloped up with four large cups of fruit punch.

"What's for lunch?" Jeremy asked. "I could eat a whale!"

"Tuna fish sandwiches on homemade bread and an assortment of fruits," Qiana told him. "Help yourselves, boys. You first–I'm only hungry enough to eat a shark."

The lunch was devoured in short order, then Luke, Jeremy, and Kimo went off to toss a Frisbee around. Qiana watched them for awhile, then growing restless, decided to try some shave ice. Walking around her three companions who were whooping with glee, she took her place at the end of the line at the shave ice kiosk.

Jeremy had seen Qiana walk past, but it barely registered until he heaved himself into the air for a particularly difficult catch and landed face-down in the dirt. Spluttering and wiping sand off his face, he found himself staring at the back of a pair of dusty brown hiking boots with bolts of lightning painted on the inner surfaces. Looking up, he saw a tall, burly man reaching for Qiana.

"Nooooooo!" he bellowed. He launched himself at the man. Jeremy hit his target at the waist and clamped onto him, driving him forward. As the man staggered and fell to one knee, a gun flew from his hand and hit the sand.

Qiana, turning, was horrified to see her nephew attached to a large oriental man with tattooed arms. Jeremy was yelling and yanking the man's hair. But she didn't get a word out before Luke was there, snapping handcuffs into place. And then two other men, wearing beach attire, materialized. One led the captive away and the other took possession of the gun almost before she could catch her breath.

"What ... ? Who ... ? How ... ?" she sputtered, unable to decide which question to ask first. She finally settled on, "What just happened here?"

Luke turned to Jeremy. "What just happened here?" he asked.

"That was the man with the lightning bolts on his boots," Jeremy said, still gasping for breath. "He was about to grab you, Qiana."

Qiana's eyes widened. "Me? Why me?"

Luke winked at Jeremy. "They must have realized they made a mistake when they let Jeremy go. They want a hostage, and you separated from our group, so they chose you."

Qiana shivered. "They were going to grab me right here on this beach in front of everyone?"

"Oh, Thor could have put his gun to your back and persuaded you to make a very quiet exit," Luke said.

"But what if I didn't? What if I started screaming? He would have been a sitting duck."

Luke frowned. "*You* would have been a dead duck. And he didn't know there were police around. He assumed all these people were nice, peace-loving souls who would have no interest in playing hero. I'm sure he thought you would be an easy mark–he would pull you around the shave ice stand and into a vehicle before anyone noticed you were gone."

Qiana wrapped Jeremy in a bear hug and held on to him for a long time. "Thank you for saving me," she said. She didn't want anyone to know that her legs were rubbery and the hug was partly for support.

Jeremy hugged her back. "Sure Aunt QiQi. Any time."

"Come on," Luke said. "Let's get back to headquarters. The boss is going to want you to listen to this bird's voice and see if you recognize it."

"So that guy was Thor?" Jeremy asked.

Luke nodded. "That's my guess."

"And who were the two men who took him away?" asked Qiana.

"Police officers," said Luke.

"You mean they were following us all the time?"

"Yes," said Luke, "but we thought the bad guys would try to nab Jeremy again. We were all concentrating on him. It was stupid of us not to realize that you could be a target too. So could Mr. Holmes, for that matter." He ruffled Jeremy's hair as they walked toward the parking area. "You can tell your grandmother that she won't have to pay for today either. I'm on the clock. It wasn't our plan to use you for bait, but we couldn't figure out any way to keep you *from* being bait without making you stay hidden for the rest of your vacation, and that's no fun."

"So do you think the danger is past?" Qiana asked. "Will that one–that Thor–lead you to the rest of his gang?"

"Good question," said Luke. "We might find out pretty soon now." He opened the front passenger door of his jeep for Qiana and the boys climbed into the back seat.

Detective Zang had waited for Luke and the others to arrive before interrogating his prisoner, in case Thor clammed up on him. But he needn't have worried. As soon as he walked into the room where Thor was being held, the big man began swearing and shouting at him.

"Where's my lawyer?" he cried belligerently. "Let me out of here. You got nothing on me."

His gravelly voice was unmistakable and Jeremy nodded at Luke. "That's him. I'm sure."

Luke nodded. "Then his nene is cooked."

"His what?" Jeremy asked.

"His goose," Kimo said, for both Luke and Qiana had returned their attention to Zang and Thor.

"You had a handgun at the beach, threatening a tourist," Zang was saying. "Your lawyer can't get you out of that one."

"Gun! What gun?" Thor roared. "If there was a gun at the beach, it belonged to you cops, not me."

Zang was calm and soft-spoken. "Then why are yours the only fingerprints on it?" he asked.

"It's a set-up. I'm being framed!" Thor's face was purple with rage. "Get me out of here. Where's my lawyer? How much is my bail? I can't stay in this cage!"

Zang shrugged. "You're the one who called your lawyer. I believe you said he's in court this afternoon."

"Then get him out," Thor ordered. "Get him out! This place is closing in on me."

"What were you doing with a gun at the beach?" Zang asked.

"I'm not talking until my lawyer gets here," Thor barked. "What do you think I am–stupid?"

"Whatever you say." Zang rose and headed for the door.

"Hey don't leave me in here!" Thor yelled. "Get me out of here."

Zang walked out, leaving Thor to rage alone. He joined Luke, Qiana, Jeremy and Kimo. "Good work," he told them. "The guy seems to be a little claustrophobic. If I let him stew awhile, I might get something out of him." He turned his attention to Jeremy. "So what do you think? Is he the guy who grabbed you yesterday?"

Jeremy nodded eagerly. "I'm sure he is. It's the same voice."

Zang nodded. "And he was going for Ms. Jamison today, right?"

"That's right," Jeremy said. "I dived for the Frisbee and ended up on the ground right behind those boots with the lightning bolts on them. When I looked up, I saw he was reaching for Aunt Qiana."

"I understand you tackled him and sent his gun sailing," Zang said smiling.

Jeremy grinned. "I would have been afraid if I'd stopped to think about it, but I didn't want him to get his paws on my aunt."

Zang nodded. "Good for you. No wonder she's so proud of you!"

"She's proud of me?" Jeremy asked. He looked at Qiana in surprise and saw the pride shining in her eyes.

"She's proud of you," Qiana said, giving him a quick hug.

"Well, I'm going to let our guest think about his predicament for awhile," Zang said. "I'll give Mr. Holmes a call on his cell if I get anything out of him that might help you."

He shook hands all around with his bone crushing grip and left Qiana, Jeremy, and Kimo massaging their hands to restore circulation. "Somebody should tell that man he's not allowed to shake hands with anyone," Qiana said, giving her hand one last rub.

Luke grinned. "He's been told, but he forgets."

"We should put a sign on him," Jeremy observed. "A pair of hands shaking in a circle and a crossbar marking it out."

Kimo laughed. "That's a good idea. We'll make one for him."

"No, you won't," Qiana said. "He's a nice man and we're not going to hurt his feelings."

The four of them strolled back to the parking lot and found Ethan climbing out of the rental car. "Ethan! Over here!" Jeremy called.

"Did you learn anything useful?" Qiana asked, as Ethan joined them.

"Thor tried to kidnap Qiana," Jeremy said at the same time.

Ethan immediately forgot Kevin Vickery. "Thor?" he asked, studying Qiana anxiously for any sign of injury. "You saw Thor? What happened?"

Jeremy reported on their adventure at the beach with an occasional comment from Qiana. When he finished his tale, Ethan turned to Qiana. "Are you okay?"

"Sure, he never even touched me," she said. "The worst part of the day for me was having to leave the reef. It was so beautiful and peaceful I could have stayed there forever. But what about you? Did you learn anything?"

"Not much," Ethan said ruefully. "Vickery was pretty much besotted with Maylea. Of course, she was Lin Choi to him. And he recognized Trolley immediately. Called her by name, but he doesn't know her real name or origin."

"How did he know her?" Qiana asked.

"Same way the rest of us did," said Ethan, "as Maylea's housekeeper."

"Really?" Qiana's forehead wrinkled in a frown. "So maybe they were a team?"

Ethan shook his head. "I didn't get that from Vickery. He thought Maylea disliked Trolley and Trolley looked on Maylea as some kind of prey."

Seeing the puzzled expressions of the others, he repeated Vickery's words, comparing Trolley to a circling owl. "I think there was something going on there that none of us knows about," he said.

"And remember the lady at the store?" Qiana put in excitedly. "She said Trolley acted as if Maylea didn't exist."

Ethan nodded. "Now if we can figure out what it means," he said.

"What are your plans for the rest of the afternoon?" Luke asked. "I know a place where the boys can take a swim with some dolphins if you two are going off investigating again. Or you can all come take a dip with the dolphins," he added, seeing Qiana's face light up.

"Oh, I'd love to!" Qiana cried. "But I have an idea that I want to check out with Ethan."

Luke's eyebrows rose. "You want to tell me about it?" he asked.

Qiana and Ethan exchanged long looks, then she shrugged. "It's one of the waitresses at Windsong Towers. She was super nervous. I want to talk to her again. What do you think, Ethan?"

Ethan was nodding. "I think it's a good idea." He turned to Luke. "Did your people ever determine who the conncction was between Windsong Towers and Thor's goon squad?"

"Not yet," Luke said.

"She might be it," said Ethan. "So you take the boys on that dolphin adventure and we'll see if we can find the nervous waitress."

Luke hesitated. "It might be dangerous," he warned. "Maybe you should tell Zang your theory and leave it up to him."

Ethan was shaking his head. "She won't talk to cops. And she probably won't talk to us, but I'd like to try."

Luke held up his hands in surrender. "You may be right. I'll have the boys back at your place in a few hours."

The two groups parted ways, but before Luke started his engine, he called Detective Zang and told him where Ethan and Qiana were going. "You didn't tell Ethan you were going to snitch," Jeremy said accusingly after Luke tucked his cell phone away.

Luke gave him a serious look. "Look kid, this isn't a game, and I'm not Magnum P.I. I do what I have to do." He turned the key in the ignition and pulled out of the parking lot.

"Are Ethan and Qiana going to get in trouble for seeing that woman?" Jeremy asked.

"Not from the good guys," Luke assured him. "I can't speak for the bad guys."

"Hey, how much is this going to cost?" Kimo blurted. The issue of snitching wasn't his problem. Paying to swim with dolphins was, he knew, a very expensive proposition.

"Nothing," Luke said. "I have some friends who train dolphins, and they're always looking for novices for their dolphins to practice on."

"Novices?" Kimo asked, frowning at the unfamiliar word.

"Beginners. Someone who doesn't swim with dolphins much. The kind of clients these dolphins will be entertaining every day pretty soon," Luke explained.

Kimo looked relieved. "Okay, then. I don't care if dolphins practice on me all the time!"

❦

At Windsong Towers, Qiana and Ethan found the head waitress, Kiana with a K. She seated them in a secluded corner, brought them drinks, and promised to send Puna, the nervous waitress, to them. In less than five minutes, Puna appeared.

"Please sit down," Ethan said. "I'd like to buy you a drink."

Puna refused a drink and seated herself on the edge of a chair. "Kiana says I must talk to you," she said. "What do you want?"

Ethan held up the drawing of Trolley. "Do you know this woman?" he asked.

Puna put her hand over her mouth, then reached for the picture. "It's Troll*ee*!" she gasped. "Where is Troll*ee*?" With her eyes closed, she suddenly pulled the picture close to her heart, as if she were hugging it.

Ethan and Qiana exchanged amazed glances. "We don't know where she is," Ethan said. "We were hoping you could help us find her."

Puna opened her eyes and glared at them suspiciously. "First you come here talking about Lin Choi. And now you ask about Troll*ee*. Why?"

"She's a witness in a murder case–Lin Choi's murder case–and we need her desperately to keep an innocent man from going to prison," Ethan said. "I'm his lawyer, and we came to Oahu, hoping to find Trolley. How do you know her?"

Puna was silent for long moments. Finally she said hesitantly, "Troll*ee* is like my grandmother, my tutu. If she wants to be found, she will be found. If she doesn't want to be found, I don't want her to be found."

"Then you *do* know where she is?" Qiana asked gently.

"No!" Puna cried. "No. I haven't seen her in months. I want to know where she is myself."

"Puna, please tell us whatever you know about Trolley," Qiana pleaded. "Lin's husband didn't kill her, but he's probably going to go to prison for a long, long time if we can't find Trolley and get her to tell us who killed her."

"Why do you think Troll*ee* knows who killed Lin?" Puna asked with a stubborn set to her jaw.

"She was living there in the house with them," Ethan explained. "But when Lin was found dead, Trolley was gone. We're worried about her. We're afraid she might have been murdered too, and her body hidden. Or else, she's hiding from the murderer."

"You want to blame Troll*ee* for killing Lin Choi," Puna said accusingly. "I hope you never find her."

She rose to leave, but Ethan caught her arm and gently tugged downward. "Puna, please believe us. We don't blame Trolley, but we *have* to find her. Please, please tell us what you know about her. Do you know her real name?"

Puna sank back into her chair. Tears formed in her eyes, but she brushed them away and said, "Troll*ee* hated Lin Choi. I hated Lin Choi. And so we were friends."

"Why did Trolley hate Lin Choi?" Ethan asked.

Puna took a deep, ragged breath. "Lin Choi was going to marry her grandson, but she didn't. Instead, she married an old, rich man. Troll*ee*'s grandson is still crying for Lin."

Ethan and Qiana waited, barely breathing, willing Puna to continue. But she was silent.

"Why did you hate Lin?" Qiana asked at last.

"Lin Choi stole my gentleman friend," Puna said. "He is a great man and very wealthy, so she wanted him. And she got him."

"Does he know Lin's dead?" Qiana asked?

"Yes, I told him that night–that night you first came here. I showed him who you were so he could talk to you himself. But he still didn't want me back, not after he's had Lin Choi!" Before Ethan or Qiana could stop her, Puna sprang up and fled.

"Maybe I can catch her," Qiana said, standing.

"No wait," said Ethan. "It's too soon. We'll come back another day after she's had time to think about it."

"After she's had time to disappear," Qiana said, seating herself again.

"Did she tell you what you want to know?" asked a soft voice. Neither Ethan nor Qiana had heard Kiana approach.

"Some," said Qiana, "but we upset her again and she ran away."

"She can be stubborn," Kiana said. "Maybe she will tell you more another day."

"Maybe you can help us," Ethan said. "Puna told us that Lin Choi stole her gentleman friend. Do you know who he is?"

It was Kiana's turn to look nervous. "I know, but I don't like to say his name. If I tell you and he finds out, I'll be with Lin Choi."

Ethan looked interested. "Really? Then maybe he's the man we're after. Maybe he's the one who killed Lin."

Kiana shivered. "He wouldn't do it, but he would have it done. And it wouldn't be the first time." She glanced around the room. Her eyes stopped at a figure in the doorway. Then she was gone.

Qiana and Ethan both strained to see the man who had frightened Kiana, but he was only a shadow. Before they could even get a good look at his clothing, he faded away.

"Whoa! That dude must be one scary character!" Qiana whispered.

"Too scary for us, I'm thinking," Ethan agreed. "Do you think we can get out of this place alive?"

"Let's try it and *now*," Qiana urged. Ethan tossed some money on the table, took Qiana's hand and led her through the shadows along the edge of the room toward the door. They stepped out into blinding sunlight and stopped to let their eyes adjust.

"Any luck?" asked a voice in a bush.

Ethan and Qiana almost jumped out of their skins before they recognized Detective Zang, lurking in the shadows. Qiana collapsed into Ethan's arms, her legs too weak too hold her. "Are you trying to scare me to death?" she asked.

"There's a coffee shop on the next block," Zang said, pointing. "Meet me there in five minutes." Then he was gone.

"I never saw so many disappearing people," Qiana said, still whispering.

"Same here," Ethan whispered back.

Zang beat them to the coffee shop. He was seated at the back of the big, sunny room where he had a good view of the door when Ethan and Qiana arrived. They slid into the booth across from him.

Keeping a careful scrutiny of the areas, both inside and outside the coffee shop, Zang asked, "Well?"

"Luke called you?" Ethan asked.

"Yes."

"Were we followed?" Qiana asked, looking nervously toward the window.

"Doesn't appear to be the case," said Zang. "Did you learn anything?" He took his eyes off the door long enough to stare piercingly into Ethan's eyes for a long moment.

"It seems," Ethan said, "that a waitress named Puna hated Lin for stealing her gentleman friend. The minute she learned Lin was dead, she notified the gentleman, apparently hoping to get him back. He wasn't interested."

Zang nodded. "And who is this gentleman friend?"

"We couldn't find out. Puna ran out in tears and Kiana, the head waitress, was afraid to name him. Puna said he's a great man and very wealthy. Kiana was afraid of joining Lin Choi if she mentioned his name."

Zang nodded thoughtfully, his eyes ever vigilant.

"You know who he is, don't you?" asked Qiana, studying his face.

"I may," said Zang, "and if so, it would be better for the both of you if he never learns you're trying to find him."

"Do you think he's responsible for Lin's murder?" asked Ethan.

Zang shook his head slowly. "I can't say. It would be in character, but who knows?"

"Then I don't have any choice except to continue trying to find him," said Ethan stubbornly. "My client will almost surely be convicted unless I can name the true murderer."

"Then I suggest," said Detective Zang sternly, "that you find someone else to name."

He stood and strode out of the shop.

Qiana and Ethan stared at each other. "Now what?" Qiana asked. "Do we have to order something?"

"I don't suppose we have to," said Ethan, "but let's do."

Qiana was eating chocolate macadamia nut ice cream and Ethan was drinking Hawaiian espresso when Qiana's cell phone rang. Glancing at the caller I.D., Qiana clicked it on and said, "Hello, Mother. How's Texas?"

"A better question is 'How's Hawaii?' " said Shelley Jamison.

"Hawaii is fabulous!" cried Qiana. "I wish you were here–I want to show you a million things."

"Qiana, Bethany Jamison just called me," said Shelley going straight to the purpose of her call. "She had heard from a Detective Zang, and she's frantic with worry about all of you."

"Oh." Qiana's good mood at hearing her mother's voice fizzled.

"I want to know," Shelley continued, "are you in as much danger as Bethany says you are?"

Qiana studied Ethan's face as if she could read an answer there. "I'm not sure. I guess it's possible," she finally said.

"I want you to do me a favor," Shelley said and her voice was very serious.

"Please don't ask me to come home now," Qiana pleaded. "Just don't ask."

"I won't," Shelley said. "I want you to take two days off. Two days. Don't poke your noses into anybody's business. Don't ask any questions. Just enjoy Hawaii for two days. Give the police a chance to do their job. That's what this Detective Zang asked for–two days."

Qiana sighed. "Mom, it's not fair to send Ethan out alone after a murderer."

"Of course not. I'm talking about all of you–you, Jeremy, *and* Mr. Holmes."

"I'll talk to *Mr. Holmes* about it," Qiana said, giving Ethan a charming smile as she referred to him as "Mr." "That's the best I can do."

She was ready to sign off, but Shelley's voice rose. "No, that's *not* the best you can do. You'll have to promise me or hang up on me–one or the other. I won't leave you alone until you agree to give the police two days while you do nothing except enjoy your holiday."

Qiana gazed speculatively at Ethan. Actually, two days of fun in the sun sounded like a little slice of heaven. "Okay, Mom, I can't promise for Ethan, but I will promise for Jeremy and me."

Shelley's whole tone had changed when she spoke again–relaxed and relieved. "Use your influence on him. I think you can bring him around to your way of thinking."

Qiana turned her most seductive smile on Ethan, as she said, "I'll do my best."

That evening, Ethan received calls from Dillon, Nettie, and Bethany, all urging him to spend two days seeing the sights and enjoying Oahu. "Qiana says you haven't been to Diamond Head or Pearl Harbor yet," was Nettie's ploy. "I want Jeremy to see both of those places while he's there. And I know you can fill two days with activities you'll all enjoy." Her tone was motherly and a little bit desperate.

Since he had already yielded to Qiana's arm-twisting, the calls were unnecessary, but Ethan responded as graciously as he could manage. After hanging up with Bethany, the last to phone, he said to Qiana. "Who's going to call me next? *Your* mother? Lt. Daly? Some pirate's pet parrot?"

Qiana laughed. "Your guess is as good as mine."

But the calls were over, and with Alana's help an agenda was settled on. They would go to Pearl Harbor the next morning, and the Dole Pineapple Plantation in the afternoon. The following day it would be Diamond Head in the morning and kayaking in the afternoon.

With Kimo and Luke for tour guides, the two-day hiatus was a resounding success. Ethan was jumpy and distracted at first, but once the tour of the USS Arizona was underway, he returned with the rest of the group to the day that is living in infamy, December 7, 1941. His eyes quit darting from face to face like a jittery sparrow, and he listened intently to the historical record of those deadly moments that catapulted the United States into World War II. Luke, on the other hand, without betraying his alertness by so much as a twitch, saw everything and everybody around him. And so by the end of Saturday, their second day of sightseeing, the Texans felt like exhausted, contented tourists. They compared notes and relived favorite moments from their excursions, then fell into bed to sleep deeply and peacefully.

On Sunday morning, Alana took Jeremy to church with Luke in tow. Qiana and Ethan slept late, but rose in time for Ethan to make a couple of futile phone calls, trying to reach Detective Zang.

"Ethan, it's Sunday. Give the man a break," Qiana said after the second failed attempt.

"He said two days. He's had two days. I want to know what's going on," Ethan said stubbornly. But he was out of phone numbers to try, so he had no choice but to wait impatiently for the next day.

And the waiting was pleasant enough, for the whole group, including Luke, ate Sunday dinner with Kimo's family. Then Kimo's father, the junior Dr. Rand, took them out onto the Pacific Ocean in his cabin cruiser. They sailed all the way around Oahu, receiving detailed reports about everything they saw from members of the Rand family. And Dr. Rand gave Jeremy a few sailing lessons, "… just in case you ever have another occasion to be the skipper," he said, setting a captain's cap on Jeremy's head.

Jeremy adjusted the cap and took the wheel, feeling very excited and very important, especially when he was allowed to dock the boat. "Thank you, sir," he said seriously. "I think this was the best day of my life."

"Oh you say that all the time," Kimo hooted. "When we hiked the trail. In the helicopter …"

Jeremy took a fake swing at Kimo. "Well, it keeps getting better and better!" he said.

And Qiana offered her enthusiastic thanks. "Every time I think this trip can't get any better, something else wonderful happens. Thank you so much for this beautiful day."

"It was my pleasure," Greg Rand said. "You know, your father was something of an idol to me. Like many youngsters, I was too stupid to appreciate my own father, but Dr. Phillip was so skillful and so cool under pressure that I thought I could do nothing better with my life than be just like him."

"How kind you are!" Qiana cried. "I can't say that I paid much attention to Dad's work so I can't reciprocate on my own behalf. But I do know that Dad had great respect for your father. I heard him say one time that he didn't know what he had done to deserve such a fine man for a friend and partner."

Dr. Rand nodded. "Yes. I'm older now, so I've managed to notice that Dad is a great doctor too. But enough of that. Please, don't hesitate to let us know if we can help you or Jeremy or Ethan in any way. If so, it would be our honor to do so."

"Thank you. And you do the same. Please call when you're in Lubbock. You and your family will have free access to Spring Up South."

Dr. Rand grinned. "I may take you up on that. I do eat too well when my mother cooks." He groaned with a hand on his abdomen, "And bakes! Ooo la la, her pies and cakes!"

Chapter 18

Ethan didn't even phone Detective Zang Monday morning. He just waited impatiently for Qiana to get ready, then they headed for Waikiki police headquarters. Luke had already picked up Jeremy. They were going to swing by for Kimo, then on to the beach for a morning of jet skiing. "It'll serve you right if Zang is out of the office and they make us sit around all day waiting for him," Qiana groused.

Ethan shrugged, never taking his eyes from the heavy traffic, streaming into Waikiki.

"The least you could have done," Qiana continued, "was to call and see if he's there instead of yelling, 'Let's go!' every five seconds."

"I only yelled, 'Let's go!' every *ten* seconds," Ethan corrected her. "And it doesn't matter where he is. They'll have to take me to him if he's not there. He owes me–I gave him his two days. In fact, he had three."

Qiana shook her head. "He *owes* you?" she repeated. "For a lawyer, you don't know much about the police, do you?"

"I know enough to make a colossal nuisance of myself," Ethan said grimly, glaring at a convertible that had pulled in front of him, forcing him to jam on the brakes. "What's wrong with these people anyway? Somebody should teach them how to drive!"

To Qiana's relief, they arrived at their destination intact. To Ethan's satisfaction, they waited less than five minutes before they were taken back to see Zang.

"Oh no!" Qiana whispered suddenly. "We're going to have to shake hands with him."

"Maybe not," Ethan whispered back. "Don't offer. Maybe he'll forget."

Upon reaching Zang's desk, Qiana sat down quickly and smiled brightly at the detective. "Good morning!" she trilled, folding her hands in her lap.

Zang smiled back. "It went well," he said. "I'd like to thank the two of you for not getting in my way."

Ethan looked sour, but Qiana said, "You're welcome. We had a wonderful weekend!"

Zang's eyebrows rose as he turned his gaze on Ethan. "And you, Mr. Holmes? Did you also have a wonderful weekend?"

Ethan gave Qiana a rueful look, then said, "Yeah, I guess I did."

"Please tell us what you learned before Ethan flies apart," Qiana urged.

"Well, first," Zang said, pointing at two cell phones on his desk, "those are the cells that were taken from Jeremy and Kimo. I'll keep them until the D.A. gives the okay, then I'll return them to the boys."

"Oh, I wouldn't worry about Jeremy's too much," Qiana said. "I doubt his mother will leave the umbilical cord unattached that long."

"You think she'll buy him a new one?" Zang asked.

"She'll have it before we get back to Texas," Qiana predicted.

Zang nodded. "Well, it is still his property, so it will go back to him eventually."

"How did you get the cell phones?" Ethan asked.

"It was part of our deal with Thor," Zang said. "They were in his possession and he turned them over to us."

"So, Thor was ready to make a deal?"

"That's right. We persuaded both Thor and Puna to tell us what they know about a man named Kun Yee. He is a businessman who owns Windsong Towers. He is involved in a number of illegal operations but, until now, we've been unable to get evidence or a witness against him. Now we have two witnesses. I will tell you the things I believe may help you with your case.

"Puna is very angry with Yee because he dropped her for Lin Choi. Thor is terrified of Yee, but he has some claustrophobia issues and would rather be dead than locked in a cell. So you can see, their testimonies may be tainted."

Ethan nodded. "That's normal."

Zang smiled briefly. "Right. Well according to Thor, Yee was smitten with Lin, partly because she didn't smother him, as Puna did. Instead, she darted in and out of his life, like a hummingbird, tasting his honey–and his money–then flitting away. She always left him wanting more. So when she did deign to honor him with her presence, he was anxious to please her. According to Thor, Yee actually gave her access to one of his bank accounts. And when she vanished, a lot of his money vanished with her. Needless to say, Yee was beyond furious."

"And did he know where she went?" asked Ethan eagerly.

"According to Thor, she told Yee she was going to Los Angeles. He and another of Yee's thugs were assigned to follow her to the mainland, but they lost her at LAX."

"Did Yee know she had changed her name to Maylea Kanaka?" asked Ethan.

"Part of his operation involves creating new identities. He's the one who provided her with the documents that turned her into Maylea Kanaka."

"If he knew she was leaving, why didn't he stop her?" Qiana asked.

"He didn't know she had looted his account until she was out of his reach," Zang explained. "He believed she was leaving because her identity theft racket was getting too hot. He had been entertained by her excursions into crime. In fact, he considered her his protégée. He gave her advice and made suggestions to help her hone her skills. So getting her a new identity and sending her off to the mainland were all part of the game as far as he was concerned."

"When did he find out his money was missing?" Ethan asked.

"Trolley told Puna and Puna–trying to regain his affection–told Yee."

"Wait," said Ethan, "Trolley told Puna what?"

"Which flight Maylea was taking and that she had helped herself to a sizable chunk of his money."

"So he sent Thor and another man after her?" Qiana asked.

"That's right, but it seems she was onto them all the time. When they landed in Los Angeles, she went into a restroom and never came out. At least, they never saw her come out."

"So she had a disguise with her," Ethan mused.

"It looks that way," agreed Zang.

"But wait. What about Trolley?" asked Qiana. "How did she find out Maylea was in Lubbock?"

"Thor wasn't sure about that, and Puna wouldn't say a word about Trolley. Thor thinks Lin must have mentioned Mr. West's name or said that she'd met a man from Lubbock, Texas–something that tipped Trolley off to her true destination."

"And Trolley didn't tell Puna?" Ethan asked.

"Forget that!" Qiana interrupted. "Why did Trolley squeal on Lin in the first place? She had to know Puna would pass the information on to Mr. Yee and Lin would be in the soup."

Zang was nodding. "Exactly. That is *the* question. As for your question," he said to Ethan, "my guess is that Trolley didn't tell Puna that Lin had gone to Lubbock because she wasn't sure. She decided to check it out herself."

Qiana was shaking her head. "Why?" she asked. "I don't get this whole Trolley/Lin Choi relationship."

"Sounds like a love/hate thing, doesn't it?" Zang said.

"Yes," said Qiana. "I wish we knew how to find out what was going on between those two."

"Yes. I believe that might provide a vital clue to your mystery," Zang agreed. He turned to Ethan then. "And now, here is a little tidbit I have for you that may help you more than anything else you've learned since you came to Oahu."

"That wouldn't be hard," Ethan said bitterly.

Zang picked up a piece of paper and glanced at it. "I had your Lubbock detective, Lt. Daly, send me Lin Choi, alias Maylea Kanaka's fingerprints. I ran them through the system, and it turns out that she's not really Lin Choi from Honolulu, Hawaii, or Maylea Kanaka West from Lubbock, Texas." He paused dramatically.

Ethan was sitting on the edge of his seat. "Who is she?" he asked.

"She is Cheryl Hoffman from Grand Forks, North Dakota."

Complete silence followed this revelation. Ethan looked at Qiana and Qiana looked at Ethan. Then both looked at Detective Zang. "What?" Ethan said, at last.

"Cheryl Hoffman. Grand Forks, North Dakota."

"But why did you check her fingerprints?" Ethan asked.

Zang smiled. "It didn't smell right. There is no letter 'y' in the Hawaiian alphabet. If Lin really came from Hawaii, why wouldn't she choose a legitimate name for her alias? Besides, I've wanted to run Lin Choi's fingerprints for a long time, but I had no way to get them until you told me her latest pseudonym and connected me to Lt. Daly."

"But if you got Maylea's real name from fingerprints in the criminal justice system, she must have been in trouble with the law before," Ethan said.

"That's right. She was arrested and tried for murdering her 65-year-old husband," Zang explained. "I'm sure you won't be surprised to learn that she was acquitted, and her boyfriend convicted. As soon as she testified against the young man, she left for parts unknown."

"Hawaii," mumbled Qiana.

Zang nodded. "Possibly."

"I'm glad it's summer," Ethan said, "since I'm headed for North Dakota."

"Ethan!" Qiana cried suddenly. "The Minnesota Vikings—Trolley's football team! She must be from North Dakota, too." She turned to Zang. "How far is North Dakota from Minnesota?"

"Next door neighbors," said Zang.

"North Dakota," Ethan mused. "How does a girl from North Dakota pass for a Hawaiian hula dancer?"

"I can't help you there," said Zang, "but I did make a few inquiries for you." He passed a sheet of paper to Ethan. "The boyfriend of Cheryl Hoffman who took the fall for her is Caleb Hancock. He is incarcerated in Bismarck, North Dakota. Cheryl Hoffman's lawyer is located in Grand Forks. The name, address, and phone number of the penitentiary and of Cheryl Hoffman's lawyer are on this paper."

Ethan looked and felt dazed. "North Dakota," he said again. He stared into Qiana's eyes. "North Dakota?"

She shrugged. "Why not? We weren't getting anywhere here."

Zang cleared his throat. "I apologize for rushing you, but I do have a busy morning. And I've told you everything I know that pertains to your case."

He rose and held out his right hand. Qiana looked at it warily. She couldn't refuse to shake his hand–that would be too rude. And so, bracing herself for the painful crunch, she held out her right hand to meet his. With the gentlest clasp imaginable, Detective Zang took her hand in both of his and said, "It has been a pleasure making your acquaintance."

Qiana looked up to see a twinkle in his eye. "I *am* capable of shaking hands without damaging them ... when I remember," he said.

He shook hands with Ethan next, saying as he did so, "Please let me know if I can be of further assistance."

"You've already done more than I could have hoped," Ethan said gratefully. "I would be happy to return the favor one day if that were possible." Putting a hand on Qiana's elbow, he took a few steps, then stopped to ask, "Are we safe now? Or do we need to stay on our guard?"

Zang, who had already seated himself and begun reading a file, looked up. "Good question. I did everything in my power to persuade Kun Yee that Mr. West knows nothing about Lin Choi's money or her illegal operations in which case it would do him no good to take one of you hostage. I did, in fact, tell him bluntly that Trolley is the person most likely to know the location of his missing money."

"Did he believe you?" Qiana asked.

"Yes, I'm convinced he did."

"Does he know Trolley's real name?" Ethan asked.

"He says he has no idea," said Zang.

"And Puna?" asked Qiana.

Zang shook his head. "She insists that she doesn't know. In fact, she claims that she begged Trolley to tell her all about her life, to be a grandmother to her. But Trolley was always evasive."

"If you ever learn anything different ..." Ethan began.

"You're the first one I'll call," Zang promised.

Ethan took a few more steps, then stopped and turned back. "Bank accounts in the name Cheryl Hoffman," he said.

"We're checking," Zang said without looking up.

"Including closed accounts," said Ethan. "Especially if they were closed by someone besides Cheryl Hoffman."

Zang nodded, still reading. Qiana took Ethan's hand and literally dragged him out of the building.

As soon as they were outside, they began a heated debate that lasted until they were seated in Alana's kitchen. Ethan wanted to take the first plane he could book passage on and get to North Dakota ASAP. Qiana wanted him to stay on Oahu with Jeremy and herself and take a vacation for the rest of the week. They had reached an impasse and were reduced to giving each other angry glares when Ethan's cell rang. He answered, suddenly became very alert and began taking notes. His comments consisted mainly of "Yes," "No," and "You're kidding!"

By the time the conversation ended, Qiana was almost drooling with anticipation. "What?" she cried. "What happened? Is Dillon okay? Is it good news or bad?"

"Wait!" Ethan ordered. He made a few more notes, studied everything he had written, then looked up at Qiana and Alana with a befuddled expression on his face. "I think it's good news," he said slowly. "Yes, it is good news. It *has* to be good!"

"Tell us before I deck you," Qiana commanded.

Ethan studied his notes a few more moments, then said, "That was a Lubbock district attorney. He said the police arrested a drug ring last week. The brains of the operation is a guy named Bruno Kroft. As the department's computer specialist was checking out Kroft's computer, he found an email from Trolley in the trash."

Qiana's eyes widened. "From Trolley?"

Ethan nodded. "It said ..." He looked down at his notes and read, " 'I need $100,000. You pay or I tell Daly why you offed Maylea West.' "

He looked up and Qiana exclaimed excitedly, "You mean, it was some Lubbock drug lord who murdered her?"

Ethan shrugged. "They haven't reached that conclusion yet. I mean, poisoning–what crime boss murders someone by poisoning?"

"A crime boss who wants to put the blame on the innocent husband," Qiana said jubilantly. "It's makes perfect sense. So is Dillon off the hook?"

"Well, the D.A. is leaning that way," Ethan said. "But our old buddy Jed Daly is pitching a fit. He says it's always the husband and the D.A. is a sorry blankety blank if he can't see it."

"But the D.A. is on our side," Qiana pointed out. "And he's the boss, right?"

"Well, it's his decision," said Ethan.

"That's it then," Qiana exulted. "We're going to play this week and fly home on Saturday, according to schedule."

Ethan grimaced. "I hate to let you win," he growled.

Qiana laughed. "Get over it," she said.

"Okay, you decide what we're going to do today," Ethan said, yielding to the inevitable. "I'll phone my office and get them started on North Dakota."

Qiana, who had started for her room to change clothes, stopped and turned. "North Dakota? What's the point? If the D.A. isn't going to prosecute Dillon, why bother about North Dakota?"

"Oh, he didn't say he wasn't going to prosecute Dillon," said Ethan. "He hasn't decided yet. And I'm not going to let any dandelions grow up around me while he's deciding."

Chapter 19

Nettie and Dillon's remarriage took place in the chambers of Judge Franklin Meyers at 11:00 o'clock on Friday morning. Nettie had an ulterior motive in choosing this venue. She wanted her Mother to see for herself that Qiana's Mother was happy and fulfilled. Accordingly, Bethany Jamison and Shelley Jamison served as witnesses to an event more precious and joyful than even the first wedding had been.

"Don't you want to have the pastor perform the wedding at church?" Dillon had asked Nettie, as they made their plans earlier in the week. "You could invite Shelley and the judge to come."

Nettie had shaken her head stubbornly. "This isn't a wedding," she maintained. "We had a church wedding. This marriage is a mere formality."

Dillon shook his head doubtfully. "It feels like a lot more than a formality to me. I feel like a phoenix rising out of ashes."

"And the ashes would be ... ?" Nettie asked, studying his face.

"All those horrible hours and days with Maylea."

"When did they become horrible?"

Dillon closed his eyes, trying to pinpoint the moment. "Oh, I'd say it was the day we told Jeremy about the divorce, and I walked out on the two of you," he finally said.

"You're kidding! Then why didn't you stay with us?" Nettie cried. "We weren't even divorced then."

"Guilt," Dillon said. "Maylea was a master at piling on the guilt." He paused a moment, then his eyes softened. "And, of course, there was the baby. At least, I thought there was a baby. And I didn't know about *our* baby yet."

"So I lost you because of my failure to inspire guilt?" Nettie asked.

Dillon opened his mouth to offer a denial, then he closed it. After another moment, he said, "Maybe so. Maybe if you'd smeared a little guilt around, I would have stayed."

Nettie glared at him. "Well, that makes you quite the wuss doesn't it?"

He nodded. "Yes, and if you want to dump me, I won't blame you."

Nettie laughed. "Oh, you're not going to wiggle out of it that easy, now that I know the secret. Guilt–I can wrap you around my little finger." She held up a little finger and waggled it.

Dillon grabbed the finger and kissed it. "Yes, my love, your wish is my command."

He was back. Her Dillon was back, and to celebrate Nettie went out and bought a new dress to wear when she remarried him. She chose a cream colored dress with turquoise accessories, and when she walked into the judge's chambers on Friday morning, she looked more beautiful to Dillon than any woman he had ever seen.

Bethany, who had driven Nettie to the courthouse, followed her into the room. Shelley and Judge Meyers were ready and waiting. "Nettie, you're beautiful!" Shelley cried, pulling Qiana's half-sister and best friend into her arms. "I'm so happy for you both," she whispered, as she held Nettie close. She hugged Dillon next, then introduced Bethany and Nettie to Judge Meyers.

The judge was shorter than Phillip Jamison had been with a decidedly thicker middle, but his eyes were bright and his smile was handy. With ease and polish he performed the marriage, then sent the newlyweds on their way. "You two run along," he said with a wink, "and pretend it's your first honeymoon." After the door closed behind them, he turned to Bethany. "And now may I prevail upon you to join us for lunch, Mrs. Jamison? Shelley has some things she wants to say to you."

Bethany sent a nervous glance toward Shelley, who smiled encouragingly. "Please do," she said. "You and I have talked often over the years, but mainly about Qiana or Qiana and Nettie. But we've never talked about ourselves or Phillip, and there are a few things I'd like you to know."

With a fluttery stomach and her misgivings well hidden, Bethany accepted the invitation graciously. She was taller and more slender than Shelley and she carried herself with a natural elegance. But Shelley's beauty, which had flourished with age, was a floodlight that washed out Bethany's best features and left her feeling frumpy. Today, Shelley's short, snow white hair framed her face in casual waves and her hot pink, silk suit complemented her rosy cheeks. Her smile reflected only good will and Bethany was certain it had not occurred to Shelley to make the comparisons that Bethany could not stop making.

Escorted by the judge, the two women walked to the parking lot and climbed into the back seat of his luxurious car. He was serving as their chauffeur, heading for his country club, nearly 30 minutes away. The two women had both time and privacy at their disposal.

"Shelley, before you say anything, I have to tell you how sorry I am for destroying your life," Bethany blurted. "I should have said so years ago, but I was always so ashamed ..."

Shelley held up a hand to stop her. "Destroying my life? Where do you think you got so much power?"

Bethany opened her mouth to reply, but Shelley stopped her. "Don't answer, but I do appreciate your speaking right up, so I could see where you're coming from. Now I know what I need to say. You didn't destroy my life–nobody has that power except me. I will admit that I may have felt destroyed at first, but it didn't last long. When I saw that Phillip was going to support us–and support us in style–and that he was going to be involved in Qiana's life, I began to enjoy my divorce. While we were married, Phillip wasn't happy with me, but I wasn't happy with him either. It took me a long time to realize it, but I need to thank you."

Bethany was almost too flabbergasted to ask, "Thank me? For what?"

"For saving me from a life with that tight-assed, superior jerk." Shelley laughed. "I said it! I actually said it instead of just thinking it. Wow, that felt good!"

Bethany began to sputter. "Phillip wasn't ... wasn't like that."

"Oh, I know, you have to come to the defense of your dead husband," Shelley said, patting Bethany's hand. "And maybe he was different with you. It doesn't matter. I just want you to know that it's time to quit carrying a load of guilt. Or carry all the guilt you want, but not because of me. I've had a grand life, and it began the day Phillip Jamison walked out of my house and set me free."

Bethany frowned and asked in a confused tone, "I was happy with him and you weren't?" It was a revelation and a miracle too vast to grasp.

"You've got it!" Shelley said, then she touched Bethany's arm and pointed at their driver, the judge, "Look at him. Now *that's* a man! And I never would have known him if Phillip hadn't left me to marry you. I have to thank you for that!"

"You thank me?" Bethany asked woodenly.

"With all my heart!" Shelley whispered triumphantly.

Nettie fell asleep in Dillon's arms that night. In all her life, she had never felt so safe and happy. Yet the yellow eyes were waiting for her in her sleep. The big white owl gazed fearlessly at her, its yellow eyes boring into her soul.

Nettie trembled. What did it want? Why had it come back now? Was it trying to warn her about something?

She wanted to hit it, shriek at it, wipe that smug look off its face. But she was afraid to approach it. Afraid to turn her back on it. Afraid even to take her eyes off it.

Just when she thought she couldn't bear the tension another moment, Nettie jerked herself awake. She lay stone still in the bed, looking around. Listening.

Dillon's breathing was regular and peaceful. With careful, deliberate movements, Nettie crept out of their bed and padded silently into the den. She settled herself in Dillon's recliner and applied her thoughts to the problem. Why was that big, ugly owl back? She hadn't dreamed about it since the night Dillon asked her for a divorce. Through the horrible loneliness and depression of their separation, no owl had disturbed her rest. Now, Dillon was back and so was the owl.

She lay motionless in the recliner for a long time, trying to understand. "It's the trial," she finally whispered to herself. "I could lose him again if he's found guilty at the trial."

She rested quietly for another long period, reliving the months that led up to Maylea's murder. She rehashed every fact Dillon, Ethan, Qiana, or Jeremy had relayed to her about Maylea or the case. In fact, she was so still for so long that she nearly feel asleep. Suddenly, with a start, she sat up. She knew what she was going to do. It was probably a waste of time, but she had to do *something.*

Easing herself and her expanded belly out of the recliner, she went to the computer and turned it on. In less than 30 minutes she had located the information she wanted and printed it out. She would take it to work with her on Monday and begin making inquiries. Leaving the pages on the desk, she returned to bed and slept peacefully the rest of the night.

Their last week on Oahu had passed in a blur for Jeremy, Qiana and Ethan. Thanks to Alana, Luke, Dr. Rand, and their contacts, the three Texans were able to go some places they could not have gone otherwise on such short notice. They hiked, biked, sailed, snorkeled, played with dolphins and visited the Polynesian Cultural Center, as well as several gardens and restaurants. When they buckled themselves into their seats for the flight back to the mainland Saturday morning, Ethan said, "It's a good thing we're headed back today. I don't think I could handle any more fun!"

Jeremy gazed at him in amazement. "Why not? I had a great time!"

Ethan grinned. "So did I, but enough is enough." He fell asleep almost as soon as they were airborne and Qiana followed suit. Jeremy gave them a pitying look, then turned his attention to a video game and the in-flight movie. About the time he drowsed off, first Ethan, then Qiana stretched and sat up.

"So you're going to North Dakota next?" Qiana asked.

Ethan stretched and yawned again before he answered. "Monday. I fly out Monday."

"You didn't ask me if I want to go with you," Qiana said.

Ethan's eyebrows rose. "Was I supposed to?"

Qiana sighed. "No, I guess not. But what if I want to tag along? Would you let me?"

Ethan studied her. "Why?" he finally asked.

"Maybe I'll be able to help you."

He gave her a skeptical look.

"It could happen!" she said huffily. "And I want to help. Let's just say I owe it to Dillon."

Ethan shrugged. "I don't know how you're going to help, but you can come if you want to."

"Mr. Know-It-All Lawyer, doesn't need anybody or anything," she said mockingly.

"You want me to kiss your feet and beg you to come with me?" he asked.

"Yes please."

Without warning, Ethan grabbed her nearest leg and pulled it up. Bending over, he kissed the top of her sandal. "Please, come to North Dakota with me," he begged. "Oh please, please! I can't possibly solve this crime without you."

"That's only one foot," Qiana observed. "You said *feet*–plural, more than one foot."

"Aw, kiss your own feet," Ethan said.

"All right. Since you asked so nicely, I'll come," Qiana said condescendingly. But there was a twinkle in her eyes that Ethan didn't miss.

The reunion at Lubbock was a touching one. Jeremy stepped into the arms of his reunited parents. The three of them held each other in a huddle for a long time before Jeremy said, "Thank you."

"For what?" Nettie asked.

"For getting married," Jeremy said huskily. "Whaddya' think?"

Nettie kissed the top of his head, which seemed higher than she remembered, then turned to Qiana. The sisters hugged for long moments, then Nettie said, "Ethan promised me that you didn't kill Maylea, so I have to apologize for thinking you did."

"I guess I can't blame you," Qiana said. "I didn't actually think of it, but if I had, I might have been tempted."

Nettie laughed softly. "Me too," she whispered.

Then Qiana hugged Dillon and offered him her apologies, which he accepted meekly and gratefully. "It's good to have you back in the family again," she said.

"It's good to *be* back," he said earnestly.

It was a short weekend for Ethan and Qiana, who had laundry to do and jet lag to overcome before leaving for North Dakota on Monday. When Qiana's alarm went off Monday morning, she couldn't remember what had made her want to continue the investigation. "Let Dillon fry," she muttered, pulling her pillow over her head. But when Ethan arrived, she was ready and waiting.

"Why don't *you* go while I stay here and sleep," he said when she opened the door for him.

"I don't think so," Qiana said. "I can't even remember why I *want* to go."

Chapter 20

Cheryl Hoffman's lawyer was a neat little man wearing a dark suit and gold-rimmed glasses. "Please call me Ted," he said as he ushered them into his office early Tuesday morning. "And if you don't mind, we'll get down to business. I have an important client breathing down my neck this morning. If I'd heard from him before your secretary made the appointment, I would have told her I couldn't see you today."

Ethan obligingly gave him a quick summary of the Maylea Kanaka West, alias Lin Choi, story. "What we'd like to know from you is her history as Cheryl Hoffman."

Ted took off his glasses and cleaned them, obviously stalling for time as he thought about his answer. "You say she is deceased now?" he finally asked.

"That's right," Ethan said.

The little lawyer studied some papers on his desk for a few more long moments before he said, "I'm afraid she fooled me completely. I believed in her innocence, but hearing you tell me what she was capable of gives me pause."

"Just tell us about her. Whether she was guilty of murdering her husband isn't our problem now," Ethan said.

Ted nodded. "Of course. She moved to Grand Forks from a small farming community west of here to enroll in the University of North Dakota. Not long after she arrived, she met the richest widower in town and was married to him before the snow melted in the spring of her freshman year. Almost as soon as he made her the beneficiary of his life insurance and rewrote his will in her favor, he was murdered. It seemed obvious she was the guilty party, but I was able to stack the jury with men and she played up to them, testifying that a young man named Caleb Hancock had committed the murder. She said he had fallen in love with her all the way back in their high school days and had followed her to Grand Forks. Before she finished, she seemed like a faithful, heartbroken widow, and Caleb sounded like the blackest sheep who ever descended from Atilla the Hun. I thought I had done a good day's work when her verdict came back 'not guilty'."

He stopped and massaged his temples. "Sorry," he said, resuming his story. "I always get a headache when I think about Cheryl. She paid a retainer–a small retainer–before I took the case, but not another cent. And she had plenty–a quarter of a million from old Mr. Hoffman's life insurance alone. She kept telling me I would be paid as soon as the estate was out of probate. Then, one day, she was gone. I never saw her again. Now you tell me she's dead."

"What about her family?" Ethan asked. "Any chance of getting them to pay the bill?"

Ted snorted softly. "Hardly. The father is a farmer, barely keeping his head above water. The mother, who's Chinese in case you're wondering where Cheryl got her oriental appearance, is a waitress. They couldn't pay me if they wanted to."

"What about Trolley?" Ethan asked. "Can you tell us anything about her?"

"Who?" Ted asked.

Ethan took a photocopy of the Trolley drawing out of his brief case and passed it over to Ted. "She goes by Trolley, shortened from Tra La La, the name her grandkids gave her because she sings when she works. Finding her is the real purpose of my visit to North Dakota. In fact, I'd be happy just to find out her real name."

Ted shrugged and handed the picture back. "Never saw her before," he said.

It was soon apparent that Cheryl Hoffman's lawyer had no more information that might help them. He told them the name of Cheryl's parents–MacKenzie–gave them instructions to the small community where she had been raised and bid them good day.

"So are we going to pay a visit to Farmer and Mrs. MacKenzie?" Qiana asked.

"Just as soon as we can get there," Ethan said.

"Town" was too grand a term for Cheryl MacKenzie Hoffman's home town. The small community consisted of an ancient gas station/convenience store and some rickety houses. Not a car nor a person was moving on the rutted streets or the crumbling sidewalks.

"No wonder Maylea wanted out of here," Qiana said with a shiver.

"For sure," Ethan agreed. "Look!" He pointed at the porch of one of the houses. Two teenage boys with wires attached to their ears were lounging on a porch swing, drinking bottles of soda pop. "There's a life form here." He pulled up to the curb.

"Two of them," said Qiana.

They approached the house with waves and cheerful greetings. "Good morning. I'm Ethan Holmes and this is Qiana Jamison."

"I'm Reg. That's Dick," said one of them. Both boys were wearing faded jeans and stained T-shirts. Reg's hair was dark and wavy; Dick's was red and curly. "Are ya'll lost?"

"Probably," said Ethan. "We were wondering if you boys can tell us how to get to the MacKenzie farm."

"We can tell you," said Reg, "but you won't find nobody there. Family moved off a few years ago."

"Do you know where they went?"

"Not me," said Reg. "What about you, Dick?"

Dick shrugged and took another gulp of his soda.

"Well, what about this lady?" Ethan asked, holding out the drawing of Trolley. "Would you happen to know her?"

"Hey, it's Trolley!" cried Reg. "Look, Dick. It's Trolley."

Dick looked and said, "Yup."

"How do you folks know Trolley?" Reg asked.

"We don't know her," Ethan said. "We're looking for her. I'm a lawyer, and I need her help in a case I'm working on."

"Think of that!" said Reg wonderingly. "A high-class lawyer needs help from ol' Trolley."

"Too bad," said Dick.

Qiana and Ethan turned their heads in tandem to face the redhead. "Why is it too bad?" asked Ethan.

"She's dead," said Dick.

Before Ethan or Qiana could react, Reg asked, "What are you talking about–dead? Trolley's dead?"

Dick gave him a scathing look. "Don't you remember? It was a hit-and-run accident. Killed her dead."

"You peanut head! It was old Mrs. Harrelson that died in a hit-and-run."

"No it wasn't, bubble brain. Mrs. Harrelson had a blood vessel explode inside her head. Trolley was in a hit-and-run somewhere. I forget where."

"Oh yeah." Reg looked thoughtful. "Man, that's right! Mom was talking about it. She said idiots who can't drive cars without running down old ladies shouldn't be allowed on the streets!"

"Look, Reg, Dick," Ethan said, "it's urgent that I find out where Trolley died. Can you remember?"

Both boys knitted their brows and made a great show of trying to think. Finally, Dick shrugged and so did Reg. "It's been awhile," Reg said. "At least–what–a month?" he asked Dick.

"I dunno'," said Dick. "Probably."

"Well, do you remember what state she was in at the time?" Ethan asked.

Both boys shrugged.

"How about her name?" Qiana asked. "Do you know her name?"

"Sure. Trolley," said Reg.

"That's not her real name," said Qiana. "Do you know her real name?"

Both boys did their trying-to-think performance again, then both shrugged. "We always called her Trolley," Reg offered.

"What about her family? Are any of them living here?"

"Nope. They all moved off too. Everybody moves off except us," Reg said. "Every night my Mom says to my Dad, 'When are we going to pack up and move to civilization?' And every night my Dad says, 'I'm not going nowhere. My father farmed here and his father before him. You go if you want to–I'm staying.' " Reg shrugged. "So we stay cuz' my Mom's goofy over my Dad."

Defeated, Ethan and Qiana returned to the car. "Well, I'm guessing we could call on every residence and business on this street before noon," he said. "Shall we try? Surely somebody can tell us Trolley's real name."

"Okay," Qiana said doubtfully. "You take that side of the street and I'll take this one."

In less than an hour, the two met again at the car. Reg and Dick were still lounging on the porch swing, observing their efforts. "We're probably the most exciting thing that's happened here this summer," Ethan said, nodding his head toward the boys.

"Well, I'm glad we could liven up their day," said Qiana sourly. She flopped into the car. "Will you start the engine and turn on some air before I fry? And by the way, if I ever want to go on an investigation with you again, have me committed!"

"Did you learn anything?" Ethan asked, turning the key.

"Nothing we didn't already know from Dumb and Dumber," said Qiana.

"Same here," said Ethan. "You'd think some of the older folks in town would remember Trolley."

"Oh, I met one of those oldsters," said Qiana. "She thought I was a neighbor bringing her lunch."

"Did she remember Trolley?"

"Oh sure! Trolley is her best friend," said Qiana. "In fact, Trolley's coming Wednesday to clean her house for her. Trolley comes every Wednesday–that's what a good friend she is."

"She doesn't know Trolley is dead?"

Qiana made a face at him. "She thinks Trolley lives around the corner from her. I wasn't about to tell her Trolley is dead. She'd probably still be crying on my shoulder if I had."

"What about the MacKenzie family?" Ethan asked. "Did you find anyone who knows where they went?"

"Maybe Los Angeles. Or was it San Francisco? One of those California towns. No, wait! Maybe it was Chicago." She shrugged. "As for Cheryl, she hasn't been back since she left for college."

"Did they know she was tried for murder?"

"Are you kidding?" asked Qiana. "That was the biggest news to hit this place since some mayor's wife ran off with some high school principal ..."

"... twenty years ago," Ethan supplied the punch line. "Sounds like we were talking to the same people. Do you think they're feeding us a line? Are they protecting Trolley or do they really believe she's dead?"

"The ones I talked to seemed genuine," said Qiana. "One teared up and said Trolley had been like a grandmother to her children. And she tried hard to come up with a name for me, but she's been calling her Trolley so long, she couldn't remember the old woman's real name. She said it might be Cora, but she wasn't sure."

"I had the same experience," said Ethan. "You'd think these people could at least remember a last name. I mean, didn't her whole family come from around here? You know, grandchildren and all?"

"We don't *know* that," said Qiana. "What I don't get is how they know she died a month ago. If they read an obit, they should know her name. If a family member told them, they should know the name of the family member."

"I can explain that," Ethan said. "Somebody passing through town told the clerk at the gas station about the hit-and-run. He's a kid and has no idea who the traveler was, but he didn't waste any time spreading the news to every customer he saw that day."

"Well, new is news, especially in a place like this," Qiana observed.

Ethan straightened and put the car in gear. "Let's head for Bismarck. I have an appointment to see Caleb Hancock tomorrow morning."

Except for his prison garb, Caleb Hancock–in his mid-twenties now–still looked like an All-American boy. His hair was neatly combed and he was clean shaven. He stood to shake hands with Ethan and said in a respectful voice, "Good morning, sir."

"Good morning," Ethan said, taking the chair opposite Caleb. "I'm Ethan Holmes."

"Yes sir. They told me. They said you are a friend of Cheryl Hoffman's."

"No, I never met Cheryl," said Ethan. "I'm a lawyer trying to solve her murder."

Caleb's eyes widened, then filled with tears. "Cheryl ... was ... murdered?" he asked before he lost control completely. Then he wept convulsively, his face buried in his arms, for several minutes.

While Caleb wept, Ethan was experiencing *deja vu*. In a prison on Oahu, he had watched a grown man bury his face in his arms and sob for Lin Choi. Now, here in a prison in North Dakota, it was happening again–a grown man weeping over Cheryl Hoffman who was also Lin Choi.

When Caleb gained control of himself, he sat up wiping away tears. "I'm sorry," he mumbled in a choked voice Ethan could barely understand.

"No, *I'm* sorry," said Ethan. "I should have realized you wouldn't know she was dead."

"Why not?" Caleb asked. "Why didn't anyone tell me?"

"It's a long story and you may not want to hear it," Ethan said.

"I do want to hear it," Caleb said stoically. "I'm all right now. You took me by surprise before. I won't blubber again."

Ethan gave him a condensed version of Cheryl/Lin/Maylea's activities for the past year. When he finished, Caleb looked shell-shocked.

"I guess I didn't know her," he said. "I thought she was just my high school sweetheart." He smiled wanly, remembering bygone days. "I was quarterback of the football team and she was head cheerleader. We were supposed to get married, have a couple of kids, and live happily ever after."

"Whoa!" said Ethan. "You sure *didn't* know her." He studied the young man, then asked cautiously, "Do you want to tell me how you got in here?"

Caleb shrugged. "It's no secret. Cheryl went off to Grand Forks to college, and I stayed home to help with the farming. My Dad had been in an accident and needed me for one year. I didn't care much about school anyway, so I didn't mind putting off college for a year. And I trusted Cheryl. I believed she would be as faithful to me as I was to her. Instead, she married somebody else her first year in Grand Forks."

Ethan nodded. "Yes, I spoke to her lawyer, and he told me she married the richest bachelor in town."

"It was the end of the world for me," Caleb said. "I would have done anything for her, but she wanted money more than she wanted me. When I found out she was married, I didn't care if I lived or died."

"So when she asked you to murder her husband, you did it?" Ethan asked.

"She didn't ask me," said Caleb. "She hinted at it, but I was so shocked at the idea that she backed off."

"Would you have done it if she'd asked?"

Caleb didn't answer for a long time. Finally he nodded. "I might have, but it would have taken some time. She would have had to persuade me that I wouldn't be caught and that we would be together forever afterwards. I guess she didn't want to take the time, and she must have done it herself."

"When did you figure *that* out?" asked Ethan.

"When she was on the witness stand. When she said I killed the old geezer. When she said I was stalking her. When she said I was obsessed with her and didn't mention that she had sworn she would love me forever." He gave Ethan a forlorn look. "Her testimony was nothing but lies."

"I hate to speak ill of the dead," said Ethan, "but lying seems to have been one of her best talents."

Caleb nodded. "It looks that way."

"Listen," said Ethan, "I'm defending the man who was married to her when she died. He has been accused of her murder, but I'm convinced he's innocent. Can you think of anyone who might have murdered her?"

Caleb looked surprised. "According to the tale you just told me, there must have been a lot of people who hated her."

"That's true," agreed Ethan, "but I've got to find the one who actually killed her."

Caleb shook his head. "I've been locked up in this place for more than five years, and I haven't heard from her once in all that time."

"So nothing happened during your high school years that might have made anyone angry enough to kill her?" asked Ethan.

"Not that I know of," said Caleb. "Obviously I was pretty blind when it came to Cheryl, but I think I would have a clue if anyone hated her that much."

Ethan nodded and opened his brief case. "Is there any possibility that you might know this woman?" he asked, holding up the picture of Trolley.

Caleb's eyes widened. "That's my grandmother!" he exclaimed.

"She's your grandmother?" gasped Ethan, barely daring to believe his good fortune.

Caleb smiled as he looked at the likeness of his grandmother. "Sure. That's my Trolley!"

"Clara Corwyn," Ethan told Qiana, as soon as he saw her. He had left her at a mall while he saw Caleb Hancock. They met at a prearranged location and began walking toward an outside door.

"Who's Clara Corwyn?" Qiana asked.

"Trolley."

"No!" Qiana cried. "How did you find out?"

"Trolley is Caleb Hancock's grandmother. He told me."

Qiana stopped walking and stared at him, then her eyes softened. "Does he know she's ... dead?"

Ethan nodded. "His mother phoned him."

"Where did it happen?"

"In Florida, but he doesn't know what city. I have an address and phone number for his mother," Ethan said.

"Where does she live?"

"In Fargo."

"I guess that means we're headed back across North Dakota," Qiana said resignedly. She had studied a map of North Dakota during their flight north.

"I've already made the arrangements," Ethan said. "We have motel reservations for tonight in Fargo, and Mrs. Hancock will see us in the morning."

"What does she do for a living?"

"She's a nurse. Right now she's on night duty. So we're going to meet her for breakfast at 7:30 tomorrow morning."

Qiana yawned at the thought. "I might as well have stayed in Lubbock and worked," she said.

Annette Hancock was a 45-year old woman who looked 55. Her dark hair was streaked with gray, and her dark eyes betrayed an exhaustion that went deeper than one night on duty. Wearing a light blue smock, she was already seated in a booth, watching the door with an expectant look.

"I think that's her," Ethan said, nodding. He led Qiana to the back of the homey little diner Mrs. Hancock had chosen for their meeting.

Greetings and introductions were exchanged. Breakfast orders were turned in. Then Ethan said. "Thank you for agreeing to see us."

Mrs. Hancock smiled sweetly and said in a soft tone. "If you'll tell me about my boy, I'll consider it an even swap. I haven't seen him in over a month."

"He looks great," Ethan said sincerely. "And he was perfectly polite and willing to answer my questions. I was very impressed with him."

Mrs. Hancock brightened perceptibly. "I'm glad. He and my Mom—Trolley—were very close. He took her death hard, and I was afraid he might become depressed."

Ethan nodded. "Yes, I could see the sorrow in his eyes when he talked about her. But he seems to be handling it well."

"Thank God!" Caleb's mother whispered.

"Mrs. Hancock," Ethan said, "Caleb seemed to have no idea what Trolley has been doing the past year. Did you know she had attached herself to Cheryl Hoffman and was working for her as housekeeper and cook?"

The weariness deepened in Mrs. Hancock's eyes. "Yes, I knew. Mom reported in occasionally. First she was in Hawaii. Then Texas. Right?"

"That's right," Ethan said. "Where was she before Hawaii?"

"She was here in Fargo. It took her over four years to track Cheryl to Hawaii. And she thought of nothing else all that time. She was determined to find a way to make Cheryl confess to her husband's murder so Caleb would be cleared."

Ethan paused before asking his next question. He had blundered all over Caleb's feelings and he didn't want to do the same to Caleb's mother. "Did Caleb call you last night?" he asked.

"Yes," said Mrs. Hancock. "He told me Cheryl is dead–that she was murdered. And I presume you're here to ask if my mother murdered her?" It was a question rather than a statement.

"Actually, we're trying to locate Trolley because we don't know who murdered Cheryl, and we think Trolley might know. In fact, we've been worried for Trolley's safety. Now, it looks as if we had good reason to worry."

"You mean, the hit-and-run was a murder, not an accident?" asked Mrs. Hancock, her eyes widening.

Ethan shook his head. "I can't say that for a fact, but it is a possibility. We have been laboring under the assumption that Trolley ... Mrs. Corwyn ... knew who murdered Cheryl and fled for her life. Or else she was murdered too, and her body dumped."

In the long silence that followed, a waitress delivered breakfast, and the trio ate in silence for several minutes. Finally Ethan said, "What can you tell me about the hit-and-run? Has it been investigated as a possible murder?"

"The police seem to have no idea who hit Mom," said Mrs. Hancock, "but I've heard no suggestion that it was anything but an accident."

"Please tell me everything you know about it," Ethan urged.

"Well, my Aunt Sarah called and said Mom had come to stay with her for awhile and one day, when she was walking to the grocery store, she was run down by a car that drove off without even slowing down. She said the police seemed to think it was some scared teenager who lost control of the car, hit Mom, and bolted."

"This happened in Florida?" Ethan asked.

"Yes. Orlando."

Ethan nodded. "And nobody saw who was in the car? Or the make of the car? Or the license?"

"It was a white car and there was mud on the license plate. Nobody recognized the make or the model. As for the driver, he was wearing a baseball cap–the kind a lot of kids wear. I guess that's why they thought it might be a teenager."

"Did she die immediately?" Qiana asked, speaking up for the first time.

Mrs. Hancock shook her head. "She died in the hospital. My Aunt Sarah got there in time to see her before they took her to surgery. She died during surgery. There were too many internal injuries to save her."

"And did they send the body back to North Dakota for burial?" Ethan asked.

"No. She told her sister to have her cremated and scatter the ashes on a railroad track. She didn't want anyone to have to bear the expense of sending her home and paying for a funeral."

"A railroad track?" Ethan asked.

Mrs. Hancock smiled slightly and repeated softly, "A railroad track." Her eyes were far away. "Trolley's dad, my grandfather, was an engineer with the railroad–back in the days when trains were an important form of transportation and freight delivery. Mom was allowed to ride with him occasionally, and she has always loved trains."

" 'I've been working on the railroad, all the livelong day …' " Qiana sang quietly.

Mrs. Hancock nodded. "Mom's favorite song." She let her gaze rest on Qiana. "Did you know my Mother?"

"No, but I've heard a lot about her."

Mrs. Hancock nodded and continued her story. "My grandfather had some construction and engineering skills, so he laid tracks through his whole house at the edges of the rooms. He made openings in the walls large enough for his model trains to go through. His whole family helped decorate the area along the tracks with towns, bridges, trees, bushes, flowers, farms, pastures with horses and cows ..." She stopped talking and let her memory return to the little wonderland in her grandparents' home. "It seemed magical to me," she finally said. "When I was a child, I would rather go visit my grandparents and their model train house than go anywhere else in the world."

She let out a long, sad sigh. "I miss my Mom, but I understood her obsession. I hated Cheryl. It was so unfair that she cheated my son out of his whole life, while she walked away free and rich! Free! And rich!" She turned her angry glare on Ethan and Qiana. "I didn't know what hate was until I hated Cheryl MacKenzie Hoffman."

"Well, somebody made her pay for her crimes," Qiana observed.

Mrs. Hancock took a deep breath. Then she nodded. "Yes, she did pay. And Caleb, at least, is still alive. Alive, but in prison for all these precious years. And for what? So Cheryl MacKenzie could get her hands on a wad of money. Money!" Her voice died away. "Just money."

"Mrs. Hancock," Ethan said after several minutes of silent eating had passed, "there are some organizations in this country that investigate unjust convictions and incarcerations. If you're absolutely certain your son is innocent, you might be able to intcrest someone in his case."

Mrs. Hancock was studying him warily. "What organizations?" her voice asked. Her tone said, *Please don't get my hopes up and then grind my heart into the dust.*

"I couldn't give you a name off the top of my head, but I will have my secretary research it and let you know."

Mrs. Hancock nodded. "Thank you," she said dully.

The monotonous tone of her voice and the weary look in her eyes told Ethan she had no hope of seeing her son delivered from his unjust fate. "What about your Aunt Sarah?" he asked. "Would you happen to know her address and phone number."

She shook her head. "No, but if you'll give me your address, I'll get them to you."

Ethan pulled a business card out of his wallet and passed it to her. Then he and Qiana asked a few more questions, but Mrs. Hancock had no more useful information for them. Seeing that he was accomplishing nothing except to exhaust Mrs. Hancock further, he shook her hand, wished her well, and let her leave.

"Now what?" Qiana asked Ethan, as they watched Mrs. Hancock drive away. "Florida?"

"I don't think so," Ethan said. "I'll call this Aunt Sarah and see if I can learn any more, but I'm not convinced I would gain enough information to justify the cost of going there."

"Orlando. That's the home of Disney World," Qiana said enticingly.

Ethan gave her a scornful look. "You're not interested in clearing Dillon. You just want to play."

"Guilty!" Qiana said cheerfully. "Well, come on then. Let's get back to Lubbock and attach our noses to the grindstone."

Chapter 21

It was the following Monday morning before Ethan was able to get an appointment with the deputy district attorney handling the Maylea West case. The D.A., a middle-aged man of great dignity and little imagination, got right down to business. "I understand you have been on a quest to locate the Wests' housekeeper. What was her name–Streetcar or Taxicab or some such thing? Have you found her yet?"

"She was called Trolley," said Ethan. "And I wasn't able to locate her in time. She died in a hit-and-run accident in Orlando, Florida, about a month ago."

The D.A.'s eyebrows rose. "She's dead?"

Ethan nodded. "Apparently."

The D.A. sighed. "In that case, I can't ask her about her threat to blackmail Bruno Kroft."

Ethan shrugged. "No, but there seems to be no doubt about the fact."

The D.A. looked sad. "Yes, so it seems, but I can't give your so-called 'fact' much weight unless I can actually interrogate ... uh, what was her name?"

"Her name was Clara Corwyn," said Ethan, "but most people called her Trolley."

The D.A. frowned and said, "Trolley. Extraordinary!"

"So what did Kroft say about Trolley and her attempt to blackmail him?" Ethan asked.

"He denied knowing her. He said he didn't know who she was or what she was talking about so he deleted the message and forgot about it."

"You didn't believe him, did you?" Ethan asked.

The D.A. shrugged. "Nobody has heard from this Trolley-woman. If he didn't pay, why haven't the police heard from her?"

"What makes you think he didn't pay?" Ethan asked.

The D.A. looked embarrassed. "Well, he said he didn't."

Ethan snorted. "What else was he going to say? Look, put your cards on the table. Are you or are you not going to prosecute Bruno Kroft for the murder of Maylea West?"

"I am not," said the D.A. decisively. "I can't get a conviction based on motive alone. There's no evidence of opportunity. Of course, he had the means, but without opportunity ..."

"Hey, hey! Wait!" cried Ethan. "What are you talking about motive alone? What was his motive?"

"Paternity," said the D.A. "Bruno Kroft was the father of Maylea West's baby."

All the wind whooshed out of Ethan's sails. "Bruno Kroft," he repeated wonderingly. "Maylea was sleeping with a gangster?"

"She must have been," said the D.A. "DNA identifies him as the father."

It was almost too much for Ethan to assimilate and deal with. But his profession required that he take surprises in stride and turn them to his advantage. "So Kroft *must* be the murderer," he said with certainty. "And my client is off the hook."

"Wrong," said the D.A. "Your client's day in court is still on the calendar."

"Based on what?" Ethan asked angrily.

"Your client had means, motive, and opportunity. Kroft had no provable opportunity. As I have already mentioned, I can't convict Kroft, but with West ... well ..."

Ethan widened his eyes in dramatic disbelief. "You're going to prosecute an innocent man simply because you believe you can get a conviction?"

"Of course not," said the D.A. "It is perfectly clear to everyone in my office that your client is guilty of murdering his wife. It has been done a million times and Mr. West won't be the last."

"Mr. West did not murder his wife," Ethan thundered. "And you're a fool if you think he did!"

"I am prepared," said the D.A. coolly, "to offer you a deal. I shouldn't but, as you say, the apparent blackmail attempt by Mrs. Corwyn does cloud the issue slightly."

"Slightly. Slightly!" Ethan roared. "Doesn't anybody in this town care about justice? Why did I have to go all the way to Hawaii to find out that Maylea West is really Cheryl Hoffman? Why didn't your police detective do a simple thing like run her fingerprints?"

The D.A. was nodding. "Yes, I was more than a little perturbed about that omission myself. Jed Daly said she looked like Sleeping Beauty lying there, a child barely out of her teens. How could he imagine that she might have a criminal record?"

"He didn't bother because he had already decided to railroad my client!" Ethan spat the words at the D.A. and stomped out of the room.

Ethan's next stop was Dillon West's office. He didn't call ahead–he simply went, fuming all the way. As soon as he and Dillon were seated with the door of Dillon's office closed, Ethan said, "I just left the deputy district attorney's office. You're still on the hook for Maylea's murder. For you they have means, motive, and opportunity. For our 'drug lord,' Bruno Kroft, they have motive, but not opportunity. In other words, they don't care who killed her. All they care about is getting a conviction. You they can convict."

Dillon's brows came together. "What's the motive for Kroft?"

Ethan sighed. "It seems they've finally identified the father of Maylea's baby."

Dillon blanched. "Is there anybody in town she wasn't sleeping with? Ethan, I could give Nettie AIDS ... or herpes ... or ... anything!"

"Didn't you check on that sort of thing before you and Nettie got married again?" Ethan asked.

"Sure, but some of those infections don't show up right away. The doctor said I was clean and he treated me with antibiotics, just in case, but what if Maylea gave me something we don't know about yet? Nettie would get it. And what about the baby? The baby could get it." Dillon's voice had taken on a hysterical note. "What have I done? What have I done?"

Ethan managed not to say something pointed like, "Well, you should have thought about *that* before you did it." After all, he was paid to be on Dillon's side. But he was at a loss for any way to comfort the man. Dillon had behaved like a colossal fool. Ethan knew it, and Dillon knew it.

"Look," Dillon said, rising, "I have to talk to Nettie. You understand, don't you?"

Whether Ethan understood or not was immaterial to Dillon. The client hurried away, leaving his lawyer to study his fingernails. With a groan, Ethan picked up his briefcase and followed Dillon out the door into the heat and blinding glare of a West Texas August morning. "Ah, for the good old days on Oahu," he muttered to himself as he slid into his car. He thought of the afternoon on Paulo's sailboat, skimming across the waves while he played a lazy game of footsie with Qiana. "Why did we ever come back here?"

Dillon was usually respectful of Nettie and her clients, but on this day he barged into her office without so much as knocking. She and her client turned to gape at him, as he lurched in, saying urgently, "Nettie, you have to divorce me again. I just found out that Maylea was sleeping with some drug-invested sleazebag. And she was sleeping with Scott Sanford. And there was that hotel owner in Waikiki and the accountant who's in jail in Oahu ..."

"Dillon!" Nettie yelled for the third time, finally halting the frantic flow of words. "Do you mind? I'm in the middle of a session here."

He blushed, put his hands over his face, then turned and stumbled out of the room.

"I'm so sorry," Nettie said to her client. "Could we possibly reschedule?" She escorted the client to the front desk where Dolly Tatum had corralled Dillon. He was sitting bent over with his face in his hands and Dolly was rubbing his back while she spoke to him in a low, soothing voice.

"Dillon, I can see you now," Nettie said.

He looked up, blushed again at the sight of the client and mumbled urgently to her, "I'm sorry. *So* sorry ..."

As soon as Nettie had shut the door, closing out everybody in the world except herself and her husband, she said calmly, "I won't divorce you again, so you can get that idea out of your head."

"You have to," Dillon said brokenly. "Look how many men Maylea was sleeping with. She must have had every STD in the world."

"What are you talking about, Dillon?" Nettie asked. "Why are you suddenly upset about Maylea's sex partners?"

"Ethan told me who was the father of her baby."

Nettie's eyes widened. "Who?"

"The leader of that drug ring ... um, Bruno something."

"Bruno Kroft?" asked Nettie.

"That's right. Don't you see? We're talking about the tip of the iceberg. We don't even *know* how many other men she was sleeping with."

"So what?" asked Nettie. "Whatever she gave you, I've already got it by now."

"Don't say that! Dear God, don't say that," Dillon cried, pulling her into his arms and crushing her against his chest. "Nettiebug, I can't bear it if I've given you and our baby some horrible disease."

"Our baby," Nettie repeated softly. "Oh Dillon, isn't that a miracle? *Our* baby. *Ours.*"

Dillon loosened his grip and looked at her. "*Ours,*" he repeated. "And Maylea's wasn't mine, thank God! Oh Nettie, you're right! It is a miracle. *Ours. Our* baby."

※

Ethan Holmes sat in his big office chair. Hunching over a desk strewn with papers and file folders, he tapped the nearest surface with a pencil in nervous agitation. He had read every item related to Maylea West's murder at least three times and still had no inkling of an inspiration. Maybe Scot Sanford had found out about Bruno Kroft and killed Maylea in a jealous rage. Wait, not a jealous rage.

A man in a jealous rage uses his hands, a knife, a gun, not poison. So call it a cold, calculating fury.

The only other possibilities were suicide and Bruno Kroft. He doubted anybody would swallow suicide. Young, beautiful, and self-absorbed, Maylea might kill somebody else, not herself. But Kroft was a viable option.

Ethan tossed his drumming pencil onto the desk and began shuffling through papers. Either Scot Sanford or Bruno Kroft had gone to Florida last month to kill Trolley. Somehow, he had to find out which one. He stopped, mid-shuffle, and dropped everything. True, Scot probably would have gone himself, but not Bruno Kroft. Kroft would have sent someone else. Ethan didn't have a prayer of learning who that someone else might have been. He cupped his chin in his hands and stared, unseeing, out the window. Was he going to have to go to Florida? He didn't want to, but did he have a choice?

With a sigh, Ethan picked up his telephone and called Spring Up South. When he got Qiana on the line after a five minute wait, he said, "You could marry me and we could go to Orlando for a honeymoon."

Qiana laughed and, he noticed, didn't ask him to identify himself. "Or we could go to Orlando for fun," she said. "It would be cheaper without the wedding."

Ethan felt his mood lighten for the first time that day. How did the mere sound of Qiana's voice have such a refreshing effect on him? "I don't really want to go to Orlando," he confessed, "but I'm hemmed in on all sides. How am I going to convince a jury that someone besides Dillon killed Maylea?"

Qiana gave a short laugh. "I've been grateful for a long time that *that* is your job, not mine."

"Thanks," he muttered.

"Well, come on over to the gym and have a workout," Qiana offered. "Afterward, I'll feed you a nasty health drink for lunch."

"How about if I skip the workout and the health drink and just take you to lunch?" he asked.

"Would this be business or pleasure?" she asked.

"Both."

"I'll be ready when you get here," she said.

Qiana was watching for Ethan at the big glass doors of Spring Up South and came out when he pulled up to the curb. She was wearing hot pink sandals and a Hawaiian floral muumuu over her leotard. Ethan knew for a fact that she had spent less than $50.00 on the muumuu and sandals, but she looked like a million dollars. Her dark hair framed her face in graceful waves and her complexion was flawless if you didn't count a few lines around her eyes.

She settled in his sports car with a little bounce and said, "I hear Orlando is beautiful this time of year."

He grinned. "August? I hear Orlando is sweltering hot this time of year."

Qiana shrugged. "Hot, but beautiful."

She directed him to her favorite Mexican food restaurant in the area where she ate a salad while he feasted on fajitas. After they had exhausted small talk, she asked, "So have you decided to go to Orlando, after all?"

"I haven't decided," Ethan said. "I'm trying to come up with an alternative." He detailed the conclusions he had reached that morning–suicide, Scot Sanford, or Bruno Kroft. "I think it's Kroft," he said, at last, "which means I'll never prove it. He's not the type to do his own dirty work, and how am I going to learn which of his gofers he sent to Florida?"

"Look, Ethan," Qiana said, "we have to consider the possibility that Trolley murdered Maylea. She was right there in the house. She hated Maylea. Next to Dillon–whom we're honor-bound not to suspect–she's our most likely candidate."

Ethan sighed. "If Trolley did it, Dillon's doomed."

"Why?"

"She's dead. Before she died, she was more like a phantom than a person. How am I going to get any evidence against her?"

Qiana shrugged. "Find the money. It's bound to be deposited somewhere in her name."

"Or her assumed name, whatever that might be," Ethan said. He gave Qiana a despairing look. "If it's not Sanford or Kroft, we're dead in the water."

"What about Kun Yee?" Qiana asked.

"I don't think so," Ethan said. "I think he genuinely lost track of her or she would have been dead a lot sooner than she was."

"Well, then, you could argue suicide," Qiana suggested. "I don't think she killed herself, but if you can think of a reason why she might have been depressed, you might create doubt in some juror's mind."

Ethan nodded. "I've considered it, but I can't come up with a reasonable scenario that ends with Maylea killing herself."

"Same here," Qiana agreed. "Well, what about her parents? Do they know she's dead? Maybe you should find them. You might find that suicide runs in the family–that would help, wouldn't it?"

Ethan shrugged. "Marginally."

"Okay, look," said Qiana in a businesslike voice, "let's go over it again–the sequence of events, I mean. I know you've gone through it over and over, but now we know more of the players. Maybe we'll come up with a fresh possibility."

"Good idea," said Ethan brightening.

"We know from Jeremy that on Friday Maylea had a week's worth of capsules in her weekly pill planner, right?" asked Qiana.

Ethan nodded.

"At that point all of the capsules held her powder from Oahu. We know that because Jeremy filled the capsules himself. So the switch must have been made between Friday night and Tuesday morning. Where were Dillon, Jeremy, Maylea and Trolley on Saturday?"

Ethan frowned in his effort to remember. "Dillon, Jeremy and Maylea spent part of the day at the mall. Dillon has no idea what Trolley did. On Sunday they went to church and out to dinner. Again, no idea where Trolley was. On Monday Jeremy went home and Dillon was at work. Maylea could have been anywhere; same for Trolley."

"Okay, here's what I think," said Qiana. "On the weekend the murderer wouldn't have known whether the coast would be clear or not. So I think he did it on Monday. All he had to do was watch for Maylea to leave. Trolley had only been living there a few days, so he might not have known about her. In fact ..." Qiana's voice rose in excitement, "... the door might have been left unlocked since she was there. So the murderer doesn't even have to break in. He just strolls in, replaces Maylea's pills with the poison pills, and strolls out."

"And where is Trolley while he's doing his dirty work?"

"Hiding. Or escaping out the back door."

"Okay, let's say you're right," said Ethan. "Why didn't she call 911 after this thug strolled away?"

"She's afraid of him. She knows Kun Yee and Bruno Kroft and is afraid to cross them," Qiana hypothesized.

"Or maybe," Ethan said, "she let him in. Maybe while she was making him a cup of coffee in the kitchen, he was back in the bedroom switching the pills. She didn't know what he had done until Maylea collapsed the next day. When Trolley realized he had planted poisoned capsules, she panicked and fled."

"If it happened that way, why didn't he get rid of her Monday?" Qiana asked.

"Like we said before, he didn't know she would be there. When he found her in the house, he improvised. But Trolley knew it was only a matter of time until he would be back for her."

Qiana was nodding. "And she was right. He found her in Orlando and murdered her."

"Or had her murdered," agreed Ethan.

"Then I believe it was Kun Yee," said Qiana firmly. "She wasn't in Lubbock long enough for anyone to know much about her–like where her sister lived. And the murderer obviously didn't follow her directly from Lubbock to Orlando or it wouldn't have taken him a whole month to do away with her."

"In other words," Ethan said thoughtfully, "Trolley had been in Hawaii for several months, so someone there might have known her well enough to know she had a sister in Orlando?"

"Yes," Qiana said, "and even though Thor and his buddy lost Maylea in Los Angeles, Kun Yee knew Trolley was his best hope of retrieving his money."

"Sure, that's what Zang told him. Remember?"

"That's right," said Qiana excitedly. "To get those thugs off Dillon's trail, he tried to put them on Trolley's trail."

"And they had to figure she was going to turn up in Orlando eventually."

"So all they had to do was wait and watch until she showed up for a visit with her sister," Qiana finished.

Ethan was nodding. "It sounds right, but I still have the same problem I had with Bruno Kroft. Yee wouldn't have gone himself, and I have no way of finding out who he sent."

Qiana looked at her watch. "I have a class in 10 minutes," she said. "I'm going to count to three, and after I say three, you say, 'I'm going to Orlando,' or 'I'm not going to Orlando.' Ready?"

"If I go, will you go with me?"

Qiana looked wistful. "Can't. I've been gone too much already. Maybe another time."

Ethan nodded. "Okay. Ready."

"One, two, three," Qiana counted.

"Going," Ethan said wearily. "I'm going to Orlando."

"Good job!" said Qiana. "You made a decision."

Chapter 22

Ethan's visit to Orlando was short and frustrating. He found Trolley's sister Sarah in a nursing home. A peppy teenager escorted him to a patio where Sarah was sitting in a wheelchair. She appeared to be much older and feebler than Trolley. Her smile was tentative and her welcome shaky.

"What's your name again?" she asked for the second time.

"Ethan Holmes," he said for the third time.

"And who are you again, Mr. House?"

"I'm a lawyer. I'm looking for your sister Clara," Ethan said, speaking as clearly as possible and boosting his volume.

"Oh, I remember," Sarah said, lighting up. "My niece said you were coming."

"That's right. I'd like to ask you a couple of questions," Ethan said carefully. He asked his questions quickly, fearing her attention would fade. But no matter how urgently he phrased his queries, Clara could give him no help. She couldn't remember the date or location of the hit-and-run accident that killed Trolley. She didn't know the name of any police investigators or a funeral home. She didn't know if an obituary for Trolley had appeared in any newspaper.

Finally he gave up, shook her hand, and thanked her for seeing him.

"You're surely welcome," she smiled up at him. "Please come back and see me again sometime, Mr. ... what was your name again?"

"Holmes," he answered before he hurried away. "Ethan Holmes."

"Good bye, Mr. House," she called after him. "It was nice meeting you. I do so hope you'll come back and see me sometime!"

Back at the nurse's station, he located the aide who knew Sarah best. And although she remembered Trolley, she was horrified to learn that Trolley had died in a hit-and-run accident. "Oh the poor thing," she kept moaning. "Oh, the poor, dear thing."

"So you're telling me Sarah never mentioned the accident to you?" Ethan asked.

"Not a peep," said the chubby young woman who couldn't have been over 25 years old. "She's carrying all that grief all by herself. I have to go to her."

"Wait!" Ethan ordered, catching her arm. "Just one more question. Is Sarah kind of ... well, out of it? Batty? Senile? Balmy?"

"Of course not," said the young aide indignantly. "She's a lovely woman!"

"Right," Ethan muttered to himself as he watched his latest informant rush toward the patio. "Lovely. But what about fruity, nutty, lost in space?"

A few more inquiries of various staff members convinced him that he was wasting his time, so he departed for the Orlando police department. To his dismay, the police had no information about the hit-and-run. Instead of persuading them to treat the "accident" as a homicide, he found himself trying to convince someone–anyone–that the incident had occurred.

"Now, Mr. Holmes," one clerk told him after he had made a thorough nuisance of himself, "if you can give us a date, maybe we can help you. But I don't have a Clara Corwyn in my data base. I don't know what else I can do for you."

He held up the drawing of Trolley for perhaps the tenth time with a pleading expression on his face. The clerk shrugged.

Dragging his feet, Ethan trudged out of police headquarters. Newspapers and funeral homes were his next targets. But he drew a blank with every effort.

Finally Ethan crawled into his rented car and pounded the steering wheel. "She's not dead," he growled. "That old woman killed Maylea and made off with the money, leaving Dillon to pay for her crime. The miserable old crone isn't dead!" He pounded the steering wheel again, then started the car and headed for Sarah's nursing home.

He found Sarah in her room this time. She was propped up in bed, watching the news. "Why Mr. House, you came back! How kind you are!" she cried. "Please come in and sit down." She indicated a straight chair next to her bed.

"Cut the act," Ethan commanded. "I want to know where your sister is, and I want to know now." He flopped into the chair–which protested with a thump and three creaks–and glared at Trolley's sister.

Sarah glared back for approximately five seconds, then she wilted. "I don't know where she is," she sobbed. "I wish I did. I miss her so much."

"Why are you telling people she's dead?" Ethan asked.

"I'm not telling *people*," Sarah said with a hurt expression. She wiped her eyes and blew her nose. "I only told my niece–Clara's daughter Annette."

"Okay, why did you tell your niece that Trolley's dead?"

Sarah swallowed hard and blew her nose again. "Clara is in the witness protection program. She ..." Suddenly Sarah gasped and clapped her hand over her mouth. "Oh no! I wasn't supposed to tell *anybody*. Not anybody." She gazed at Ethan wide-eyed, then looked wildly around the room. He could see her hand under the covers, trying to locate something.

Standing, he tossed the covers back and saw that she was holding her call box. Before he could stop her, she pressed the button to summon help.

"Why did you do that?" he asked, flopping back into the chair. "Trolley's not hiding from me. I want to help her."

"If you wanted to help her, you would know where she is," Sarah said.

Ethan sighed. "She's not in the witness protection program, and I would never hurt her," he said.

"Then why are you here?"

The door opened and an aide entered. Ethan looked up at the tall, muscular young man who had obviously been a football player *and* a basketball player in high school. "It's Orlando," he growled at Sarah. "I've always wanted to see Orlando."

He stood, said "Howdy," to the titan, and walked away.

∽✵∼

Dillon and Jeremy were down the street playing basketball when Ethan phoned. Nettie answered, and he unloaded on her. "Trolley's not dead," he told her. "She's just pretending to be dead, and that means she killed Maylea."

"How do you know she's not dead?" Nettie asked. "Did you see her?"

"No, but I had a heart-to-heart talk with her sister." Ethan described his day in Orlando, explaining why he had come to the conclusion that Trolley, far from being an innocent bystander, was the murderer of Maylea West.

"What's next?" Nettie asked.

"I have no idea," Ethan said despondently. "I'll have to think on it."

"I have an idea," Nettie said eagerly. "In fact, it's more than an idea. I know where she is. Well … I know where you can find her."

Nettie's bold announcement was followed by a long pause. Finally Ethan said, "I guess I need to clean out my ears. I thought you said you know where she is."

Nettie laughed. "Don't clean out your ears. I just finished reading an email that gives her location. In fact, I was going to call Qiana and get your cell number so I could call you."

"Well, spit it out!" Ethan cried. "I'm so depressed over failing my client that I was about to go throw myself in front of a locomotive."

"Go ahead," Nettie said. "You would be on the right track then."

"Ha, ha, the right track," Ethan said. "Would you please quit toying with my emotions?"

"Okay," Nettie said. "Here's the deal. The night Dillon and I got remarried I couldn't sleep because I was worried about the trial. So I spent a lot of time thinking about the case and came up with the crazy notion–what if Trolley committed the murder?"

"Not such a crazy notion, after all," Ethan observed.

"Anyway, Jeremy told me how Trolley was always singing, 'I've Been Working on the Railroad,' so I got on the internet and looked up all the railroad systems I could find. I printed out their phone numbers and email addresses. The next Monday I made some phone calls and sent out some emails, giving Trolley's description. I asked for engineers and personnel departments to watch for her. I thought she might try to get a job on a railroad. Or she might be sitting around somewhere watching the trains go by."

"And you got an answer?" Ethan asked eagerly. "Someone knows where she is?"

"There's a little town northwest of Lubbock," Nettie explained. "The town has only one park and it's located next to a railroad track. She's there at noon, eating her lunch, almost every day. And she always waves when a locomotive goes by."

"How do you know it's Trolley?"

"She's usually wearing her Vikings jersey," Nettie said.

"Purple?" Ethan asked.

"With a big white number 10 on it," Nettie said.

Ethan whistled. "So where is this town?"

"Give me your address, and I'll forward the email to you," Nettie said. "I thought you should be the one to talk to her."

"Mrs. West," Ethan said, "right at this moment, you are my favorite person in the whole world."

Chapter 23

Two things happened late on the morning of August 29th. Nettie West went into labor and Ethan Holmes found Trolley. Having already scouted the area, Ethan pulled a rental car up to the curb and switched off the motor two blocks from the place where Clara Corwyn–Trolley–liked to eat lunch. Unable to get on an immediate flight to Lubbock, he had flown instead to Dallas the previous night, then rented a car to drive to a tiny town in the Texas Panhandle that he'd never heard of before.

He scooted down in the driver's seat, so that he could just see out the window. At fifteen minutes before noon, he saw her coming. She was a tiny woman, wearing a purple jersey and black slacks. In her hands were a plastic bag and a paper cup. He waited until she had seated herself at a covered picnic table and begun to eat before he got out of the rental car.

The sky was powder blue, stretching to infinity. The scorching sun was August hot, chug-a-lugging every drop of moisture out of the landscape. Trolley, her toes barely touching the ground, looked like a dried up twig of a human being.

Ethan studied her as he approached from her right side. Occasionally, she picked up a half sandwich and nibbled at it listlessly. Ethan's throat closed as he watched her. She looked like a tiny, lost soul. But he knew from her reputation that she could be feisty and tough. Cheryl Mackenzie Hoffman-Lin Choi-Maylea Kanaka West had done this–sapped the joy and strength out of her. Suddenly he knew with a depth of feeling rare for him that he could have killed Maylea himself. He could have closed his hands around her skinny neck and strangled the life out of her for devastating the lives of so many good people. And not just his client. There was Caleb Hancock. And Kevin Vickery. And everyone who loved Dillon, Caleb, and Kevin. Including Trolley.

He stopped. He didn't want to destroy Trolley. He wanted her to be free. He wanted her to be able to enjoy her grandchildren and visit her sister. He wanted her to spend the rest of her life cooking for her family and singing, "I've Been Working on the Railroad."

"Don't just stand there," Trolley called suddenly. She held out the untouched half of her sandwich without looking at him. "You can have half of my sandwich. I'm not hungry."

Ethan didn't want the sandwich, but he joined Trolley and accepted it. He sat down and took a bite.

"You took your time," Trolley said. She didn't sound like an old lost woman. Her voice was firm and pleasant.

"It wasn't because I wasn't trying," Ethan said.

Trolley looked at him then. "You're Dillon's lawyer, aren't you?"

"That's right. I'm Ethan Holmes, and it's a pleasure to meet you at last, Trolley."

Trolley shrugged. "I'm sorry I've caused you so much trouble."

"You're not the one I blame," he told her. "Maylea deserves the blame."

Trolley nodded. "You won't get an argument from me."

He thought he was going to ask a thousand questions when he found her. Instead, he sat beside her trying to decide what the sandwich tasted like–flour paste? pablum? cat food?

"Go ahead," Trolley said.

"Huh?" Ethan's head jerked up. "Go ahead what?"

"Ask your questions."

He frowned and put the sandwich down. What were his questions? "Well, let's start at the beginning," he said after some thought. "When did you get to Lubbock?"

"About a month after Cheryl–Maylea–left Oahu."

"But you didn't move in with Dillon and Maylea until a month later."

Trolley smiled ruefully. "She wouldn't have it. She said she couldn't stand the sight of me, and if I didn't quit stalking her, she would report me to the police."

"So what did you do?"

"I kept stalking her," Trolley said. "She wasn't going to call the police on me. I knew too many of her secrets. Finally she said she couldn't take it any more. She wanted me to move in so she didn't have to see me everywhere she went."

"And so you could do all the cooking and housework?" Ethan guessed.

Trolley laughed. "That was probably the main reason she decided she could tolerate me."

"Then what happened that Monday night after Dillon left–the night before Maylea died?"

Trolley grimaced at the memory. "She was in a fury. She'd never had so much trouble getting a man to obey her every whim. Even the mafia types were putty in her hands. But she tried every wile she had on Dillon, and he wouldn't turn into mush for her."

"Good for Dillon!" said Ethan.

Trolley nodded. "Yes, good for Dillon. But dangerous for Dillon, too. After she finished screaming at me, she left. I followed her, of course, and she went straight to Bruno Kroft."

"Kroft? Why Kroft?"

Trolley looked troubled. "I think she was arranging for Dillon's murder. She didn't say so, but I was afraid for him. After I saw where she had gone, I went back to the house and cleaned it from top to bottom. When she got home, way after midnight, she was all calm and serene. Too calm after the screaming fit she'd had earlier."

"When did you plant the poisoned pills for her to take?" Ethan asked.

"That night while she was out. I'd made my plan, and I decided it was time to carry it out."

"Did you talk to Maylea at all on Tuesday?"

Trolley nodded. "I went in at the usual time with her usual breakfast–hot tea and toast. I got her pills and put them on the tray. It was a typical morning. She sat by the window to eat while

I made the bed. Then she said she was still tired and thought she would lie down a little longer. If she fell asleep, I was to wake her at 10:00 so she could get ready for her lunch date with Scot." Trolley paused to brush away a tear. "She was almost too tired to make it to the bed. She sort of collapsed across it and lay there, looking like some beautiful fairy tale princess."

"Then what?" Ethan whispered when her voice faded into silence.

"I left."

"What about that note the police found on the refrigerator?" Ethan asked. "The one that said Maylea should remember to call Scot. Was that for real?"

"No."

"So you mentioned him in the note just to make him a suspect?"

Trolley shrugged. "I was hoping if there were enough suspects, no one could be convicted for murdering Maylea."

"And you put Bruno Kroft into the mix with your blackmailing email for the same reason?" he asked.

Trolley nodded. "Sure, why not? Besides, he's a lowlife."

"But an email like that," Ethan objected. "He just deleted it. How was anybody supposed to know about it?"

Trolley grinned a lopsided grin. "Didn't you hear? The police received an anonymous tip about Kroft and his gang."

Ethan's eyebrows went up. "From you?"

"Who else?"

"And you knew they would go through his computer, looking for evidence?"

"I hoped."

"Okay, what about the timing? Why did you choose that exact moment to ..."

"To murder Maylea?"

"Well, yes," Ethan said, "to murder Maylea."

Trolley sighed. "In the beginning I believed I could talk her into confessing that she had killed her first husband and that Caleb had nothing to do with it. But she wouldn't even discuss it.

I kept hanging around her, working on her, trying to make her understand how much she was hurting Caleb."

"You thought she really loved Caleb?" Ethan asked.

"I saw them together all those years. I would have bet my life on it," Trolley said.

"But she didn't?"

Trolley shook her head. "Not enough."

"What happened to her?" Ethan asked. "How did she get so heartless? Was she abused? Were her parents messed up?"

"I've wondered about that a lot," Trolley said thoughtfully. "She had three older brothers and they all treated her like a princess. So did her father. And I suspect her mother was jealous of her beauty. But there was no big trauma in her life, just a sense of entitlement, especially from men. And perhaps a bit of neglect by her mother."

"Anyway," Ethan asked, directing the conversation back to its previous course, "you gave up hope that you could get her to confess to murdering her husband?"

"Not only that," Trolley said. "I gave up hope that she would ever quit using men–stripping their money and their dignity then tossing them away when she was through with them. And I like Dillon. I couldn't watch her do to him what she did to Mr. Hoffman and the man in California. ..."

"California?" Ethan asked. "What man in California?"

"Oh, you missed him?" Trolley asked.

"I'm afraid so."

"When she left North Dakota, she went to California and found a billionaire to marry. Of course, she had to woo him away from his previous, gold-digging wife, but she managed it in a couple of months. They were married before the ink on his divorce papers was dry. And she found a gangster to assassinate him before the ink on the wedding license was dry. She had learned her lesson in North Dakota–she wasn't going to do it herself and be tried for murder. It was in California that she learned to court powerful gangsters, who could order a hit with a snap of their fingers. Cheryl–Maylea–was lunching with the publisher of a newspaper when her husband was shot through the head. She was never investigated and, as soon as the will cleared probate, she was gone, leaving her gangster lover to wonder where she went."

"How do you know all this?" Ethan asked. "Annette said you didn't find Cheryl until she moved to Hawaii."

"Cheryl told me," Trolley said. "Most of her headaches were bogus but when she had a real migraine, she was like a drunk, spilling every secret she had. I caught her at a weak moment and dragged it out of her. She would have told me anything to get me to turn off the light and leave her in peace."

Ethan frowned. "But once she was the widow of a billionaire, why did she keep on? What was the point of stealing credit cards and ruining lives for a couple of dollars here and there?"

"I think it was a game for her," said Trolley. "She got addicted to the thrill of the hunt, I guess, and I *know* she didn't care who she hurt."

Ethan was nodding. "And you really believe she was going to have Bruno Kroft kill Dillon?"

"Of course she was," said Trolley. "Dillon wouldn't play her game, and she hated him for it. She was through with him, and she wanted a clean break with him–his days were numbered."

Ethan's face was white. "You're saying that killing her was the only way to save him?"

Trolley gazed at him with clear, intelligent eyes. "Yes."

"Where did you get the morphine?"

Trolley shook her head. "Cheryl's friends were my friends. She got cozy with the big bosses and I made friends with their older, trusted buddies. Or uncles. Or cousins. Morphine was easy–I could have gotten it from dozens of sources, and I won't mention any names." She observed Ethan's intense expression and chuckled. "How do you think I was able to give the police the hot tip that got Kroft's gang arrested?"

"How?" Ethan asked.

"I had what you might call inside information," Trolley said with a grin. Suddenly she cocked her head and listened. Her eyes went to a point on the horizon where the railroad tracks appeared and within moments a freight train appeared there. Its rumble turned into a roar as it approached, and when the locomotive was next to their picnic area, Trolley waved. An answering wave and three long whistles acknowledged her greeting. As the engine pulled away, Ethan watched Trolley watching the train–flat cars, boxcars, tanker cars. Her face was alight with joy, and he wondered if she was thinking of her father.

When the last rumble had faded and the last particle of dust from the train had settled, Trolley turned back to Ethan and asked, "When are you going to ask me why I took the law into my own hands instead of turning Maylea over to the police?"

"I think I know the answer to that one," Ethan said. "After Caleb was convicted–and Kevin Vickery, too–you didn't trust another jury to recognize her guilt. But you have to be fair. She might have been convicted on Oahu if she hadn't vanished onto the mainland."

Trolley nodded. "That's part of it. But Mr. Holmes, she was afraid of prison. She was afraid that guards would rape her. Afraid that being in a cage would make her crazy. One reason she went to Oahu was because of the birds there–so many kinds of beautiful, *free* birds. When she was about 12 years old, she had a canary. One morning she found it dead in its cage. She always believed she would be like that canary if she went to prison. She begged me more than once to make sure she never went to prison."

"But you can't imagine she meant she'd rather be dead!" Ethan objected.

Trolley shrugged. "No, but for Cheryl there were no good choices. If she lived free, she was always going to ruin lives. So which is better–to be a caged canary or Sleeping Beauty?"

Ethan sighed. "I'm glad it wasn't my decision to make."

"It wouldn't have been mine except for Caleb. When she took away my grandson's freedom, she took away my options."

Trolley's voice was bitter, and Ethan frowned, trying to understand an emotional pain so intense that it could drive a law-abiding grandmother to murder. When he remained silent for several minutes, Trolley asked, "What else do you want to know?"

With an effort, Ethan moved on to the next issue. "What about the money? Maylea's money–do you have it?"

Trolley's expression grew stern. "That money belongs to a lot of people. Old man Hoffman's children. Kevin Vickery's clients. Some of the waitresses and guests of the Windsong Towers. I don't even know everybody the money belongs to."

"So where is it?" Ethan asked.

"It's in a lot of places. I'm not saying where. Not yet."

Ethan nodded. "Look Trolley, please don't tell anyone I said this, but I hope you'll set some aside for Caleb's defense. He doesn't deserve to be in prison for loving the wrong woman."

Trolley's eyes softened. "Thank you for caring about my grandson," she said. "He'll be taken care of. I think I've found him the right lawyer."

"And how do you propose to get all that money back to its rightful owners?" Ethan asked.

Trolley grinned at him. "I don't know about that. Maybe you'll help me."

Ethan grinned too. "I'll help you if I can." Then he grew serious again, "Okay, this is my biggest question of all. Why didn't you just let Kun Yee take care of Maylea? If you'd told Puna where she was, Yee would have taken her out, and you wouldn't be guilty of murder."

Trolley didn't answer and he turned to look at her. Tears were rolling down her cheeks. Swiping the tears away, she said, "For awhile that was my plan. Every day I took out my phone to call Puna. But I couldn't do it."

"Why not?"

Trolley took a deep breath before she said, "Cheryl used to play with my grandkids when they were little bitty things. One day I was baking cookies for them and she came into the kitchen to watch me. I had a batch fresh from the oven and cool enough to eat, so I handed her a cookie. She took a bite, looked up at me with her beautiful dark eyes, and said, 'Trolley, would you be my Trolley, too?' I hugged her and told her I would. Of course I would."

Trolley pulled a tissue out of her pocket to wipe her eyes and blow her nose before she continued. "Kun Yee would have demanded his money back. Maylea would have denied taking it. He would have tortured her until he got it back. Then he would have killed her. I couldn't bear for her to be tortured. I was still ... I was always ... her Trolley, too."

"So you put enough poison in her capsules to make her go to sleep forever," Ethan said softly.

Trolley nodded. "Now she can't hurt anybody. And nobody can hurt her."

Images of a canary lying dead in a cage, a crying child, and a beautiful woman in a pink negligee lying dead on her bed flashed through Ethan's mind. Trolley had done the wrong thing–his head was certain of it. But his heart ached for the old woman who had felt compelled to destroy a woman she had once loved. When he was finally able to get the words past the boulder in his throat, he asked, "What's next? Are you going to come back to Lubbock with me and turn yourself in?"

Trolley shrugged. "Why not? My kids and grandkids think I'm dead. Sarah thinks I'm lost in the witness protection program. I don't want to live like this." She grimaced. "Besides, Kun Yee would have found me eventually–then I would be dead."

"Do you want me to drive you?"

She nodded and lifted what was left of her half sandwich toward her mouth. He snatched it away, stood, and tossed it into a nearby trash container. "In that case, I'm buying your lunch. What's your favorite restaurant in Lubbock?"

"One last meal for the condemned convict?" she asked with amusement.

"No," Ethan said seriously. "A thank you from me to a woman who has more guts than I'll ever have."

Trolley rose and tossed the nearly full cup after the sandwich. "Okay then," she said, taking his arm, "I like the Bless Your Heart Restaurant."

While he drove, Ethan punched in Dillon's cell number. Dillon, dressed in surgical scrubs and cap, answered with a distracted, "What?"

"Where are you?" Ethan asked.

"In a labor room with Nettie."

"Now? I thought she was due next month."

"She's early," Dillon said, watching his wife for signs of the next contraction.

"I'll make this quick then," Ethan said. "I'm on my way to Lubbock, and Trolley is with me. She's going to turn herself in."

Dillon's attention left Nettie and focused on the phone. "She's with you right now?"

"Yes."

"I want to talk to her," Dillon said.

Ethan passed his cell to Trolley. "It's Dillon," he said. "He's in a labor room with Nettie."

"Hello, Dillon," Trolley said. "I'm sorry."

Dillon heaved a deep sigh and cleared his throat before he could get the words out. "Look, Trolley, I want you to know that if there's any way I can help you, I will. I'm back with my family now, and my life is much better than I deserve. I shouldn't be glad Maylea is dead, but …"

"I understand," said Trolley softly. "I'm glad you're not angry with me."

"No, I'm not angry," Dillon said, his eyes back on Nettie. "And I will be forever in your debt."

Before Trolley could answer, he said. "I have to go. Nettie needs me. Tell Ethan he's my hero."

Trolley handed Ethan's phone to him and said, "He says you're his hero."

Ethan shook his head. "I don't think there *are* any heroes in this fiasco." Then he gave Trolley an impish grin and added, "You know, I think I'm falling in love with Nettie's sister. I guess I have you to thank for that. I might never have met her if it weren't for this case."

Trolley smiled sadly. "I'm glad something good has come out of Cheryl's life."

"And her death," Ethan said softly.

Chapter 24

Jeremy's baby sister was born at 5:09 that afternoon. Although she was two weeks premature, she was healthy and beautiful with an excellent pair of lungs. When she let out her first wail, Dillon's heart almost burst with joy. He was peering over Nettie's knees, counting fingers and toes, before the first cry ended.

"All there," he reported to Nettie. "Eight fingers, two thumbs, and ten toes."

Nettie smiled, squeezed his hand, and fell asleep.

They named the baby Regina Bethany after her two grandmothers. To avoid confusion, she would be called Ginny since her Grandmother West was commonly known as Reggy.

Dillon and Nettie brought Ginny home the following evening. Holding her, Jeremy thought about crying for joy because his family was together again. But, of course, he didn't. No way he was going to be so lame! But his eyes were aglow when he looked at his Mother and said, "She's the most beautiful baby in the world."

Nettie nodded and said, "I know." Then she yawned.

Dillon took the hint and led her to the bedroom. Soon Ginny was in a cradle on Nettie's side of their bed, Nettie was washed and gowned, and both were sleeping peacefully.

Jeremy had gone to his room, but he went to the kitchen for a snack around 11:00. To his surprise he found Dillon sitting in the den, reading a Bible and weeping. "Hey, Dad, what's the matter?" he asked. Only a few hours ago, he had thought his was the happiest family in town.

Dillon brushed aside the tears and looked up in embarrassment. "I'm so sorry I didn't read this and believe it before I put you and your Mom through a living nightmare."

"What is it?" Jeremy asked, trying to read the words upside down.

"The book of Proverbs in the Bible," Dillon said. "It talks about adultery. I hardly ever noticed these verses because I thought they could never apply to me. But now they sound like they were written just for me. Listen to this one. It says an adulterer is 'like a bird darting into a snare, little knowing it would cost him his life'. That was me–I went rushing into Maylea's trap like my life depended on it, and the next thing I knew, I'd lost everything I cared about."

"I guess you got lucky in the end," Jeremy observed, barely knowing what to say.

"Jeremy, would you sit down with me for a few minutes?" Dillon asked.

"Sure."

"I've been so worried about you all summer," Dillon confided. He explained about the Vacation Bible School lesson that dramatized King David's life and sins. "Now, if anything goes wrong in your life, I'm going to feel like it's my fault," he concluded.

"That's a pretty heavy load, Dad," Jeremy observed. "Don't you think you're making too big a deal out of it?"

Dillon sighed. "Your Mom says I have to turn it over to the Lord, and I try, but I still feel so guilty."

Jeremy shrugged. "I'd like to be perfect for you, Dad, but I know I won't be. So what do you want me to do?"

Dillon smiled sadly. "I'd like to make you promise to read Proverbs 5-7 every day and believe it can happen to *anybody* so you have to be prepared for it ahead of time. But I know I'm being unreasonable, so how about if you read it every now and then. Maybe once a month. Or a few times a year?"

Jeremy nodded. "Okay. I'll read it sometimes, starting tonight."

Dillon let out a relieved sigh. "Thanks, son."

"But, Dad. You have to promise me something, too."

"What?"

"You have to promise you won't blame yourself every time I mess up. I can't handle that kind of pressure for the rest of my life."

Dillon stood up and held out a hand. "It's a deal." They shook hands, then hugged.

Jeremy went on into the kitchen and Dillon went up to bed. Tiptoing into his bedroom, he stood over Ginny's cradle and marveled at her perfection. Then he undressed and climbed into bed with Nettie. She never stirred and, although he wanted to take her into his arms, he contented himself with holding her hand until he fell asleep.

Nettie was in the middle of a dream. The white owl had returned. It focused the full power of its yellow eyes on her. Dream Nettie just smiled at it and closed her own eyes. It didn't frighten her any more. When she opened her eyes again, the big white bird spread its wings, as if it had been waiting for her attention, and soared into the air. She watched it flying silently through the night sky until it came to a freight train. The big owl matched its speed to the speed of the locomotive and kept pace with it as it rounded a curve and disappeared from sight. As Nettie waited, she heard the locomotive give out a long, haunting whistle.

The dream ended, but Nettie didn't wake. However, she did move closer to Dillon. Waking, he snuggled up close to her and inhaled the sweet, fresh scent of her hair. "Dear God," he whispered, "please help me to be the man she wants me to be–the man *You* want me to be."

That night in Oahu prison, Kevin Vickery began, at last, to plan a life without Lin Choi. In a Bismarck, North Dakota, prison, Caleb Hancock reviewed every detail of a phone conversation with his mother about a legal group that might be able to get his conviction reversed. In a small house in California, Cheryl MacKenzie's parents, unaware of their daughter's death, slept peacefully. And in a jail cell in Lubbock, Texas, tears drenched the withered cheeks of an old woman called Trolley. No one was mourning the passing of the Hawaiian wildflower, except the woman who had taken her life.

The End

Made in the USA
Charleston, SC
03 August 2010